'Mater Biscuit

A Homegrown Novel

Julie Cannon

A TOUCHSTONE BOOK
Published by Simon & Schuster
New York   London   Toronto   Sydney

TOUCHSTONE
Rockefeller Center
1230 Avenue of the Americas
New York, NY 10020

TOUCHSTONE and colophon are registered trademarks
of Simon & Schuster, Inc.

For information about special discounts for bulk purchases,
please contact Simon & Schuster Special Sales:
1-800-456-6798 or business@simonandschuster.com.

Designed by Jan Pisciotta

Manufactured in the United States of America

10   9   8   7   6   5   4   3   2   1

Library of Congress Cataloging-in-Publication Data
Cannon, Julie, date.
    Mater Biscuit : a homegrown novel / Julie Cannon.
        p. cm.
    "A Touchstone book."
    1. Female friendship—Fiction. 2. Women—Georgia—Fiction.
3. Tomato growers—Fiction. 4. Georgia—Fiction. I. Title.
PS3603.A55M38 2004
813'.6—dc22   2003070724
ISBN 0-7432-4606-3

For Iris, Gus, and Sam,
who bring me joy beyond words

Contents

'Mater Biscuit

Prologue

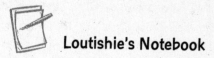

Loutishie's Notebook

One warm June evening after supper I was sitting in the green iron lawn-glider underneath the pecan tree listening to the loud, electric orchestra of the field crickets and katydids when my aunt Imogene stepped out on the back steps to scrape the drippings from supper's pork chops into Bingo's dog bowl. She straightened up, holding a skillet, and her eyes swept the yard until she spotted me. Grabbing the handrail, she moved deliberately down the steps in my direction. I knew she had something to say.

As she got closer, I couldn't help noticing how troubled she looked with her mouth in a grim line and her forehead all wrinkled up. No one would blame her, what with all the things she's had to shoulder on her own.

"Hoo-wee. That Imogene's certainly had a hard row to hoe lately," the folks around Euharlee always said whenever we went into town to the Kuntry Kut 'n' Kurl, or to Calvary Baptist on Wednesday nights and Sundays. "Can you imagine?" They shook their heads in wonder. "Burying a husband and a fiancé in under two years! But would you just look at how strong she is! Managing beautifully. Smiling away like she doesn't have a care in this world!"

That's why her serious face that evening alarmed me so much. Imo prided herself on the way she'd bounced back into life, and how she kept her "chin up in the air."

Her chin certainly wasn't in the air as she sank down beside me. She sighed, kicked off faded navy Keds, and rubbed the big toe of one foot over the bunion on her other foot.

"Loutishie?" she spoke my name like it was a question and then her bosom rose as she took in a deep breath, "we need to have us a little talk about something real important."

The hairs on the back of my neck stood up. Anybody who knew my aunt would've been scared, too. Imo wasn't one to discuss serious issues. When it came to her telling me and Jeanette about our uncle Silas's cancer, she could hardly bring herself to say the words. Then, when she fell in love so soon after he was in the ground, and also when we discovered Jeanette was having an illegitimate baby, it was like pulling hen's teeth for Imo to get the necessary words to come out of her mouth.

I don't blame her. I have to excuse Imo because I know she just wants to protect everyone she loves from painful and disagreeable things. I know she would be happiest in a world where nothing unpleasant is ever discussed—like Reverend Peddigrew says it's going to be up in Heaven; where there is no more pain, weeping, or suffering. I respect Imo's faith in a happy eternity. However, I have learned that there are some things down here on Earth that you can't stick your head in the sand and ignore forever, pretending they don't exist. Some things in this life come to a head and there's no escaping them.

That evening Imo turned and fixed me with one of her super-serious looks. "Please run and fetch Jeanette off the front porch, Lou. She needs to hear this, too."

"All right," I said, springing to my toes, glad for the delay and for the safety in numbers Jeanette would bring.

I made my way around the side of the house, past the septic tank and Imo's muscadine arbor, my brain buzzing with thoughts. What in heaven's name could this be about? Bingo bounded up to run circles around me, his snout shiny from the pork chop grease. He nudged the back of my hand. "C'mon, boy." I ruffled his neck as we walked to the front yard and stopped in front of some dusty azaleas.

Jeanette was standing on the front porch, smoking a cigarette with one leg up on the railing, painting her toenails bright red. Little Silas was sitting near her, wearing only a diaper, beating a wooden spoon against a pot lid.

"Imo has something *important* she needs to talk with us about," I said.

To my surprise, when I motioned for her to follow me back around the side of the house, Jeanette didn't utter a word of protest. She tucked her cigarette between her lips, scooped up Little Silas, perched him on her hip, and walked on her heels in a cloud of smoke down the steps.

Used to be, everything riled Jeanette. She was as headstrong and as contrary as an old goat. Still was sometimes. But since Little Silas's birth she'd mellowed a bit. It tickled Imo no end to see Jeanette's pale cheek mashed up against his tiny brown one while she crooned lullabies. Little Silas's face, with its plump cheeks, twinkling dark eyes, and full lips, was the spitting image of his long-gone father—the man from India who ran the Dairy Queen.

The sun was sinking, and the cicadas sent up an ominous buzz from the acuba bushes as we headed to hear who knew what. The thought that flashed through my brain first was that maybe we were going to have to sell the farm. I knew money was tight. Boy hidey, that was going to be tough! Imo was born and raised right there on the farm and she loved the land the same way I did—with all her heart.

Then I got to thinking Imo had some terrible disease, that she did not have long to live. She had been waiting till her time was almost up to tell us about it. That would be just like her.

My fingernails were digging into my palms as Jeanette and I sat down on either side of her. I felt miles away from everyone as I watched Little Silas holding out his arms, saying "Mi-moo." Imo pulled him onto her lap and sunk her chin into his jet-black halo of hair. We sat there a long moment while Imo stared straight ahead.

"What's up, Mama?" Jeanette said kind of quiet. "Why'd you call us?"

Imo blinked. "Well, I can't put off telling you this any longer, girls. I reckon it's for sure." She bit her bottom lip and said no more for quite a spell.

I saw Jeanette's face go pale and it dawned on me that tough old

Jeanette was as scared as I was. I crossed my arms, willing myself to look unconcerned. Wondering if Imo were ill or we were leaving the farm gave me butterflies in my stomach. It would almost be worse to lose the farm. Imo would be sick anyway if she had to leave here. I looked out across the back pasture, drinking in the brilliant streaks of a gold and crimson sunset stretching above the horizon.

I couldn't leave here. I loved this place, too! I loved the river bottoms where the Etowah meandered through the lower hundred acres. I loved the old farmhouse full of warm memories. And more than anything I loved working in our garden.

"Loutishie, you have my same love of growing things. We are like two peas in a pod," Imo had said to me on many a spring day. We'd be side by side out in the garden, warm earth crumbling in our hands like cake mix as we set in seedlings. I knew this was true. Gardening came as naturally and as joyfully to me as breathing. I always believed that this was what gave me and Imo such a strong connection. Stronger even than if I'd sprung from her own belly, instead of her younger sister's, who had passed away the day I was born.

Plus, I knew the therapy a garden could be. I had already witnessed the healing power of digging in the dirt. When Uncle Silas died, just two short years ago, after forty-eight years of marriage, it was the garden that eventually pulled Imo back into life. That woman literally poured herself into the soil; hoeing, planting, mulching, weeding, watering, and harvesting. She'd spend hours out there every day, coming back in the house at nightfall, smelling for all the world like crushed tomato leaves and warm marigolds, and just a-smiling. Sure enough, Imo turned out to be a lot like those tomato plants in our garden—the plants with the strongest survival instincts. What would Imo do without her beloved garden?!

It was the hardest thing in the world to sit there waiting like that. I kept willing Imo to just spit it on out. Whatever it was, I could handle it a lot better than the not knowing.

Finally she glanced in the direction of the well-house. She cleared her throat. "Looks like I need to pinch back those begonias, doesn't it, Lou?"

Begonias?!

Jeanette and I exchanged confused glances. Now I couldn't help thinking

Imo was losing her mind. Going off her rocker like Ernest Kitchens, an old man who constantly rocked and thrust his dentures in and out on the tip of his tongue during preaching at Calvary Baptist. I snuck a glance in Imo's direction. There was proof! Her hair was a bit tangled and the cuffs of her cotton housedress had some grease splatters on them.

I sat there trying to picture the homeplace without Imo in her right mind. My imagination went wild; I saw myself cooking, scrubbing, washing, folding, and ironing. Tending to the animals and the garden all by my lonesome. Down on my knees begging Jeanette to drive me places as I was still half a year shy of sixteen. I saw Jeanette lounging on the couch watching daytime soaps because she couldn't go back to finish high school without Imo to look after Little Silas.

Mixed with all the fear I had been feeling, I felt a lump of sadness forming in my throat. Tears pooled on the lower rims of my eyes. I snaked my arm up and around Imo's shoulders and squeezed. I searched her face, thinking, *I'll take care of you, Imo, when you become like a little child. You took care of me and I'll do the same for you.*

In a distracted way, Imo reached over and patted my knee. Then she gazed off into the distance again, unblinking. "Girls," she said, "it's going to be a mighty lot to handle what with getting the garden harvested. She's going to be moving in here real soon. When we're just covered over with snap beans and tomatoes and okra. You girls will have to be big helpers."

"Yessum," I said, holding my breath.

Jeanette gave Imo a quick, suspicious glance, but she didn't say a word. She scratched at some stray polish on her knuckles. I could almost see the wheels turning in her head. Imo sure sounded sane to me, but I wondered who in tarnation she was talking about. Was Jeanette scared to ask who, too? I sat there with my hands folded in my lap, listening to a fly buzzing around us. I figured I could count on Jeanette, who was three years older than me and always knew what to say. She never minced words. Apparently, though, she was going to let me down this time, and if we didn't get this thing out and discussed to Imo's satisfaction, it would be too late for me to make a run down to the banks of the Etowah River with Bingo, which is what I liked to do when I had things I needed to think over.

Like he could read my thoughts, Bingo straightened up on his front legs, pointed his snout toward the sky, and let out a sad "arrroooo."

"*Who's* coming?" The words flew out of my mouth in one breathless pop.

My question hung there and Imo drew a deep breath. She sighed a bit and tightened her hold on Little Silas. Finally she cleared her throat. "Mama," Imo's muffled voice came out of the cloud of Little Silas's hair.

Mama? Mama was coming? Imo was Mama, and she was already here. It took me a minute, but slowly it dawned on me who Mama was. *Imo's* mama. My grandmother. A woman we referred to as Grandmother Wiggins when we spoke of her at all. I had never laid eyes on the woman in the flesh. She and I had absolutely no kind of relationship—there were no heartwarming chats over the phone or tender birthday cards in the mail.

The only thing Grandmother Wiggins ever seemed to give Imo was a bad humor. Whenever they spoke, Imo left the phone with a stubborn thrust to her jaw, blinking away tears. I knew that her crying was due more to anger than sadness. Sometimes it took days before she was back to herself. Usually a mild sort of woman, chats with her mother could turn Imo into someone as feisty as Dusty Red, our Bantam yard rooster who was always itching for a scrape. Jeanette and I had learned to give Imo a wide berth and lots of time after her interactions with Grandmother Wiggins.

As this information sunk into my brain, I felt my heart booming in my chest and I tasted the metallic *ting* of fear. Hard as life had been around there, it was just fixing to get healed up real good. I didn't think I could stand any more things that upset Imo.

No, no, no, a thousand times no! I would have said if anyone asked me, but of course I had no say in the matter. I sat there, picking at a parchment-thin paint flake on the glider and watching Bingo scratch out another cool hole in the dirt.

When the full impact of what Imo had said reached Jeanette's brain, she shook her head like gnats were in her eyes. "You're shitting us, aren't you?" Her mouth hung open for a second. "Grandmother Wiggins?!" she hollered then, with such a shrill tone that Little Silas started crying.

Imo put her hands over Little Silas's ears. She drew her shoulders up tall and straight. "Watch your mouth, Jeannie," she said, her voice rising to a warning tone. "We've got to go and fetch her. She's family. She needs us, and I need you girls to understand."

"I seem to recollect you telling us that the woman is crazy," Jeanette hissed, one hand on her hip.

"What I said is she's not in her right mind."

"Sure enough, Mama," Jeanette said, leaning forward and looking deep into Imo's eyes, "that means she's *crazy.*"

Imo wrapped her arms tighter around Little Silas. "It's called senile dementia. Lots of folks' minds slip when they get old."

Jeanette thrust her chin out and huffily crossed her arms across her chest. "How old is she anyway?"

"Well, I'm sixty-five and she had me when she was nineteen. So that makes her eighty-four."

"That's ancient," Jeanette breathed. She leaned forward to peer around Imo and Little Silas. "Hey Lulu," she said, giving me a swift, venomous look, "we've got us a crazy old biddy coming to live with us. Isn't that just wonderful? And won't life around here be fan-damn-tastic with her and Mama under the same roof?"

I didn't say a thing. I only breathed a sigh of relief, happy that Imo still had her mind and that we were staying on the farm. My thoughts were spinning and what I needed to do more than anything was to run like the dickens down the dirt road to the river bottoms, sit down on the bank of the Etowah, wrap my arm around Bingo's neck, and think for a long spell.

Imo shook her head slowly. "We will just have to make the best of it, girls," she said in a trembly voice.

In the half-light, I saw her eyes grow shiny and watched her lips starting to tremble. I could not ever stand to see her cry, so I piped up in a preacherly tone, "I think this'll be wonderful! My own granny coming to live with me. I can't wait to meet her," and at that very moment I made a vow to myself to love the woman. After all, she was my own flesh and blood, and what harm could an old lady do? A grandmother? *My* grandmother. Surely things couldn't be as bad as they seemed.

Jeanette frowned. She huffed. She reared back and straightened one leg, holding it aloft and turning it this way and that to admire her red toenails. Then she leaned forward, put both elbows on her knees, and began twisting her hair around her fingers and muttering in low tones to herself—it was a funny way she had of thinking. I figured she was beginning to soften when I saw her head nodding ever so slightly. "Okay, then," she said finally, "okay. I reckon I ain't got no choice in the matter. But I thought she lived in one of those old folks' homes."

"Well, she was," Imo said with a sigh, "she is, I mean. But she's causing trouble there."

Jeanette sat bolt upright. She turned to Imo. "What kind of trouble?"

"I'd just as soon not say," Imo said in a low, composed voice.

"You have to!" Jeanette's eyes glinted with delight. "Tell us, Mama. Tell us what kind of trouble that crazy old biddy's getting herself into."

"Well," said Imo, patting a sprig of gray hair into place, "she's been running off. Escaping."

"You serious?" Jeanette giggled. "Where to?"

"Let's just say she's been causing quite a bit of a ruckus in Pamplico, South Carolina."

Jeanette laced her fingers behind her head and swung her legs. "Give us the details," she said.

"What it is, is, Mama keeps turning up at the Waffle House down the road apiece from the old folks' home." Imo's voice broke off and she began playing a silent pat-a-cake game with Little Silas.

"Hmph. That ain't no big deal." Jeanette poked out her bottom lip.

Imo brought Little Silas's plump fingers up to her lips to nuzzle them. She gazed off into the distance. She closed her eyes, then drew a deep breath to add in the faintest whisper, "when she's wearing only a little bitty see-through nightie."

"Woo-hoo!" Jeanette hollered. She shot up, stamping her bare feet, and clapping her hands; a small jig of delight that startled Bingo. "Bet that's a sight to put folks off their feed!"

Imo's face was beet red. In a high, thin voice she said, "So, girls, we've *got* to go fetch Mama. There's no other choice, really. She's family and it is our duty."

Bingo pressed his nose between my knees, blessing me with a ripe dog smell as we sat there in the twilight, quiet for the moment, while that word—duty—zinged around in my head like a ricocheting bullet.

I'd heard Imo talk about duty plenty of times, and always it was in the context of something unpleasant, like paying taxes or serving on a jury. I glanced over at her profile, at the determined set of her jaw, and I knew it didn't matter if she was half-dead or the house was on fire, that woman would do her duty.

My heart began beating so hard I could hear it throbbing against my eardrums. Suddenly I was imagining what was around the bend for us and bracing myself for the wildest trip of my life.

One

❧

Homecoming

*I*mogene Lavender never imagined her mother would be coming back. When she left, she said to Imogene that she was shaking the dust of Euharlee, Georgia, off her feet. She didn't even stop to pack her things. Left a dresser and a closet full of clothes, a bathroom drawer overflowing with curlers and combs and creams, and, most amazing, her prized antique trunk stuffed with photographs, letters, ticket stubs, and corsages. Locked tight, but just sitting there in one corner of her old bedroom.

Imo stood in the kitchen at dawn, coffee cup in hand, paralyzed by this recollection coming so fast and thick. Normally an act of her will, along with constant busyness, could keep this and other painful memories at bay. But today, the day she and Lou were to drive to Pamplico, South Carolina, to the Carolina Arms Apartments, to bring her mother back to Euharlee, she couldn't fight them.

In another recollection she was an apple-cheeked five-year-old. She was following her mother outside into the hushed grayness of early morning to gather eggs for breakfast. Her mother's voice floated back to Imogene as she stepped carefully along a path through beds of tiger lilies. "Look at all the tiny spiderwebs between the lilies, Imogene!" she whispered as she knelt down. "Just covered in that sparkly dew! Looks like a fairy world outside, doesn't it?" Gently she touched Imo's shoulder, turning her small frame to look out over the lawn. "See? A fairy world right in our own yard." Her voice trembled, breathless, coating the words like a soft blanket, breathing into them such awe that the lawn in the lifting fog of morning seemed to have an almost magical quality.

Standing there, Imogene clutched the egg basket tighter. She looked out at the glittering world and back at her mother and said softly, "Oh! It really is, Mama. But where do the fairies go when the sun dries the dew up?"

Her mother laughed and kissed her cheek. "Why, they curl up inside the very center of the lilies. They go to sleep and wait for the darkness to come back out. They have to keep their skin purely white."

"Pearly white?"

"Yes, sugar pie. Purely white and pearly white." She held out her hand to take Imogene's. "Let's go fetch those eggs. We'll carry them on in the house and then you can help me roll out the biscuits and we'll rub one with butter while it's hot and sprinkle on a little cinnamon-sugar for you."

Imo tiptoed along, squeezing her mother's hand to say, *Yes, a cinnamon-sugar biscuit would be good,* exhilarated by the sharpness of the cool morning air and the sparkling fairy world.

This was Imo's first real memory, and so full of tenderness and safety that she wouldn't have minded being able to crawl back into it and stay awhile. There were no words to explain the contentedness in her heart back then, the sweet mystery of having each need met, of feeling secure and loved no matter what. There seemed no need to doubt that things would always remain that way.

Stay here awhile. Just stay in this particular moment of your memory, she pleaded with herself, determined to savor the feeling of security. *Not all of your memories of Mama are sweet, so don't you go any further, Imogene Lavender. Don't you cross that line into where the pain began!*

She gripped the front edge of the sink and ground her teeth together. She willed herself to focus on the amber liquid in the Palmolive bottle: "Tough on Grease, Soft on Hands!" she read. But it was too late. Her eyes were drawn to the windowsill, to a small black-and-white ceramic Holstein cow that was a cream pitcher. As she studied the jagged lines of glue at the cow's neck and hoof, her sweet memory dissolved into one that was disturbing.

Imo watched herself at eight years old perched high on a kitchen stool, sipping coffee-milk while Mama stirred grits and turned ham in a skillet. Her daddy was sitting at the small wooden table in the kitchen drinking his black coffee and listening to the radio as the county agent talked about the peach crop. He wasn't very talkative or playful in the early mornings, but Imogene was just as happy to have her mother's full attention.

"More coffee, Jewelldine," he said when the weather report was over. He had the earnest look of a man waiting for inspiration, for energy to begin his day. "Reckon I'll work down in the bottoms this morning, in the corn. Sounds like we got us a purty day coming."

Jewelldine nodded and poured coffee for him. Next, she set the boiler of grits down onto a folded towel near his elbow, stood a minute flapping her hands over the pot, then turned back to get the pot lid left on top of the stove. "Flies sure are bad this summer, Burton." She settled the lid in one swift stroke. "Shoo!" She stuck her bottom lip out. "They're pesky little things!"

"I'm putting a bounty on these flies. Penny a piece." He grinned and took a fresh gulp of coffee. "I'm gone hire Imogene here to catch 'em, and bring 'em in, dead or alive. Put the girl to work."

Mama only grunted, but Imo was pleased by this notion of herself working. She figured she could swat all the flies in the house before her daddy came back in for lunch at noon. He'd be proud and Mama would be happy.

Imo's biggest ambition was to make her parents happy, especially Mama. When her toys were not neatly put away or she was too loud and hurt Mama's head, or when Mama scowled at the muddy stains on her dresses and shoes, she was stricken to the heart. What made her take up this burden of worry, Imo couldn't quite say, but perhaps it was on account of being an only child for so long. Mama tried hard to have another baby, and she cried often about it when no more came for years and years. Then she stayed in bed for weeks on end, not speaking and barely eating, after the birth of one that died before it was born. His tiny grave had a lamb carved into the headstone. There had been other babies lost, too, and Imo knew her mama wanted a baby boy more than anything else on Earth. She said he would carry on the family name and help Imo's daddy work on the farm. The fact that no living boy babies ever came made her mother feel sad and angry.

Sometimes Mama didn't smile all day. Sometimes she acted mad at Imogene's daddy. Today, though, Imogene was delighted when she bent and kissed him on his whiskery cheek. "I swannee, Burton. A bounty on a fly!" she said, and there was something joyous in the way she wrinkled her nose and bustled over to the oven wearing a red hot mitt on her hand to grab the biscuits out. She slid a golden biscuit onto a cheerful plate with the alphabet marching around the rim. She set this down in front of Imogene and tied a dish towel around her neck.

The three of them ate with the warm smell of sizzling ham circling the tiny kitchen, and the happy twang of Earl Scrugg's banjo over the sound of a second pot of coffee percolating. When his plate was clean and his coffee cup empty, her daddy stood, pushed back his chair, and stretched. He bent over Imogene and kissed the top of her head tenderly. "See you later, Jewelldine," he said to his wife, patting her hand. He left them still sitting at the table.

A fly settled onto the cow cream pitcher in the center of the table. Imogene studied the fly's vibrating wings. She figured she could kill that fly. Please her mama.

She lifted her hand, moved it above the cream pitcher, and held it motionless a moment to fool the fly. In one split second, she brought her hand down fast as lightning. Too clumsy, she struck the cow and it clattered onto its side, the head and one leg breaking off and cream splattering everywhere.

Imogene froze. She stared at the white puddle seeping across the oilcloth and underneath their breakfast plates. Mama loves that cow, she thought. She sought Mama's face to say she was sorry and tell her it was an accident.

Mama's eyes flashed angrily. "You broke it!" she hissed, reaching for Imo's thin arm and holding it hard.

Imo drew her shoulders up to her ears. "I'm sorry, Mama," she said finally in a hoarse whisper. "Stop, please, you're hurting me."

"Hurting *you*?" Mama cried through clenched teeth, squeezing Imo harder. "Hurting you? Listen, missy, you broke my lovely pitcher! Ruined the table!" She pushed her stern face right up into Imo's and whispered, "And now I will have to teach you a lesson. You need to learn how to behave!"

Imogene's heart was racing. Her mother had spoken harshly to her on many occasions, but this was the first time she had lifted a hand to her.

"Yes! I need to teach you!" Each word of Mama's threat felt like a slap.

Imo stopped breathing. "Mama," she pleaded, tangling her fingers in her hair, "Mama, I'm sorry. So, so sorry. I mean it. I promise I won't ever do it again!"

Mama didn't seem to hear. "I'll teach you, Imogene Rose Wiggins!" Mama released Imo's arm and used both her hands to press Imo's head down onto the table, into the cool cream puddle. She held her face in it for a long while, mashing it hard against the wet oilcloth.

So stunned she could barely breathe, Imo stopped resisting. Her chest ached from her swallowed sobs. Her blouse was cold and wet and the ends of her hair sodden.

Finally Mama released her, swiped her hands on the pockets of her apron, and said calmly, "Okeydokey, let's get this cleaned up, dear." She strode over to the screen door that led out onto the back porch, opened it, and shooed a fly out. "Do it immediately," she said, staring out across the yard.

Imo nodded, patting her face dry with the hem of her blouse. Clumsily she slid from the tall stool and went to the sink for the dishrag. Mama was a scary presence behind her as she washed and dried the table and the dishes and then collected the pieces of the ceramic cow.

She had never seen Mama quite like that before—so furious, and possessed by this terrible, cruel thing that took shape and began to live in her then. After that morning in the kitchen, Imo knew her life would be different somehow. A barrier had been knocked down, one that had been the dividing line between Imo's former innocence and her new uneasy life with Mama.

Imo didn't know exactly what seized Mama at certain moments, but it seemed like she became an entirely different person. Something told Imo that nothing she could say or do would head things off during these spells with Mama. She just had to wait them out. Endure. After these fogs passed, Mama acted as if nothing out of the ordinary had happened. You would have thought she might say "I'm sorry, sweetie. I must've lost my head," or try to make amends of some sort, but Mama blazed right on ahead with the day's agenda. Come bedtime, she turned back the covers on Imo's trundle bed and patted the pillow before tucking Imo in. She'd kiss her cheek and listen as Imo said her prayers.

"What time are we going to leave?" Lou's voice jolted Imo out of her memory.

"What, sugar foot?" Imo asked, shaking her head and looking at Lou standing barefoot in her nightgown.

"I said, what time are we leaving? I'm going to go get ready."

Imo tried to calculate the distance from Euharlee, Georgia, to Pamplico, South Carolina. "Nine-thirty or so," she said. "That ought to give us enough time. Don't wake Jeanette and the baby. We'll leave them here so we'll have room for Mama's things."

The truth of the matter was that Jeanette hadn't stopped fussing since yesterday morning when they'd moved her and Little Silas into Lou's room to create a spare bedroom. She'd hollered and kicked the walls and let out a string of filthy words that made Imo's ears burn. All Imo could do was hope against hope that when the girl and the old lady were face-to-face they would click, and pray that if this miracle didn't occur, then Jeanette would just learn to accept her over time.

"Alrighty, Imo." Lou smiled. She knew the real reason to let Jeanette sleep. "Where is it we're going again?"

"Going to the Carolina Arms Apartments in Pamplico, South Carolina," Imo answered, untying her apron. "Located along the Great Pee Dee River."

"She lives on a river?"

"That's what Mr. Dilly said."

"The Pee Dee River," Lou mused. "I wonder if it's as pretty as the Etowah."

Imo watched Lou leave. *I don't have the faintest,* she thought to herself as she sank down into a chair at the kitchen table, mashed up a crumb with her pointer finger and absentmindedly rolled it around on her thumb. She was trying to make sense of it all, thinking about what Mr. Eugene Dilly, the manager of the Carolina Arms, had said about Mama and the Great Pee Dee River.

He said they'd found the old woman more times than they could count, either swimming in the river or setting out on a flat rock in the middle, fishing with a bamboo pole. Mr. Dilly said he did not want to be responsible for a resident drowning. "We simply cannot restrain Miz Wiggins. It is bad enough," he said, "to have a patient with such a severe case of senile dementia, but during her spells of what the doctors here are calling extreme paranoia, she is amazingly strong. Crafty, too. Plus, her money's run out again. She's a month in arrears."

This was not a surprise to Imo. She and Silas had been sending money off and on for years, and since his passing she hadn't refused the old woman's demands. Thank the Good Lord in Heaven that with the money from Silas's life insurance policy, and her monthly check from social security, combined with a small inheritance from Silas's uncle Bud, they managed to get by. She had supposed she would go on sending money any time Mama called. That was the only time she ever called, when she was broke, but to Imo's mind, the checks she sent were a small price to pay for the peace the distance between them brought. Gladly she would have sent every last penny she had not to be going today.

Oh, the hole Silas's passing had left in her life. He would have been her rock to lean on during all this. He would have made things better. He always knew what to do.

Imo desperately held on to the notion that Mama couldn't be "getting even worse, if you can believe it," as Mr. Dilly claimed when he described her latest escapades. He said that Jewelldine Wiggins must be going back in time to her childhood because she was now calling him Pepaw whenever he hauled her up out of the river. "Tried to hop up in my lap oncet," he laughed. "I rode down to the river in my pickup truck when somebody said they seen her out there in the middle, up on that big ole rock, and I got her back to the bank, up the hill, and opened the passenger door for her and told her 'Hop on in and I'll carry you back home,' and then I went around and got behind the wheel and before I knew it, Miz Wiggins was trying to get in my lap! Calling me Pepaw and pouting about me making her go inside and it not dark yet. Telling me to carry her on home with me and Memaw and not to make her go back home to her folks' house. Said her father would whip her good. Course, she wouldn't fit, what with the steering wheel and all." He exploded in laughter. "Gol doggit! Was funny, it sure was. Got to have a sense of humor to work with old folks like I do. But even we can't keep your mama safe and secure no more, Miz Lavender, and I sure would hate to see her drownded. They's another place, near here, where they've got it more secure. They keep all kinds of old folks in there what have lost their minds." He chuckled again. "Want me to get the number and set up a meeting time? I know the feller who runs it."

"Let me call you back, Mr. Dilly," Imo stalled. "I'd like to talk to my pastor and seek his advice." But after she thought things through, she decided against mentioning Mr. Dilly's conversations to Reverend Peddigrew. Something about saying these things aloud seemed disrespectful toward her mother, but mostly it would make tending to it unavoidable.

So Imo bought a bit more time by sending several good chunks of money directly to the Carolina Arms Apartments, and then for quite a while, she just ignored the reports from Mr. Dilly. She contented herself with the knowledge that they were professionals there at the Carolina Arms and that the little bonuses she was adding to the checks must surely compensate them for their troubles. Wasn't providing for her mother's sustenance all that duty required as far as being a good daughter? She told herself that she'd done more for her mother than anybody else would have under similar circumstances. Lots of people would have turned a deaf ear to someone who'd done them the way Mama'd done her.

Another reason she didn't want to mention her dilemma to the Reverend Peddigrew was that commandment about honoring your father and mother. The Fifth Commandment. What did it mean anyway? Was she breaking it? It nagged at her occasionally, but she managed to keep busy enough to outrun it—thinking of the day-to-day business of caring for the girls, the farm, the Garden Club, her vegetable garden, the shut-ins she tended to, and that precious, perfect light-of-her-life, Little Silas.

Three weeks ago Imo was standing in the kitchen making a scrambled egg for Little Silas's breakfast when Mr. Dilly called once again and said very firmly this time that Jewelldine Wiggins could not stay at the Carolina Arms Apartments no matter how much money Imo sent. A million bucks wouldn't be enough.

"You've simply got to come and fetch your mother, Miz Lavender. You're the only family she's got. Only soul listed on her forms here."

This can't be true, Imo remembered thinking, *this can't be happening.* She couldn't even imagine seeing her mother, much less carrying her back to Euharlee after all this time. She asked Mr. Dilly for the number of the maximum security personal care home that he had mentioned earlier. She called, and after they quoted prices to her, she picked her jaw up off her chest, thanked them, and hung up. That night she lay on her bed and cried like she hadn't since Silas passed.

When Imo had the kitchen tidied up, she sat at the table with her hands folded in her lap, waiting for Lou to finish feeding Bingo and Dusty Red. She winced when the phone rang.

Tentatively she picked up the receiver. "Hello?"

"Well, hello to you, dear!" It was her best friend Martha Peddigrew's cheery voice. Martha was the Reverend Lemuel Peddigrew's wife, as well as the president of the Garden Club. "How are you? I feel like I haven't talked to you in a month of Sundays!"

"Yes, well, I've just been real busy," Imo said.

"Pray tell what's been so important you can't pick up the phone and call your dear buddy?" Martha teased.

"Uh . . ." Imo had to think fast, "just, you know, tending to the girls and Little Silas and all."

"I see. I hope you're not too busy for a visit later on today, this afternoon sometime. I want to bring you a loaf of my sourdough bread and jar of homemade strawberry jam."

"That is so sweet of you to offer, Martha, but I've got to, uh . . ."

Imo faltered, "I've got to run into town and pick something up and I don't know when I'll get home." This was not actually a lie, Imo told herself.

Though a part of her wanted to confide in Martha, she just couldn't bring herself to do it. Facing the vast unknown made her anxious, and she didn't quite know how to put everything into words. "We'll have to catch up later," she said, "gotta run now."

Martha sounded hurt as she said good-bye.

It didn't take ten minutes to get out of Euharlee, and not half an hour more to go down through the cornfields and vast stretches of kudzu that were Acworth and Elizabeth, Georgia. By eleven o'clock they were completely out of the farmlands and in Atlanta, heading for I-20, which would take them all the way to Florence, South Carolina.

Imo gripped the steering wheel. Pamplico along the Great Pee Dee River! All at once a vision flashed into her imagination and she saw the slippery red-clay banks of a brown body of water running beside a string of buildings that included a post office, a five-and-dime, a beauty shop, and a courthouse. Crowds of people were strolling down the sidewalk that ran between the shops and the river, and Imo's attention was drawn to the solitary figure of an old woman among them.

It was Mama. Imo strained to picture her more clearly, to make out what, or more aptly *who*, she was these days. This was an impossible task.

"What are we supposed to call her?" Lou piped up as they turned onto I-20. "Granny? Grandma? Tara calls her grandmother Memaw, and so does Linda May."

Oh, what a question! Imo scowled. Grandma and Granny had a certain feel to them—loving, warm, and embracing. A granny, as well as a grandma, was someone rocking on the front porch with a lap full of butter beans to shell, or some mending, who, when she sees a grandchild, pushes aside her task to pat her lap and say "Come right on up here and let me see you, honey-child!" And Memaw was a big-bosomed woman in a checked housedress covered by an apron made from a feed sack, wrapping you in her arms between sweeping and frying up a skillet full of okra. None of these fit Jewelldine Wiggins.

"Well, Loutishie," Imo said, wondering how to explain her mother to the girl, "you know that her given name is Jewelldine Wiggins, and since she's my mother, that would make her your grandmother Wiggins."

Lou's face was serious as she contemplated this. "Grandmother Wiggins?" She frowned.

"Well, I reckon we ought to just think on that for a spell then, hmm, sugar foot? Maybe when you see her for the first time, it will hit you what you ought to call her." Imo did her best to give the girl a reassuring smile. She felt she'd managed to put on a pretty good face about things so far, but ever since Mr. Dilly's last call, she'd been literally dreading this day and hoping the way she felt inside wasn't showing. Every single time she thought about seeing Mama, her heart sped up so fast she got swimmy-headed, and now, here they were, actually on their way to fetch her. Imo had to face the facts; there was no way to sugarcoat things for Loutishie and Jeanette anymore. *Give me strength, Lord,* she breathed.

They spent the next thirty miles in silence, watching strings of signs for fast-food places and gas stations pass by. Imo thought, wouldn't it be nice if you could just turn your brain off sometimes and move through life unaware? Then a body could have some peace. She was still thinking of this when they cruised through a Dairy Dawg for hamburgers, french fries, and Cokes. With one hand Imo settled her drink, unwrapped her burger, and took a bite.

Of course, that's not the way life works, she mused as she chewed and drove along four lanes of thick lunchtime traffic. There were constant streams of cars just full of folks driving along to who knew what. Folks who no doubt had troubles of their own, except Imo could not imagine that any of them would face something as hard as she was heading to today.

"Sure are a bunch of people around here," Lou said in a wondering voice, almost like she could read Imo's mind.

"Yessirree," Imo said. "Reckon how the Lord keeps up with everybody?" She looked at Lou's slumped little shoulders. "I reckon we know just about every soul in Euharlee, don't we?" she asked to lighten the mood.

Lou shrugged.

Sadness rose up inside Imo—a painful lump that began in her heart, moved to her throat, and then brought a shine to her eyes. She felt a twinge of concern for dear Lou. How could she make this easier on the child? Why did life have to be so hard for such a sweet girl? She had already lost her mother, didn't know who her father was, and was now on her way to get some grandmother she'd never known. A woman with a mean, dark streak no one could change—not doctors; not Imogene's dear, long-suffering daddy, God rest his soul; and not Imogene. She had a good mind to make a U-turn and just ignore Mr. Dilly. Tell Jeanette and Lou it was all a big joke.

Things had been healing up around their house finally. Jeanette was back at high school, going to graduate and make a life for herself and Little Silas. Lou wasn't moping around so much and Imo herself was back in the groove of life. Though memories of dear Silas and Fenton Mabry were as close as the photos lining the mantel, or a walk down the dirt road to the river bottoms of the farm, Time had been a great and wonderful healer in regard to their passing.

She drove on, knuckles white on the steering wheel. How many years had it been since she'd last seen her mother? At least fifteen, because Lou was fifteen. Must be closer to sixteen. As she calculated this, forcing herself to remember, her pulse began to race and breathing became difficult. She was not fit to be driving, she told herself as she eased over to the shoulder of the highway and stopped completely to pat her chest.

"What's wrong?" Lou's eyes were wide as she laid a hand on Imo's arm. She shook her gently when she didn't get an answer.

Imo sat and stared blankly. She couldn't think. Images flashed through her brain as cars whizzed by.

"Oh!" Lou squeaked, shaking Imo harder to get an answer. "Are you okay? What's wrong?!"

"I'm okay," Imo managed finally, "just had a little spell. Things are going to be fine." She peered into the child's narrow face and somehow gathered herself together and managed to ease back out onto the highway. They drove for a long while in silence. "A whole 'nother state!" Imo called out exuberantly as they passed the Welcome to South Carolina sign. "Isn't this exciting?"

"Yes ma'am," Lou replied, with a suspicious look on her face.

When they reached Florence, Imo dug into her handbag for the scrap of paper where she'd written Mr. Dilly's directions. "Not much farther," she said, mashing the accelerator as they sped through Windy Hill and Claussen. She gripped the wheel tighter, with trembling hands, when she saw the first mileage sign with Pamplico on it. She maneuvered past an auto body repair shop, a tiny white clapboard house that read Bella's Flowers, and two barbecue shacks—the totality of the city of Orum. "Be the next town," she whispered under her breath.

Imo's head was a tangle of excitement and dread as they entered the Pamplico city limits. The appointed time was here. She wondered whether her mother would be in the present, or be the little girl Mr. Dilly spoke of. And what would she think of Lou, her very own grandchild? Would she still be so quick to fly into a rage and spew out painful words?

Before long she spied the Carolina Arms up on a sloping hill. It was a long two-story white cinder-block building with a flat black roof and a strip of green grass out front. Behind it stretched a thick wall of pines. Imo decided that the Great Pee Dee River lay beyond that.

No turning back now, Imo thought as she pulled the Impala onto a gray half-circle of asphalt in front of the Carolina Arms. Slowly they cruised by the glass entrance, which jutted out like a hotel lobby. A small sign in the grass read "Manager/Office" and had an arrow pointing down a narrow walkway. She idled awhile until her heart stopped racing. She couldn't let Loutishie see how upset she was. She had to be a calm bulwark. Slowly she pulled in a deep breath. "Alrighty, Lou!" she said, "we certainly are in the right place!" She patted the child's knee and pulled around to park in a row of visitor's spaces.

They stepped out into suffocating heat, marched up the walkway, and pushed open double-glass doors. The sharp smell of antiseptic and a blast of cool air met them as they entered the Carolina Arms. Old folks lined the walls of the long, burgundy-carpeted foyer; some slumped in wheelchairs with their eyes closed, some leaned on walkers, and a few sat in plastic-covered wing chairs. A large middle-aged lady wearing a smock printed with teddy bears and rainbows looked up at Imo and Lou from behind a receptionist's desk. "Hello, ladies," she said, smiling brightly. "What may I do for you today?"

"Hello. I'm Imogene Lavender, and this is Loutishie, and we've come to fetch my mother, Jewelldine Wiggins." These words tumbled out of Imo by themselves. Was she imagining it when she thought this woman's eyes grew wider at the mention of Mama's name?

"Wonderful!" the lady gushed, peering hard over her bifocals at Imo, quickly straightening a pile of papers and stuffing them into a folder. "I'm Miz Johnson. You two make yourselves at home and just give me a second to get her things together here."

Imogene selected a butterscotch lozenge from a cut-glass dish and sat down on a wooden bench. She touched a plastic flower arrangement on the table at her elbow. "How lovely!" she exclaimed, pretending this was nothing but an ordinary exchange of pleasantries.

"I'll call Mr. Dilly," Miz Johnson said, reaching quickly for the phone on the wall while keeping her eyes fastened on Imo. "Let's get him right on up here. I imagine he's got things all ready for the final checkout."

"Thank you kindly," Imo said, reaching for Lou's small hand. She felt that this was one of those moments she would revisit time and again, one that would separate her life like the chapters of a book.

 ## Loutishie's Notebook

When Mr. Dilly came around the corner with his arm leading this ancient woman, Imo jumped in her seat and squeezed my hand. I stared hard at the old lady's humped back and then at her pot belly beneath what looked like a frilly Easter dress. Her chin stuck out sharply and she had dark beady eyes underneath a straw hat. She wore white gloves and black patent-leather Mary Janes.

This is Imo's mother, I thought, *my grandmother.* This woman standing here is bone of my bone, flesh of my flesh, as folks in the Bible said whenever they were relatives.

Before Mr. Dilly had a chance to introduce himself, the old woman yanked away from him and scooted forward to grab Imo's arm. "Memaw!" she said into Imo's face, "I sure have been missing you!"

"Mama," Imo finally murmured, "I've come to carry you back home to Euharlee."

"Well, where's Pepaw at then? Why didn't he come with you?" She turned her attention to me. "Hi cousin Annalea. Why didn't y'all bring my Pepaw?"

"Um, I . . . I . . ." The cat had my tongue.

"Mama," Imo said firmly, "this is Loutishie. Your Vera's daughter. Your granddaughter."

"Hello ma'am," I squeaked out. "Nice to make your acquaintance."

"Why, Annalea!" the old face looked me up and down hard, "you know you don't call me 'ma'am,' and just look at you, you're skinny as a beanpole. You aren't eating enough to keep up your strength." This said, she turned and wrapped her old withered arms around Imo, burying her face in Imo's blouse. "Memaw, you really ought to make Annalea eat more, and also you ought to have brought my Pepaw."

Mr. Dilly set a red suitcase on the floor. He smiled and pulled the woman away from Imo. "We're having one of our confused spells, aren't we, Miz Jewell?" he said gently, grasping her wrists and speaking directly into her face. "Remember, you're going home today."

"Home, home, home!" she said firmly, then clapped her hands, leaned over to me, and whispered, "Wanna play dolls when we get home, Cousin Annalea?"

I held my breath as Mr. Dilly tried to steer her away. I guess he could tell I was terrified.

"Let go of me!" She crossed her arms, pouting.

"Mama," Imo said, biting her lip and shaking her head. "Mama."

All I really wanted to do at that point was to run away fast and far, but I managed to stay put while Imo kept calling out "Mama! Listen to me, Mama!" and Mr. Dilly said "Jewell, Jewell! You're going home!" until they managed to get her settled down.

That's when I decided to call this person Mama Jewell.

All of a sudden Mama Jewell stopped fussing. Her eyes opened really wide and she nodded. "I'm ready!" she crowed, "ready to get myself on back home! I've been waiting for this day for a long time."

"Be just as soon as we get your papers together and your things loaded up." Mr. Dilly slapped the side of the red suitcase happily. Turning to Miz Johnson, he instructed her to get out a paper for Imo to sign as well as an invoice that would settle the account.

Leaning against the wall and trying not to look at any of those other old folks who were staring at us, I thought about the crazy scene. I couldn't decide whether to think it was funny or to feel sorry for Imo and be sad about it. I knew she was feeling poorly, because she kept pausing now and then to press her hand over her heart while Miz Johnson gave her instructions on the procedure to claim Mama Jewell.

Finally Mr. Dilly came back to us, looked over the papers, stuffed them into a folder, patted it, and nodded. "Alrighty. We are all good to go here!"

"Well!" Imo said.

Mr. Dilly grabbed Mama Jewell's elbow and steered her toward the front door and said for us to pull right up to the steps there. We did and he eased Mama Jewell into the backseat, darted back inside and returned to fill up the trunk with her belongings. "Going home," Mama Jewell sang. "I'm going home."

Imo clipped her sunglasses onto her bifocals and we pulled away from the Carolina Arms. All I could think about as we headed into the late afternoon sun was that when Jeanette met Mama Jewell she was going to be fit to be tied! Jeanette's tolerance level was pretty low, and I had only lately learned that there were certain times to just stay out of her way, and if I couldn't manage that, to bite my tongue and endure patiently.

Back out on the main road things got quiet and I cast a glance toward the backseat. I saw that Mama Jewell's eyes were closed and her jaw was hanging open.

"She's got the dropsy, I reckon, Lou," Imo said. "Lots of older folks get the dropsy." Then, kind of sad, she added, "Lots of older folks go back to their childhoods, too."

"You mean like when she thought you were her Memaw?"

"Well, yes. Mr. Dilly said it's senile dementia. As well as a touch of what's called paranoia, combined with Alzheimer's. Anyhow, she goes back and forth in time a good bit, according to him."

"What?"

"Occasionally she'll be in her right mind," Imo said, "in the here and now and she knows who she is, but most of the time she doesn't." She scowled. "Goodness, Lou, those clouds yonder are moving in, aren't they? Looks like we may get us a sprinkle."

I nodded, knowing she had closed the discussion on Mama Jewell. It gave me a funny, scary feeling to think Mama Jewell could be different ages and not realize it. She sure seemed harmless enough as the young girl. I wondered how it would be when she came back into her right mind and was her true self.

I soon found out. Half an hour later she snorted real loud. She lifted her head and closed her mouth. Then her eyes opened so wide you could see whites all around. She turned her head this way and that and she like to have had a fit when she discovered the seat belt fastened underneath her pot belly. You'd have thought she was being kidnapped and tortured by the way she started yelling at that point.

"What in tarnation is going on here!" she bellowed, grabbing at the seat belt and flailing her little bird legs around.

"Hungry!" Imo said. "Mama, are you hungry? You must be hungry. I'll pull over at this Shoney's and get you some supper," she offered, slowing down a bit.

"I want to know just what is going on here. Where in heaven's name are we going?" Mama Jewell looked wildly around, her hands still clutching the seat belt buckle. "I surely didn't want to go nowhere. Where's Mr. Dilly at? He said—"

"He said for me to come and fetch you, Mama," Imo said. "You've been misbehaving."

Judging by the way Mama Jewell bit her lip, crossed her arms, and scowled, I knew she was thinking. She looked flustered, like she was trying to decide exactly who she was. Finally she leaned up, grabbed the back of the front seat, and looked hard at Imo. "I know who you are," she said finally, pointing a bony finger at Imo, then she turned toward me, "but I don't know you, little girl."

All this time I had been real quiet, praying Imo wouldn't start crying or having one of her heart-racing spells.

"Well, who are you, little girl?" Mama Jewell tapped my shoulder.

I turned to meet her eyes, dumbstruck.

"Tell!" she insisted.

Imo came to my rescue. "This here's Loutishie." She blew out a long whoosh of air. "Now, Mama, she's Vera's girl. Your own granddaughter. We've talked about Loutishie before. You remember."

"Turn back around here to me, girl," Mama Jewell demanded, "so I can get a better look at you."

I clamped my teeth together, turned, and looked at her as respectfully as I could.

Her eyes bored into me. "You must favor your father's side," she declared, then made the ugliest face you could imagine, scowling and thrusting out her old spotty lips. "'Cause you sure don't look a thing like my Vera did." She sat back and crossed her arms and I heard her add "that little tramp" under her breath.

I couldn't decide if not looking like Vera was good or bad for me in Mama Jewell's eyes. One thing I did know, and that was the fact that I did not like *this* version of the woman one tiny bit. As we drove along, I decided I'd try and do her like I did Jeanette when she was disagreeable. I would ignore her as best I could.

It was near dusk when I saw the familiar red and white of the Dairy Queen sign that was a mile from our road. Mama Jewell was asleep again and Imo and I rode in silence. The anticipation of our homecoming sat between us like a big fat person we couldn't see around. I was filled with horror and excitement. What would Jeanette think when she came face-to-face with Mama Jewell? Or, more to the point, what would she do?! They both obviously had a chip on their shoulder, along with a strong sense of self-entitlement.

I grabbed hold of my cool door handle even before Imo eased the Impala underneath the shed. What I wanted was to get out of there and run to the sanctuary of my room. Then I remembered I didn't have a room to myself anymore.

"Hold your horses, Lou." Imo reached for my wrist. "I need you to help me tote Mama's things in. Hopefully she'll just stay asleep while we unload and then we can get her inside. Mr. Dilly gave me some tablets that help relax her and I reckon I'll give her one soon as we can get her into the house. Buy us a little time anyway."

"Yessum," I said.

Imo hefted the red suitcase out of the trunk and I followed along behind her carrying a clothes bag and a small vanity case. We made several more trips back and forth to unload the car, and thankfully Mama Jewell's old chin stayed on her chest as she snored away.

When we roused her enough to ease her out, one on either side, steering her by the elbows toward the house, she was silent. Her eyes were open wide as silver dollars, looking to and fro, but she made no move to pull away or protest. *Thank you, God, I breathed. You know what a hard time Imo's having, so would you please keep this woman quiet until she gets to her bed and then let her go right on back to sleep for a long, long time.*

I spotted Jeanette with Little Silas sitting in her lap. They were on a quilt spread out over the floor of the darkened den, watching a rerun of *Diff'rent Strokes.* Light flickered from the TV onto Little Silas's sleepy-eyed face.

As Imo fastened the dead bolt, Jeanette pointed the remote at the TV to silence the laugh track and spun around to face us. Imo and I steadied Mama Jewell there in the kitchen.

For just a moment, the five of us were frozen in time. We all just stared. I decided Mama Jewell was thinking she was in a dream and would be waking up any minute to find herself in Mr. Dilly's lap along the banks of the Great Pee Dee River.

"This here is Imo's mama," I said finally, feeling a strong need to break the silence.

"No shit, Sherlock," Jeanette set Little Silas down gently, folded her arms across her chest, and studied Mama Jewell.

"There'll be no cursing in my home, missy," Imo piped up.

Mama Jewell suddenly sprung to life. "I'm *home*?!" She wrenched her arms free from me and Imo, and boy, was she strong. "Why, I surely *am* home!" she said as she flew over to the window behind the sink. "But somebody's been doing some redecorating in here. Where are the lacy curtains? The shamrocks along the windowsill?" She skipped forward into the den. Her hands flew out in the darkness, automatically and precisely reaching for the light switch. The adjoining den/kitchen lit up in bright fluorescent light.

Startled, she peered hard at Jeanette. "What's this girl doing in here? Father always sends the kitchen help on home directly after they finish clean-

ing up the supper. Like to get them home to their shanties before dark falls."
She turned her attention to Little Silas. "That little colored baby shouldn't be
in here either. Let me get someone to tote it on home."

Jeanette was on her feet in an instant. First she just stood there, looking
stunned, then her face turned furious. "You senile old warthog!" she snarled,
stamping her foot so hard that Mama Jewell jumped. She slid her hands under
Little Silas's armpits, scooped him up, leapt forward, and held him up close to
Mama Jewell's face. She waved him around a little. "Let's get a few things
straight around here! First of all, I ain't no kitchen help, and second of all, this
here's Little Silas and his daddy was an Indian from India. So don't you never
ever say one more ignorant word *to* or one word *about* my boy, and don't
you never, ever lay one of your ancient, warty fingers on him neither!"

"Goodness gracious me!" Mama Jewell blinked and her hands flew up to
her mouth. "Why, Father never allows the kitchen help to talk back." She
stood taller, pointed at Jeanette, and in a condescending tone said, "You'll
lose your position here, young sassy, if you don't watch your tongue."

Jeanette strode right up to Mama Jewell and she poked her pointer finger
into her chest. "I don't take no crap off of nobody, and you can go to hell!"

Mama Jewell's hands flew up in the air. "Mother! Father!" she screamed.
"The kitchen help's rising up! It's a revolt!"

"I done told you I ain't no kitchen help!" Jeanette hollered. "I ought to—"

Mama Jewell bristled. "I've a good mind to tell Father to carry you out
behind the woodshed!"

Jeanette got this wild look in her eyes and she bounced on the balls of
her feet with her free hand curled into a fist.

"Jeanette," I pleaded, "stop. Don't. Look at Imo over there."

Imo had collapsed into a kitchen chair at this point, with her legs in a
spread-eagle position. Her mouth was open in an O and a vein throbbed in
her temple.

"She's having one of her spells," I said. "Please just let it go with Mama
Jewell."

Jeanette sighed and bit her lip. "Oh, all right," she said reluctantly, backing off a bit.

I sidled over next to Mama Jewell and stroked her arm. "There, there, now," I murmured. "Everything's going to be okay. You're with family now."

At last Imo came back to herself. "Thank you, Lou," she said.

Mama Jewell turned to Imo. "I need to tell Mother or Father about the sassy kitchen help."

"Your folks passed away a long time ago, Mama," Imo said. "Let's get you on into bed right now, and tomorrow we'll all get a chance to talk. We'll also introduce everyone properly." She scowled over at Jeanette.

"But Mama," Jeanette's voice was quavery, "she disrespected me and Little Silas! Didn't you hear what she said?"

Imo looked back and forth between Mama Jewell and Jeanette, and I had the feeling she was wondering which one of them to pacify. "You'll just have to learn to overlook some things, Jeannie," she whispered. "I told you she's not well." She tapped at her temple with her finger.

"Stick her crazy ass in a crazy house then," Jeanette muttered as she whirled around and huffed off to our room.

I stood there thinking how Imo told us we didn't have enough money to send her off. I swallowed hard. How in heaven's name were we all going to survive in this house together?

"Give me a hand getting her to her room and into bed, will you, Loutishie?" Imo tilted her head and gave me a pleading look. Her shoulders were drooping, like the oomph had been knocked right out of her.

With all that had just transpired, I was pretty wiped out, too, and my feet felt glued to the floor.

"*Please,* sugar foot?" Imo pleaded. "And then would you look in my handbag and fetch those tablets for Mama that Mr. Dilly gave me? He says she has to be lying down to take one."

Somehow I got my feet moving. As we were on our way to her bedroom, Mama Jewell turned to Imo and she said, "Listen, I need to talk to Burton."

"Daddy's passed away, too, Mama," Imo said matter-of-factly.

"No, no, no," Mama Jewell cried, her knees giving way. Imo and I both staggered under her weight. We looked at each other helplessly.

If I can just get a tablet in her, Imo mouthed to me and I nodded. We managed to drag her to the bed and quickly Imo administered the tablet.

It didn't take long and Mama Jewell was out. I put my arm around Imo's shoulder. "Everything will be better in the morning," I told her.

"You're my right-hand man, Lou," she said. "I don't know what I'd have done without you today. And surely, with the good Lord's help, the two of us will be able to manage things."

I swallowed the knot in my throat and nodded.

Two

Field of Stone

*I*mogene tossed and turned that night, straining through the darkness to make sure all was well. As long as she heard nothing but the creaks and groans of the old farmhouse and an occasional owl, she figured she was holding things together. Maintaining the peace.

Long before first daylight, she grew weary of trying to sleep and pulled a flashlight from underneath her pillow, flung on a bathrobe, and crept outside. Silvery light from a full moon illumined the path out to the garden.

She walked first along the side of the garden closest to the house, where she aimed her beam of light to see bumblebees hovering amid the showy baseball-sized yellow blooms of the African marigolds. Here she bent and drew in a calming peppery breath.

Her slippers damp with dew, she walked among the rows of tomatoes. Next she checked the okra, the squash, and the melons, then knelt to scoop up a fistful of soil near the sweet corn to see if it was time to water. As she did, she spied a weed at her knee and paused to pluck it up. She noted that the Kentucky Wonder pole beans were doing well. Patiently she had trained them to twine around the stalks of sunflowers she planted beside them. When the garden was young, she'd sprinkled powdered lime around all the plants to keep the snails and slugs away. She'd also planted scented geraniums and tansies to attract ladybugs, since they ate their weight in aphids every day.

It was like fighting a battle to garden, Imo mused as she stood in the gray haze. Strategies had to be devised and implemented. Her hoe always stood at the ready, along with the water hose and the fertilizer, and she kept a barrelful of manure tea, aged and waiting, ready to revive an ailing plant.

Despite all this, birds and slugs would inevitably claim a few of the tomatoes, and blossom-end rot was a constant foe. The weather did not always cooperate, nor did the red Georgia clay.

But, Imo decided as she stopped to pinch a few suckers from a Brandywine tomato, if it *were* easy, it wouldn't be worth anything. That was how life was, too. All the way from raising children, to being married, to taking in an aging parent. You had to stay on top of things. You couldn't leave life any more unattended than you could a garden. Lord knows how much elbow grease she'd put into rearing her girls and Little Silas; still was, for that matter. And now it seemed that she had a fourth child to tend to, and a very demanding one at that.

How could she get through to Mama? Bring her back into reality? She kept telling herself that surely there was some way to make a tiny crack, to let the light shine in. If only she could discover it. She hunkered down between the cucumbers and the gourds to pray and to give it more thought.

What a peaceful sanctuary the garden was! Sometimes all it took was a leisurely stroll down the rows, pausing to straighten a tomato stake here or to mash a pesky hornworm there, and she could almost feel her blood pressure dropping. Tensions fell away as she unwound among the serene plants. Even weeding could clear her head, she mused as she tugged at a stray blade of grass.

Think, Imogene, *think,* she told herself as dawn came into its fullness and she made her way back to the house to start coffee. She paused a moment to admire the soaring spires of delphiniums beside the birdbath. She reached out to run her hand across their velvety petals, and as she did, an idea exploded into her brain.

Now, she was no psychiatrist, but it seemed to her that a visit to the family plot was the answer! She could show Mama her mother's and her father's graves. She would lead her over to Daddy's grave, too. Maybe even Vera's. Prove to her that all those folks were dead and snap her out of this confusion. She bet Mr. Dilly had never thought of that. Why, they could all ride up to the cemetery together!

Imo went into the bathroom to splash cold water on her face. She walked down the hallway and peered in on Mama. The light of dawn was just creeping across her bed. She certainly looked peaceful with her eyes closed, like someone capable of being reasonable.

Imo squared her shoulders and headed for the kitchen to brew some extrastrong coffee. Two cups later, she entered Mama's bedroom. She paused for a moment at the foot of the bed, to run her hand along the old trunk, the one Mama'd left so many years ago. It was still locked tight. Gently she shook her mother's shoulder. "Mama," she said, "wake up! I'm going to carry you to see your Burton this morning."

I wish I really could see my daddy, Imo thought, *he always made things better.* She sat down on the edge of the bed to wait, feeling twelve years old again. "Come on now, Mama, time to wake up."

"My Burton?" Mama's eyes fluttered open. "You really mean it?"

"Yes, Mama. You're going to see your Burton." Now Imo felt deceitful, though it wasn't exactly a lie.

Mama was subdued and quiet as Imo helped her dress. She sat Mama in the La-Z-Boy in the den while she went to boil grits for breakfast.

Things were going along smoothly enough, but for one brief moment Imo let herself review last night's ugly scene. She knew Jeanette could easily make a mess of this, too.

As it turned out, Jeanette shuffled silently to the kitchen in her nightgown, opened the Frigidaire, popped the pull-top on a can of Tab, and walked back to her room without even so much as a glance in Mama's direction.

Jeanette drove and they trundled along between pastures up to the main road. Little Silas flung Cheerios and mooed at the cows while everyone else was silent. It was going to be a real scorcher later, Imo noted, but it was cool enough for the windows to be down this early. She admired the pink crepe myrtles along Paris Street, still blooming proudly along, though July had been fairly dry.

They drove by Calvary Baptist. There was a new message on the rolling marquis that sat in a clump of fescue between the road and the parking lot. Imo strained to see what the Reverend Lemuel Peddigrew had come up with this time.

FREE TICKETS TO HEAVEN!
DETAILS INSIDE.

Catchy enough. Imo decided Martha had thought this one up. The Reverend Peddigrew was a simple, no-nonsense type of man. Not one given to flashiness or sensationalism. After all, he'd grown up a hayseed farm boy from a tiny town down in South Georgia, and Imo'd heard him say on many occasions that when he felt the call to be God's mouthpiece at the age of fifteen, he was out picking cotton and he just stopped right then and there and preached the gospel to the cotton stalks as he stuffed bolls into a burlap sack.

And to this day, he still dressed like a farmer: khakis held up by suspenders, clunky work boots, and a chambray shirt. Except for Sundays when he stood in the pulpit and wore a nice suit and tie.

Imo knew she ought to go to Reverend Peddigrew for wisdom to help her through this particular trial. Something in her said she should seek spiritual counsel, just as she should have when Jeanette was with child. At the very least, she ought to call Martha and tell her that Mama was here.

Just deal with one thing at a time, Imo, she told herself, and right now, merely recalling Jewelldine Wiggins's fits of anger, her quick hand with the hickory switch, and, most of all, her stinging words, was painful enough. Plus, if she were to lay it all out there for the Reverend or for Martha, it might very well stir up even more terrible memories.

Anyway, she wouldn't need to burden the Reverend Peddigrew once Mama got to the cemetery and snapped out of this current craziness. Imo would be able to manage her on her own after that. Her main task would be to keep the peace between Jeanette and Mama, and surely she could handle that.

They rounded a corner and Imo bent to retrieve Little Silas's pacifier. She handed it over the seat to him and turned her attention out the window to Euharlee's downtown. It was primarily a wide place in the road, with a covered bridge that carried folks across the Euharlee Creek. There was also a fire station, the tiny library, the courthouse, Dub's Gas, the Health Clinic, and the Dixie Chick, a restaurant that served frogs' legs fresh from the creek. Mama's dark eyes darted from side to side, but she remained quiet, clutching a large black patent-leather purse on her lap.

Bits of gravel pinged against the underside of the car as they turned onto the unpaved road that wound up to the high rocky spot of the family cemetery. The road made a sharp turn at the crest of the hill and ended at a wide circle underneath some mimosas and pines. From this vantage point, you could look up a weedy knoll of fifty feet or so and see the patch of tombstones. Some tall and leaning, like crooked teeth, and some stout and short, planted solidly among sprouting weeds. In the light of early morning, the stones had a bluish cast.

Imogene was the first one out of the car. She pressed a hand against her heart and stepped through dirt as dry and fine as talcum powder to open her mother's door. *You're on your way to wholeness now, Mama,* she thought as she studied the old woman's face.

Now that they were here, Imo wondered briefly just how she was supposed to do this. She sucked in a breath. "Well," she said, "here we are! And such a pretty day, too!"

Mama's eyes were wide open and unblinking when Imo reached in to set the purse aside and unfasten her seat belt. "Let's get you on out of there, Mama."

"Uh uh uh! Hands off!" the old woman snapped. She bunched her shoulders up close to her ears and bent forward over the purse.

"Sorry." Imo stepped back.

"What the hell's going on back there?" Jeanette turned to look over the seat.

Imogene sized up the moment. She willed her face to relax. "Oh, not a thing, Jeannie. Just having a bit of trouble unfastening this pesky buckle here!" She smiled to beat the band.

"Got some things for my Burton in here," Mama fussed as she patted her purse. "Do I look purty enough to see him?"

"You're lovely, Mama," Imo said.

Jeanette looked over at Lou, circled a finger in the air next to her ear, rolled her eyes, and whistled like tiny birds.

"Mi-moo!" Little Silas cried out from his restraint beside Mama. This brought a fierce look from Mama and Imo could almost see the wheels turning in her brain about the previous evening. She didn't want Jeanette involved in any way and so to head off trouble Imo dashed around to the other door, leaned across a startled Loutishie, and unclipped and scooped Little Silas up and out of the car in one swift motion. She nuzzled her nose on his soft brown cheek, kissed his head, and settled him onto her hip. "Now we'll get your great-granny out, darlin'," she whispered into his ear. She returned to Mama's door and carefully slid a hand underneath the purse and unlatched her, grabbing her elbow and helping her out.

This, too, shall pass, Imo reassured herself as she struggled along, one arm toting Little Silas and one arm hooked through Mama's, toward a narrow footpath leading up the small incline to the cemetery.

She could make it. If she stopped now to think about how exhausted her body was from a night of no sleep, and on top of that, how fuzzy her mind was from the terrible memories, she may as well just lay on down and die right now. Be convenient here, anyway. She smiled for the first time in days.

They moved along between overgrown weeds until her Keds and socks were wet with the dew. She glanced over her shoulder for Jeanette and Lou. They were sitting in the Impala. It was just as well, she thought. It would keep Jeanette and Mama apart. She'd holler for them to join her when she'd accomplished her mission.

She climbed higher, heading into the rising sun, picturing Mama's deliverance at Daddy's tombstone.

At last they reached the low stone wall that enclosed the cemetery, and they sailed through a rusty iron gate sagging on its hinges.

"Well, here we are," Imo said, panting. She pointed at a wide, thick stone. "Yonder there is Burton Ivey Wiggins."

Mama squinted. She pulled away from Imo and darted forward, stopping abruptly at the headstone. She turned to eye the flat stone that marked the foot. She tapped at the dirt with her shoe. She turned and fastened her questioning gaze on Imo's face.

Imo's heart was hammering. She bounced Little Silas on her hip. "Daddy," she said, pointing to the stone. "Your Burton."

Mama stood, nervously raising up and down on tiptoe, as a look of disbelief spread across her face. She shook her head like a wet dog drying himself after a dip in the creek. She stomped one foot. "I reckon it's not my Burton!" she cried. "It's not!"

Imo knew that it was probably unwise to argue with her in her present condition, but what else could she do? "Why, it surely is him, Mama," she said in her gentlest voice as she bounced Little Silas on her hip. "Daddy passed away the year before sister had

Loutishie. You've been up in Pamplico for going on sixteen years! I am sixty-five, Mama, and you are eighty-four, and Daddy, I mean Burton, is dead. He's gone to be with the Lord." She took a long, slow breath.

The old woman stood slack-jawed, squinting at Imo through streams of sunlight.

"You remember, don't you, Mama?" Imo coaxed. "He died of emphysema. You sat by that dear man's sickbed and nursed him for close to six months of your life. You were good to him. You spoon-fed him. Turned him to keep the bedsores from coming. Sang to him, even. You barely left the farm. Don't you remember his funeral?" she urged.

Mama clutched her purse closer. She maintained her perfect silence.

"See? You do see, don't you, Mama?" Imo's voice sounded shrill to her own ears as she sidled over to rub Mama's back. "This is 1999. Loutishie back yonder at the car is your granddaughter. You're a grandmother. Over there is your daughter Vera's stone. She's dead, just like Daddy. Gone to be with Jesus, too."

Mama took tentative steps closer to Burton's headstone, still shaking her head. She rubbed the marble in disbelief. "It's not him! You lied to me, Imogene Rose. I come up here to bring him this and he's not here!" She thrust out her chin as she pulled a small silver object from her purse and shook it around. "I've a good mind to switch you good for lying to me, girl!"

Imo saw that she held a can of Vienna sausages. "Mama," she pleaded, hearing an edge of fury in the old woman's words that turned her blood to ice and froze her limbs. "You have *got* to understand, Mama," she begged. "Burton is dead. He's right there underneath your feet."

She looked down. "He is most certainly not under my feet!"

Imo bounced Little Silas on her hip even harder. "Well, you're right. He's with the Lord, as I said before. But he's not with us anymore." She suddenly grew weary. Her plan was not working. She walked over to Vera's stone to set Little Silas down upon it. "Hey sister," she said, sighing and stroking the cool marble.

Mama Jewell glanced at her with suspicion. "What's that you're saying?" she asked, wrinkling up her forehead.

"Just talking to Vera, Mama."

"Vera Wiggins?"

"Yessum. Your daughter. Passed on, just like your Burton."

"Girl was a tramp," Mama Jewell snarled.

Imo waited. Then she said, "Why can't you let that go, Mama? She was young."

Mama Jewell pushed out her bottom lip. "Ran with that fast crowd from Buzzard Mountain. Those low-life white trash." She shook her head. "Hussy!"

"You shouldn't speak ill of the dead, Mama," Imo whispered softly.

Mama put the sausages back into her purse and snapped it shut. She fingered the faux gold clasp.

"Mama, you've got to *understand*," Imo said, "you're living in the past."

Mama looked at her quizzically. "What?"

"Yessum. You are living in a world that's gone."

"It's gone?"

"Plum gone!" Imo nodded for emphasis. "You need to snap out of this . . . and you also need to—"

Mama looked wildly about. "Liar!" she spat.

"I'm not," Imo said, rage flaming over her cheeks. Little Silas laughed.

"Yes, you are lying to me," Mama Jewell insisted. "I'll learn you to lie to me, girl," she said, coming toward Imo and Little Silas like a spider.

Imo sucked in a breath. Instinctively she picked up Little Silas and backed away. He cried out, a loud "Wah!" that startled Mama. Abruptly Mama stopped and she peered hard. "You brung the little colored baby? Why come you to do that?" Her voice got softer. "Why, he's just darling," she pronounced, dropping her purse and reaching out for Little Silas. "Let me hold him."

It couldn't hurt, Imo thought. Clearly Mama was enchanted by him, and she couldn't get far with him if she did decide to do anything contrary. Gently Imo nestled Little Silas into Mama's arms.

The change in Mama was remarkable. Her eyes lit up, she smiled ,and she began humming and swaying back and forth with the boy. Imo whispered a silent prayer of thanks to God that Jeanette was nowhere in sight.

"They're mighty cute when they're little," Mama said as she stroked his cheek tenderly. "Aren't they, Imogene?" She turned to Little Silas. "Yes you are. You're mighty precious. You surely are." She squeezed him and Imo feared he might squeal and push her away. But he seemed fascinated by her wrinkly face as he patted at her cheek and then her neck.

Mama giggled. "Yep," she said to him, touching his nose to hers, "cute you are. Wish't I could freeze you like this! 'Cause when little colored babies grow up, they get sassy!"

Imo shook her head. She was furious, but she was not shocked. This was the Mama she'd grown up with. Narrow-minded and prejudiced. She was one of the old white southern women who thought whites were better than everybody else.

Imo searched Little Silas's tiny brown face. If Jeanette hadn't told them that the father was an India Indian, she'd have bet money herself that he was half black (or Afro-American as the young folks said nowadays).

Fascinated, Imo listened as her mother talked baby-talk to Little Silas and he laughed. Her high, quavery voice said, "Oh, yes you are simply darlin'. First moment I seen you I said to myself that you was just an itty-bitty precious little sweetheart. I could just about eat you up!"

Then all of a sudden Mama stopped speaking. For a moment she stood there dead still. She searched Little Silas's face intently and sought Imo's eyes next. There was an abrupt shift in her face, a change like night to day. "Is this *my* baby?" Mama asked, her forehead knit up in bewilderment.

Imo looked at her. She was pitiful, really. An old lady, befuddled by senile dementia. Her eyes seemed to scream out *Help!* Imo eased over toward the two of them. She gathered Little Silas and set him onto her hip once again. She touched Mama's shoulder. "He belongs to Jeanette," she said gently. "Come on, Mama," she said, "let's get you back to the house. It's getting to be right hot out here."

Mama stared at her a long moment, then let herself be shepherded back along the path. "Father will be mad at me for being late," she warned. She took a faltering step forward. "He's liable to take the hickory switch to me!" With that statement, her eyes widened and her little bird legs flew along the path toward the gate. "Come on, Memaw!" she yelled to Imo. "Hurry! Please carry me to Pepaw's store and let him hide me from Father!"

Imo stood there, staring at her mother's back, an awful realization forming inside. This senile dementia could not be rooted out by a visit to the family graveyard or by wishful thinking. She spied Silas's headstone out of the corner of her eye, still new enough that there was no moss yet. Imo blinked away a tear, feeling sorry for herself without him. He'd certainly had a way with Jeanette.

Jeanette! Imo sucked in a breath as she pictured Mama and Jeanette in a fistfight back at the car. "Wait up, Mama!" she cried, running after her.

God, give me strength, Imo prayed as they drove along toward home. She surveyed the faces depending on her. She could use someone to talk to about all that was going through her mind right now, someone to roll alternate ideas off of. Very briefly she considered Loutishie. No, it would not be fair to burden the child. She deliberated on Martha Peddigrew once more. No, though she was a longtime friend, her big mouth could not be entrusted to keep all of the details to herself. If Imo told Martha, every one of the girls in the Garden Club would know, and most of the congregation at Calvary Baptist.

Surely there was some way just to block out all these painful memories that were sprouting like dandelions.

Growing up, Imo's goal had been to steer clear of her mother whenever she was on one of her frequent rampages. She would run down to the river and stay there for hours, letting the water wash away the terrors and the heartaches.

And when Silas Lavender asked for her hand in marriage at the tender age of sixteen, she'd leapt at the chance to enfold herself in his strong arms. They'd moved into a tiny, rickety caretaker's shack not a hundred yards away from the farmhouse and from Mama and Daddy, but far enough away to be Imo's sanctuary and her heaven. This meant that Imo was close when Vera was born ten years later. Mama was forty-five then, and hardly in a condition to tend to a newborn, and Imo was more than willing to help out.

Poor Mama. It had been bad enough that she had suffered through a succession of miscarriages and a harrowing stillbirth, along with the dashed expectation of ever giving birth to a son that lived, but on top of that, and perhaps in part due to that, she was plagued by a state of sadness that was not acknowledged as clinical depression way back then. This depression moved on to the deeper level of despondency and then worsened further to despair.

It was in a period of this deep despair, marked by an absolute loss of hope, that Mama had attempted suicide shortly after Vera's birth. Some said her near-fatal overdose of sleeping pills was due to postpartum depression, but Imo knew its roots were much earlier and went much deeper than that. Imo often recalled something she'd read by a psychologist several years ago as she waited for an appointment in the dentist's office. Dr. Harvey Goldman wrote that "despair is sometimes connected with violent action, even rage."

It was this sentence she recited over and over again, hoping to find in it some origin for forgiving her mother. Surely Dr. Goldman was saying, in a roundabout way, that Mama wasn't responsible for her fits of temper. But the fact remained that this knowledge did nothing to help Imo forgive or forget.

She stared out the window. They were passing Calvary Baptist once again. She pictured Reverend Peddigrew inside his tiny office at the rear of the chapel, barely bigger than a broom closet, with his ever-present cup of coffee in a stained enamel cup and a stack of Bible commentaries at his elbow.

As a young girl, she had believed that her minister, the Reverend Elmer Webb, now gone to glory, actually talked aloud with God, and that God answered him aloud, much like any other human conversation. She was told ministers had direct lines and answers from heaven.

Silas might have had the answers, but he was no longer here, and Imo realized now that however hard she tried, and as much as she just wanted to block it all out, she could not handle this alone. She could not deal with her own anger and her helplessness over that anger. She had to get some help. Not just for her own sanity, but for Jeanette and Lou and Little Silas and, yes, even for Mama's sake. It was Imo's duty to shepherd these people.

Plus, the Bible said she was to honor her mother and father. Well, she had no trouble honoring her daddy. He had been gentle and kind, did all in his power to give her a good life. He knew what Imo suffered at the hand of her mother, and always he came to her after Mama's fits of rage, and said to Imogene that they were not her fault and she should not blame herself at all. Daddy always reassured her that they had nothing to do with her. He said that Mama was helpless to stop herself.

And Imo was helpless to obey that commandment about honoring her mother without a direct connection to the Almighty. When they were home, she was going to make an appointment with Reverend Peddigrew. Surely he would not tell Martha about Imo's secrets. Ministers were like doctors, sworn to secrecy.

Loutishie's Notebook

It was early that first morning of Mama Jewell, and I sat at the kitchen table waiting for everyone else to get ready to go up to the cemetery. I peered out at the rusty bell beside our mailbox. A long dirt road led from the highway through the upper two hundred acres of the farm and then looped around beside the house, like the eye of a needle, so that the mailman could deliver our mail and then turn right around. A worn dirt path ran from the back steps to the mailbox and the bell. Whenever Imo rang the bell, you could hear it clear up to the edge of the fields along the highway, and also if you were way down in the bottoms, one hundred acres of corn and soybeans through which the majestic Etowah River flowed.

I longed to be running down to the river bottoms that very moment, but Imo had this crazy idea that a trip up to the cemetery would be healing for all of us. She was on a tear inside the house, running around and doing things like wiping the top of the Frigidaire until it was spotless and organizing the silverware drawer.

I figured that was her method of dealing with Mama Jewell. It was the same way she dealt with all the crises of life. During those long, lonely days she had to get through after Uncle Silas died, and then her fiancé, Mr. Fenton Mabry, I remember Imo just keeping herself constantly busy. She never slowed down enough so we could sit and have a heart-to-heart talk about our grief. We didn't pause to discuss Jeanette's walk on the wild side either, and we certainly weren't discussing Mama Jewell's condition. That's why I was so leery when all of a sudden, Imo said we had to head up to the cemetery to help her.

I looked out across the pastures as we traveled along, trying to decide if this trip was so Mama Jewell could pay her respects to her parents, her husband, Uncle Silas, or my mother. I knew for a fact she wasn't there for Uncle Silas's funeral, and from the sound of things, she didn't come back for her daughter's funeral either. Her very own flesh and blood!

We rolled to a stop and Imo collected Little Silas and Mama Jewell from the car. It didn't seem polite to go up there and gawk while a person paid their respects, so I decided to stay in the car with Jeanette.

She lit a cigarette. "Ain't you going up there, Lou?"

"Nah. I'm just going to wait."

"What are they doing up there? I didn't see no flowers." Jeanette blew a long stream of smoke upward.

"I reckon they're visiting graves so Mama Jewell can pay her respects," I said. "Imo said coming here would be healing for her."

Jeanette made a little noise of disgust. She glanced up at the rearview mirror to catch my eye. "She's a weird bird, ain't she, Lou? You get a load of her crazy ass last night? Calling me the kitchen help, and calling my baby colored? I hate the old warthog already."

My cheeks got hot. I didn't think Jeanette ought to be saying those things about Mama Jewell. Didn't she heed the Reverend's warnings about how we ought to set a guard round about our lips and only use savory words, speech that is good for the edifying of others? I didn't call her on it because she didn't take well to godly counsel, and also because there I sat, despising Mama Jewell myself. Bad thoughts were like wild horses in my head, horses I just couldn't slip a bridle onto.

Jeanette took a last long suck on her cigarette and then flicked the butt out the window. "I know what!" she said. "Let's go spy on them. We can get behind that clump of trees up there at the edge of the graves."

I considered this for a second. "Well . . . okay," I said. "I guess it couldn't hurt."

We climbed the short hill and stationed ourselves in a wide patch of mimosa trees. Neither Jeanette nor I said much for a while. I spotted Imo, Little Silas, and Mama Jewell a ways off, standing near my grandfather Burton Wiggins's grave. I never knew him, since he died before I was born. All I ever thought of when I did think of him was one old black-and-white photo of a weather-beaten farmer standing beside an old-timey hand plow, and the words that were etched into his stone beneath his name: Gone to Glory.

I knew the words on every stone up there. I'd been to visit Uncle Silas's grave so many times since he'd passed on that the stones were like friends. They were also like listening to one great big sermon. Two stones always made me stop and catch my breath when I read what they said. One of them belonged to a great-aunt named Eula Mae Binney. In big, bold letters cut deep in the stone and furry with moss, it read "In the twinkling of an eye, at the last trump: for the trumpet shall sound, and the dead shall be raised incorruptible. 1 Corinthians 15:52." The second was about the Rapture of the saints, too. Underneath Isaac Didymus Wiggins's name and his dates it said, "Get ready! Jesus is coming."

The Rapture was one of Reverend Peddigrew's favorite topics. He said that getting ready for heaven took constant attention. It was not an easy task. "You must do battle with your thoughts and your tongues!" he liked to say. He also said Jesus was likely to descend on his cloud of Glory any minute, and He would blow his trumpet, and the dead saints would be raised up to immortality first, and then the living saints would be caught up together with them in the twinkling of an eye.

Whenever the Reverend described death, he made it sound like a good thing. Well, a good thing if you made it into heaven, that is. A place free of all sorrow and weeping and sickness and frailty. It helped me a little to know that Uncle Silas was free of the cancer in his body. Those last few months of his life on this side of the grave were hard. He liked a peaceful, unadventurous life, and when he got overcome by the pain and all those doctors, nurses, and tearful relatives coming by to see him in his hospital bed, he didn't quite know what to do. My heart ached for him. I knew Uncle Silas longed to retreat to the farm with the sky spreading over him like a healing salve.

When he was surrounded by fields and livestock and the farm equipment he knew inside and out, he was a happy man. Happiness that started in the Euharlee soil and worked its way up through the soles of his boots and right into his heart. I was like that, too. But even though I knew heaven was supposed to be beautiful, the streets paved with gold and jewels everywhere, secretly, in my heart, I believed it couldn't possibly hold a candle to a morning on a country dirt road in the springtime. I bent to pick up one of the pink blossoms that looked like powder puffs strewn all over the ground underneath the mimosas. I cradled it in my hand as I studied Jeanette. Someone needed to rattle her cage. I could think of no one more than her who needed to be warned about the Rapture. She never considered her eternal destiny. She lived entirely in the moment.

"Isn't this pretty, Jeannie?" I placed my palm with the mimosa pouf near her face. "Pretty for earth, I reckon. But heaven's going to be a whole lot prettier. And won't it be great to see Uncle Silas again when we get up there?"

A cynical smile crossed her face. She was sitting cross-legged in the dirt, lining up the pink blossoms out of boredom. She lifted one high, released it, and let it flutter down. She began talking, almost like I wasn't even there. "I miss him, sure enough," she said. "I miss Daddy more every day and I wish he could see Little Silas." She swiped a tear away with the back of her hand. "But what I'm gonna do is hunt me a man to take care of me. Love me. *Me and* Little Silas. He'll git us our own place. Place with a yard and one of them swing sets with a seesaw. Away from that crazy old biddy yonder. Little Silas is going to have himself a daddy to carry him fishin'." Jeanette's foot swept out and sent the mimosa blooms scattering. "Mmm-hmm. Gonna find me a man is what I'm gonna do." She gave her head a determined nod.

"You should find one that's not married this time, Jeannie," I said, speaking before my brain got in gear. I knew it was a real sore spot with her that Dipafloda left the country and went back to his wife in India before Little Silas was born.

"You little idjit!" Jeanette shot me the meanest look.

"Well, it's a sin to take other folks' husbands. That's adultery," I continued, now that I was already on her bad side, "and you won't rise up during the Rapture if you commit adultery."

"Aw, hush your preachin'." Jeanette rolled her eyes and sighed. "I done told you there ain't no heaven." She stood and placed her hands on her hips. "All your stupid talk about some heavenly father. Well, if there is a father up there and he's so good, why did he take Daddy?" She paused a moment.

"Hmmm? Answer that one, Lou. Anyway, we make our own heaven right here on earth and I aim to find me a heavenly man!"

I shrugged and picked up a stick. I wasn't good at quick comebacks.

"Went to Lacey Whitcomb's wedding last Saturday, you know," Jeanette said. "My friend from junior high? One with the long, black hair?"

Just barely listening, I nodded. I was focusing my attention on Imo and Mama Jewell, who looked like they were having angry words about something.

"Wore me that little blue dress with the slit up the side," Jeanette was saying, "Lacey married a boy from Alabama named Dusty, and he was *such* a stud muffin in his tux. But his brother, the best man . . . mmm mmm mmm, talk about meltin' my butter!" Jeanette shook her head in wonder as she closed her eyes.

I groaned over her choice of words. She gave me an exasperated look and scooted over beside me to fluff up my hair. "You know what, Lou? You could be gorgeous if you ever gave it half a mind. With all this thick chestnut hair and your big eyes," she gushed. "Let me cut you some wings tonight, and give you a highlight. I'll get one of them kits from the Buywise that you paint on golden streaks with and I'll do you a makeover. How 'bout it, kiddo?"

I didn't answer her. I had no use for primping and fussing with how I looked, and to Jeanette, that was a sheer waste of being. She loved makeup and perfume, was always dieting and rubbing in thigh-firming gels and crow's-foot removal creams. Her favorite thing to say lately was "Soon I'm gonna get my figure back. I'm gonna get down to below my prebaby weight! Yep, I'll be hotter than I ever was!"

From the corner of my eye I noticed Imo scurrying after Mama Jewell. Mama Jewell was shaking her head and waving her fists.

Suddenly Jeanette laughed. She leaned back, shaking her head in wonder. "Remember when Mama got herself that makeover, Lou? Blew my mind, but man, she looked sharp. And then she started dating all them men."

That question sat heavy on my shoulders. Back when Imo was gussying herself up and on that crazy manhunt so soon after Uncle Silas had passed away, I said and did some things I am not proud of today. Then she actually went and fell in love with one of the men. But what was even crazier is that I fell in love with Mr. Fenton Mabry, too. Though it was not romantic love like Imo had. It about tore all of us up when he was killed right before their wedding.

Almost like she could read my thoughts, Jeanette patted my arm. "That was terrible when Mr. Mabry got shot by deer hunters, weren't it, Lou? Broke poor Mama's heart all over again."

"Yep, it was terrible all right," I said into the rays of sunlight streaming through the mimosas.

Jeanette shook her head. "Two dead folks. Reckon who the third one's gonna be?" She laced her fingers together and then turned her arms up and her hands inside out to stretch.

"What?" I looked up in alarm at her.

"You know, Lou, how bad things come in threes. There's gonna be another dead body. You can count on it."

A terrible feeling came over me. Sometimes I hated Jeanette, she sure knew how to get my goat. "Hush," I said. "You shouldn't even *say* that."

"Well, it's true. Maybe it'll be old Mama Jewell who's dead body number three, and if it is, I'll tell you what I'll do, Lou, I'll dance on her grave! Hell, I'll throw the biggest friggin' party in the whole friggin' world!" Jeanette lit another cigarette. "But, of course," she said, smiling, "it could be me. I bet I die young."

"Stop it now," I said. "Don't say stuff like that!"

"Well, I hope it's not true—I have Little Silas who needs me," she said, smoke from her cigarette curling up through the mimosas, "but it could happen." She nodded and rubbed her chin. Clearly she *had* thought about this before.

"You die young, you leave a beautiful corpse!" she sang out as she waved a fly away. "Who wants to get old anyway? Old and crazy like Mama Jewell!" She stood up, walked to the edge of the shade and held a hand over her eyes. "Hey, come here, Lou. Look at them! They're hanging out at your mother's grave."

I scrambled up and over to stand beside Jeanette.

"Your mother died young and beautiful, Lou," Jeanette said.

I watched Mama Jewell growing very animated there at my mother's headstone. She was shaking her head, and I saw Imo patting her back and trying to calm her down. The graveyard no longer looked peaceful and friendly to me, and after all that talk about dead folks and dying, all I wanted was to get home.

When we did get back to the house, Mama Jewell stepped out of the Impala, slapped her thighs, and hollered out "El-mer! Dewy Ro-ose! Come here, babies!"

Jeanette started laughing. "What's the old girl doing?"

Imo winced. "Those were some peacocks she used to have here."

Mama Jewell got all worked up looking for them until Imo was able to distract her by saying they ought to go out to the garden and see about picking the okra.

Mama Jewell grabbed a feed bucket off a shelf in the shed. "I'll fry us up some okra for our supper," she said, marching toward the garden. "Burton sure loves his fried okra."

The cemetery stirred up memories for Mama Jewell. As we all sat down for supper, she began to rant and rave about my mother.

"What was the name of that trashy girl Vera was running around with?" Mama Jewell asked Imo. "Girl was nothing but a tramp! I told Vera time and again, I told her not to mess with them loose girls. Shameless! Every last one of them. Little Jezebels!"

"Here, have some meatloaf, Mama," Imo said. "Got some mashed potatoes down here, too."

"Oh yes," Mama Jewell continued, "went and got herself knocked up. My Vera did. Hussy!"

"That's enough, Mama," Imo said, piercing Mama Jewell with a stare.

"Boy never did show up to claim his little bastard child."

Shame flooded over my cheeks.

"Shut up, warthog!" Jeanette came to my defense, slapping the table so hard all the plates rattled. "Don't you say one more word about a *bastard.* You hear me?!"

I held my breath.

"Do you?!" Jeanette stood, knocking the table forward.

"I think we're all just hungry," Imo said. "Have another roll, Mama."

Well, Mama Jewell blinked and started in on her supper, but my mind went zooming back to a long-ago memory. I was six or so, and I had been playing in the pantry—a tiny room off the kitchen where the shelves were lined with red and green rows of quart jars bright with tomatoes, pickles, and beans. It was peaceful in there, quiet and cool as I silently stacked and restacked a white column of Chinette plates we used for church potluck suppers. Imo puttered around the kitchen, cleaning up and baking two of her famous girdle-buster pies for a neighbor who'd fallen and broken her hip.

There was the sharp rapping of someone's knuckles on the door. Then I heard Imo calling "Come in, dear," followed by Miss Willie Pardini, an ancient woman who had come to lend a hand when I was a newborn, saying all breathless, "Imogene Lavender!"

Miss Willie's voice had a scolding, shame-on-you sound to it. "How come you didn't tell me? Had to hear it from Mr. Preston down to the bank!"

I stopped breathing and moved from my squatting position and sat quietly. Forgot all about the city I was making out of the plates.

"Just beat all I ever heard," Miss Willie went on. "I had to get myself on over here and see if it was true."

Imo didn't answer her a word. I could only picture her standing at the sink and scrubbing the mixing bowl over and over.

"You ought not to have to take that off her, hon. You and Silas oughtn't be sending your mama money. You don't have it!" Miss Willie's strong, indignant words hung in the air and the way Imo got so quiet, I thought maybe Miss Willie had convinced her.

Anyway, she was right. We didn't have any money. Uncle Silas took over the farm when Granddaddy Wiggins died and I had figured out a long time ago that he didn't make a bunch of money.

"It's okay," Imo countered softly. "She's sick."

"Doesn't give her the right to do you and Silas this way."

"Well," said Imo, "it's not my job to judge Mama."

"Not your job to support her either. And after the way she's done you over the years."

"Here, let me get you some tea, Miss Willie."

I heard the freezer opening and ice chinking into glasses and then chairs at the kitchen table scraping back and the two women settling themselves down.

"Just tell me you didn't bail her out this time," Miss Willie said.

"Mmm-hmm," admitted Imo.

"She'll never learn if you keep on," said Miss Willie. "Sometimes you have to be cruel to be kind."

"I had to. She'd have been out on the street if I didn't."

"Listen, hon, you don't owe that woman a thing. She'll take everything you've got and then some," warned Miss Willie. "And she won't feel one twinge of guilt. The way she did when Vera was expecting little Loutishie."

Those words hung in the air for a moment. My ears got hot. I stared at a blue box of salt Uncle Silas sprinkled on the ice when he churned ice cream. I put my arms around my knees and hugged myself.

"This is the way I look at that, Miss Willie," Imo finally spoke, firmly and softly, "Mama did me a favor that time. Raising Lou has been my pride and joy."

Miss Willie sucked in a deep breath. "Well, don't you think I know that, dear? But it doesn't change the fact that she up and *left* her family! Left y'all when her own daughter was expectin'. Now you listen here to me, Imo. Your mama's selfish. That's what I've been saying all these years. She's made her bed and now she ought to have to lie in it. If they put her out on the street, they put her out on the street."

Imo's voice was quivery with emotion. "It was the beginning of her undoing, Miss Willie," she said, "when sister got pregnant with Lou. She was twenty-four, but she was not married, and Mama really lost it. She just went to pieces. She tried to hide sister's condition from the Baptist women. I remember her crying and saying how she was a failure at raising a virtuous daughter. My Silas didn't care. He adored Vera. He drove her to the hospital when she was ready to have Lou, and he just dared anybody in Euharlee to say one word about her not being married."

I wasn't listening any longer. I tuned them out so I could think. At six years old, I had never really stopped to ponder the fact that I didn't actually come out of Imo. She was my mother and that was a fact. It sounded really strange to hear about this Vera, who was Imo's sister, and who was, supposedly, my mother. Vera was just a name and a tiny face in random pictures around the house; she meant nothing to me.

That moment in the pantry is when I lost my innocence. One day I was without a care in this world, and the next I was confused and feeling a little guilty about some type of scandal that was associated with my birth mother, Vera, who was Imo's little sister, and with my grandmother, Jewelldine, *their* mother and my very own grandmother. Judging from the conversation going on in the kitchen, however, what my grandmother did was much worse than a woman with no husband having a baby.

"I simply can't believe it, Imo." Miss Willie sighed. "I remember you telling me you practically raised Vera. You and Silas. What was your mama thinking?"

"Don't get yourself so worked up, Miss Willie. Mama was sick then, too. She cried practically all the time when she was pregnant with Vera. And she kept on saying how she wanted to die for a while after Vera was born and her not a boy, and Dr. Thursby saying she couldn't have any more children." There was a pause. "Poor little Vera," Imo said reverently, "never had hardly a chance in this world."

"Even if your mama was sick, she didn't have to put all that off on you, Imogene. Never looked sick to me when I saw her, stout as she was."

"Sick up here is what," Imo said, and since I couldn't see where she meant, I could only guess.

"Then she just up and run off for good when Vera got in her predicament!" Miss Willie fussed, "and has never even laid eyes on her only grandchild. Didn't even bother to come to Vera's funeral."

By that time my legs were aching. But I couldn't move as I listened to Imo arguing that it was her mother's sickness that made her do all those things. A sickness that she had no control over. "Mama was so mad when Vera wouldn't bring the boy, the father, out to the house, Miss Willie. I never knew if she wanted to force him to marry Vera and make an honest woman out of her, or if she just wanted to do away with him."

"What happened with the father?"

"I don't know. But it doesn't matter anymore. Silas is Loutishie's father and that's all that matters. He couldn't love the child any more than he already does."

"Lou, dear, aren't you hungry?" Imo's voice pulled me back to reality and I nodded, forked up some butter beans and placed them in my mouth. But I could barely swallow a bite that evening.

Three

❧

Wisdom from Above

*I*t had been an exhausting two weeks.

With settling Mama in and trying to keep peace in the household, there had been times when Imogene didn't know which end was up. She had intended to make an appointment with the Reverend Peddigrew a thousand different times. But every time she was on the verge of doing just that, something or someone else needed her attention.

Little Silas was fussy, Jeanette petulant and sassy, Lou deep in one of her periodic fits of the mully-grubs, and of course, she never knew what she was going to get when it came to Mama. Sometimes she was a quiet, easily pacified child-woman, and sometimes a belligerent, willful elderly lady.

All of this left Imo feeling frazzled. It didn't help that the house was a wreck and the yard gone to seed, either. Imo kept telling herself that there was only so much a body could do, but still, a glance around made her feel panicky. So she sat down and wrote herself out a list. This always helped her sort her mind even when she didn't get around to doing everything on it right away.

First she wrote *Call the Reverend!* in great, big letters at the top, and under that, *Call Mr. Dilly!* After the trip to the cemetery and several other escapades, Imo figured Mr. Dilly might have some pointers in dealing with Mama.

She also wrote down *Call Wanda Parnell.* Wanda was Martha Peddigrew's sister and the owner of the Kuntry Kut 'n' Kurl. Imo wanted to hire Wanda to come to the house to set and style Mama's hair once a week or so. The old lady's hair was dry and sparse and had a mind of its own, and there was nothing Imo could do but tie a scarf over it.

After this, Imo listed her outside to-do's. She wrote *Pinch back leggy begonias.* Next came a reminder to *Cut okra that's ready each morning* and then *Slice and freeze what we don't eat.* Then it was *Cut watermelons, snap beans, and peppers,* which were all still making fairly well, though she'd spent next to no time out in the garden lately. The tomatoes were waning, and they'd eat what they could of what was left and share the extras. Thankfully she'd already put by enough for winter before they'd gone to fetch Mama.

Lastly, she wrote *Plan fall garden,* and below that, *Mulch garden.* She made another list of things she needed from the Feed 'n' Seed and then she stuck all the lists up on the Frigidaire. She needed to keep them in plain sight. She began to wonder if she'd even have the time for a fall garden—the girls started school on Monday and she'd have Little Silas to tend to during the day, along with Mama.

It took all a body could give just to shepherd Mama along through life and Imo couldn't imagine how she would be able to handle the two of them by herself. But she would not allow herself to dwell on that now. How did that saying go? Don't borrow sorrow from tomorrow? Yes, that was it. No use fretting over it early.

Plus, once she'd sought the godly counsel of Reverend Peddigrew, item number one on her list, things would certainly go smoother.

When she heard his voice coming through the receiver, Imo was so nervous she couldn't think what to say. She was sitting at the kitchen table with Little Silas on her lap, staring at their reflection in the oven door.

"Hello? Hello? Calvary Baptist," the Reverend's voice came again. "Hello?"

Imo felt like hanging up, but she clutched the phone harder. "Hello," she managed, "it's Imogene Lavender."

"Well, how are you?" he said in his gentle tone.

She sucked in a breath. It would be a sin to lie. "I'm not good," she said. "I mean, we're not sick or anything like that, and we are blessed with enough money, and food . . . but . . ." Imo choked up as she tried to put her mental anguish and physical exhaustion into words.

Reverend Peddigrew swallowed loudly. "I see," he said. "Perhaps you'd like me to come to see you and we can talk?"

Imogene let her mind go to him seeing the mess in her house, the people in it a mess. "No!" she said, "um, I mean, I'd like to come to Calvary! I'll come see you there, please." She sunk her chin into Little Silas's soft hair.

"Alrighty, then. Let me get to my calendar here." There were shuffling noises. "How about tomorrow at eleven?"

Mama moaned from the sofa. Imo certainly couldn't take her along. Her mind raced over the practical options of Mama-caretakers. She thought of Lou right off the bat. She couldn't ask Lou, could she? She stopped to ponder. In the back of her mind she decided that she could. The ends would justify the means. If she herself were happier, it would spill over into Lou's life. Plus, she could give Mama one of those tablets to relax her, and it would probably be no trouble at all for the girl.

"Hello?" Reverend's voice was searching.

"Oh! Yes," Imo said, "tomorrow is Saturday. Tomorrow will be fine."

Imogene's pumps were unsteady as she walked across the gravel parking lot of Calvary Baptist. The morning was already hot and she paused to admire the liriope lining the front walkway and then to smell a yellow rose. She smiled. Martha Peddigrew had done a wonderful job landscaping the church yard.

Early in the morning Imogene had gone out to the garden and gathered some tomatoes, okra, and a mess of snap beans to carry to the Reverend. She'd also clipped a small bouquet of the marigolds bordering the gourds to send to Martha. In part, this was to assuage her guilt over not calling Martha even once since Mama's arrival.

She pulled open the wide front door and stepped inside, standing while her eyes adjusted to the dim vestibule. She felt vulnerable in the quietness.

"Hello?" she called, listening to her voice bounce off the wooden floor. For an instant Imo thought he'd forgotten, so she set her offerings down on a small table draped with a purple cloth and turned to go.

Footsteps came from behind her. "Imogene? Is that you?"

She straightened her blouse and smoothed the seat of her skirt. "Hello, Reverend," she said, "thought maybe you weren't here."

He smiled. "I was in prayer," he said. His overalls and work boots gave him a fresh-off-the-farm look. "It's nice to see you." He held out his arm to say Imogene should walk before him.

"Brought some things for you and Martha." She gestured toward the table.

The Reverend smiled. "You are the seventh member of this congregation who's brought me things from their garden this week!"

"Oh my!" Imo said, "then you don't need these. I'll just go put them back in the car. The flowers are for Martha, though."

"Nonsense. I'm delighted to have them! Thank you. A body can't ever get enough homegrown tomatoes, and Martha will be tickled to get the flowers." He reached out for the shoe box full of tomatoes and when they reached his tiny office, he set them down on the corner of his desk.

"So, how's your family?" he asked Imo as she sank onto the cool metal of a folding chair hauled in from the fellowship hall.

Imogene steeled herself. "Busy," she breathed, which was the gospel truth. "And I am just about wore out."

Reverend Peddigrew dipped his head for a better look at her through his bifocals. "Weary, huh?"

"Yes, Reverend. I'm plum tuckered out."

"Please," he said, "call me Lemuel."

Imogene nodded, though the truth was that calling him by his first name felt too familiar for a man of God. Too intimate. Well, she reasoned, at least he didn't suggest she call him Lem. He swiveled around in his chair to some shelves behind him and lifted an enamel coffee mug. He filled it from a stained carafe and leaned across the desk to set it before Imogene. A bit of his aftershave mingled with the aroma of scalded coffee.

"Cream or sugar?" he asked.

"Cream, thank you," she said. "This is real nice of you."

"Well, perk you up anyway." He swiveled again and produced a cardboard cylinder of powdered creamer and a spoon. "So you're weary," he said as he placed it before her and sat back to wait.

Imogene couldn't think of a good lead-in after the weary comment. She spied a piece of paper with the words *God Answers Knee-Mail* written in the center. "What's that?" she asked.

He chuckled. "Martha thinks I need to be more modern," he said, "bless her heart. She wants me to put that outside on the marquis next month." He shook his head. "I don't even know how to turn a computer on!"

Imogene laughed. "Me neither. The girls keep saying we need to start out by getting us a microwave, but I swannee, I just don't know what I'd do with one. Creature of habit, I reckon. Some things never change."

"But times are changing," he said. "Things change." He glanced over at the tomatoes. "Speaking of changes, did you know that preachers used to stand up in the pulpit and condemn the tomato?"

Imo stared at the Reverend. "Are you serious?"

"They certainly did." He nodded. "Back in the 1780s, they used to called the tomato a love apple. By virtue of resemblance—it looked like the human heart, you see. Voluptuous and provocative, is what they said about it. Folks thought it was an aphrodisiac, and it was feared by virtuous maidens. Wasn't till the 1820s or so when folks would even eat a tomato."

Imo felt her chest flush. "Imagine that," she said. Was this something a Reverend should bring up? She decided to change the subject. She searched the tiny office. "What pretty curtains!" she said. "Those new?"

"Martha made them last year, I believe. You haven't been to my office since . . ." He ran a finger along some green ball fringe sewn on the hem of the curtains.

"Since Fenton and I came to you for prenuptial counseling," she finished the sentence for him.

He was quiet. Imogene folded her hands in her lap for a moment. There was only the scattered sounds of birds outside the window. All of that seemed like another life. No, another person! She was in the bloom of love then, walking on air with a song in her heart. If she'd only known what was coming—that Fenton wouldn't live to see their wedding day.

Love. Romance. She had discovered that it really could happen a second time, only to have it yanked out from under her. Now that Mama was living with them, she couldn't even *think* about such things as a relationship with someone of the opposite sex. Just surviving and tending to the bare basics of life was all she could manage. And she wasn't even doing that very well at the moment. Her heart began to race.

The Reverend looked thoughtfully at her. He sipped his coffee. "Well," he said, "tell me what's going on. How can I be of help?"

"I'm not sure." She took a swig of her lukewarm coffee.

"Not sure what's going on, or not sure what I can do to help?" He picked up a pen from his desk and toyed with it.

Imogene saw that the only way to do this was with the painful, straightforward approach. She would have to say the words. "My Mama's come to live with us and she's off her rocker!" she spewed out.

He laced his fingers together. "I see," he said.

Imogene could read nothing from his expression, but once she'd started things off, the rest of the talk she'd planned seemed to come out easily enough. "It's senile dementia and sometimes she can't accept that my daddy's dead. She's convinced they're newlyweds. And sometimes she goes back so far in time she calls *me* Mama. Or Memaw, even. Sometimes she runs off and hides from us. Found her sitting out in an old junker pickup truck in the backyard yesterday evening. Said she was going to drive to Niagara Falls."

His eyes widened a bit.

"Sometimes she carries around a sack of flour, like a baby doll. Calls it Imogene and sings to it." Tears, never very far away, began to trickle from her eyes.

Reverend Peddigrew slid a box of tissues across his desktop to her.

"I'm sorry," she said, sniffling.

"Think nothing of it. God feels your pain," he assured her quickly. "Just let it all come on out."

But that was the problem. A wild surge of emotion like this could never get it all out! The pain, the memories, and the scars ran too deep.

"You've experienced a lot of grief in a short time, Imogene," he told her, "losing a beloved spouse of forty-eight years, and then dealing with Jeanette's pregnancy, and then losing your fiancé. You have every reason to feel this way."

Imo stared at him. This wasn't about her grief over losing Silas, or Fenton, or the heartache over Jeanette's pregnancy out of wedlock. Sure, she still felt pangs of loss at times, but God had granted her peace over those parts of her life. The memories of the two loves of her life were good companions to her now. And Little Silas, why, he was the joy of her life.

"What I need help with is one of the ten commandments," she said finally.

Reverend Peddigrew raised his eyebrows to ask.

"It's number five," she said.

Julie Cannon

"Honor thy father and mother?"

"That's the one."

"But . . . I thought you just said you'd taken your mama in. And your father's passed on, hasn't he?"

"He has," Imo said, "and I am. Taking Mama in, I mean. But I cannot *honor* her."

"I beg your pardon?" said the Reverend.

"Well," Imo said, "once, it was yesterday actually, I had this daydream that she had accidentally swallowed a whole bottle of her relaxing tablets and she passed away." She paused for this to sink in. "And I was happy." She buried her face in her hands. "I've prayed. I've read the Good Book. What it says is to *honor* thy father and thy mother." She buried her face in her hands on the corner of his desk. "Lord, forgive me," she whispered as she peered up at the Reverend with pleading eyes.

Reverend Peddigrew cocked his head. He did not seem shocked.

"There's no way around that honor bit, is there?" she asked.

"No exemption clause anywhere in the Bible," he said.

"Listen, Reverend—"

"Please, call me Lemuel," he said. "Honor? Honor thy father and mother." He tapped his temple with a pencil. "Honor means to revere and respect and obey. Obey them in all proper conduct, of course. But when parents behave contrary to the Word of God, and demand their children to do likewise, it could then be understood that they have grounds for not obeying them in such matters."

Imo supposed she didn't have to obey Mama, since she certainly wasn't behaving like the Word of God said to, but what about the revering and respecting part? She knew she did not revere and respect Mama. The mean thoughts in her heart were the ugliest things imaginable, and they were spilling over into the rest of her life. She swallowed. "I can't revere and respect her," she said.

"These things can't be forced, Imogene," he said. "What is it about her that you despise? Is it the heavy load of caring for someone with senile dementia? It's a lot of work. Taxing physically, I know that." He paused and got a breath.

"No, I can manage that load just fine," she said. "I've never been one to shy away from hard work."

He acted like he didn't even hear her when he kept on. "One thing you could do, when you get weary, is to just remember how she nurtured and cared for you. Think about how she brought you up, and sacrificed herself for you."

Lemuel Peddigrew pressed his hands together, touched his fore-fingers to his chin, and looked benignly into her eyes.

Imo could feel her heart booming so hard it shook her whole body. She took a quick swig of her tepid coffee. After a long mo-ment, she said, "When I was growing up, Mama would get so furious with me over *nothing*, and I was scared to death of her. Literally shook in my shoes around her. It was a horrible way to have a child-hood!" She paused for a breath, hoping he would draw the words out of her.

He only sat there listening, his face as placid as the Etowah River. "Well, what you need to do," he said at last, "is you need to set your affections on things above. Long for Heaven, Imogene, and just view this terrible time as a temporary thing. This is not the only life you'll have, you know, and it says in Luke that one day you'll be repaid for all this grace you're bestowing on your mother. You'll get your reward in Heaven."

Imogene looked hard at him. Well, that certainly had not made her feel any better. It was fine to think she'd get a reward in Heaven, but what about the here and now? How could she make it through while she was on earth? How could she wait for Heaven? Who had that much patience? She wanted a healing for *this* life. She looked at him incredulously. She rose up quickly out of her chair.

"God can help you, Imogene," the Reverend said plaintively. "He can still calm a storm at sea."

"What?!"

"Don't attempt to do this by yourself. Give it to God."

Imo stared at him.

"So many folks constantly struggle in the flesh. They attempt to do it all by themselves. That's the American way. Doing it ourselves. 'I'll do it on my own!' we cry. What we need to do is yield ourselves to God," he said, waving one arm now. "Cast yourself on His mercy and stop trying. Ask Him and then trust Him to help you."

Imo wondered if he'd really heard her. "Mama used to whip me with the hickory switch," she whispered.

"My daddy whipped me with the hickory switch, too," he said. "Caught me smoking back behind the woodpile and gave me a licking I'll never forget." He laughed. "I'm glad, too. I've never touched another cigarette."

"She switched me so bad once I couldn't sit down for days. All on account of the fact that I let the corn bread burn. I was in the kitchen watching it, and I went outside to see about one of the heifers that got out of the fence, and when I came back in the house it was burnt. I told her I'd be happy to make some more, but—" Imogene couldn't go on.

Lemuel rolled his lips inward until there was just skin showing and took one solemn nod. "Ask God to help you release it, Imogene. Only He can give you the freedom to forgive your mother and take that heavy burden off of you."

Imo sat there like a knot on a log, his words falling like meaningless chatter.

Suddenly the Reverend's eyes lit up and he hopped out of his chair to strut up and down the room. "I've got it!" he said, "let me add this to help you along in your journey. The fifth commandment is the first commandment with a promise attached to it."

She willed herself to smile and ask, "What is it?"

"Honor thy father and thy mother," he said slowly, "that it may be well with thee, and thou mayest live long on the earth."

Imo stared at him. She guessed she'd heard that somewhere

before, but it surely sounded new to her now. Live long on the earth? No thanks! She'd just as soon cross on over to Glory where there were no more tears or suffering. But then her mind flitted to a picture of Mama, alone on this earth. If Imo went on to Glory, would Mr. Dilly take Mama back? No, there was no hope of that. Vera was gone. Daddy was gone, and Mama had no siblings or cousins or aunts or uncles left anywhere. No blood relatives.

No one but Loutishie. Heaven forbid that the burden would fall on Lou! Imo would just have to suck it up and do her duty. But she needed some good advice to see herself through, and Lemuel Peddigrew didn't have one clue in this world. He had failed her. He had offered her nothing to help her carry her burden. She felt like jumping up and running back to the Impala, flooring the accelerator and spinning gravel as she zoomed out of Calvary's parking lot. How dare he call himself a shepherd of a flock, and why did she ever imagine that he could help her in the first place? He was nothing but a hayseed plowboy!

Politely she pushed her chair back, thanked the Reverend, and excused herself. She would hunt a pastor who didn't give out such stodgy counsel. She needed one with a fresh approach, some hip, modern ways of looking at things. Where could she find one like that? Wait a minute! What about that minister from the Rockmart Church of God who had preached Fenton's funeral? What was his name? Reverend Montgomery Pike! That was it. She'd hunt up his number and give him a call. She recalled his dynamic words at the service and his unique perspective on things. Hadn't everyone hung breathless on his sermon? And it was not your usual funeral fare, either. Surely he would be able to help her, to offer her some newfangled, revolutionary advice.

When she got home, she drew a line through "Call Reverend Peddigrew" on her list, and rummaged through some papers on the counter for Mr. Dilly's number. He picked up on the second ring.

"Hello. Eugene Dilly speaking."

"Imogene Lavender here, Mr. Dilly. How are you?"

"Fine, fine. The million-dollar question is how is your *mother*?" He guffawed.

"We're managing," Imo said, "but I've got several questions." She was breathless with desperation.

"Okay. Shoot," he said.

"You've dealt with Mama's condition, and I surely do appreciate the relaxing tablets. But I need some more advice. It says I can't give her but one of those a day." Imogene tapped a pencil against the back of an envelope she was planning to use for writing down his words of wisdom.

"Alrighty, Mrs. Lavender. I'll see what I can do. What's the problem?"

"How did you distract her when she got going on one of her rampages?" she asked.

He chuckled. "Hmmm . . . well, let's see. She likes to watch the stories on TV. What are they called? Soaps. Likes the soaps and *The People's Court* and *Judge Judy* and all those talk shows, too. God bless the television."

Imogene turned this over in her mind. "You mean all those *trashy* shows?"

"Yessum, that I do," Mr. Dilly said. "That right there will give you some more peace."

Imogene was almost speechless. "Maybe so," she managed. "Well, thank you for your help, Mr. Dilly. Good-bye." She hung up and studied the gray-black screen of the TV, and then her mama's slack jaw as she slept in the La-Z-Boy. She supposed it was a practical enough solution. Buy a little bit of time anyway. Time to work in the garden, she reckoned. Time to chase Little Silas.

She crossed off "Call Mr. Dilly" and hunted the number for Wanda at the Kuntry Kut 'n' Kurl. She told herself that once she'd crossed that one off, she could go outside to the garden.

"I can't hardly wait to meet your mama, hon," Wanda told Imo. "I bet she's just as sweet as you are! I love old folks. I specialize in old ladies' hair, you know." She giggled. "Wash, roll, set, and spray on enough Super Hold to get 'em through the week! I guar-an-tee you, Imogene, she will be beea-u-ti-ful!"

The next day Imo planned to get her housework done quickly so she could get outside to the garden while Mama napped. She breezed through the breakfast dishes and was tossing a load of whites into the washing machine when the doorbell rang. Scowling, she hurried to the door.

"Hello, dear!" Martha stood on the welcome mat, balancing a Pyrex dish in one hand and a boiler in the other. "Brought you all some vegetable soup and baked apples. Lemuel told me your mother was here." She poked her head past Imo and peered in.

Taken off guard, Imo nodded, stepped back, and held the door. "Come in," she said.

"Shame on you for not telling me, hon," Martha said as she set the dishes on the table. "Where is she? I can't wait to meet her."

"She's sleeping," Imo said quickly. "Have a seat and let me get you a cup of coffee." She found herself praying silently *Please Lord, let Mama stay asleep till Martha's gone*. She could not unburden herself, could not reveal her vulnerabilities to her friend. Then it crossed her mind that perhaps the Reverend Peddigrew had already filled her in on Imo's history. "Lemuel tell you anything else? Anything about Mama?"

Scowling, Martha cocked her head. "Nope, just that you had your hands full. But, honey, I know just how it is. Lemuel's mother lived with us for eighteen months before she passed away, and let me tell you, it was worse than having a newborn. Sweet as she could be, she was, but near about blind and deaf, and could barely creep around. It'll surely take it out of you, and so I told Lemuel, I said, 'I'm going to carry supper out to Imogene tonight.'"

"This was so thoughtful of you," Imo said.

"Tell me about her." Martha stirred a spoon of sugar into her coffee.

Imo blinked. "Well, she'll be eighty-five in December. Widowed, you know. Raised me and Vera right here on this very farm. Has been gone sixteen years or so. Left two years before you and Lemuel moved to Euharlee."

"Can she get around all right?"

"Oh, yes, she's spry enough."

"That's a blessing, hmm?"

Imo didn't know how to answer. She didn't associate the word *blessing* with Mama in any way.

"How's her mind?"

"Oh, it's okay," Imo said, intentionally vague, as she leapt up to fetch a box of Fig Newtons. "Here, have a cookie, dear." Martha ate her cookie as Imo's mind raced over possible distractions. "You and Lemuel going to try to get away anywhere before the busy fall sets in?" she asked.

"We may try to head up toward Chattanooga for a spell."

"Well, good," Imo said absentmindedly. She stood up quickly to peer out the window over the kitchen sink. "Oh my! Looks like we might get us a little sprinkle. Hope it holds off, though. I surely need to get out there to the garden before Mama wakes up."

Martha looked up then to search Imo's face. She drained her coffee and set the mug down sharply. "I imagine I ought to run then, and let you get to it."

Imo didn't protest. "It was sweet of you to drop by, Martha," she said, "too bad Mama was asleep."

"I'm sure I'll get to meet her at Calvary on Sunday."

"I don't know if I'll be carrying her to church."

Martha turned and drew in a sharp breath. "Not taking her to the Lord's house? You have to!"

"But I—" Imo said.

"Of course you'll bring her, Imo. You're just wore out is all, and you're not thinking clearly. I thought something seemed strange about you. Believe me, I know it's not easy."

You don't know the half of it, Imo thought. "I am right tired today," she said.

"I'm going to go now. You ought to lay down and nap while you've got the chance," Martha told her as she put the soup into the Frigidaire. "That garden will wait and you don't have to fix supper now. A little nap would do you a world of good."

As soon as Martha's Dodge was out of sight, Imo flew outside to the garden. She stepped in between the gourds and the okra, fished her gloves out of her pockets and pulled them on. She sucked in the earthy scent and felt the sun seep through her blouse.

Sidling up to the okra stalks, she cut the tender fuzzy rocket shapes and dropped them into the gaping pockets of her apron. She allowed herself to live in this moment. No other thoughts could intrude. While she was gardening, she could forget the rest of her life. She felt a little calmer as she touched one of the pale yellow blooms of the okra. She'd always marveled at how they favored a hibiscus. At times, she'd even been tempted to cut some of the okra blooms and carry them inside for a centerpiece.

She gathered a few random tomatoes, some butterbush squash, and an armful of peppers. Finally, she set to tending all the stray gourd vines. She didn't know what it was about her gourds this year, but their twining vines had engulfed the marigolds, the watermelons, the cantaloupes, and even the row of tomatoes nearest them. Seemed like they threatened to squelch out everything but themselves if she didn't cut them back regularly.

Gently she unwound a tendril of gourd vine that was strangling a pretty orange marigold. The curling green runners from the gourds were as strong as steel! She bent and sunk her nose into the warm center of the marigold, like a lion's mane, sharp, spicy, and full of the sun's colors. Imo let herself linger here and for the first time in over a week, she felt like her old self.

*   *   *

Wanda Parnell pulled her mint-green camper trailer into the yard on a sunny Saturday afternoon. The commotion wakened Dusty Red and he flapped down from his perch atop the birdbath and went strutting furiously off toward the chicken house. Loutishie glanced up from the front porch, where she was reading a book.

"Howdy, Lou!" Wanda called as she climbed out of her pickup.

"Hi," Lou said.

"I'm the mo-bile Kuntry Kut 'n' Kurl today, hon," Wanda said in response to the girl's puzzled look. "Imogene called me to come and do her sweet mama's hair."

"Oh. You ever *met* Mama Jewell before?" Lou asked, bounding down the steps.

"Uh-uh. Sure haven't. But I know she's got to be a living doll if she's Imogene's mama. Y'all call her Mama Jewell? What a cute name! I can't wait to meet her."

"Listen," Lou said, glancing hurriedly over her shoulder at the house, "I better run fetch Imo. Tell her you're here."

By the time Imo returned with Mama, Wanda had run a garden hose from the camper up to a spigot at the house, folded down the steps, opened the windows, and started a tiny oscillating fan.

"Hello Wanda," said Imo.

"Howdy there, Imogene!" Wanda said in her breathy, singsong voice. "And this lovely creature must be Mama Jewell! It's a real pleasure to make your acquaintance, ma'am."

Mama eyed Wanda hard for a long moment, taking in her clingy tube top, short denim shorts, her platinum hair piled on top of her head, and her glittery green eye shadow to match her eyes, along with the cigarette in her hand. Imo waited for an ugly outburst, but Mama smiled, took a step forward, and clasped Wanda's free hand between her own.

"Aren't you a purty lil' ole thing?" she gushed. "Just like a doll. Remind me of that country music singer with all the blond hair and the big bosoms . . . Dolly Parton!"

Wanda giggled. "Well thanks, hon. Too bad I cain't sing a lick, but don't you worry, I got a transistor radio in my salon. Got a little bitty TV, too."

"My goodness," Imo said, "how do you fit all that in there?" She eyed the tiny trailer.

"It's a miracle, I reckon." Wanda smiled. "Same as my beauty makeover service."

"I sure do appreciate you coming out all this way to do Mama's hair, Wanda."

"Oh, you think nothing of it. Seniors are my favorite. I've got more bottles of White Minx and Spray Net than you can shake a stick at!" Wanda stubbed out her cigarette and hooked her arm through Mama's. "Let's get you on up and in here, darlin'. Now, what is it we want to do for Mama Jewell today, Imogene? The full beauty treatment?"

"Yes, yes. Do the full treatment." Imo followed them up the steps and sank onto a fold-out stool next to a Formica table covered with Styrofoam cups, a coffeemaker, cream, and sugar.

"Start that coffee there at your elbow, would you, dear?" Wanda said as she settled a cape around Mama's shoulders and clipped it at her throat. "Alrighty, Mama Jewell, we're in business. First let's spin you around and get that hair washed."

A fruity herbal fragrance filled the trailer and mixed with the pungent coffee. Wrapping a towel turban-style around Mama Jewell's head, Wanda whirled her back to face the mirror. "Why, Imogene!" she said, drawing in a quick breath, "you two favor each other so much! Through the eyes and the nose."

Imo looked up, startled. She'd never been told that she looked like Mama. She'd always heard people say that she favored her daddy, and she had believed it, clung to it, in fact. Hesitantly her eyes searched Mama's face and she was startled to see herself. "Maybe so," her voice faltered.

"Ain't no maybe about it. I can definitely tell you're a chip off the old block here."

Imogene sat up straighter. "So, who's ready for coffee?" she asked quickly. She fixed three coffees and settled down to watch Wanda work.

"I'm going to turn you into one real hot number," Wanda teased.

"You are?" Mama's hands came out from under the cape and she squeezed them together. She looked delighted.

"Yes indeed. Make you look just like a movie star."

"I imagine Burton'll be tickled to death when he sees me."

"Who's Burton?" Wanda asked.

"Why, Burton Wiggins. You know, my fiancé."

He's dead, Imo mouthed silently to Wanda.

This did not seem to phase Wanda. She said, "Burton'll be real tickled." She patted Mama. "Probably carry you out for supper to show you off."

"Might," said Mama. "He doesn't have much money, though. And plus, Father said this morning that I was too ornery to get to go anywhere. Said he had a good mind to whip me good and send me out into the fields to work with the hired hands."

"Don't you worry, dear," Wanda patted Mama. "You were probably just feeling ornery 'cause you didn't feel pretty. I know how bent out of shape I get myself when I'm feeling dog-eyed ugly."

"Oh, I bet you're *never* dog-eyed ugly," Mama gushed. "Bet you were born purty. Say, do you think you could do some makeup on me like yours?"

"For sure I will, babe," Wanda said.

Imo gazed out of a postage stamp–size window and sipped her coffee. Was this really her mama sitting here? The same woman who once forbade her girls to wear even lipstick? As Wanda sectioned Mama's sparse hair and twined it around rollers, Imo decided it was the senile dementia kicking in that made Mama act this way.

Wanda sprayed each roller generously with something that made Imo's eyes water, then aimed a hot blow dryer at it.

"So, tell me about this Burton fellow," Wanda said when she turned the dryer off. "He a doll or what?"

Mama's face brightened. "Oh, he's a dear, dear man. Poor as dirt, but I don't care. I don't care if he is poor as dirt. I'm in love."

"I can see that," said Wanda as she unrolled a section of hair from a curler to test it.

"Father's rich, you know. Owns this here farm lock, stock, and barrel."

"Mmm-hmm." Wanda rewound a hank of hair.

"Says he'll cut me out of the will if I marry Burton."

"Why, that's awful, sweetie!" Wanda's hands stopped in mid-movement. "Did he? I mean, will he?"

"Sure as shootin'." Mama thrust her jaw forward.

"Poor, poor dear." Wanda stroked Mama Jewell's wrinkled cheek.

"But I adore Burton and I don't want to live without him. I'll do *anything* to be with him," Mama said resolutely. "We'll just have to live on love, that's all there is to it. If Father disowns me like he says, I won't care. I *won't* miss the kitchen help like he says I will. I *won't* miss the laundress. I *won't* miss the fancy trips and the nice clothes." Her eyes glittered with unspilled tears. "We'll manage somehow. Burton's got a job as farm manager out at the Carson place and a farmer's wife is a respectable position. I can learn to cook and sew and garden. Then we can eat out of the garden and also I can learn to put by things from the garden for the winter. Me and my Burton'll raise us up some strappin' sons, and they'll help out on the farm, too. We'll manage. I'll show Father!"

Imogene was cut to the heart as she listened to Mama. She'd heard the story of how Mama had grown up in the lap of luxury many times. Mr. Reginald Pridemore, Imo's maternal grandfather, had made a killing in cotton and his only daughter, Jewelldine, had had every advantage, except for a loving father. He did indeed sever all ties with his daughter at her marriage. However, not long after that, Mr. Pridemore fell victim to an untimely death, and within five years Mrs. Pridemore was penniless. She soon became ill, passed away, and left the farm to Jewelldine and Burton Wiggins, as a sort of late wedding gift and as a way of mending things. Happily, the poor young couple packed up their belongings and left their rental home on the Carson place to put down stakes at their very own farm. None of this was news to Imo, but this was the first time she had ever heard or seen the depth of love Mama felt for her husband and Imo's father.

"Live on love," Wanda mused. "That's so sweet!" She patted a roller above Mama's ear. "We've still got another few minutes on your curls, baby doll, and then we'll comb it out, tease it, and spray it. Shall I do your makeup while we wait?"

Mama sat up. "Oh, yes!"

Jeanette appeared in the doorway of the tiny camper as Wanda wrestled out a huge basket overflowing with cosmetics.

"Hi Wanda," she said, "what's shakin'?"

"I'm just doing a glamour job on this little doll here."

"Gonna take a lot more than makeup," Jeanette said, laughing and slapping her thigh.

This was all lost on Wanda. "Come on up here, baby doll, there's room," she said. "Have a look around."

Jeanette stepped inside. With her mouth open, she examined Wanda's shelves full of shampoos and dyes and permanents. She stroked a row of nail polishes and acrylic nails, bent over a palette of blue eye shadows. "Cool," she whispered in an awestruck voice. "This is just *fantastic* in here! Man, I'd give anything to have all this stuff!"

Wanda beamed. "Pays my bills," she said.

Jeanette slowly nodded her head. "Not all your clients are old fart—uh, I mean, elderly, are they?"

"No, cutie pie. I also do girls, women, boys, and men. And a poodle here and there."

Mama's eyes caught sight of Jeanette in the mirror. "Why, there's one of the kitchen help right now," she said.

Jeanette's eyes narrowed. "I done told you, you old warthog, I ain't no kitchen help!"

"Now, now, girls," Wanda fussed, drawing back with her hands on her hips to size up the situation. "There's no need for fighting. I tell you what, Jeanette, you run in the house and fetch me some iced tea and a sandwich and when I get done with Mama Jewell, I'll do you a makeover, too."

Amazingly, Jeanette turned and scampered back to the house. Wanda quickly unrolled, combed, teased, and sprayed Mama's hair into a lacquered gray bubble. She stroked on bronze powder, cranberry blush, wine-red lipstick, and azure eye shadow and dabbed on a quick dot of liquid eyeliner to serve as a beauty mole. She unclipped the cape and swept it away in a dramatic flourish. "Just look at you!" she said. "Burton's not going to believe his eyes! Ain't no better cure for a case of the orneries neither." She looked over at Imo and winked.

Imo stared in the mirror at the transformation that was her mother. Wanda's handiwork had literally peeled away the years. It had opened up Mama's sagging eyes and replaced her withered cheeks and delineated her faded lips so that the outcome conjured up a certain image.

Imo looked back in time and she saw a young Mama, in the prime of her life, standing on an embankment in the front yard, with one hand on her hip, wearing a blue paisley sprinkled dress. It was a fresh-washed morning in summertime and she was admiring a burnt-orange sea of daylilies that had opened overnight. There were also great masses of Japanese irises, foxgloves, wild daisies, and snapdragons blooming away along the drive and on the bank. Their yard was a literal chaotic profusion of flowers.

"I'm going to let you in on a little secret, Imogene," her mother had said, beckoning Imo over as her lovely face still gazed at the flowers with genuine delight. "Money can't buy happiness. I'm telling you truly, these are prettier than any manicured lawn. Worth every bit of the elbow grease." She looked down at the calluses across her palm.

Looking now at Mama, Imo felt her chest expand with a sense of compassion. "You worked hard, didn't you, Mama?" she said. "I never really understood how much you sacrificed to marry Daddy."

There was no reply and Imo drained her coffee. She crossed her arms, leaned back, and closed her eyes to think about all of life's interwoven dramas.

 Loutishie's Notebook

For weeks and weeks after Mama Jewell came to live with us, she would wander outside and holler "El-mer! Dew-y Ro-ose!" and then get in a snit when her peacocks didn't come running. At first, Bingo would sidle up to her, his tail tucked between his legs and his head bent, humbly waiting for a kind hand to ruffle his rib cage. But after being disappointed so many times, he just stayed in his soft bed of dirt underneath the pecan tree.

After all that time and various attempts at distractions, Imo decided Mama Jewell would never hush up about her beloved birds and so she decided to go on ahead and get a peahen and a peacock. "I reckon it's a small price to pay for our sanity," she said with a weary sigh. "Let me call Teresa Luckasavage."

Miss Luckasavage was our county agent. She pulled up in the yard waving the latest Market Bulletin and assured us that peafowl were even better than watchdogs. "That's right, ladies. They let out an ungodly, ear-piercing scream that can raise the hairs up and down your spine if they see or hear anything out of the ordinary. Also," she said, without hardly taking a breath, "such a nice, simple, and clean way to handle the pest control in your garden. It's certainly a nasty job when you have to handpick those bugs and plop them down into a bucket of kerosene, isn't it? Specially those big, soft, green-horned cutworms! Yep, you get you some peafowl and you can just let them do all the dirty work. And they'll love it."

Well, that sold Imo, and she called a fellow who'd advertised some birds, and that very afternoon we were the proud owners of a peacock and a pea-hen. Jeanette didn't even bother to come outside and meet them once they arrived. I clung to Bingo in one corner of the barn as he and I surveyed them from a distance. They were strutting around inside of a stall, blinking their eyes at ancient, calcified salt-lick blocks and shreds of hay hanging like icicles from spiderwebs in the rafters.

Imo led Mama Jewell out the back door of the house and into the barn.

"Why, I remember when that tombstone salesman come through here and gave me that there block," Mama Jewell said, pointing to a big piece of granite among the concrete blocks that made up one wall of the barn; "1930" was carved into it.

"It was last spring and Burton was in the middle of building the barn here. Feller was an itinerant salesman that peddled tombstones. I told him we weren't planning on dying anytime soon, but it was getting dark outside so I invited him in the house for pork chops and grits. He ate four of my biscuits with sorghum." Saliva glistened in the corners of Mama Jewell's mouth. "Said his wife was ex-pecting their seventh young'un. Had her a goiter, she did. Well, it was pitch dark by the time we got to our pie. Fixed us a chess pie, I surely did. So I invited him to stay on for the night. Next day, the feller tried to pay me, but all I could think of was that poor wife of his with number seven on the way and a big ole goi-ter, right under her chin here." Mama Jewell touched her withered neck. "And I said 'No, no, you cain't do that. Go with our blessings,' and a few weeks later, he up and sent us that block yonder and Burton put it in the wall."

I found Imo's face and she was smiling. I suspected she enjoyed stories about the good ole days as much as I did. In a way it was strange to hear Mama Jewell talking like that, remembering all those details like it happened yesterday, but that's how she was. She might not be able to tell you what she'd eaten for breakfast, or even what day it was, but she could tell you who'd won a blue ribbon for their pickled squash at the 1942 county fair, or the type of ear-bobs her third-grade teacher wore on Valentine's Day.

I watched Imo gently steer her over to the stall. "Mama," she said, "Elmer and Dewy Rose have been asking to see you."

Mama Jewell clasped her hands underneath her chin and giggled—a schoolgirl's gesture. "My babies!" she gushed as Imo opened the stall door. I hung on to Bingo and watched the incredible scene. Mama Jewell leapt into the stall, dropped to her knees, flung her ever-present purse onto a heap of dusty antifreeze jugs, yanked off her gloves, and was frantically reaching for a terrified bird. "My baby," she cooed toward the blue-chested male. "Come to mama, Elmer." The bird backed himself into a corner, fluttering his soft grayish wings. Mama Jewell walked on her knees and hemmed him in. Nervously he marched his long white featherless legs in place and blinked two beady dark eyes in his blue-green head. Imo stood back a ways, scared of the stiff, sharp spurs right above both of Elmer's feet, I reckoned.

The peahen strutted back and forth behind Mama Jewell, watching anxiously. She was not so splendid. A brown head and a white neck. But her breast and her back, also brown, did have some pretty speckles of green.

"Come to Mama, Elmer," Mama Jewell kept saying in baby talk. "Come here and give your mama some sugar." Elmer stomped and fussed a while more, but finally, he cocked his head and calmed down enough to let Mama Jewell stroke his head. She did this a while and then she eased on over close to wrap her arms around him and hug him. Bingo and I stood there and witnessed ourselves a bona fide miracle as the peahen sidled over to Mama Jewell, too, and wedged her head underneath Mama Jewell's arm. You never saw anybody as happy as Mama Jewell was at that moment. She stroked and cooed and had herself a beautiful reunion as darkness slowly drifted across the barn. Finally, she gave them both one last big squeeze and said, "The sun's setting, sweeties. You'd best get yourselves on up to your roosting branches, you hear? We'll play together tomorrow."

Imo glanced over at me. "Help me get Mama to her feet, Lou, please?" she asked. "I need to give her a tub-bath and get her on into bed."

I left Bingo and scurried over. Mama Jewell was peaceful as we hefted her up. "Those birds are worth their weight in gold," Imo whispered to me as we headed back inside.

Imo and I were helping Mama Jewell into her nightgown when suddenly her face changed from its enraptured state. She sucked in a loud breath and grabbed my wrist. "Sheila, did you remember to get those croker sacks?" she asked, her eyes wide. "You know we need them for the cotton."

"Oh, yes," I reassured Mama Jewell as Imo buttoned a row of small pearlescent buttons at her wrinkly neck. "I got the croker sacks just like you said to." She released my arm and let out a small sigh of satisfaction.

When Mama Jewell first moved in, I would freak out during those times she went backward in time and thought that I was her friend Sheila, who has been dead for forty years. But by that evening, I had realized that her backward trips were basically harmless. Sometimes she referred to me only as "girl" or her cousin Annalea. The only times that still freaked me out were when she called me Vera, my late mother's name. I tried to play along, though, and give her the right answers that would keep the peace and make her happy.

Imo patted my arm when we had Mama Jewell all tucked in and were back out in the hall. "Thank you, Lou, dear. You've been a big help to me tonight. You get yourself on to bed now. Sweet dreams!"

I wish I could have sweet dreams, I thought to myself as I climbed into bed, listening to Jeanette and Little Silas's steady breathing.

Despite being so wore out, I was afraid to close my eyes. I'd been having this awful dream a bunch, ever since the Reverend Peddigrew preached a particular series of sermons. In this dream, it always started out with me and Jeanette on the earth. Jeanette is a rich ruler, and she is clothed in purple and fine linen, and she is feasting on a banquet table full of delicious food. I am a beggar, just like Lazarus in the Bible story, and I lie at Jeanette's gate, pleading for the crumbs that fall from her lavish table. I beg and beg her for a crust of bread while I lie on the ground, clutching the ornate gate of her big mansion. Jeanette is enjoying her grand earthly life, running around and living for the moment and all its temporal pleasures, and she never gives a single thought to tossing me a crumb, or to laying up treasures in her heavenly account either. She lives entirely in the moment and turns a deaf ear to my cries of hunger.

Toward the end of the dream we both die and I go up to heaven, where I feast on figs and pomegranates in my white garments. Jeanette is cast down into hell, where she is weeping and hollering out "Lou! Lou! You've got to bring me some ice!" Begging me just to touch the tip of her tongue with a cool cube. And I keep trying and straining to get a cup of cold water down there to her, but I can't reach her.

I always woke up sweating and scared to bits from this dream. That night I decided the dreams were God's way of urging me to witness to Jeanette. He wanted me to be bold and tell her that she needed to let Him in her heart and turn from her sins. Because if she didn't, and the Rapture happened, she would be left behind.

I slid out of my covers and walked on my knees over to the edge of her bed. I placed my hands on her shoulders and gently shook her awake. "God can be a father to Little Silas," I said bravely into her startled face, "and He can be a father to you, too."

Jeanette swiped the back of her hand across drool on the corner of her mouth.

"What in hell's name are you babbling about?" she said, squinting up through the glow of Little Silas's night-light.

"You *said* you wanted to find a father for Little Silas."

"What I said is I'm gonna find me a *man.* A man to take care of us and get us out of this crazy shit hole."

"You also said you wanted to find a *daddy,* Jeannie," I said, "for Little Silas."

Jeanette turned away from me and yanked the sheet up over her head. "Go to sleep, Lou, and cut the God Squad crap." Her muffled voice sounded mad. "Anyway, you ain't no one to talk about daddies when you don't even have one your own self. Why don't you go find *your* real daddy?"

I looked away. My nose tingled as the tears threatened, and I concentrated on not letting them fall. But it was no use. The tears came pouring down and I sniffled.

Jeanette peeled back the sheet to look at me. "I'm sorry, kid," she said as she reached over and put her arm around my shoulders. "I shouldn't have said that. It hurts, don't it?"

"It's all right," I said. "I'm all right."

"Don't you ever want to find him?"

"Sometimes," I admitted.

"It's okay," she said. "It doesn't mean you love Daddy, uh, I mean, Uncle Silas, any less. You know that, don't you, Lou?"

"Yeah, but it would probably hurt Imo's feelings if I was to hunt my real father."

"Look, kiddo, I learned a long time ago that you've got to live your own life. You can't go around always worrying about what other folks think." Jeanette rolled over and pulled the sheet back over her head. "Now, get back over there and get yourself some sleep."

I crawled into bed, staring at her shape under the covers as I pondered her words. My real father was out there somewhere, maybe not even far from where I was that very minute. I'd often wondered about him—what he looked like, what he did for a living, and maybe that I had some half-sisters and -brothers. Would it be wrong if I did try to find him? Wouldn't that be disloyal to Imo and my uncle Silas, who raised me?

But then again, maybe Jeanette was right. Why, of course she was! I decided that I really did have a right to know about him and that I would try to find him. The opportunity would come along one of these days and I would get a sign that it was time.

Early the next evening there was a loud knock at the back door. "Come right on in, Reverend," Imo insisted, holding the door open. "Hot out there, isn't it? I should have told you to come in the morning. I'll fix us some tea."

I looked up from my homework spread out across the kitchen table, expecting to see Reverend Peddigrew. Instead, there was this young, dark-haired man I'd seen somewhere before but couldn't quite place.

Watching a soap opera from her La-Z-Boy, Mama Jewell jumped at the stranger's voice. She turned and stared at him like he was an alien. She strained forward, but couldn't quite get up. "Cain't pay nobody," she hollered at him. "This is the Depression. Have to take food as your wages."

"I'll do that. Thank you kindly, ma'am," he smiled, and winked in my direction. My heart did a flip-flop. He was so handsome!

"It's okay, Mama," Imo called. "This here is the Reverend Montgomery

Pike from over in Rockmart, Georgia. Preached Fenton's funeral service. I asked him to come see me about something."

So that was where I'd seen him! I kept my head down, working on my math problems.

"Have a seat, Reverend," Imo said. "I appreciate you coming on such short notice. That's my mother, Jewelldine Wiggins."

He said hello to the side of Mama Jewell's head, but she was back watching her story.

"And I believe you met Loutishie after the funeral service."

"Sure did. How are ya?" he said, smiling with big white teeth enclosed in dimples.

"Fine," I mumbled.

Reverend Pike did not look like any minister I'd ever seen. There was a tattoo of a snake curled around his forearm and he wore a T-shirt! He also had holes for earrings in his earlobes and this dramatic swoop of black hair like old pictures of Elvis.

I thought he looked like a rock 'n' roll star, and that was something Imo didn't approve of. But she was treating this man like royalty. Fixing tea with lemon wedges and shaking Pecan Sandies onto a silver tray we used at Christmas to hold pink and green mint pillows.

"I don't believe I met your mother at Fenton's funeral service," he said as he reached for a cookie.

"No. Mama wasn't able to be there. She's only just moved back to Euharlee."

"I see."

"Mama's not in her right mind, Reverend," Imo whispered, "and she's just about to do me in. She's the reason I asked you to come out."

I didn't realize I was staring or eavesdropping until Imo fixed me with a sideways glance and lowered her voice even more, continuing to talk to the Reverend Pike with the most serious face. I caught a few bits and pieces of their conversation, mainly her telling him that Mama Jewell was difficult and that talking with Reverend Peddigrew hadn't helped her one bit, and that she'd heard he had a good reputation for settling family squabbles.

When she was through talking, Reverend Pike nodded, was quiet for a minute, then he took a deep breath and said reverently, "Well, Miz Lavender, you're doing exactly what the Good Book says to do. Says we're supposed to look after orphans and widows in their distress." He took a swig of his tea, glanced over at Mama Jewell and then back to Imo. "But it's tough, huh?"

"Without a doubt," Imo said.

"It's definitely not easy to do the right thing sometimes," he said. His eyes grew sad. He shook his head slowly. "Yes, sister, we all have our battles to fight."

"I imagine we do," Imo said, "and I imagine you hear a lot of them."

"Yes," he said, wrinkling up his brow. "Got my very own." His eyes flashed. "Daily I battle the temptation to fall back into my old lifestyle. Rock 'n' roll, booze, drugs, and women."

I was shocked. Imo didn't say anything to that. She just poured more tea and offered more cookies.

"Let me tell you something about life, Miz Lavender," said Reverend Pike after a spell, "sometimes all we can do is just keep on plugging along. Making our way like pilgrims along the journey. Doing what we know in our heart is right, despite our urges to turn back. Despite our human longings or our aching backs."

Imo stiffened at that. "I just need some sort of wisdom or guidance. It's hard work taking care of her, yes, it is, but that's not . . . well, you know, you've just got to realize—"

He held up a hand. "You can go crazy trying to figure stuff out. Now, I know all this seems like a terrible struggle when you're smack dab in the middle of it, but when you move on down the road a bit, you'll look back and you'll see it had a purpose. That's the way it is with me. I'll get down the road apiece, and I'll say, 'Now I've got it! Now I see why I was having to work through that!' and I'm a much stronger person because of the hard places I've had to go through."

"But you don't understand!" Imo blurted.

"Oh, I do understand!" he said. "Let me tell you something, sister. Life is hard down here. We've got to encourage one another to just keep on plodding along. Like I said earlier, you're doing what's right here—looking after a widow in her distress. Just keep on saying to yourself 'Everything's going to be all right in the end. Keep on going. Work harder.'"

Raising my head, I saw Imo's slumped shoulders and her lips in a thin, exhausted line. I could tell that she hadn't found any comfort in the Reverend Pike's words. She stared down at her hands in her lap.

This did not seem to faze the Reverend. "Yes," he said, "I fight the temptation to go back to rock 'n' roll every day of my life. But I'll have you know this, Miz Lavender, music itself isn't sinful." He held up both of his palms in a surrender pose. "No, no, no. Music is a gift to us and I have set my heart on playing uplifting music. Music is a healer." He eyed Mama Jewell. "Hey, is it okay if I play a song for your mother? Got my guitar out in the truck."

"That would be real nice," Imo said in a flat voice, her eyes still on her hands.

Next thing I knew he was back with an amplifier and a triangular-shaped guitar that looked like it came straight off The Jetsons cartoon. "Any requests?"

"She used to love 'O for a Thousand Tongues to Sing,'" Imo said.

Well, the Reverend lit into playing this real lively rendition of the hymn so that it sounded just like rock 'n' roll to me. He crooned and strutted and squinched up his eyes and sung the words in a voice that was liquid honey. The walls of the farmhouse throbbed with his strumming and I had no doubt he could've been a star if he'd wanted to.

Suddenly Mama Jewell came up out of her chair and grabbed hold of an end table and cut the rug in a fashion. She waved her free hand, bent her knees in time with the music, and on every other beat she tipped one foot up on its heel.

All that loud music lured Jeanette into the den. She leaned against the wall holding Little Silas, wearing her AC/DC T-shirt and some skimpy shorts Imo kept trying to put into the rag bag for dusting. She looked awfully interested in the Reverend. I watched her run her tongue over her top lip and flip her hair over her shoulder as she watched him, her eyes sparkling.

Little Silas began to fuss before too long.

"Hush your mouth!" Jeanette stamped her foot and wagged a finger at him. "I done told you I'm fixin' to change you!"

The Reverend glanced up. He stopped singing. "Hello," he said.

"Howdy," Jeanette crooned. "You sure can play that thing!"

"Thank you kindly," he said, "who's that handsome fellow in your arms?"

"This here's Little Silas," Jeanette said, bouncing the fussy boy on her hip. "He didn't come with us to Mr. Mabry's funeral on account of how loud he gets."

"I see. He hungry?"

"Naw. He's got messy pants," Jeanette said, "and he don't want me to have a minute's peace. It's always something."

"That's how young'uns are, I imagine," he said. "Don't have any of my own. Like to someday, though."

"Is that a fact?" Jeanette said with a giggle. "Mama," she said, keeping her eyes on Reverend Pike, "you seen Little Silas's Bible storybook? I need to do my daily reading to him out of it."

She's showing out, I said to myself, lying and showing out in front of the Reverend! She never reads to Little Silas out of that Bible storybook. It's been collecting dust on top of the bookshelf since Imo gave it to him over a year ago.

"Do I look fat, Lou? You can be honest with me," Jeanette asked me that night after she'd gotten Little Silas to sleep. She was doing twirls in the den, releasing a cloud of strong perfume, and pinching her thighs.

"You look fine," I said, knowing that would make her mad.

"I don't want to look *fine*," she snorted. "Hey, wait a second! You're not even looking at me, Lou."

"You look great," I said as I glanced up from my book.

"Really?" She was beaming. "Think Reverend Pike thought I looked okay? Mmm . . . mmm . . . mmm . . . talk about a stud-muffin . . . ooo-wee, now that man melts my butter!" She hugged herself. "It's enough to make me join the Praise Squad at his church. Isn't that what he called that group of singers he kept on talking about, Lou? Those ones he gets to do special God numbers?"

"Hush," I said sternly. "You shouldn't talk that way about a preacher or his ministry."

She smiled and bent her wrists to fan out her nails under my nose. "Passion pink," she said. "Got me a mud-pack, too, to tighten up my pores." She touched her nose, then her hair. "And I bought some conditioner that cures split ends. Let's put some on together tonight."

"Nothing doing," I said.

"Well, alrighty then, Lu-lu. You can just keep right on being a plain-Jane if you want to, but I've got to catch me a preacher man!" Jeanette spun around, laughing, and grabbed my hand. "Gonna join me the Praise Squad and sing for Jesus!"

I just stood there, pleading silently with God to hold off on the Rapture for a while. I had my work cut out for me.

Four

Praise Squad

It was a week too late when Imogene remembered Martha's birthday. What was the matter with her? Forgetting someone so dear to her. The fear of Alzheimer's struck at her heart. Being in charge of Mama had made her stop and think more than once that perhaps it was something you inherited, like big thighs or going prematurely gray.

Somehow she would make it up to Martha. Carry her a cake and introduce her to Mama. She didn't have to tell Martha the entire history of her childhood, however. Just say the old woman had to move in on account of illness. Better yet, just let Mama's actions speak for themselves. How did it go? A picture speaks a thousand words?

It was twilight when Imo went out to the feed shed where the deep freeze was. Cool outside, like the early part of October always is late in the day. She shivered a little as she opened the freezer and quickly found a tinfoil-wrapped rectangle marked "Pound Cake." She thought she'd get the cake thawed and squeeze some icing on it to say Happy Late Birthday and carry it to church the next morning, which was Sunday.

As she headed back across the yard, she spotted the iridescent, rainbowlike feathers of Elmer in the low branches of the great oak tree. She looked around for Dewy Rose. She was behind a gingko tree, preening. Both of them spent a lot of time using their long necks to aim their beaks for fluffing and smoothing feathers.

God bless you two, Imo thought, as she stood there watching the pair, her hands numb from the frozen cake. There was no question about it, they could really calm Mama down. They adored her and she adored them. So many times Imo had used them to divert Mama from unpleasant scenes. These scenes frequently began when Mama and Jeanette disagreed about which TV show to put on. Jeanette favored trashy shows, too, but her favorites were MTV and some really sleazy talk shows, which often conflicted in time with Mama's stories.

Generally, all Imo had to do was walk to the back porch, open the door, and holler out, "Oh Mama, Elmer's crying for you!" or "Dewy Rose is feeling lonely, Mama!" and Mama would heft herself up and out of the La-Z-Boy and make a beeline for the backyard.

Between the peacocks, the trashy shows on TV, and her tablets for relaxing, Imo had the routine of getting Mama through each day down fairly well. Still, though, it was tiring work, and if you added in chasing little Silas while Jeanette was off at school or running around with her friends, sometimes it was hard to know which end was up.

Plus, if you added in her increasing forgetfulness, so that things like birthdays, Garden Club meetings, Circle meetings, and all the other routine things she used to know like the back of her hand were slipping her mind these days, you could get downright anxious. Perhaps she would have to start writing out a daily to-do list each morning, because if she wasn't able to keep up with her own life, it would be like the Good Book said with her and Mama—"The blind leading the blind."

Imo carried the cake inside, unwrapped it, and set it on a cookie sheet to thaw. Mama was on the couch, watching the Home Shopping Network with her black patent handbag perched up on her round stomach. She heard Little Silas waking from his nap. He kicked the side of his crib and hollered out "Mi-moo? Mi-moo?"

You would think he was Mama's own little boy by the way the old woman galloped to his room to scoop him up each afternoon following his nap. She changed him, fed him, sang to him, rocked him, and fussed over him. Imo smiled at the memory of Jeanette explaining why she'd changed her mind about letting Mama touch the boy. "Ain't it more blessed to give?" she asked Imo. "When I seen the way she took to him, I knew it would bring joy to her old heart. Anyhow, it ain't the *Christian* thing to do. She wouldn't hurt him. She adores him."

There were more changes in the girl as well. Besides this amazing act of generosity, she'd up and joined the Wednesday night Praise Squad at Reverend Montgomery Pike's Church of God in Rockmart, Georgia. At first, Imo was floored by this news, and when Jeanette came home from her first choir rehearsal wearing a silky royal blue robe and a smile from ear to ear, she listened as the girl flounced around the den, crooning "Rock of Ages." But, bless her heart, she was tone-deaf and couldn't carry a tune in a bucket. The only hope was that as one of six women on the Praise Squad, this deficiency in talent would not be too obvious. And surely, it was the intent of one's heart to praise and glorify God that mattered.

Imo was thinking of this as they all piled into the Impala on Sunday morning. It would be Mama's first real public outing.

The sun was climbing up in the sky as they drove toward town. They cruised along past wave after wave of kudzu that was slowly but surely turning brown for fall. The crepe myrtles along the center strip of Euharlee were turning, too, and the Japanese maple in front of the courthouse was the most gorgeous red of all as the morning sun shone through its leaves.

Mama was presentable in a red gingham dress and a green cloche hat with a plastic daisy fastened to its side. Her white gloved hands rested on the huge shiny black purse perched on her knees. Wanda had come again and worked magic on her hair.

As they turned into the parking lot, Imo spotted Martha talking to some ladies near the front door. She patted the cake, took a deep breath, and uttered a quick prayer that Mama would behave herself.

Pulling around to the side of the church to park out of sight, Imo gave one final glance into the backseat. Jeanette was unfastening Little Silas from his car seat. Mama was opening her purse. "Here we are!" Mama exclaimed as she pulled two cartons of Marlboro cigarettes and a red plastic lighter from among a jumble of things.

"Oh, Mama!" gasped Imo. "Why do you have those?"

"I reckon Burton's taking up smoking again." Mama thrust out her chin.

A wave of despair washed through Imo. "What are you planning to do? Give out cigarettes to the whole congregation?"

"Dear me, no. Going to lay these evil torches of Satan on the altar for Burton. He couldn't come this morning. Had to get in the corn. But I know the Lord will cast out the demon of nicotine in him from afar."

"Hey, those are mine!" Jeanette's eyes were slits as she pounced over Little Silas's car seat and snatched them from Mama's surprised hands.

"You sassy young'un!" Mama turned and hissed. "Give those back to me!"

"You old senile goat!" Jeanette stuck her tongue out and held the cigarettes behind her back.

Imo's heart slid to her feet. What in heaven's name could she do here? Turn around and head on home? "Jeannie, please," she ventured, "don't get her all riled up. Just let her place them on the altar." Then she added in a whisper, "I'll get them back for you after the service."

"But I've been looking all over for these!" Jeanette wailed, hugging the cigarettes to her chest.

Sitting ramrod straight in the front seat, Lou shook her head. "Dern it, Jeanette," she said, "I agree with Mama Jewell on them. They *are* bad for you! God doesn't want you to defile your earthly temple. So there." Arms folded, she squinched her eyes shut.

"You stay out of this, Loutishie! You can't tell me what to do!" Jeanette screamed so hard the windows throbbed. "And neither can you!" She aimed her face at Imo, then collapsed backward against the seat.

"Please," Imo begged, "don't you girls fight like this, not at Calvary. I simply cannot bear it." She turned to face Jeanette. "Nobody's telling you a thing to do, Jeannie. Now you know what we're dealing with here and I'm asking you to just please let her tote them in." She squeezed the steering wheel so tight her fingers hurt. Her legs were feeling shaky and she wasn't even sure she *wanted* to go in anymore until the opening hymn drifted out from the church's open doors.

> *Rock of Ages, cleft for me,*
> *Let me hide myself in thee;*
> *Let the water and the blood,*
> *From thy wounded side which flowed,*
> *Be of sin the double cure, Save from*
> *wrath and make me pure.*

The chorus of voices bathed Imo in hope. "Come on and give them to her, Jeanette," she coaxed once again.

Still, Jeanette shook her head.

> *Could my tears forever flow,*
> *Could my zeal no languor know,*
> *These for sin could not atone;*
> *Thou must save, and thou alone.*

In a flash of blinding insight, Imo placed a hand on Jeanette's arm. "Hey, how come I never hear you singing that second stanza there? Is it because Reverend Montgomery Pike likes to stick to just singing the first stanzas for Praise Squad?"

Jeanette blinked. She became as still as a statue at the mention of Reverend Pike. "Montie . . ." she breathed in a reverent whisper.

"Please let Mama carry the cigarettes inside, Jeannie," Imo said. "I'll get them back for you after the service. It would be the *Christian* thing to do. I'm sure Reverend Pike would approve."

Jeanette started to speak, but instead she looked off into the distance, and with an otherworldly smile, she released the cigarettes.

They slipped into the very back pew once the opening hymn was finished. The Reverend led everyone in a prayer, and his familiar voice steadied Imo. Certainly things would go smoother now, Imo decided, even if Mama did remember to lay the cigarettes on the altar. Anyway, being at Calvary was like being with family. Most of the folks in here Imo'd known for what seemed like forever. Calvary had been her home church since she had married Silas here fifty years ago. Some had known Mama, too, just because Euharlee was so small that almost everyone was on a first-name speaking basis, though she and Daddy had attended Bethabara Baptist in a nearby county.

Yes, some there would remember Mama, though they'd know nothing about her mental troubles and the nightmare Imo had lived through. Imo had suffered in silence. The whole family had. You just didn't announce those kinds of things to the world. You carried your own burdens. Surely these folks would see only an elderly woman who was not connecting with reality. Plus, Imo reminded herself that a church would not judge, and that they would welcome the feeble-minded.

When the Reverend got to announcements, Imo stole a look in Mama's direction. She was pooching out her lips and smacking the back of a church bulletin. "Mama, stop that," Imo whispered, noting that Mama's lap was full of little white Avon lipstick samples that Wanda had given her.

When it was time for lifting up prayer concerns, requests were taken from the congregation, and Imo prayed silently and fervently that Mama was not paying attention and that they would get through to the end of the service without incident. The sermon began and the Reverend likened human bodies to earthly tents. Then he read a poem with a line about the fact that each day a person pitched their earthly tent one step closer toward home. He went on to say that because they were bound by the flesh, there would be days for each believer that seemed futile. But then he assured everyone that there would be peace when you finally died, crossed over Jordan, and pitched your tent on the other side.

The words were very pretty and Imo sat there waiting for peace to enter in and refresh her weary soul. But just as Reverend Peddigrew wound down, she remembered that this was communion Sunday and her heartbeat quickened when he extended the invitation for everyone to come forward to the Lord's table.

"Come all," his gentle voice urged, "come forward to sup at the Lord's table. Do this in remembrance of our Savior's sacrifice. Come and lay your burdens down. You will find rest in time of need."

Imo wished they could scoot out early instead of waiting for the inevitable scene. What a Sunday she'd picked for introducing Mama! Row by row, ushers directed the congregation to enter and leave the altar, and here they came to Imo's pew, sweeping hands to beckon them to rise and come. She rose solemnly. There was nothing to do now but get it behind her.

Mama blinked. She stirred. She looked up at Imo's face, and dramatically gathered the cartons of Marlboros and the lighter in her gloved hands. She got to her feet and side-stepped out to get in line behind Imo. Imo did not allow herself to even think. *Keep moving,* she admonished herself, *keep moving,* until she was kneeling at the altar rail. When Mama arrived, she made a big show of lifting the cigarettes and the lighter up high, waving them about, then placing them on the altar. Next she held on to the rail to lower herself to her knees and then raised her hands up, fluttering them in the air. Imo noticed with horror that the fingertips of her gloves were stained red from the lipsticks.

"Lord, deliver my Burton from the demon of nicotine!" Mama cried out.

The congregation was breathless. Imo's toes curled in her pumps as the Reverend Peddigrew made his way toward Mama. He placed a hand on her head. "Yes, Lord," he said with exaggerated care, "meet the needs of this dear child of yours who's come before you to place her burdens at your feet. Carry these burdens for her as You promised You would. Amen."

"Amen!" the old woman cried, her hands still up, now clenched into fists. "Hallelujah," she added, and dropped her head to her chest. She seemed satisfied.

Imo felt dizzy as they made their way back to the pew. She avoided the eyes of the rest of the congregation, especially Martha. She could barely breathe. Her heart was racing. She managed to assure herself that now the worst was over and not a single soul had laughed.

This was Imo's day to get everything out in the open. She would mend things with Martha. Yes, she thought, feeling her burden lifting a tiny bit, soon grace would be hers again. Deliverance would surely come now that Mama was at Calvary.

As the Reverend pronounced the benediction, Imo straightened her shoulders, took a deep, cleansing breath, and fixed a warm smile on her face. She helped Mama put up the hymnal and gather her purse. She turned to collect her own purse and saw Martha bustling down the aisle, coming toward them with her arms wide open. "Imogene Lavender! You've been hiding from me. How in the world are you? And here's your dear mother!" She smiled warmly at Mama and moved to grasp her hands. "Anybody who gave birth to Imogene must be a living saint!" she gushed.

Imo was quick. She reached for her friend's wrists. "I'm so sorry I missed your birthday, dearie," she said, "and I've got a little something out in the car for you. So don't you leave till I go fetch it."

"Well, aren't you sweet! Number sixty-five it was. Lemuel brought me sixty-five red roses and he carried me to Raymond's Fish-House for supper."

Imo smiled. "He surely does adore you, Martha."

Soon Imo and Mama were surrounded by folks. She thought she saw amusement and compassion in the eyes of the crowd as she introduced Mama around. They visited for quite a spell until Imo remembered the cigarettes. "Y'all keep an eye on Mama for me," she whispered to Lou and Jeanette as she pulled herself away to go and slide the cigarettes up underneath a panel of her crocheted vest. She eased out to the Impala, slipped them into the trunk, and fetched Martha's cake from the front seat. Straightening her shoulders, she took a deep breath and carried the cake carefully up the front steps of Calvary.

Inside, the postchurch crowd had moved to the tiny fellowship hall to socialize. Mama sat in a folding chair, holding a Styrofoam cup full of black coffee, surrounded by everyone. "Lord, yes. Burton's been working dusk till dawn and then some," she was saying. "'No rest for the weary,' I always say. He says if it weren't for my famous fried fatback and milk gravy, and my 'possum and taters, he'd probably just *stay* out there in the fields and not ever come back in the house. He calls my cooking 'lovin' from the oven!'" She cackled and slapped her thigh.

Everyone let out a hearty laugh right along with her. Encouraged, she continued. "Burton weighed 152 pounds when we got married. He was skinny as a bean pole. But he didn't stay that way for long! Nossirree. I fattened that man right up."

Imogene leaned against the wall, closed her eyes, and shook her head.

"Honey, she's darlin'!" Martha's voice pierced Imo's thoughts. "Just look at her over there charming folks. She tickles me to death! I don't know when I've laughed so hard, and I don't know what in the world you've been doing hiding her from me."

"I'm sorry, dear. Please forgive me. Here, take this birthday cake. I'm sorry I'm late with it and I'm sorry I haven't written you a thank-you note for that delicious supper you brought by, and I'm sorry I haven't returned your dishes either."

"You're just a sorry thing today, aren't you, Imogene Lavender?" Martha teased as she reached for the cake.

"Yes. I don't know what's wrong with me. Forgive me?"

"Course I do. You're just flustered is all. Got too many folks depending on you. Come outside here with me while I put this lovely cake in the car."

Imogene followed Martha outside and they stood in the gravel parking lot. "She's a hoot!" Martha smiled. "A real charmer."

"Think so?"

"Why, I certainly do! Where in the world has she been all these years?"

"You know. I told you she was up in Pamplico, South Carolina."

"Well, shame on you. How come she never came to visit before now? I don't even recollect seeing her at Silas's or Fenton's funeral."

"Um, she was busy," Imo said. "Couldn't get away." Her neck flushed warm with the lie. "Listen, has Lemuel ever told you why I came to see him right after Mama moved in?" She held her breath.

"Like I already told you, hon, he said you was just wrung out. Said you were so plum exhausted you couldn't even see straight, much less make any sense. Two teenage girls will do you that way, huh?" Martha laughed.

"Yes, yes." Imo nodded, breathing out a sigh of relief. "Thanks again for the supper."

Martha patted Imo's arm. "Well, you think nothing of it. It was my pleasure. I'm always ready to help. 'Specially for my dearest friend in all the world. Thank *you* for the lovely cake."

Imo drove home with a lighter heart.

It was a crystal-clear, cool morning in late October and Imo stole a moment to step out onto the back porch for a calming breath. She studied the stark branches of the pecan tree. Winter was definitely around the corner now and there was so much that needed tending to outside, she didn't know where she should start. Among other things, it was time to refurbish the mulch on the garden, start adding leaves and other materials to the compost pile, and dig her dahlia and gladiolus bulbs.

She decided she'd bring Mama and Little Silas outside to soak up some sun while she worked in the yard. It did cross her mind briefly that things might be difficult if they decided to run in two different directions, but she told herself that they couldn't stay cooped up in the house all day, every day, till Jeanette got home from school. She helped Mama into her dress while Little Silas played at their feet. She changed and dressed him, too, fed them both, and then in slow motion they crept out to the backyard. From the well-house Imo got a folding chair. She set it up near the clothesline and lowered Mama to sit in it.

"Girl, you need to tote that laundry in, so's I can wet it and iron it!" Mama grabbed Imo's sleeve. "You hear me?"

"Yessum," Imo said in a gentle voice, "I'll be sure to take care of it in just a little bit." She would not let herself lose patience with Mama today. She went to the shed for the garden fork and as she was returning she glanced up to see Little Silas with one knee up on the rim of the wheelbarrow at the barn. "Yoo-hoo, get down, sugar foot!" she called, "that big old thing will tip right over on you!"

He watched her running toward him, laughed and pulled his other knee up. Imo was just able to catch him and right the wheelbarrow before it tumbled over on top of him. "Whew," Imo breathed as Little Silas giggled wildly, swinging his legs to get down. "You come with Imo, sweetie," she said, "and I'll let you help dig up the dahlia bulbs. Don't you want to play in the dirt with me?"

"Yes," he said emphatically.

"Get this here laundry in, child!" Mama ordered from her chair before they could even make it to the birdbath.

Imo held Little Silas tighter, desperately searching for the peacocks to distract Mama. She could not see them anywhere. *Where were those birds when you needed them?* "Here, here, here!" she called, slapping her thigh with her free hand. "El-mer! Dewy Roose!" From underneath the glider Bingo came bounding up to speak to Imo, nearly knocking her and Little Silas over with his front paws on her knees.

From Mama came another grunt and a sharp "Imogene Rose! Come here this instant!"

"What is it now?" she panted, running up.

"These trees here are dead."

"What?"

"These!" Mama waved a hand at the oaks to her right, which were dropping their leaves for winter. "Just dead as a doornail."

"But Mama . . ." Imo started to protest, only she felt so frustrated that all she could do was close her eyes against the old woman ranting in the lawn chair.

"Better cut them on down, by cracky!" Mama insisted. "They're losing leaves left and right. Liable to fall down on top of us and knock us dead."

"Okay, you're right, Mama," Imo said. "I'll tend to it soon as I can get my saw out of the shed."

Thankfully Elmer wandered up shortly and distracted Mama enough so that Imo could set to work digging up her dahlia bulbs. She ran the garden fork across the ground, carefully removing the soil layer by thin layer so as not to damage the bulbs. When this was done she knelt beside Little Silas and felt for the smooth treasures, remembering their intense colors in August and September with a smile. "Wipe the dirt off these for me, please, sir," she said to Little Silas, handing him two bulbs along with an old hand towel. "We're going to let them sleep all winter long in the cellar. Let them hibernate just like an old bear. They won't survive the cold if we leave them out here."

He nodded and wiped the dirtiest bulb intently.

"We'll also have to put the garden to bed for the winter before too long. It's winding down, you know."

"To bed," he said, with an amused twinkle in his eye.

Imo smiled. Fall always filled her with a pleasure that was tinged with sadness. The garden was about done for the year, and the memories of the sowing, planting, tending, and harvesting were sweet and satisfying, but the bad part of it was knowing she had to wait so long for spring to come again. She pushed the wheelbarrow full of bulbs out of the sun and led Little Silas to the garden's edge. She walked around it, sizing it up, and he followed like her shadow. "Shall we mulch the garden or rake up leaves for the compost first?" she turned to ask him.

"Leaves!" he shouted, clapping his hands.

"That's right, darlin'. We'll make the biggest pile of leaves for you to jump in, and then we'll load them all up and put them in the compost bin."

"Goody, goody." Little Silas hugged Imo's knees.

She led him to the barn. "Here we are," she said, handing him a short bamboo rake, "let's get busy."

Imo felt her heart growing lighter as she swiped strips of oak leaves into a pile. Little Silas exulted in jumping into the crunchy heap and Imo reveled in the warm sun on her shoulders as she worked. Lately she'd been so stifled as far as getting outside, and the beautiful thing was that out here there were no walls, there were only wide-open spaces and the lovely blue sky stretching above them without limits.

"Yoo-hoo!" Mama waved both hands at Imo. "It's time for my stories!"

"Hold your horses," Imo called, "just give me a few more minutes here."

"Now, by cracky!" Mama exploded in frustration. She began rocking backward and forward, futilely trying to gain enough momentum to get to her feet.

In a heartbeat, Imo's warm feelings vanished. "Calm down, Mama!" she shouted. "I promise I'll get you inside in just a bit."

"Make haste, Imogene, or I'll miss the beginning," she fussed, "you're slower than Christmas."

Imo dropped the rake, hustled over, looped one arm through Mama's, and hauled her along. "Upsy-daisy," she said as they reached the cement steps at the back door. She settled Mama into her La-Z-Boy and turned the TV on to a Tide commercial. She could let down part of her guard now, at least. She would have two hours of playing in the leaves with Little Silas, and then when she got him good and tired she could get the leaves on the compost pile and work on mulching the garden. But there was one problem. What if Mama took a notion to get up and wander out the front door? She did this on occasion. Imo pondered this and was torn.

"Oh, thank you, Jesus!" Imo cried as she remembered the baby monitor near Little Silas's crib. Sprinting down the hall, she grabbed both parts of the contraption and returned to plug one in next to Mama's chair. She settled the other half of it in her pocket.

Now she could get back to the garden without worries!

But before she and Little Silas could get out the door, the phone rang. She hesitated only a moment, then headed outside. It rang and rang and rang.

"Mama!" Little Silas shouted.

Imogene stopped. "I reckon Mi-Moo does need to answer that, doesn't she, sweetie?" she said to Little Silas, "it really could be your mama or your aunt Loutishie calling from school."

It was Martha.

"How are you, hon?" Martha said. "You sound out of breath."

"Was on my way outside with the baby," Imo replied. "I'm okay. How are you?"

"Fine, fine. Sure was nice to meet your mama Sunday. Lemuel and I enjoyed that nice cake you made me, too."

"Well, good," Imo said.

"Imogene, did you get ahold of all the girls about Thursday?"

"What?" Imo's chest tightened.

"You were supposed to call all the girls about Garden Club on Thursday."

Imo drew a sharp breath. "I *knew* there was something I was forgetting!" she said. "I had it on my to-do list, Martha, I promise I did. But I can't find my list. Maybe I can get around to it this evening. It's just Tuesday. Surely I can do it by tomorrow. I'll go write it down right now. I'm sorry."

"Well, dear," Martha said, "you're mighty busy. I'll tell you what, I'll get Myrtice to do the calling. Will I see you there on Thursday morning?"

"Oh, I don't know, Martha. I don't believe I can manage getting these two out of the house together and I can't leave them. I'll just have to miss this one."

"We need you, Imogene Lavender," Martha reprimanded, "and you love Garden Club."

"I know." Imo fumbled with the receiver.

"Listen," Martha said, "I know what we'll do! We'll just have to have our meeting at your house."

"No!" Imo shouted. "I mean, no thank you, dear. That just isn't possible."

"Well, for goodness sake, why not? It seems like the perfect solution to me."

"Because this place is an absolute wreck," Imo confessed, "it's just fallen to pieces in the house and the yard's near about gone to seed. I can't let you or the girls see this place. You'll kick me out of the Garden Club for being a disgrace."

Martha chuckled. "Listen at you!" she said. "We stand beside each other, come what may. You should know that better than anybody. I'll tell Myrtice to tell the girls just to come on to your place Thursday."

"Uh . . . no . . . I mean I may just take a break this month. Get myself together. I told you, Martha, I am just so busy chasing Mama and Little Silas."

"Hold on one minute here," said Martha. "What about Imogene? You need to do something for *yourself,* hon."

"I don't have *time* to do anything for myself," Imo said, fighting a hint of irritation.

"You know what you are?" Martha drew a sharp breath. "You are a prime example of the Sandwich Generation!"

"What?!"

"I just read this article in my latest *Woman's Day.* It was all about the Sandwich Generation," Martha said. "That's when you're caring for an aging parent and chasing grand-young'uns at the same time. Get it? Your mama and Little Silas are the slices of bread, and you're the middle. You're the filling!"

"Well," Imo said as this new thought settled over her. There was nothing she could think of to say back to Martha.

"Well yourself," Martha said gleefully, "the article said that you, the middle of the sandwich, need to be sure and carve out time for yourself. Or you'll get squished. Now, I'm going to tell Myrtice to tell the girls ten o'clock Thursday at your house."

The minute she hung up, Imo began cleaning house as best she could between keeping an eye on Mama and chasing Little Silas. She would shine things up inside and when Jeanette and Lou got home, maybe then she could get outside again for a while.

By four o'clock when the school bus rumbled to a stop at the mailbox, Imo felt drained. She had spent every last bit of strength sweeping, dusting, and scrubbing.

A bit after five, she found the energy and freedom to get outside as Mama sat glued to *The People's Court.* She picked up sticks left from the storm weeks ago, and then made a dash for the garden. Gathering two late tomatoes, she hurried back in the house to fix supper.

She rolled up her sleeves to sift some flour with salt, sugar, soda, and baking powder. Then she cut in shortening and added buttermilk for biscuits. She rolled the dough out the same way she had for fifty years, but her thoughts were elsewhere. It was going to take all she had to get the house suitable for Garden Club in two days. She was only treading water as it was, not moving ahead in life at all. She was close to panic as she sliced the tomatoes into pretty red circles and arranged them on a plate. Operating on automatic, she pulled the cookie sheet full of golden biscuits from the oven and slid them into a towel-lined basket.

She settled a platter of pork chops on the center of the table and placed a boiler of butter beans dotted with okra onto a folded towel beside it. In her mind, it was Thursday morning and she was at the door welcoming the Garden Club girls, apologizing for the state the house and the yard were in. Then it hit her, she would have to bake something for them, too! Not tonight, however. She had just enough oomph to feed everyone supper, get it cleaned up, and get Mama into bed. She'd have to run to the Clover Farm Grocery tomorrow and get some things to bake a coffee cake.

When they were all seated for supper, she asked the Lord's blessing. "This is our last fresh tomatoes till next year," she said after the amen. "I was just out in the garden and I didn't see any more coming along, so we'd better enjoy them."

They ate in relative silence, with only Mama's dentures clicking as she chewed and Little Silas banging on the table with his spoon. Mindlessly Imogene split open her biscuit and wedged a slice of tomato between the two halves. She took a bite and laid it down on her plate. She looked across at Jeanette and Little Silas and Loutishie, and then beside her at Mama's jaw working her pork chop and then down at her own tomato biscuit, or 'mater biscuit as her Silas used to call them.

Then it hit her. Why, she *was* that slice of tomato! Just like Martha said, she was sandwiched in the middle of two very demanding generations. Every day she fell farther and farther behind in her own life; there was less and less time for the filling.

Imogene bit off another chunk of her 'mater biscuit, chased it with a gulp of iced tea, and told herself that things simply must change.

 ## Loutishie's Notebook

One afternoon in October Imo asked me to keep an eye on Mama Jewell while she went to the Clover Farm to buy some things to make a coffee cake for the Garden Club.

Two emotions shot through me at once. One was gratefulness at the chance to lend Imo a hand, by being in charge of the thing that was wearing her out. The months of caring for Mama Jewell were really taking their toll on Imo. Often at night I'd find her nestled down in her bed, exhausted after getting Mama Jewell to sleep, too tired to even read or talk. So I wanted to help her. I just didn't know what I could do besides lending a hand with cooking and cleaning, and some general things like laundry. She was the most appreciative, however, when I helped with Mama Jewell's baths or dressing her.

The other emotion was fear. Imo was getting very forgetful. She said she was running around the way she was that afternoon because she'd forgotten about her Garden Club meeting. Once I'd even found her purse in the Frigidaire. Jeanette agreed with me that Imo was losing her grip. Imo seemed to be getting more and more frazzled each day and I sure didn't want to think of her heading in Mama Jewell's direction.

I waved good-bye to Imo from the porch and walked back in to eye my charge. Mama Jewell was watching *Judge Judy* with her jaw hanging open. I figured she would stay in her La-Z-Boy, just like she was, since that's what she usually did, so I went to my bedroom to hunt a book.

But when I got back to the den, her chair was empty. First I checked the kitchen and the bathroom and then each of the bedrooms. No luck. "Mama

Jewell! Where are you?" I hollered real loud as I ran into the dining room and the pantry. They were empty, too, so I flew out onto the back porch to scan the yard. Nothing there.

For a while I stood, paralyzed, watching three buzzards circling in the air above the hay barn. She couldn't have gotten far, I kept telling myself. I hadn't even been gone five minutes. I peered out across the back pasture, absolutely motionless, with knees that felt full of jelly, until my brain zeroed in on this conversation I'd overheard the week before. It was Imo telling her friend Myrtice that Mama Jewell had run off, more than once, and that each time she had found her sitting in an old junker pickup truck up on cinder blocks out behind the silo.

As soon as I rounded the silo, I spotted her. She was sitting in there just like a statue. "It's time to go to the fair," Mama Jewell said once I managed to get the door open.

"The fair?" I asked, bending forward to hold the stitch in my side.

"Yes!" she told me in a voice that showed me she thought *I* was the crazy one.

"Come on out," I said, "there's no fair this time of year." I tried to pull her out by the elbow.

"Stop that!" She yanked her arm away. "We're going to be late if you don't get in here and drive right this minute, Sheila."

There she was, thinking I was Sheila again. I was going to look pretty stupid driving a truck with no wheels, but I crawled over her into the driver's seat and perched up on some lumpy springs with yellowed cotton batting oozing out. It stunk to high heaven in there, but I had learned that you just had to play along with Mama Jewell's mind-trips until you got her to a place where you could distract her.

Mama Jewell wore a gaudy floral housedress and rubber boots. An old Feed 'n' Seed cap of Uncle Silas's was perched sideways on her head. "We've got to hurry, Sheila," she said, "the river's going to rise soon."

What she was talking about was every afternoon around five when the Army Corps of Engineers released water from a dam at Lake Allatoona to generate power. This made the water level of the Etowah rise up to five feet.

I slipped an imaginary key into the ignition and bounced my fanny on the seat for special effect. Mama Jewell was content. She was bona fide crazy but seemingly happy, sitting there on her way to the fair with the most expectant face I ever saw.

"What you got there?" I asked her, nodding at a paper sack on her lap.

"Muscadine preserves."

"That your lunch or something?"

"Of course not, Sheila. How silly you are! You know good and well I got a ribbon with this at last year's fair. I aim to do it again."

"Oh yeah," I said, wondering how long I had to keep driving.

Mama Jewell gazed out at the weeds, not a glimmer in her eyes that we were sitting still. There was no way I could tell what was going on in her mind.

"We're here!" I said after I had counted slowly to a hundred.

Mama Jewell nodded. "Well, let's tote this to the judging barn, then." She patted the sack. "We can go see the heifers once it's all signed in."

I nodded. I wondered when Imo was going to get home. I slid over Mama Jewell and landed in the grass, grabbed her arm, and helped her out. We walked around the pasture a while and then Mama Jewell set her bag on a stump. I got a chance to peek inside. There was a can of fruit cocktail in light syrup.

"Where's the fun house at, Sheila?" She grabbed my arm.

I inched her along a dirt path to all that was left of an old swing set. It was a rusty slide attached to a couple of bent poles, lying on its side next to a broken-down plastic seesaw. "Here we are at the fun house!" I said. Elmer and Dewy Rose had found their way to us and Elmer was pestering Mama Jewell's ankles.

"Shoo!" Mama Jewell hollered. "They need to keep the livestock penned up better than this, don't they, Sheila?"

"I know it," I said. "But, hey, it is getting kind of late, Jewelldine, and we'd better get on back home and tend to supper."

Reluctantly she let me lead her back to the truck. The hat had fallen off her head. "I surely hope I get me that blue ribbon again, Sheila."

"Me too," I said.

"I'll put it in my scrapbook. Burton is so proud of my winnings," she said. "But, Sheila, he's so worried about our little Vera. She's running around with white trash folks."

I held my breath. She was talking about my mother! I had begun to treasure the bits and pieces about my mother that I sometimes gathered from Imo and from snippets of conversation I overheard at Garden Club meetings. However, anytime Imo mentioned her sister these days, it got Mama Jewell all worked up and so Imo'd stopped talking about her completely. We'd even had to go around the house and put all the photographs of her out of sight. I was starved for talk about my mother, and feverishly I searched my brain for ways to get Mama Jewell to stay in that period of her memory.

"Well, that's just awful, Jewelldine," I said. "Who are these white trash folks?" I patted her old back kind of hard. *Please stay on track*, I prayed.

Her hands started shaking. "It's that bunch of riffraff from up on Buzzard Mountain," she said. "Vera's took up with some old boy with long, stringy hair."

This bit of information had me starving. I wanted names. I didn't know anyone who lived up on Buzzard Mountain, so I made up a name real quick. "Is it that no account Bobby Pardue?" I asked.

But Mama Jewell'd given out on the subject. She was scratching Dewy Rose's head. "Go find your honey bunch," she said to the blinking peahen. "Run and tell him you want to see his play purties."

Just my luck! I was so mad that I caught myself wishing Mama Jewell would drop down dead. That would certainly solve a lot of our problems. But I knew it was wrong to think like that, and I stood there desperately trying to harness my ugly thoughts. Ever since Reverend Peddigrew's big slew of sermons on the Rapture, I thought of my life like it was this big chalkboard divided into three parts; the good things in my heavenly account, the bad things working against me, and then the neutral stuff. I didn't actually do many bad things. I smiled at everyone, even the mean, snotty girls at school. I didn't kill or cheat or steal or lie. And I didn't say most of the ugly things I wanted to.

The main place I was having trouble in was my thought life, especially wishing ill things on Mama Jewell. I had willed her to die lots of times, even after reminding myself that the Rapture could happen any minute.

"Hungry," Mama Jewell said, yanking me out of my thoughts. I hooked my arm through hers and steered her back inside, to the kitchen table. Her teeth clicked. "Fix me some corn bread and buttermilk, girl."

"Yessum," I said. "Want onion with that?"

"I surely do."

She was ravenous and I found myself fixing two heaping bowls of buttermilk, corn bread, and chopped onions for her. "Your show's on," I said when she'd finished.

"Wait, Sheila, let's go look at my scrapbook." Mama Jewell reached for my arm. "You can see my blue ribbon from last year's fair." She shuffled to her bedroom, to the tall trunk at the foot of her bed, and grunted as she tugged at the latch. I stared down at the ancient pine trunk. It had never occurred to me till now to open it. Always before it had been just this nondescript piece of furniture with a stack of Imo's quilts on top, but all at once I had no doubt that it held many secrets from the past. Maybe even the clues that I needed to fill in the lost puzzle pieces of my life.

The trunk was locked tight. Energized by my curiosity, I went to the bathroom for a bobby pin and wiggled it around inside the hole. This allowed the lock to swing free, but I had to beat all around the top of the trunk with my fist until it gave way. It let out a creaking sound and a musty, flowery smell as I lifted the lid, letting it flop back against the mattress.

There were stacks and stacks of dusty books, papers, and old-timey photographs held together in clumps with faded ribbons. In one corner of the top a cardboard square held needles, and there were spools of thread and a crocheted cross-shaped bookmark in the lid of a tattered pasteboard box.

Mama Jewell's eyes lit up. "My things!" she cried. "My wonderful, beautiful things. Nothing was lost on the train!"

"Nothing was lost," I said, eyeing the contents curiously as she began pulling things out and laying them on the floor.

She picked up a string of red beads and held them to her withered neck.

"Look, Sheila! I wore these to the May Day dance! Remember? Had me some matching ear-bobs, too. Let me hunt them." She ruffled through several layers and all of a sudden I noticed the top of this photo sticking out from under an old postcard of the Great Smoky Mountains. I bent closer and I could have sworn it was me until I slid it out a little more. A chill ran along my spine—it was my eyes and forehead all right, and my nose, but the mouth and the hair were unfamiliar. It was a picture of a young man with scraggly long hair who looked to be high school age. Quickly I stuffed it into my pocket.

Mama Jewell entertained herself by digging through the trunk till Imo got home. When I was free, I ran to the barn and pulled that photograph out and stared at it hard, memorizing every bit of the teenage boy. Could this be my father? It had to be! I knew it was wrong for me to take the photo from Mama Jewell's trunk, but I suppressed my guilty feelings by telling myself I would put it back later, and that then I would also confess it to God and repent of it.

I sat there in the dusty stall, dreaming of finding my father. He was grown up by then, no doubt. A big, strong man who would enfold me in his arms and shake his head in disbelief that we hadn't been reunited earlier.

Dewy Rose strutted into the barn to say hello. "Lookey here, girl," I said as I pulled her onto my lap to show her the picture. "This could be my father. What do you think? He cute or what?"

She looked into my face and cocked her head.

"I'm glad you agree. Jeanette thinks I ought to try and find him. She says I owe it to myself. What do you think?"

Dewy Rose blinked.

"You do, huh?" I said, patting her head. "Maybe I will then. But we have to remember, Jeanette's not always the best person to get advice from. She's not very smart about some things."

I sat there wishing that Dewy Rose could really talk to me. I needed some feedback. But still, it helped me somehow to put my thoughts into words and say them aloud like that, and so I continued. "Jeanette calls me a holy roller if I even mention her not being ready for the Rapture. Can you imagine that, Dewy

Rose? That right there proves she's not the brightest person on earth. Well, we'll have to get that girl onto the straight and narrow path, won't we?"

Just then, Elmer wandered by the barn door and Dewy Rose scrambled out of my lap to meet him. They walked breast to breast toward the pecan tree. I felt a pure loneliness seeping into my bones as I watched their tail feathers.

"You've got each other," I mumbled under my breath as I jumped up quickly, dusted off the seat of my pants, and made my way along the dirt road that led across a small pasture, through a bit of woods, and down to the riverbank. I crunched through dry leaves and rotting muscadines to get to my favorite spot in the whole world, and I settled down to think for a spell. Just watching the Etowah run along could push Jeanette's mean face and Mama Jewell's crazy voice out of my thoughts. It carried away my hurts, at least for a little while. I looked out over the brown water, watched it running by so easy. The river had never let me down.

"Jeanette wrote a nasty love letter to Reverend Pike," I said out loud over the water, and the words sunk down into the Etowah and rolled away. For some strange reason, she had insisted on showing it to me the night before, and I read it right before she spritzed it with Jean Naté cologne and smacked her lips coated in hot pink lipstick all around the border.

"Mama Jewell's crazy as a loon!" I shouted over the water, "and she's wearing Imo plum out. And I'm feeling like I'm all alone." I knew I was acting stupid. *Grow up, Lou,* I said to myself. *When you were a little kid it was okay to think that you and Jeanette and Imo and Uncle Silas would all live forever on this place with things going right on like always, but those days are long gone.*

I got quiet a minute to think about those perfect days. When Imo and Uncle Silas adopted Jeanette, I was three and she was six, and it was great to have a sister. Me and Jeanette were always jumping around in the corn inside the silo together, playing school in the well-house, and exploring the farm. As we grew older, one of our favorite things was collecting arrowheads down in the bottoms along the banks of the Etowah. Uncle Silas showed us the perfect vine to swing out into the river and we used to have the finest time you can imagine splashing around in the water. Jeanette never even set foot down at the river anymore.

That lonely afternoon at the Etowah, I decided that finding that photograph in Mama Jewell's trunk was my sign. I would focus my thoughts on finding my father. I told myself that nothing in this world could steal my joy as long as I had the secret of finding my long-lost father bubbling up inside of me.

Later that evening I was in the kitchen getting a glass of water, when I saw this shadow dancing around the wall behind my own, all crazylike. Suddenly Mama Jewell leaped forward, grabbed my arm, and squeezed it a bit.

"Huh?!" I was startled.

"Where's Burton?" Her face was in mine. "Why didn't he feed the cows today?"

"I . . . I don't know," I said quickly, shrugging and shaking off her dry fingers. "Maybe he's busy. On a trip. Or maybe it's 'cause he's sick."

Her eyes got huge. "It's his emphysema acting up again!" she gasped. "The man can barely draw breath sometimes." She turned from me, yanked open the silverware drawer, and grabbed out a butter knife. Then she groped around underneath the sink for two onions. She plopped the onions up on the cabinet and began wildly whacking away at them with the blunt knife.

"Stop!" I said. "What are you doing? Imo just cleaned this place up."

Chop, chop, chop! "I'm mekking an onion poultice for my Burton," she said. "Going to lay it up on his chest to loosen up the phlegm. To where he can get his breath back."

I tried to tell her that he was already dead, but the words wouldn't come out. "Stop," I said instead, more firmly than the first time. "Go back to your bed, Mama Jewell. Imo's tired and you're going to wake her up."

"But Burton'll die if I don't get this poultice on him!" Mama Jewell spun around and looked at me with horrified eyes. "I just can't live without my Burton." She turned back to her frenzied chopping. When she was satisfied, she wrapped the bits of onion up in a dishrag and spun around to face me. "Alrighty, where is he, girl?" she asked. "Where's my Burton? You take me to him this instant. I've got to lay this up on his chest right now."

I was dumbstruck. I was also filled with pity for the fearful and befuddled old woman in front of me.

"What's all this commotion about, Loutishie?" Imo came through the kitchen, barefoot, rubbing her eyes. Then she spied Mama Jewell. Gently she took the dishrag from her hands and set it in the sink. "Mama," Imo said, "what in heaven's name are you doing?"

"She thinks Burton's on his deathbed," I said softly.

"Listen, Mama, Daddy's passed away," Imo said gently, turning her around in one smooth motion. "He's dead, and you need to get your rest." They shuffled off down the hallway.

"Who died first, Sheila? Me or Burton?" Mama Jewell turned to ask me over her shoulder. Her face was stricken.

I could not utter one word in response. I had never seen such a pitiful sight. I couldn't understand Mama Jewell's private battles, but I knew I had to find some way to keep myself moving ahead in life. I had to seek some wholeness, find some answers to the questions that followed me.

Jeanette came around the door frame laughing. She sat down on the telephone stool. "Crazy old goat, ain't she, Lou?"

"Sad, isn't it," I said. Breathing in deeply, I tried to focus my thoughts on other things. "How was your choir practice tonight?"

"Fuckin' heavenly." She closed her eyes and sighed.

The blood in my veins froze up. "Jeanette!" I breathed. "You shouldn't talk that a way!"

"Why not?" she said. "It was. Montgomery brought his guitar and his amp and I stayed late after all the other Praise Squadders left." Jeanette was smiling big, and silver flecks in her eyeshadow caught the light in the kitchen and made her look sparkly. "Mmmm mmmm, Lou, I'm in love sure enough this time," she said in a dreamy voice. "I don't think I could ever look at another man the way I do him!" She closed her eyes, leaned back against the counter, wrapped her arms around herself, and squeezed.

"Jeannie!" I spluttered. I couldn't help the picture that formed in my mind then—of her assaulting the Reverend Pike and taking advantage of him. I had to put a stop to this. "Well," I said meanly, "he may be the loving and leaving type just like Little Silas's father was."

A startled, hurt look spread across Jeanette's face. "Just tell me who peed in *your* cornflakes this morning!" she said as she turned on her heel and stormed out of the kitchen.

For some reason I felt pleased with myself to have wounded Jeanette. She deserved it, I reasoned, laying her trap for a preacher!

That night before I fell asleep I slid my hand up under the mattress to feel the stolen photo.

Everything was going to be better when I found my father.

Five

Giving Thanks

*T*he morning of the Garden Club meeting turned out to be windy and cold. At dawn, Imogene put on her cardigan and went outside to sweep the leaves off the porch and walkway. She hadn't slept most of last night for fretting over the house and yard. Plus, she still had to bake the coffee cake.

Elmer strutted over to her to check out the activity. Because of his long legs, he was having trouble keeping his balance in the strong winds. To stay up, he spread his train, swaying and strutting around Imo. Dewy Rose kept her perch in a nearby tree, surveying them from a safe distance.

"Now don't you two go to hollering and scare the Garden Club girls," Imo warned. "I don't want anything to spoil this meeting today, you hear me?"

The peacock swayed to her left, turning his head to stare at her. He appeared to be smiling.

"Shoo! Go on, now!" Imo said with a sharp wave of her broom. "I've got too much to do to fool with you right now."

Elmer scuttled forward and plopped himself right on the porch steps, looking accusingly at Imo.

"There's enough foolishness around this place already. Now shoo!

Go on! Get!" Imo said, aiming the brushy end of the broom at him. The bird fell all over himself climbing down, then made a dash for the barn. She checked her watch. It was time to get the girls up for school.

She hurried inside. When she got to their bedroom, she found Lou already up and dressing. She bent to gently shake Jeanette's shoulder. "Wake up, Jeannie," she said.

"I don't feel very good," the girl moaned from beneath her cover.

"Well, get on up," Imo urged, "surely you'll feel better once you're up and moving around."

Jeanette rolled over and edged one eye open. "Cain't get up," she said, "I'll have to miss school today." Her nose was pink and swollen, and her eyes had dark circles beneath them.

Imo sighed and cleared her throat. "You're sure then?"

"Mmm-hmm," Jeanette said, "positive."

"Alrighty," Imo said finally, "I'll bring you some juice and aspirin in a little bit."

Imo went to peer into Little Silas's bed. He stirred, so she placed a hand to her mouth and stepped back soundlessly, willing him to sleep just a tad longer. Well, she thought, if there was a silver lining to Jeanette's feeling under the weather and staying home from school, it was that she could keep an eye on Little Silas during the Garden Club meeting. This thought was comforting.

In the kitchen Loutishie was hunting a box of cereal and Mama sat vacant-faced at the table, waiting for her coffee. Imo flew around, starting the percolator and setting out cups, bowls, and spoons. Onto the counter she placed her mixing bowl, the sugar, the flour, and two eggs. Next she rummaged through the cabinet for some aspirin, poured a cup of orange juice, and raced back down the hall.

"Here, swallow these," Imo whispered to Jeanette, "you'll feel better directly."

Little Silas cried out, "Mi-moo!" and a knot pulled in Imo's stomach. She had not had time to freshen up the bathroom. She took a deep breath and picked up his heavy, sleepy shape.

She said to him, "You're just going to have to come on into the kitchen and help Mi-moo this morning. Yes you are, sweetie pie. We've got ourselves a cake to bake."

She changed Little Silas's diaper on the couch, set him in his high chair in the kitchen, and filled his sippy cup with juice. She poured coffee and milk into Mama's cup and set it before her. She heard the school bus rumble up, glanced out the window above the sink to see Loutishie climbing aboard.

Imo glanced at her watch. Seven-thirty. Her mind raced forward to ten o'clock as she set a skillet on the stove to fry eggs for Mama and Little Silas. Both sets of their eyes were fastened on her, waiting for their breakfast. They depended on her! Her selfish feelings of wanting to get through with them and on to baking her coffee cake made her feel ashamed. Look at Little Silas's sweet face, the sparkle in his eyes, the dimples in his hands! And that old woman there, Imo's very own flesh, the woman who had given birth to her. Completely dependent now on Imo's mercy and provisions.

Wiping her brow, Imo measured flour, salt, and baking soda into the mixing bowl, and in the next split second she turned the two eggs sizzling on the stovetop. She surveyed the chaotic house as she plopped the eggs onto plates and cut them both up into bite-size pieces. *Eat quickly,* she urged them in her thoughts, *so I can get you out of here and get this mess cleaned up before the girls arrive.*

". . . pass me the salt and pepper for my egg, girl," Mama said as Imo stirred the batter for the cake. "You know I need me the salt and pepper." She banged her fork on the table.

Imo got still. A memory was elbowing its way in. Rigid, she stood, desperately trying to will it away. What was it that had triggered this one, she wondered. What had unlocked it against her will? The lilt of Mama's demanding voice?

It wasn't something she wanted to remember—a clear October

afternoon when she was twelve or so, with some gray clouds scuttling away after a quick rain shower. Mama was angry because the apple slices she had laid out to dry on an old sheet atop a piece of tin perched on the roof of the shed got wet. Imogene felt her mama's anger as she swatted at Imo with the hickory switch, raising a pink welt on her thigh. "If you'd have just paid attention, Imogene Rose," Mama snorted, with her face red and her body practically shaking, "if you would've brung in the apples before it sprinkled on them, I wouldn't have to fuss at you! You are so irresponsible. Don't have the sense God gave a monkey sometimes." Imo cowered behind a watering trough outside the hog pen, knees trembling, choking down any retort, believing her mama's words, and squeezing her eyes shut tight.

How could she pull herself out of this memory? Imo stared hard at a silly picture of a rooster along the top of her recipe card. Next, she focused on the word *butter*. Butter, butter, butter. She spelled it aloud, b-u-t-t-e-r. Touched it until the memory began to fade. But now there was the heartache in her chest, and the tears in the back of her throat, teetering on the rims of her eyes. A tear escaped down her cheek, and with it, the image of herself later on that terrible day and that following week, fearful of anyone seeing the red slash on her thighs, and knowing how bad she must have been to deserve that mark.

Thank God her girls never had to endure something like that. Or even to know about it. She glanced at Little Silas. He was through with his egg and he flung his plate to the floor. Thud! Imo bent to retrieve it and as she did she began to shake free of the awful feelings. She wet a paper towel, wrung it out, and bent again to wipe up the greasy mess on the floor. Keep busy! That was the trick! The trick she needed to keep these memories at bay, and it was surely an easy thing to do around this place. She'd leave no time, just keep hands and mind occupied constantly.

She flew around the house, busier and busier the closer it got to time for the Garden Club girls to arrive. She left no idleness for thoughts. No, no, she'd not leave a foothold for those memories.

At 9:55, headlights shone beyond the pines at the curve of the drive, and then Martha's Dodge pulled to a stop beyond the mailbox. Imo watched Martha emerge, and then gather bags and more bags from the backseat. Now that she had her arms full, she bumped the car door closed with her fanny. She walked along past the birdbath, wobbling on her heels in the pea-gravel, until all of a sudden Elmer snuck up behind her and let out an ear-piercing scream.

Imo stood helpless at the sink as she watched Martha's arms fly out and the bags go sailing through the air. Pinecones and ears of colored Indian corn landed everywhere.

"No!" Imo cried, throwing up her hands from the dishwater and spraying Little Silas. He laughed as Imo hollered for Jeanette to come and tend to him while she flew out the door to Martha's side.

"Oh, hon, I'm so sorry," Imo breathed. "I should have warned you about them." She bent to pick up Martha's things, gathering a stack of papers that read "Hollies Are Sturdy and Colorful" across the top.

"What in heaven's name was *that*?" Martha gasped with wide eyes.

"That was Elmer. Mama's peacock."

"My lands!" Martha looked put out with Imo already.

"I'm sorry," said Imo. "I've been so busy getting ready for the Garden Club meeting that I just didn't have any time to think, much less call you about them." She stuffed the last red ear of corn into a bag to drive her point home. "Let me go pen them up inside the barn."

"What in the world are you doing with a peacock, Imogene?" Martha asked when Imo returned.

She shrugged. "Calms Mama down. Lou's taken a fancy to them, too."

"Them?!"

"We've got us a girl as well. Dewy Rose. I imagine she's hiding out somewhere with Bingo. I swannee, sometimes she thinks she's a dog." Imo laughed.

Martha laughed, too. "I cannot imagine, Imogene," she said, shaking her head. "Two of them." She cast an eye around the yard, fixing Imo with a sideways glance. "'Bout to get out of hand around here, huh?"

"Oh Martha, I told you. I just can't do it all."

"Need you some help around here. Need you a man. I couldn't make it a day without my Lemuel."

Imo looked hard at Martha. "Shame on you, Martha Peddigrew!" she said sharply over her shoulder. "Don't even say something like that! Hear me? Now come right on inside and have some coffee." The last thing she needed was someone else to tend to, Imo thought to herself. She had four people, besides herself, to take care of now, and she simply had no time for a man.

The kitchen was empty when they got inside. "Two peacocks!" Martha exclaimed. "You certainly have got your hands full." She sank down onto a chair at the table. "Well, not to worry, dear. A friend in need . . . Here, let me show you what we're making today." Carefully, Martha reached into one of her bags and pulled out a pinecone with strips of colored construction paper stuck in for a tail at one end and the shape of a turkey's head wedged in at the other. "This is our example," she said, placing it in the center of the table. "And this"—she held up three ears of Indian corn fastened together with a slender bit of corn husk—"is what we'll make to hang on our doors."

"They're pretty, Martha," Imo said.

"Well, I figured it would be nice to have it with Thanksgiving right around the corner."

Imo nodded, feeling dazed. She forced a smile. Thanksgiving. Who could even think of Thanksgiving? Well, she couldn't be expected to get it together to do her usual celebration. She'd seen complete prepared family meals advertised at the big grocery stores in Cartersville. Maybe that would be the solution for their Thanksgiving dinner. She was grateful just to make it through ordinary days. Sometimes lately she had even served cornflakes and milk for supper.

From the den came the sound of the TV, too loud, with Little Silas fussing over that and then Jeanette's nasal voice saying, "Yessum, sweetie boy, we surely do need us another TV if this old fart's gonna hog it like this!"

Imo excused herself and went to the den to head off a sure fight. Jeanette sat on the couch in a Pepto-Bismol–pink robe with a lap full of crumpled tissues. She had the remote control in her hand and was flipping the channels while Mama protested.

"My show's fixing to start," Mama cried, looking to Imo for help.

"Jeannie," Imo pleaded, "*please*. Let her watch this one. Maybe you and Little Silas could go and play in your room a while."

Jeanette's eyes narrowed. "You mean *I* can't even watch TV in my *own* house?"

"Please, sugar foot," Imo said, "take turns with the TV."

Jeanette stomped her foot, but she rose, grumbling, scooped up Little Silas, and shuffled off down the hallway.

When Imo got back to Martha she heard a knock. She put on a wide smile, marched to the door, and opened it to see Florence Byrd and Maimee Harris.

"Hello girls," she said, "come right on in."

"Mmm-hmm," said Maimee, "something sure smells delicious in here!"

"It's cinnamon coffee cake," Imo said as she led them to the dining room table. "Make yourselves at home. I reckon I'd better run and see if the cake's ready to come out now."

Martha was certainly making herself at home. She was already in the kitchen, pulling the cake out of the oven, and had a fresh pot of coffee brewing. She had arranged cups, saucers, spoons, sugar, and creamer on a tray. She placed the tray in Imo's hands.

"Here, hon," Martha directed, "you go on in there with this and I'll bring the cake and the forks and napkins. I'll tend to the door, too."

Imo looked down. It was a tray she hadn't been able to find for months.

It was close to ten-thirty when eight members of the Garden Club were all settled around the dining table with coffee and cake in front of them.

"Where's Glennis?" Maimee Harris turned to Florence Byrd. "Didn't she ride with you?"

"She's gone in for some surgery," Florence said matter-of-factly.

"Oh my," gasped Maimee. "She didn't say a word to me about it. What kind of surgery is it?"

"It's nothing serious," Florence explained, "just a little face-lift."

"Face-lift?" said Viola. "That can too be serious. Any surgery is serious. Who would take a chance like that? Glennis is lovely just like she is. Plus, I'm proud of my wrinkles. I earned them!"

"Amen!" said Maimee. "I can tell you where every single one of my wrinkles came from. These here," she said, pointing to her creased forehead, "are on account of being a middle school home-ec teacher for forty years!" She paused a moment. "And the rest are from being married to Fred for forty-nine years!"

Everyone laughed.

"Got most of mine when Charlie took that job down at the Ford dealership in Rome," Florence exclaimed.

Brenda raised her eyebrows and waved a hand in the air. "Mine are all from the grand-young'uns. 'Specially Lacey."

"She's a handful, huh?" Viola said.

Brenda nodded her head vigorously. "Lands, yes. That girl keeps us all on our knees."

"She'll make out okay, given time, dear," Martha reassured her.

"I know, I know," said Brenda. "Hey, girls, how 'bout we all carry some food out to Glennis. Then we could get a look at her!" She laughed.

"I don't think so. You know how Glennis is," said Florence. "She doesn't want anybody to see her when she's not at her best. When you were once the Camellia Queen, and it doesn't matter how long ago it was, you have an image to uphold." She touched Martha's wrist. "Don't quote me on this, hon, but I believe she said she's going to get herself a liposuction on her tummy and thighs, too."

Viola sucked in a quick breath. "Liposuction?! Why, we may not even recognize her!" She gave a lame little laugh. "And how will that make the rest of us look?"

Maimee helped herself to another piece of cake. "Well," she said, "*I* think it's a fine idea to improve yourself like that. No different from repainting your kitchen or putting new carpet in your den. If you've got the money, it's a nice gift for yourself and also a nice gift to give to those who have to look at you. If I could eat all I wanted and then just suction off the fat, I'd do it in a heartbeat." She chuckled as she slid a bite into her mouth.

"Me too," said Martha. "Now that would be nice."

"Mmm-hmm," agreed Florence. "Can you just imagine? Eat whatever and whenever you wanted, and not think a thing about it."

"I think I'd start by eating the rest of that cake there," laughed Brenda. "It's delicious, Imo!"

They all sat quietly for a while, drinking coffee and finishing their cake. "All right, girls," Imo said after a bit. "Time to get down to business. Let's hear the minutes from our last meeting and the treasurer's report, and then we'll get started on our activities."

"Now," Imo said after the minutes and the treasurer's report were done, "Thanksgiving!" She placed Martha's pinecone turkey example on her palm and held it aloft.

Myrtice adjusted her glasses and peered at it. She chuckled. "Haven't seen one of those since I was a little bitty thing."

"Isn't it precious!" Imo said. "Didn't your granddaughter make this one, Martha?"

Martha nodded, beaming.

Imogene glanced at all the eager faces. "Well, let's get busy, then. We can make extras to carry to Glennis."

They worked on their turkeys and gradually the conversation turned to Thanksgiving recipes. "You going to try anything new this year, Imogene?" asked Brenda. "I found a recipe for a new Jell-O salad. Calls for pecans, cranberries, and Cool-Whip."

Imo pondered this thought for a moment. "No!" she said during a moment of sharp inner discernment, "I'm going to do all our old favorites. Not going to change a thing." And as fast as these words were out of her mouth, Imo had changed her mind about Thanksgiving. She began to imagine that just getting into her usual routine of the season would itself bring back the feelings necessary. She reckoned if she could just make herself get in the kitchen and hunt up the recipes and smell the familiar smells, she could put together a happy holiday for her family. Things weren't going to be instantly perfect, but they surely could not get any worse.

The girls traced and cut and stuck in bits of construction paper to create two cheerful pinecone turkeys apiece. They fastened three ears of Indian corn together for their front doors. Imo enjoyed feeling like she was back in grade school and she loved hearing each of the girls talk of their holiday plans.

"One thing I always do at my house," said Brenda, "is I go around the table and I make everyone say three things they're thankful for. You should hear some of the things they come up with. Some of them don't bear repeating." She blushed. "But you know how boys are. Sure does liven up our Thanksgiving, and keeps us mindful of all our blessings!"

Imo decided she would try this, too. She drained her coffee, resolved to give her family the best Thanksgiving they'd ever had. The girls and Little Silas would need the good memories to keep them company when they got old.

The conversation turned to fall crops of collards and turnips. From the den Imo heard Jeanette and Little Silas's voices getting loud again. She felt a pinch of alarm and glanced at her watch—eleven o'clock. Must be Jeanette's turn to look at the TV. Was the transition to Jeanette's show upsetting Mama? She strained to make out the words over the Garden Club's happy chatter.

She heard Mama's raspy, indignant voice and then Jeanette's nasally voice going back and forth like gunfire. Pow-pow! went Jeanette's voice. Pow-pow! went Mama's in reaction. The words were indistinct, but the intent was not. Pow! Pow! Pow! Pow! Imogene could only imagine what they were saying. Then something hard hit the floor in the den and Mama cried out sharply, "No!"

"Excuse me, ladies." Imogene stood quickly. She could feel her pulse accelerating like crazy. *The jig's up now, Imogene. The whole world's going to see how out of control your household is,* she said to herself as she strode through the kitchen and into the den.

Mama's face was bright pink as she struggled to pull the remote control out of Jeanette's hand. Little Silas sat on the couch watching.

"It's our turn," Jeanette hissed, "you had your turn, you old selfish fart!"

"Jeannie, Jeannie," Imo said, gently grasping the girl's arm, "please give her the remote."

"Since when does *she* own the TV?!" Jeanette spat out. "Seems like you love her better than us. Ever since the old warthog showed up—"

"Shhh," Imo pleaded. "*Please,* sugar foot, please. You've got to understand. I don't love her better. I don't even . . . Anyway, Jeannie, you're away at school all day and she's gotten used to watching these shows. It's her routine. She thinks the folks in them are real. And lately, Jeannie, you've been gone to Praise Squad rehearsals about every night of the week, and Lou and I don't even look at TV, and Mama's gotten used to watching it whenever she wants to." Suddenly a wonderful thought occurred to Imo. "Hey, don't you have Praise Squad rehearsal tonight?"

Smiling, Jeanette nodded. "Yep, it's tonight." She had that faraway look in her eyes she got every time someone mentioned the Praise Squad.

The girl sure did love to sing those Christian songs. Imo was still rejoicing that God worked in such mysterious ways. "Well," Imo said, "I imagine I'll watch Little Silas for you to go then, as usual, and let you drive the car. Provided you help me deal with Mama here." Imo locked eyes with Jeanette in a meaningful way and gently pulled the remote from her hand. As she slid the remote into Mama's hand, she spied the familiar red and white of one of Jeanette's Marlboro cartons jutting out from beneath the cushion wedged in beside Mama's fanny.

Lord help us all, Imo breathed, quickly tugging the cushion over to conceal the box. No telling what would happen if Jeanette saw that.

"Speaking of Praise Squad, you'd better get on to bed, Jeannie," Imo said quickly. "If you want to feel well enough to go and sing tonight, you need to rest up." She put on her serious face. "Here, I'll watch the baby for you to go and get a little nap in. Rest your voice."

Imo held her breath and returned to the dining room with Little Silas on her hip. As she settled herself back at the table, the girls did not even glance up. They were busily chatting away and collecting snippets of construction paper for the wastebasket.

Light-headed with relief, Imo listened as Martha wrapped up the meeting. "Okay, ladies, now listen up," Martha said, "as you all know, our next meeting will be our Christmas party. Everyone needs to bring a finger food to share and something under five dollars for our gift exchange. We'll be meeting at Viola's—"

"Now wait just one darn minute here," Viola interrupted, her deadpan face making everyone stop and look hard at her. "I don't think we ought to have a December meeting."

There was silence.

"You don't?" Maimee said at last, her eyes wide.

"Nope," Viola said, fighting to hold a grin back. "What I'm figur-

ing is we ought to agree to cancel it on account of we'll all be needing to get ourselves some liposuction surgery after Thanksgiving!"

"Ain't that the truth, sister!" Brenda said, laughing and slapping
her thigh until they all joined in.

Jeanette sashayed out of her room at six, dressed in a pair of clingy
black pants and a shiny red shirt that was more suitable for a night-
club than the Lord's house, but Imo decided not to say one word
about it.

"Feeling better?" Imo called.

"Feeling finer'n frog hair," Jeanette sang out as she applied her
lipstick in the mirror over the mantelpiece.

That instant when Jeanette unscrewed the cap on a cylinder of
lipstick and puckered up her lips and leaned forward into the mirror
summoned a long-buried memory for Imo. Her sister Vera was fifteen or so, standing in high heels and a short black slip, swiping on
lipstick under the glow from the lone lightbulb in the tiny bathroom.
Mama came down the hallway and spied her. She stopped. Her
mouth opened in surprise, then closed.

"Jezebel!" Mama shrieked. The whites of her eyes were warning
enough, but her hands were clenched into fists.

"Please, Mama . . ." Vera cowered, the words dying on her
tongue, a long gash of red trailing down her chin.

"You know we don't allow face paint in this house!" One hand
shot out and smacked the lipstick out of Vera's hand.

Vera winced as it clattered to the floor.

"Bad enough you disobey me, but inviting trouble like this . . .
Tramp! Hussy!"

"I'm sorry," Vera whispered, "I'm so, so sorry." She cowered down
onto the cold tile floor, wiping her lips on the back of her hand. She
looked to Imo, who was standing behind Mama. Imo could see thin
white rivulets of tears flowing through Vera's tan face makeup.

When Mama was out of earshot, Imo placed a hand on Vera's

thin, childish shoulder, saying softly, "Come on, sweetie, let's get you to your feet and get you a washrag and clean your face up."

Vera nodded, clasping Imo's hand shakily. Imo gently wiped the tracks of Vera's tears away. "Everything's going to be okay. She'll calm down sooner or later."

Vera stared at Imo for a long bewildered moment, and then she nodded.

Imo stood at the kitchen sink with an ache pulsing in her chest at the remembrance of Vera's face that night. It hurt to realize that she didn't know then what she knew now. Now she would not stand for what she had then. But Vera was free now. Yes, Imo thought, as she began to gather recipes for Thanksgiving, Vera didn't have to deal with Mama in this befuddled condition. She was spared the memories and the pure labor of it all.

A fresh wave of hope surged through Imo as she sat down at the table to plan their feast; a beautiful brown turkey breast on her Delft platter, a boat of giblet gravy at its side, tiny marshmallow and pecan-encrusted sweet potatoes, steaming corn bread dressing, sides of cranberry sauce, green bean casserole, Waldorf salad, yeast rolls, and pumpkin pie. But most of all, faces smiling around the table. A good, happy memory would be made this year. Deliverance for a time from painful memories, from the hardships of life. Grace would come around the Thanksgiving table.

Imo was putting down shredded leaves for mulch when the Reverend Lemuel Peddigrew's blue pickup came putt-putting down the driveway. It was the day before Thanksgiving and all of her preparations were right on schedule. The cranberries were inside, simmering on the stove, she'd made the corn bread to crumble into the dressing, and the turkey was thawing in the Frigidaire. Jeanette was gone off somewhere, Lou was down in the bottoms, and Little Silas sat in the wheelbarrow beside her while Mama watched one of her stories inside the house.

She wondered what in heaven's name had brought the Reverend out today. He was a walking reminder of their unpleasant and unsatisfying conversation about Mama. She took a rake and smoothed the surface of her mulch.

"Imogene!" The Reverend bounded up to her, carrying a plastic bag from the Piggly Wiggly. "How are you? And hello to you, young man." He thrust his pointer finger at Little Silas. "Pow! Pow! Got you!"

Little Silas laughed and clapped his hands.

Imo grabbed the handles of the wheelbarrow. "Hello, Rever— I mean, Lemuel," she said.

Slinging the plastic bag to his forearm, he took the wheelbarrow from Imo. "Allow me."

"Certainly," she said, her heart suddenly pounding with anticipation. What in the world was he doing here?

Like he read her mind, he said, "I came out today because I feel like I let you down at our last visit together. You seemed so distraught when you left, and I just can't rest knowing you're having a problem." He parked the wheelbarrow at the back steps and swung Little Silas up to his hip. He cleared his throat, waiting for her to respond and open the door.

"Wonderful," Imo said without meeting his eyes. What she really wanted was him gone, she had many things to do, but she opened the door and led him into the kitchen, where the noise of Mama's show was so loud she had to shut the door from the kitchen into the den. Imo paused to stir the simmering cranberries. The kitchen smelled of cinnamon and nutmeg from a warm pumpkin pie on the counter.

"Martha said y'all had a nice Garden Club meeting here," he said as he set Little Silas onto a chair and unburdened himself of the bag.

"Yes, we did." Imo eyed the bag sitting in the center of the table. It was sweating.

"Brought us a little treat," he said, watching her face. "Some ice cream."

Imo stood there, wondering what it was he'd come to say that needed sweetening up. Her heart was booming like crazy.

"Butter knife?" he asked her.

"Knife," she repeated, gesturing at the silverware drawer.

He slid a carton of Neapolitan ice cream from the bag, set it carefully in the center of the table, and peeled down the cardboard sides to expose the brown, pink, and white striped rectangle. Next he ran a butter knife under hot water and used it to quickly slice off four rectangles. "Saucers?" he asked.

Imo gathered the saucers.

"Your mother?" The Reverend searched the room.

"In yonder, watching TV."

"Go get her, too. She likes ice cream, doesn't she?"

Numbly Imogene made her way to the den. "Preacher's here, Mama," she said, switching off the TV.

"Preacher?" Mama gasped, turning her head back and forth rapidly. "Come to tell me about Vera, I imagine. But I already know all about Vera. She's running with that bad crowd of white trash. Heading down the wide road to hell. Tell him I cain't come, Imogene." Her knuckles were white on the chair arms. "Tell him . . . I'm feeling too poorly to talk. Having my monthly."

Imo shook her head as she mashed the button to put the TV back on. She paused at the kitchen door to draw a deep breath.

"Mama's sick," she said, sitting down at her rectangle of ice cream.

The Reverend nodded and slid a napkin her way. "So, how goes the battle, Imogene?" he asked, spoon poised. "I've been so burdened in my spirit over what you told me about your mother, and I've been getting down on my knees and praying hard about it."

In the tumble of the Reverend's reassuring words and the kindly light from his eyes, Imo began to relax. "It's hard. Really hard," she said, looking at him finally. "Some days I don't know how I can keep putting one foot in front of the other." She bit her lip. "The bad memories, they just keep on a coming."

Nodding, he leaned across the table and patted her wrist.

"I don't know what to do anymore." She lowered her face, wiped her eyes. "I am just plum give out. Mama's been running off a good bit, and Jeanette fights with her all the time. And poor little Loutishie. I have to count on her to help me. . . . She doesn't complain, mind you, but I know it's hard on her." She looked at him again.

"You've got a lot on your shoulders, Imogene," he said finally. "So much pain. It must be an awful load to bear."

"Yes, it is," Imo sighed, "it most surely is." She took a deep breath. Things were getting uncomfortable. She wanted to get this over with and get back outside to her mulching.

"Well, like I said, I've been praying so hard for you my knees are getting calluses. And I just feel it, in my spirit, Imogene, that your healing, your peace, will come." He smiled at her and blotted his lips on a napkin. "There. I had to come out here and tell you that."

"You do?" She sat up straight. She wiped Little Silas's hands. He slipped down from his chair and over to a pile of blocks on the floor. "You think I'll get some peace?"

The Reverend nodded as he spooned up some strawberry ice cream and settled it onto his tongue.

Imo ran a finger around the edge of her saucer. She felt a glimmer of something very close to faith that she would make it through forming inside of her. With his reassuring words, and she could tell he was convinced of their truthfulness (and wasn't that what faith was?), and with his earnest and plenteous prayers behind her, things could end up okay! Her situation was certainly not as difficult as parting the Red Sea. Overcome by an immense burst of gratitude, she felt the need to engage him in further conversation. Come to think of it, she realized that she'd never heard about his growing-up years, his raising.

"Tell me about your childhood, Lemuel," she said, patting her lips with a napkin and leaning forward earnestly.

He rubbed his chin. "Well, I grew up with two loving, God-fearing folks who gave their all for me. We weren't rich by any means. No, I don't mean that. I mean I had their unconditional love and their sacrifice.

"Daddy worked night and day, it seemed, just to put food on our table, and my dear momma worked her fingers to the bone for the ten of us young'uns. Never traveled more than fifty miles from Stinchcomb County in her entire life." His face was reverent. "Momma," he breathed, "the Lord rest her soul."

Imo felt a pang of envy. But was it for his wonderful childhood or for the fact that he carried no burdens?

"Yep, I feel like I've had more than my fair share of blessings," the Reverend continued. "I've never wanted for a thing in this earthly journey. I've had the love and companionship of my Martha for forty-nine wonderful years. I don't know what I'd do without her. I'd be lost, that's for sure."

"Well, that must be mighty nice," Imo sputtered, "now, if you don't mind, I've got some things I need to tend to." She stood abruptly and set her spoon down on the saucer with a loud clink.

He lowered his head and sank it into his hands. He was quiet for quite a while as his ice cream melted into a brown puddle. "I don't even long for heaven like I should, Imogene," he murmured finally.

Imo couldn't believe what she was hearing. She studied the top of his head—sparse hair combed in neat furrows over a shiny bald spot. Imagine being God's mouthpiece and not longing for Glory! She felt like she needed to comfort and counsel *him*. She sat herself back down. "Oh, I'm sure you long for heaven, Lemuel," she offered, leaning forward and placing her hand on his wrist. "You just don't realize it because you stay so busy. You're right where you're supposed to be! *That's* why you're not longing for heaven. Think what life would be like for your flock down here if you did leave us." Now she patted his arm in what she hoped was a reassuring way. "And I surely appreciate you coming out to see me today, and for the ice cream, too. Plus, you're really helping me!" she blurted with a teary laugh. "Your prayers and your words of encouragement and all."

She rose to carefully stir the cranberries. "So you stop talking like that, Lemuel," she said, "we wouldn't know what to do if you weren't around, you hear?"

She waved good-bye from the porch as he pulled out of sight, and she stood a moment, reflecting on their visit. She was touched by his prayers on her behalf, of the way he'd offered his own pain to her.

It was four o'clock on Thanksgiving when Imogene went outside to ring the dinner bell. A clear, sunny day in the seventies with a slight breeze. There couldn't be a more picture-perfect setting, she decided, and even after cooking for two days straight, she felt energized and had even managed to fashion a centerpiece out of one of the smaller pumpkins from Lou's garden and the pinecone turkeys.

Lou came running up the hill from the river bottoms with Bingo and Elmer and Dewy Rose at her heels. She washed her hands with the garden hose and ran inside. Imo decided to wait until everyone else was situated before she collected Mama from the La-Z-Boy.

By the time Jeanette made it to the table with Little Silas it was four-twenty and the dressing, the rolls, and the soufflé were no longer steaming. The ice in the tea glasses was melting. But this did not bother Imo. It was, she decided, her new way of reacting to the circumstances in her life. Things were going to roll off her like water off a duck's back. She would be flexible and focused on all the blessings in her life. Thankful.

She glanced around the table to count her blessings. Loutishie sat smiling, freshly scrubbed clean and dressed in a brown corduroy jumper with a white blouse. Jeanette was wearing faded, skintight blue jeans and a glittery black T-shirt that read "Guns 'n' Roses," and it looked like she had teased her hair into a tangly mess. Little Silas sat in his high chair—sparkling eyes, round honey-brown cheeks, a tousle of black hair, and that ever-present impish grin.

Imo went to fetch Mama from her La-Z-Boy. Her eyes were fastened on a Thanksgiving Day parade in some distant city.

"Hungry, Mama?" Imo said, kicking the lever to lower the footrest, hooking her arm through the old woman's, and easing her up. "We've got a table full of goodies."

Mama swooped one hand down to fetch the remote. "We got victuals?" She turned and peered hard into Imo's face. "I haven't had a morsel to eat in two days. It's the middle of the Depression, you know." The lime-green Feed 'n' Seed hat she'd been wearing lately was askew up on top of her head and made her look like one of the old-men apple dolls they sold at the Bartow County Fair each fall.

"Yes, we've got victuals," Imo said, forcing cheerfulness into her voice.

Jeanette laughed at the sight of Mama Jewell as she entered the dining room. Imo started to throw her a *hush up young lady, and show some respect* look, but decided against it.

As soon as she was seated, Imo cleared her throat. "I have an idea," she said, "let's all go around the table and say some things we're thankful for before I ask the blessing."

She paused and searched each face. The room was silent except for the faraway sound of a motorcycle. Undaunted by the blank faces around her, Imo said, "Well, I am thankful for all of you!"

She thought she saw Jeanette roll her eyes, but she decided to ignore that. "Lou?" She turned to her right.

"Yessum?"

"What are you thankful for, sugar foot?"

"I'm thankful for . . ." Lou looked up toward the ceiling like she was trying to see the answer. "For . . . let's see . . . for Elmer and Dewy Rose!" She slapped her palms onto the table. "And for Bingo and my 150-pound pumpkin that was the county winner and got third in the state." Little Silas chortled and beat his spoon against his high-chair tray. She looked over at him. "And for Little Silas, too," she added.

Imo nodded and turned to Mama. "How about you, Mama?" she asked. "What are you thankful for?"

Mama gave her a startled look. "Why, I'm thankful them looters didn't get our silver during the War Between the States. Auntie Bess buried it in the chicken house." She cackled and waved a fork, which was actually part of an Oneida stainless-steel set of flatware from JCPenney.

Imo blinked. "Oh, well, good for you." She turned to Jeanette. "What about you, sugar foot?"

"Hmmm," Jeanette mused. "I need to think a spell on that." At last she smiled. "Shoot!" she said. "I reckon I am thankful to have such a precious, classy, and smart old woman as Mama Jewell living in my home."

Imo sensed that this was a test and she felt a little cross with the girl and would have called her on it except for the fact that Mama was clueless to the remark's intent. In fact, she was beaming.

"Well, good," Imo said, casting a quick warning glance at Jeanette. "Now, let's all bow our heads and thank the good Lord for our blessings and the bounteous table He has set before us."

While Imo said the blessing, Jeanette cut Little Silas's hot dog into bites. Imo decided to ignore the clink of the knife on the plate. She reasoned to herself that the Bible didn't say you had to be still or close your eyes to pray.

"Now," Imo said, drawing a deep breath following the amen, "let's eat." She passed the plate with the turkey on it, eager to admire each biteful, each smile.

When the platter reached Jeanette, Imo saw that she passed it on to Mama without helping her own plate to any. She did the same with the sweet potato soufflé and the rolls. After everything had been passed, all her plate held was a smidgen of green beans and a tiny dollop of cranberries.

Imo could not contain her disappointment. "You're not hungry, Jeannie?" she asked. "I've been cooking for two whole days!"

"I didn't ask you to cook for two days," Jeanette said offhandedly. "I'm on a diet."

"But this is *Thanksgiving*! Surely you could eat turkey and dressing on Thanksgiving. And rolls and soufflé."

"Can't do it. Not with my ass as big as it is."

"No cussing in my house, missy!" Imo blurted.

Jeanette rose. "Fine," she said, and scraped her chair backward. "I'll just leave then. Take Little Silas with me."

"Listen, Jeannie," Imo said as she half leaned across the table to plead. "Forgive me, please. You don't have to eat it. It's just that I've worked so hard to make us this feast."

"Thanksgiving ain't about food anyway," Jeanette said and thrust her bottom lip out.

She had a point there. Imo said, "You're right, so let's forget all this and you just sit right back down there and eat your green beans and your cranberries. I won't say another word about what you eat."

But Mama had more to say. A pack of Marlboros in Jeanette's shirt pocket had caught her eye when Jeanette was bent over unbuckling the belt of the high chair. "The work of the devil!" she hissed as she reached out a bony hand to pluck them from her.

"Shoo!" Jeanette slapped her wrist.

"Sassy young'un!" Mama rubbed the pink splotch left by Jeanette's hand. "I'm gone carry you out behind the woodshed and get me a hickory switch."

"Oh yeah? Try it!"

Along with the tartness of cranberries spreading over her tongue, Imo could feel every nerve in her body standing alert. She stood up and the napkin in her lap floated to the floor. She grabbed Mama's arm and held it tight. Standing there paralyzed, she heard Elmer's ear-piercing scream from the front porch, and for that moment she was speechless.

Finally, she was able to whisper, "Please, please try to overlook it,

Jeannie, please, for me." She managed a small smile. "She's sick. She can't help it. I know how you feel, though. Believe me."

"She cannot tell me what to do!" Jeanette hissed. Her furious expression did not change and Lou looked like she was about to burst into tears.

"There's pie," Imo said hastily. "Anybody want some pumpkin pie with whipped cream on top?"

Lou flinched, then nodded. "Sure," she said, glancing anxiously at Jeanette. "Everything is delicious, Imo. Thanks for all your hard work."

"Well," she said, "you're certainly welcome. It was my pleasure." She turned to the sideboard for the pie. "Who else wants pie?"

"Pie!" Little Silas exclaimed as Jeanette sat sullenly in her chair.

"The little colored baby wants him some tater pie!" Mama exclaimed. Imo felt her heart stop.

"I have done told you and told you," Jeanette stood up and screeched, "he's half Indian! So get it right next time, you fucked-up old warthog!" She leaned forward and grabbed a fistful of sweet potato soufflé, pulled off Mama Jewell's cap, and mashed it on top of her head. Then she wiped her hand clean on the old lady's back, extracted a cigarette, lit it, sucked in loudly, and blew smoke into her surprised face.

Mama coughed, and then with lightning-quick reflexes, she thrust out her own hands and scooped up the remainder of the soufflé, slathering it across Jeanette's startled face. "An eye for an eye!" she crowed.

Jeanette's mouth hung open in surprise, which turned to glee in one quick moment. "You wanna play dirty, do ya, old woman?" she said. "Well, that's just fine by me." She leaned forward, smiling, to pluck up a roll. She pressed it firmly on top of the soufflé on Mama Jewell's head. She reared back and smiled like a Cheshire cat. "There. Now you're a queen!" she exclaimed.

"Why, I surely am," Mama Jewell said gleefully. "I'm queen of *this* household, and when I tell Father that the kitchen slattern's been acting up again, he'll fire you for sure."

"Oh yeah? I'll be so, so sad," Jeanette said. "He's gonna fire me, huh?"

"Without a doubt," Mama Jewell said, nodding her head. "We'll surely miss the extra hands around the place, but we will just have to make do. I can learn to cook. Clean, too. Maybe Sheila here can help out." She pointed at Loutishie.

Lou, a bite of pie poised in midair, looked up and nodded. Then she began to giggle at the sight of the roll perched on Mama Jewell's head and the soufflé dripping from Jeanette's nose. Little Silas flung a coin-shaped piece of hot dog across the table to land on Imo's plate. He slapped the tray of his high chair, laughing.

For a moment, Imo sat stunned, gazing at everything in a sort of detached manner. Then she found herself smiling, too. It was crazy, but around the table, in the midst of the chaotic scene, she glimpsed an indefinable joy. Who else would have a Thanksgiving dinner like this one? And at this table—this table of wounded, hurting folks, where they each faced their own trials and setbacks, where there was a gracious plenty to complain about, and miles to go before any real, lasting peace—there were also things to be grateful for.

Imo bowed her head and closed her eyes; she whispered a quick prayer of thanks for the laughter, and then one asking for courage for the journey ahead.

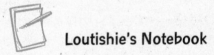 **Loutishie's Notebook**

December turned out to be the longest month of my life. Though we had two weeks off from school for Christmas break, that just made things worse. Not only did I not see my friends, Jeanette was gone off chasing Reverend

Pike practically all the time, and Imo stayed so busy with Mama Jewell and Little Silas that she may as well have been gone, too.

The first part of December was still short-sleeves weather. It got up to seventy degrees in the afternoons, and was wonderful for running out the back door and down to the river bottoms. The pansies lining the walkway and circling the birdbath were pretty, their little faces turned up cheerfully like they were trying to say to me, *Have fun!* The unseasonably mild weather had even confused Imo's spring narcissus, and they began to bloom. Imo just laughed it off and said we should enjoy the Indian spring.

But by the middle of the month Euharlee began to cool down, and on the morning of December 19th I had to break the ice on Bingo's water bowl. I had carried a rind of ham biscuit outdoors to him and I wondered how the peafowl liked cold weather, so after he had licked the saucer clean, we went looking for them. We crunched across dry leaves from the pecan trees in the backyard, blowing white breath and peering up into the branches for their shapes.

Bingo was still my best buddy, but Elmer and Dewy Rose came in at a close second, and because of this, he loved them, too. He was careful to watch over them. In exchange, they hung out with him and treated him like their king. Often I found the three of them lounging together between two rows of Blue Moon hydrangeas next to the well-house.

Elmer and Dewy Rose had won Imo's affection, too, because not only did they pacify Mama Jewell, but they also gobbled up the mice and snakes around the barn and the well-house. Jeanette, on the other hand, hated them with a passion. Not that she'd ever even tried to get to know them. She despised them because Mama Jewell loved them. She referred to them as "a pair of shit-birds," since their droppings literally covered the whole yard.

I spotted them huddled together in the crotch of a double-trunked cedar. When I reached out and touched Elmer's tail feathers, I said, "Y'all are half froze! I'm gonna have to carry you in the house and thaw you out."

Jeanette and Little Silas and Mama Jewell were still asleep and Imo didn't even notice I had Dewy Rose in my arms when I came back inside. She was at the kitchen table with her calendar, scratching out her daily to-do list.

"There, there, now, girl," I whispered into the bird's white neck as I settled her on a towel on the floor of the pantry. She looked up gratefully, her eyes glittering jewels in her brown head. I stroked her brown breast and her back, admiring the lovely speckles of green in her feathers there. "I'm going to go fetch your sweetheart now." I patted her cold, smooth cheek. I wondered if she ever got jealous of her Elmer and the regal brush of blue feathers that sat atop his head like a crown. Back outside at the cedar tree, my teeth chattering from the cold, I lifted my arms. "Hurry up," I said, and Elmer scrambled down. I managed to sneak him in safely past Imo, too. Bingo stood at the back door whining while I draped a stack of kitchen towels over the birds. It took so many for Elmer because in September he had begun growing his long, beautiful train feathers with eyes of deep-blue circles surrounded by green-blue and gold-brown rings. I loved the way his train reflected the light. It seemed to glow with the iridescent colors of the rainbow.

When they'd thawed out enough, Dewy Rose and Elmer crawled out from underneath the towels and moved together around the pantry, peering down in the potato bin and at the rows of shiny quart jars. I sat down on the floor to rest, wrapped my arms around my legs, and settled my chin on my kneecaps to watch, thinking how nice it must feel to be part of an inseparable pair like that. When I found my father, I reasoned, I would have somebody.

Jeanette had somebody. She lived on a cloud, always talking about Montie this and Montie that, and every chance she got she was heading off to that Church of God in Rockmart. You'd think some of the Reverend Pike's sermons would have started soaking down into her, but from what I could tell, they sure weren't working at home; she still cussed like a sailor and laughed in my face if I ever mentioned God or the Rapture of the Saints. However, I was fairly certain that she was playing the part of Miss Pious whenever she was around the Reverend.

She'd said to me the night before that she couldn't understand why things between them were coming along so slowly. "I just cain't get enough of that man, Lou. I run the wheels off the Impala going to see him and you'd think he could take the hint."

"He's a busy man," I said. "Preachers have to work hard. Plus, I thought you said that he's putting together a Christmas musical *and* a pageant."

"He is, Lou. I'm playing the part of Mary." She stood there frowning, dressed to the nines in a red bodysuit trimmed in faux fur and some knee-high black boots with stiletto heels. Her hair was up in a sophisticated French twist, her lips a startling blood-black red.

I stifled a laugh. *Jeanette as Mary?* "So, you're playing Mary?" I said.

"Sure as hell am, kid, but the problem is he's such a damn Goody Two-shoes. A friggin' Samaritan!"

"What's the problem with that?" I asked.

"The problem is he's always got to run right off after rehearsals and see about somebody who's sick or troubled. Constantly carrying gifts and food to indignant families."

"You mean indigent. Maybe he just doesn't want to spend time with you," I said, playing the devil's advocate, "maybe he doesn't like you that way."

"He does! I can tell about stuff like that!" She sighed. "Seriously, if Montie'd just loosen up some, stop treating me like such an angel, things would be fantastic."

"But that's good, Jeannie. Means he respects you."

"That's good, yeah, I guess, being treated like an angel is. But Lou, what I really want is for the man to love me like the devil! I'm going crazy trying to figure him out."

I said not to try and figure him out. "Can't you just be patient, Jeannie?" I asked her.

"I'm not a patient person. You know that. If I have to sit through one more rehearsal in that makeshift stable without so much as a wink from him, I'm going to puke!" She lit up a cigarette and closed her eyes to suck in deeply. "Two hours sittin' on a pile of straw! Looking all pure and saintly. Can't smoke . . . mmm mmm mmm"—she paused to shake her head—"the things I do for love! Tonight I was sitting in that scratchy old stable and every time he'd look my way, I'd smile and I'd—"

"Wait a minute," I said, "did you wear *that* to be Mary in?" I looked hard at the way the snug bodysuit revealed her curves.

"'Course I did." She grinned. "Dress rehearsal's not till the twenty-third, and you should see the drab feed sack I'm s'posed to wear for the pageant. I mean, it is god-awful ugly!"

"Jeannie!"

"Well, it is."

"I don't think your heart's in playing Mary," I said.

"My heart's in playing Montie's wife. Know what, Lou? I've been praying he'll give me an engagement ring for Christmas. Can you believe it? Me, wanting to settle down . . ."

I looked at Jeanette's face and could hardly believe my ears. Jeanette praying? Jeanette wanting to be a preacher's wife?! Miracles did happen, because I'd just witnessed the most marvelous one of all.

One morning, a week before Christmas, Imo said she could not put off shopping for presents any longer. She had one list for groceries and one list for the strip mall stores in Cartersville. Jeanette was away somewhere with Little Silas and Imo stopped me as I was on my way out the back door to feed Bingo. "You don't have any special plans for the day, do you, Lou?" she asked with a weary smile. I shook my head, and I waited for what I knew was coming next. "Would you mind keeping an eye and an ear out for Mama today while I shop, please, sugar foot?"

"Yessum," I said quickly, "I'd be happy to do it." This was no lie. Part of me could never refuse her desperate requests for help; plus, I reasoned that this could be an excellent opportunity to get Mama Jewell talking about my mother or my father some more. Anyway, I told myself, maybe the day wouldn't be too bad. When Mama Jewell's shows were on the TV, she was virtually a zombie, sitting nice and quiet in her La-Z-Boy.

Mama Jewell spent most of that morning behaving fairly well, fussing only occasionally at some actress on TV. I fed her a bologna and mustard sandwich for lunch as we watched the news at noon together. Then she wanted to watch *The People's Court* and *Judge Judy* and things were easy enough. I sat on the couch reading a book.

The hours passed and around five I was getting kind of antsy to go outside and stretch my legs. I stood up, contemplating a quick run around the house. Mama Jewell cocked her head and looked hard at me.

"You going to prayer meeting with me tonight, Vera?" she asked out of the blue. "Reckon we'd better get an early supper if you are."

"Uh, yes!" I answered. "Going." I flew into the kitchen to heat some TV dinners for us. My hands shook as I set two trays of Salisbury steak and mashed potatoes on the table. We sat down across from each other and began to eat in silence.

"It's good you're going, girl," she said when she got to her applesauce. "You need to. You're heading off down the wide road to ruin."

My heart started beating like a woodpecker on a hickory. I would try to get her to say the name of my father, the boy in the photo underneath my mattress! Without batting an eye, I said, "Oh Mama, is it my bad boyfriend you don't like?"

She stared blankly for a moment while I held my breath. *Please*, I begged silently, *please stay where you are.*

"Well, is it him?" I urged, gripping my fork so tight my hand hurt. "Is it my white-trash boyfriend you're worrying about?"

She nodded. "Yes," she said, "it's him and all that other bad crowd you run around with, Vera. A man is known by the company he keeps."

"Oh, you are right about that, Mama." I was nodding to encourage her. "They are *so* bad. Please help me. Pray aloud to Jesus for each one by name with me." I was shameless.

"Possessed of the devil," she murmured.

I latched onto that. "Oh, he is. He's possessed of the devil, desperately wicked, Mama. You've got to pray real hard for him. Pray for . . ." I urged.

"Lord," Mama Jewell intoned, with eyes cast downward, hands raised, as her plump upper arms jiggled with fervency, "let your grace and mercy touch Randy and draw him to you. Yes, touch all them white trash up there at the Dusty Springs Trailer Park where he lives. Let all those low-accounts that live up on Buzzard Mountain repent and be saved."

I watched her bow her old head with its sparse gray helmet of hair and my heart lifted up. *Randy.* Maybe my *father* is Randy, I thought. She began to plead louder. "Father God," she cried, "flood Randy's heart with light. Wash away the filth from him. And Lord, you know me and Burton tried to raise this girl here right. Restore my Vera to her salvation." She trailed off and sagged down into her chair. I dabbed the wet corners of her mouth with a napkin and got her back to her La-Z-Boy, where she fell asleep.

Randy from Dusty Springs Trailer Park on Buzzard Mountain. I turned this information over and over in my brain. When Mama Jewell started snoring, I looked out the front windows to make sure Imo wasn't headed down the drive, and then I dashed into Mama Jewell's bedroom. I turned on a lamp and opened her trunk.

As I sat there staring down into it and smelling that musty, sweet smell of old things, I couldn't help but feel God's great big all-seeing eyes looking down on me. I decided to ignore the feeling as I rifled through the yellowed piano recital programs and dried corsages. After all, she had let me see in there earlier, and besides, nobody had told me I *couldn't* look inside her old trunk. It was certainly not the same thing as spying or stealing, I told myself.

I spotted a strip of those black-and-white photos you get for a dollar when you step into the little booths at the fair. This beautiful woman was beaming into the camera, head-on in the first two shots, then left profile and right profile. A heart-shaped movie star's face; young and smooth, with wide-apart Jackie Onassis eyes and an upturned nose. Shiny full hair curling at her shoulders.

I tried to think who it might be. Some actress? With that confident smile and straight white teeth? I flipped it over. It said "Jewelldine, 19 years" in ink pen on the back.

I shook my head. It couldn't be! But as I looked more closely I could see a shred of semblance through the eyes and I knew that it was a young Mama Jewell. I sat there for a long time shaking my head in utter disbelief as I stared at it. The worst part of all was realizing that getting old happened to every single living creature, unless they died young, like my mother had. I searched through the piles of stuff for more pictures of my father, but what I came up on was an envelope of pictures of this round-headed baby with a curl above each ear. It said "Vera at 6 months" on the back of one. I decided my mother had been a cute baby as I flipped through them, figuring it must be nice to be so new and untarnished. A clean slate just waiting.

This put me in mind of my own heavenly account and my conscience was seared once again. I had led Mama Jewell on falsely for my own interests, and here I was rifling through her possessions. I got so overcome by guilt at that moment that I stuffed everything back inside and closed the trunk, thinking of the any-moment possibility of the Rapture. I jumped when I heard the back door slam and I went to help Imo carry her packages into the house.

Later that evening my head was spinning so fast I did what I always do when I need to think real good. I ran out the back door, past the sumac and pyracantha, which were laden with berries, down the dirt road to the Etowah. The air was crisp and for a moment I thought to myself that I would just keep on running. I could live in the woods, get my food from wherever I could find it. I would leave that crazy, sad household behind me.

Bingo trotted up beside me. "Arrroooo," his throat quivered as he howled seriously.

"Hi boy," I said, stopping to kneel down and put my arm around him. "How ya doin'?" He licked my cheek. "I've been thinking of looking for my father," I said. "But maybe I shouldn't. It seems to be making me do things I think are wrong. I reckon I ought to pray some about it, huh?"

Bits of the full moon sparkled on the water as I dropped to my knees and lifted my face and commenced to praying aloud. "Dear God," I began, "I am sorry for using Mama Jewell for my own purposes and for digging through her personal things and for stealing that photo." But I did not go on because I could feel my words falling down. They were not rising up to heaven. They were bouncing all around me and making the cold, red clay bank spin way too fast beneath my feet. Even Bingo's warm breath on my neck didn't help.

At first, I figured my prayers weren't getting an audience with God because of how bad my heavenly account looked. But slowly I was able to convince myself that God was just ignoring me so I'd go out and hunt my real father, Randy! God knew I needed him and this was His way of turning a push into a shove. I held Bingo's smelly neck as I sat there on the dark bank of the Etowah.

But now the problem was going to be finding him, and I felt really chicken about that part of the plan. That's when I determined that I would have to call my friend Tara in on the hunt.

Six

A Christmas Miracle

Y'all are coming to see me in my big acting debut, aren't you?" Jeanette said. "Montie . . . um, I mean Reverend Pike says I'm a natural. He says I'm almost as good at being an actress as I am at singing. But the guy playing Joseph, you should see him. He's this pimply-faced kid who's sooo nervous. And he just worships me! Stares at me all goo-goo eyed and forgets his lines. It's such a hoot! Really cracks me up. I said to him at the rehearsal tonight, I said, 'You've got to get a grip, Lester. You know you can't do this on December twenty-fourth, or you'll ruin the play.'"

Jeanette was gesticulating wildly with her hands and bouncing on the balls of her feet as she talked. "One time he about near dropped baby Jesus. The three wise men came up to bring their gifts and I was fixing to hand Jesus over to him so I could kneel at their feet and say my line, and when I turned to Lester and said 'Hold our son,' he got so flustered. His neck turned beet red, and when our fingers touched he jumped and let go of Jesus. I managed to get a hold of him, however. Good thing it was only a doll."

Jeanette and Imo were standing in the kitchen. Jeanette still had her winter coat on, and the car keys in her hand. It was December

20 and at last the air was crisp enough that things were beginning to feel more like Christmas.

"So are you?" Jeanette said. "There's going to be refreshments served afterwards."

Imo drew a deep breath and studied the girl a moment. "Well, now, dear," she said, "of course I'm going to come. But you know that if I come, Mama'll have to come, too."

"Yeah, sure. I know, and that'll be okay." She smiled and nodded her head in a convincing manner. "We'll *all* go and have us a fine old time."

Imo nodded. "I suppose we'll all go, then," she said evenly, searching Jeanette's face. She wondered if the girl was thinking straight. Surely she hadn't been drinking. Imo leaned in closer and drew a deep breath. No, there was no smell of alcohol. But how could she say she would go anywhere out in public with Mama? Perhaps she was just full of the Christmas spirit.

It was not quite a week ago that Jeanette and Mama had had themselves a knock-down, drag-out fight in Shiftlet's Grocery, over candy, no less, and Jeanette had sworn she'd never go anywhere else with the woman again.

Thinking back on that fight now unnerved Imo, and she worried that all of them going somewhere together would never work. It was hard for her to imagine a pleasant holiday outing to the Christmas play.

"Let's all go out for pizza beforehand, too." Jeanette's face brightened even more at this thought.

It seemed unreasonable to say they couldn't. "Well, certainly dear," Imo said, "what a nice idea."

It was Christmas Eve and the play was at 7:00 PM. Imo planned to leave the house at 5:00 so they could drive into Stilesboro for pizza and then get to Rockmart half an hour before showtime so Jeanette could get into her costume and assemble with the rest of the cast.

At 3:00 Imo began to get herself ready to allow time to get Mama bathed and dressed. She put on her slip, her white silky blouse, her green wool skirt and jacket, and red beads with matching ear-bobs.

She stood in front of the mirror, tugging the collar of her blouse into place. She certainly looked festive! The very picture of Christmas.

"Mi-moo pretty," Little Silas said as he came around the door frame.

"Why, thank you, sweetie pie," she said. "We'll dress you up, too. We're going to see your mama in a Christmas play."

"Play?" he said, crouching down to pat one of Imo's shiny black pumps.

"Yessum. She's going to be the baby Jesus' mother in a play. We're all going to go together and we're going to have a nice time!" she said, forcing enthusiasm into her voice. And maybe they *would* have themselves a fine time like any ordinary family out for a festive evening. Miracles happened at Christmas.

"Where we going?" Mama asked, peering out the back window as they pulled onto Paris Street.

"I told you earlier," Imo said, "we're going to eat pizza and see a Christmas play."

"Mama's in play!" said Little Silas.

"That's right, baby," Jeanette said. "I'm playing the Virgin Mary."

"Hmph!" Mama said. "Now that's a laugh."

Imo squirmed and gripped the wheel tightly with one hand while she turned up the radio loud with the other. Wayne Newton came on crooning "Silent Night" and blessedly, Jeanette ignored Mama's barb and joined him—"all is calm, all is bright," she sang.

At length Imo felt herself relax and she peered out the window at the tiny town of Stilesboro. Lights fashioned into the shape of wreaths hung from the telephone poles all along Main Street, and in the center of town a light display of Santa and his sleigh sat next to a Nativity scene.

"Look, Santa!" Little Silas exclaimed. "And Rudolph!"

"Tonight Santa's coming to see *you*." Loutishie turned and leaned over to the backseat to pat his knee. "We'll have to put out some cookies and milk for Santa, and something for his reindeer, too, won't we?"

"Santa eats candy canes!" Little Silas said gleefully.

"Ain't no Santa," Mama stated emphatically. "Ain't no Rudolph neither. Folks shouldn't tell that nonsense to their young'uns. That's the devil's doings. Santy Clause and reindeers, my foot."

Imo tensed again as Jeanette turned toward Mama and opened her mouth to say something. But then, just as suddenly, she shook her head and closed her mouth.

Imo took the turn to Highway 13 and the road ran along a thickly populated stretch where festive lights shone in the windows of the houses and on various yard displays. Glenn Campbell came on the radio singing "I'll Be Home for Christmas" as they passed a Family Dollar store where a brave soul stood out front ringing the Salvation Army bell beside a red bucket.

Around the next curve the Pizza Hut appeared, a sloping red-roofed oasis, with snowy scenes spray-painted on the windows. Imo turned onto the asphalt lot and glided carefully into a parking space.

"What are we doing here?" Mama asked.

"We're having pizza for supper," Imo said.

"Peas?" Mama said, puzzled. "For supper?"

Imo turned around to speak to Mama. "I told you, we're going to eat pizza and then we're going to see Jeanette in a Christmas play."

There was an uncomfortable moment as Mama clutched her purse and hunched down in the seat stubbornly.

"Pizza, pizza!" Little Silas demanded.

"We can't leave you in the car, Mama," Imo said. "It's too cold out here. Come on in and get you some pizza."

"Green peas or black-eyes?" Mama sunk lower and poked out her bottom lip.

To Imo's surprise, Jeanette leaned across to explain. "They've got spaghetti here, too," she said. "You love spaghetti."

Mama blinked. "Spaghetti?" She sat up, grabbed the handles of her purse, and strained against the seat belt. "I like spaghetti better'n peas any day."

"Hold your horses, Mama," Imo said, slipping the keys out of the ignition. "I'm a coming."

Inside the door of the Pizza Hut, a plump girl wearing a Santa hat asked if they wanted a booth or a table. They settled into a booth in the corner, which suited Imo fine. The restaurant had a twinkling Christmas tree next to the salad bar, and this, combined with the red carpeting and candlelit tables, provided a cheery atmosphere. The waitress appeared with five waters and large plastic menus. Imo sipped her water and decided to let the others choose the pizza.

"Cheese pizza!" Little Silas declared. "Coke."

"How about you, Lou?" Imo asked.

"Mmm, how about pepperoni and mushroom?"

"Jeannie?"

"Anything's fine with me. Little Silas can just pick the stuff off his and have plain cheese."

"Mama? You want spaghetti?"

Mama was silent. She was staring hard at the pictures of pizza on the menu cover, tracing the outline of one with her finger. It occurred to Imo that perhaps she'd never had pizza before. They'd certainly never had it when Imo was growing up. Her first taste of it had been when she was in her thirties, with Silas, at a little Italian restaurant in Alabama.

"Pizza, Mama," Imo said, "is crusty bread with tomato sauce and cheese on top. You'd like it. You like cheese."

"Oh, well . . ." Mama said vaguely, still looking at the picture.

"Aw, come on," Jeanette said, poking her arm playfully. "You've never had *pizza*? Try some then. You'll think you've died and gone to heaven."

Mama blinked. She cocked her head to the side. "All right," she said finally, "I reckon I could try it. I don't imagine Burton's ever had it either. I'll carry him home some for his supper. He's been ailin' a while, you know."

"Pizza! pizza!" Little Silas bounced happily in his seat. He was scribbling on a paper place mat with some crayons the waitress had left for him.

"I'm betting you're going to like pizza, Mama," Imo said. "And Daddy will, too." She smiled at the happy scene. It was all made even better by the relief that Jeanette hadn't sparred with Mama over the mention of Burton like she usually did. Jeanette just never could get it through her head, the way Loutishie could, that there were some things you couldn't reason with Mama over. Burton was one of them. And each time Mama mentioned him within earshot of Jeanette, Jeanette took it upon herself to try and set Mama straight. "He's dead," she'd declare, "nothing but dust in the graveyard," sending Mama into spasms of tears.

When the pizza arrived, Mama was served the first piece and everyone waited as she lifted her slice and took a tentative bite. She chewed very slowly, her forehead wrinkled in contemplation. At long last she swallowed and took a long drink of her tea. She patted her lips with her napkin and rolled her lips inward. "Well," she sputtered, "this here pizza . . . beats peas and corn bread and buttermilk hands down!" Her eyes twinkled as she lifted her piece for another bite.

Jeanette couldn't stop giggling over this as they all dug in to the steaming pizza. Everything was going along better than Imo'd ever dreamed. Everyone was smiling and they looked like any family group out for an evening of holiday fun.

"We'd better hurry on to Rockmart," Imo said when they'd finished. "Get our actress to the stage on time."

Mama shook her head. "Cain't go," she said, "get me home *this instant*. Burton will be starving for his supper." She waved a triangular shape wrapped in a napkin sheer with grease.

Imo's eyes darted anxiously to Jeanette's face. *Please,* she wanted to say, *don't let her get to you this time. Don't tell her he's dead and turning to dust or rotting in his coffin.*

A shadow of irritation passed over the girl's face, but at length she sighed, drew in a deep breath, hunched forward, and said in a conspiratorial whisper, "Listen, Mama Jewell, Burton said for me to tell you he's got to work late in the fields tonight. He said to tell you to go on and party. He's got to get in the uh . . . the corn! No rest for the weary, like you always say."

"The corn?" Mama said suspiciously.

"Shoot, yeah," Jeanette said. "He's up to his ears in the stuff." She collapsed onto the table in a fit of laughter and Lou stifled a giggle.

"Well, all right, then," Mama said, unfastening the gold clasp on her purse and stuffing the pizza in.

They appeared to be following the full moon as they drove out beyond the city limits, passing a junkyard, a scraggly stretch of pines, a filling station, and a tiny cemetery. Traffic was sparse. Imo hadn't been out this way since Fenton's funeral.

"The Reverend Pike's church is still in that little shopping center out this a way, isn't it?" Imo asked Jeanette. "Right up this road a piece?"

"Mmm-hmm. We're 'bout there."

"Well, good. I guess y'all will be having a little run-through before the performance?"

"Yeah. It's going to be outside, you know. In the corner of the parking lot. That's because we've got live chickens and sheep going to be in it."

"We'll be outside in this cold?" Imo was alarmed. "What about the old folks?"

"It only lasts twenty minutes," Jeanette said.

"Why, a person can freeze in twenty minutes!"

"I'll sit in the car with Mama Jewell," Lou offered.

"Shoot," Jeanette said, "she can sit right inside the church and look out the big window at us."

Well, that was a good idea. Things would work out fine, Imo thought as they swerved into the parking lot of the Golden Gate Shopping Center and right up to the door of the vacant Sleep-Well Mattress Warehouse that served as the Rockmart Church of God. She needn't have worried at all. She should just relax and enjoy the show.

"Y'all come on inside and stay cozy till showtime," Jeanette said, beckoning them with her arm.

Climbing from the car, Imo noted a crude stable fashioned from sheets of plywood and some natural fabric that looked like muslin. Bales of hay lined the walls of this and also jutted out ten feet or so on either side to form an arc. Several chickens peered sleepily at them from the shadows. There was a man busily adding chunks of wood to a bonfire at the edge of a pool of folding chairs. When she got closer Imo saw that this was the Reverend Pike.

"Merry Christmas!" she called, waving gaily.

"To you, too," he returned.

When they were inside, Imo spied a card table set up with cocoa and cider. "Sit down, Mama," she said, "and I'll fetch you a hot drink." Jeanette had disappeared behind a door at the rear and Lou led Little Silas to a colorful Christmas tree in the center of the room.

Imo fought the impulse to remember the last time she was here. This was turning into such a joyous evening and she was determined to keep it that way. She hurried back to Mama with two Styrofoam cups of cocoa. "Cozy in here, isn't it?" she asked.

"Yessum. You say this is supposed to be a church?"

"Mmm-hmm. Church of God."

"Don't look like no church *I* ever saw."

"Well, Mama, they're growing. Jeanette tells me they're saving up to pay for a building. They've got several acres of land out on Goshen Road."

Jeanette emerged from the rear with a scrubbed-clean face, and looking miserable in a scratchy potato-colored shift and some flat brown sandals. She held a tinfoil halo.

Mama looked up at her and drew a quick breath. "You look a heap nicer, girl," she said, nodding her head.

"Well, thank you very little," Jeanette said in an exaggerated syrupy voice that Mama didn't catch. She did look much younger this way, and as she made her way outside, Imo noted that Reverend Pike stopped to catch his breath when he saw her. Imo watched out the long plate-glass window as more cars arrived and the folks spilled out of them, some taking a seat in the folding chairs set up facing the stable and some obviously cast members in their shaggy earth-colored tunics. She scanned them for a nervous, pimply-faced Joseph and decided he was the skinny boy wearing what looked like a bathrobe and a striped tablecloth fastened to his head with a braided rope. Everyone's breath outside came in white puffs and the sky above them was a clear navy blue with twinkling white stars.

"Let's head on outside, Mama," Imo said after a bit, "get us some seats up by the fire." She motioned to Lou that they were going and Mama rose without a fuss.

"Right purty out here," Mama said as they settled themselves on the cool metal chairs. "I reckon those are real sheep yonder."

A chorus of baas rang out from a small corral. "Yes, the chickens are real, too. Jeanette said a local farmer brought them for the kids to enjoy."

"That a real baby up there?"

Imo turned to look where Mama pointed. The head of a large wide-eyed baby doll stuck out from underneath a makeshift trough. "No, it's a doll. I imagine they'll set it in there when the play commences."

"Jeanette's playing Mary," Mama said. "That the preacher-man she's carrying on with there by the fire?"

"Yes it is," Imo said. She smiled. "I imagine he's giving her some last-minute acting tips."

"Looks to me like he's doing himself some courtin'."

Imo shrugged. She watched him lay a hand on Jeanette's arm as they leaned in toward one another, laughing. Probably they were just enjoying some Christian fellowship. Lou and Little Silas plopped down beside her. Little Silas's cheeks were bright pink with the cold.

"I was just thinking, Lou, dear," Imo said, "isn't it amazing how Jeanette's become so dedicated to her faith these days? I mean, all the time she spends here at the church."

Lou shifted awkwardly in her chair. She looked away from Imo and slowly shook her head from side to side. Imo figured this meant that the girl was as awestruck as she was.

"Mama! Mama! Mama!" Little Silas hollered, standing on his chair, bouncing on his tiptoes, and waving up to the stage.

"Shh," Imo whispered. "Sit down. Your mama wants you to be quiet out here." She pressed two Mary Jane candies into his palm.

The Reverend strode up to a microphone and tapped it. "Testing, one, two, three," his voice rang out through the cold air, over the sheep's bleating. The crowd settled down a bit, peering eagerly toward the front. Imo stamped her feet silently to warm them.

The cast took their positions and an expectant hush fell. A spotlight appeared, which fell on Mary and Joseph as they entered the scene from the shadows and followed them as they traveled along wearily toward a sign reading "The Bethlehem Inn—No Vacancy." They turned away and Mary's cumbersome belly swung from side to side as they dejectedly made their way to the stable where Jeanette was delivered of her burden, screaming convincingly in childbirth. Lester's Adam's apple rose and fell nervously as Jeanette held the doll to her bosom.

The spotlight moved to the sheep. "Behold the angel of the Lord," said a figure clad in white, standing on a bale of straw. Two boys, holding walking canes, fell down to the ground, covering their heads in mock terror.

"Fear not, for I bring you good news!" shouted the angel in a nasally twang that made "bring" sound like "brang." Lou tittered a bit and clamped her hand instantly to her mouth. Mama peered intently toward the scene as the shepherds made their way to the manger to fall at the babe's feet. Next came three men wearing tall crowns and bearing brightly wrapped packages. They drew near to the manger. Jeanette looked pointedly at Lester as she nestled the doll in his arms and turned to kneel at their feet. He blinked hard and managed to keep ahold of the baby Jesus.

At the close of the play, Reverend Pike pushed a button on a large gray boom box and the melody for "What Child Is This?" scattered over the parking lot. The cast lined up across the front, holding hands, their voices surging upwards as they began to sing the words. Imo made out Jeanette's thin off-key tone soaring above the rest.

Suddenly Mama cleared her throat. She got to her feet, opened her mouth, and joined loudly in the singing, all the while threading her way along through the folding chairs to the edge of the stage, where she hopped nimbly up to join the cast. Imo was on the edge of her seat, one arm stretched forward, whispering loudly, "Hush, Mama! Get yourself back down here!" But, as it turned out, the cast welcomed Mama, and her high tremulous soprano actually sounded good as it fell in with the group.

Imo leaned back, smiling, and closed her eyes to fix the scene in her memory. She knew she would have no finer Christmas gift than tonight.

Loutishie's Notebook

One Saturday in early March I found Elmer and Dewy Rose hanging out with Bingo between Imo's Blue Moon hydrangea hedges. It was a beautiful day, sunny and crisp, with a sky so blue it looked unreal. I watched as Elmer paused to spread his train straight up into a gorgeous fan. Hundreds of eyes glowed, their iridescent rainbow colors reflecting the sunlight, changing as he shimmied his plumes.

When Elmer was getting ready to mate, which was supposed to happen in late summer, he was beautiful. He'd already been calling out with loud screeches and strutting like crazy in front of Dewy Rose, rattling his splendid train until it sounded like pecans falling down onto red clay.

However, a lot of the time, Dewy Rose twisted her long neck up and away from him, pretending not to even notice how gorgeous he was.

I hated it when she ignored him that way. "Hey, Elmer, don't you fret," I crooned, walking over to him and getting down on my knees. "She's playing hard to get is all. You're the most gorgeous boy in the entire world." I swear he smiled at me when I said that.

Bingo's wet nose found its way to my arm. "Hey, Jealous," I said, turning to ruffle his ribs. "What I meant to say is *you* are the most beautiful dog in the world and Elmer is the most beautiful peacock in the world." I sat down between those two, drinking in the warm sunshine in hopes that it would clear my fuzzy brain.

Dewy Rose paid us no attention. She was busily hunting for leaves and flowers she could nibble on. "She's just silly," I reassured Elmer, flopping over to lay my head on Bingo's rib cage and close my eyes. After a bit I felt myself sinking, my head giving a sudden jerk, then gliding downward into sleep.

I dreamed I was knocking on a door and when it opened, the handsome man from the picture came out and enfolded me in a great big bear hug. He stepped back, his gaze traveled over my face, and he said, "My darling daughter, my very own flesh and blood. I'm glad you're here. I've been searching for you. Won't you stay with me forever?"

Before I could answer, the bell at the house went bonggg! The bell was Imo's way of summoning me and Jeanette for meals or telephone calls. Climbing up out of that dream, I was so disappointed. I would just as soon have stayed there. I ambled toward the house, fussing under my breath. Imo stood out on the back porch, in one of her red-checked aprons, with her hands on her hips and looking just like a picture of Betty Crocker on the front of one of her old cookbooks. "There you are, Lou, dear. I was beginning to think you'd gotten lost." She laughed. "I made tuna casserole and steamed carrots for supper. Run wash up."

I went down the hallway to the lavatory and Mama Jewell stood in the doorway of her room, leaning against the door frame. All she had on was a short, flimsy light blue housedress that snapped up the front. "Girl?" She reached out and clutched my arm. "You done my laundry yet? Can't very well go into town buck-nekkid."

"Oh, sure you can," I said with a straight face. "Folks are doing it all the time these days." She nodded with wide eyes, and I pulled away, smiling, to continue down the hallway. I decided that there was something special about that dream, some lingering feel of it that followed me along and made me brave and sassy.

As I washed my hands, I decided that the time to find my father was at hand.

"What are you and your friend Tara planning to do on this pretty afternoon?" Imo innocently asked as she drove past our mailbox.

"Well," I said, "we're going to study for our science test tomorrow, and . . . work on our English papers."

Imo stepped on the brake. "Then don't you need to run on back in the house and grab your schoolbooks?"

"Um . . ." I said, "we're planning to use Tara's! And the English paper is just something out of our imagination. Three paragraphs on what we're planning to do over the summer."

That old devil had me right where he wanted me. Now I had lied to Imo, and the more terrible thing was that I could not work up one speck of repentance. Even when I kept on telling myself that the Rapture could happen any second and there I'd be, left behind with the sinners.

Mama Jewell sat quietly in the backseat, her black patent-leather handbag perched on her knees. Imo flipped down her sun visor, gunned the engine, and headed for the highway. She switched on the radio and Tammy Wynette sang in her nasally voice, "*D-I-V-O-R-C-E*." . . . I fingered the photograph of my father that I had stuffed into my pocket, my heart accelerating at the thought of finally meeting him. It would be so wonderful to connect with him, like finding where that last piece of a puzzle went.

When I'd called my friend Tara Higginbotham to ask if she wanted to help me search for my father, she laughed gleefully. "Would I?" she said. "I wouldn't miss that for the world!"

We pulled onto the long, curvy driveway of the Higginbothams' place, a brick ranch house on five acres. Mr. Higginbotham managed the Shoney's in Chenille and Mrs. Higginbotham raised Shelties and six children. Tara was the only girl and so their house was running over with footballs and BB guns and dirty socks. Except for Tara's room. She was like the princess there, tucked into a bedroom filled with thick pink shag carpeting and a white canopy bed and a long white chest of drawers with gold pulls that had a fold-out mirror over it so you could see yourself from all angles. I loved hanging out in Tara's room, but that day, the best thing about the Higginbothams' place was the fact that it was less than a mile from the foot of Buzzard Mountain, and halfway up that was Dusty Springs Trailer Park.

Tara and I had spent many Saturdays scaring each other by walking partway up Buzzard Mountain and daring each other to go in the entrance of Dusty Springs, which was marked by a rotting wooden sign surrounded by weeds. Mrs. Higginbotham forbade us to even go near the place. She always said to us, in hushed tones, with her eyebrows raised high, "A rough crowd lives in Dusty Springs."

"I'll come back for you at six," Imo said as she pulled up beside the half basketball court. "You girls be sweet."

"Oh, we will," I said, bounding out and giving her and Mama Jewell a quick wave with both hands.

Tara's mother was outside, in a pair of shorts and an old football jersey, moving some rocks from around a flower bed. "Hello Lou," Mrs. Higginbotham said, "looks like you girls couldn't have ordered a prettier day. Go on around back. I believe Tara's on the deck waiting for you."

I glimpsed Tara's red hair first. "Hey," I called out.

"Hi Lou. Let's go sit in the hammock," she said, scooping a puppy from her lap, plunking him on the ground, and beckoning with her arm. I followed her past the kennels where a surge of barking followed us. Beyond that was a muscadine arbor, a picnic table, and a cement bench, and then, a bit farther, a hammock stretched between two cedar trees. Tara grabbed a rope tied to a tether ball pole beside the hammock, we climbed in, and she tugged on the rope to get us swinging.

"Okay, let's see it," she said.

I fingered the edge of the photograph. "I know this is him," I said. "I'm positive." Slowly I pulled it out of my pocket, cupping it out of her sight. "He looks a lot like me," I said, smiling.

Tara yanked us to a stop. "Give it then, Lou." She reached over toward the picture now in my palm. "Let me see him."

"First you gotta promise me something," I said, holding the picture just out of her reach. "Promise me two things, actually. The first one is you've got to double-swear, hope to die, stick a needle in your eye that you won't tell a soul about us going looking for him—until we find him, that is."

"Okay, Lou," she said, "I won't tell anybody. What's the other thing?"

"You have to go up to Dusty Springs with me today and help me look for him."

"He lives in *Dusty Springs*?" Tara opened her eyes wide and put her mouth in the shape of a big O. "Mama don't allow, you know." She withdrew her hand from me and folded her arms across her chest and stared straight ahead.

"If you won't go up there with me, then I won't let you see the picture," I said, watching her out of the corner of my eye.

She started us to swinging again. "Well . . ." she said slowly, then put out her flat hand on my stomach, "all right, Lou, I'll go. Now hand over the goods." She wiggled her fingers until I placed the photo into her palm.

Tara looked at that picture like she was a blind person who had just received her sight. At last she nodded her head. "Yep, Lou, he *does* look like you! He really does," she said, "through the eyes, and the nose, and your hair's the same, too." She looked impressed. "He's kind of cute," she added.

"You should see how gorgeous Mama Jewell used to be!" I blurted.

"You're kidding!"

"If I'm lying, I'm dying," I said, trying to remain modest about my good-looking family. Just the thought of Tara saying this maybe-father of mine was cute made me feel important.

"What if he's got old and ugly like your grandma did?" Tara threw back her head and laughed. "Or what if he's white trash or in jail. Or dead, even."

Sometimes Tara made me furious. "He's not!" I heard myself trying to sound certain but instead sounding desperate. I sat up in the hammock, slung my legs over the side. "All I know is I've *got* to find him."

"How come?" Tara said finally.

"I just do," I said, pausing and taking a deep breath. "He's all I'll have left."

"What are you talking about?" she said. "You're not alone."

"Well," I said, trying to think of how to word it. "I may as well be. Imo won't be around forever, you know, and Mama Jewell's crazy, and Jeanette's set her cap on a man. Where does that leave me?"

"Who?"

"Who what? I'll be all alone in this world," I said.

"I mean who has Jeanette set her cap on?"

"A preacher."

Tara bent double laughing. "You're kidding me!" she said once she got her breath. "What's his name and what does he look like?"

"He's the Reverend Montgomery Pike and he looks like a movie star."

"She dating him? A reverend?"

"Well, actually, she's *chasing* him. She was praying for an engagement ring from him at Christmas, but she didn't get it. Made her so mad, she was spitting nails. She's still mad, but she hasn't given up. Now she's in his Easter musical. She's the angel who appears to Mary at the tomb."

Tara giggled. "Jeanette as an angel," she said. "I'd like to see this guy. But you're pulling my leg about him being a preacher, aren't you?"

Sometimes I despised Tara. "I'm *not* kidding," I said. "Now are you ready to talk about *my* big news?" I pulled away from her and crossed my arms.

"Sorry," she said, flopping back as she slung her arm across my shoulders and squeezed. "Forgive me, Lou?"

I turned to study her face. I sniffled to add impact. "I reckon," I said, "but only if you'll keep your promise and go up to Dusty Springs with me."

"Now?"

"Now."

"Okeydokey," she said, jumping from the hammock. She was across the yard, down the front lawn, and past the mailbox before I knew it. I ran to catch up and we hurried along until the shape of Buzzard Mountain became visible around the first bend in the road. Suddenly the few wispy clouds above us let go of a sprinkle of rain while the sun continued to shine.

"Devil's beating his wife," Tara said, dropping to her knees and pressing her ear to the dirt on the shoulder of the road. "Mama says you can hear him beating her down there."

"That's silly," I said, hooking my arm through hers and trying to pull her up. "Come on, get up. Time's a-wastin'."

"It's not silly either." She pulled away. "If it rains while the sun's shining, he's beating his wife." She patted the dirt next to her cheek. "Get down here and listen with me."

I shook my head. "The Bible doesn't say he even has a wife."

"So."

"So then he doesn't." I patted my pocket with the picture inside. My patience was wearing thin.

A battered Pinto wagon passed us, with what looked like a dozen children's faces pressed against the grimy windows. "Mama would be so furious if she knew where we were," Tara reminded me as we stared at its tailpipe trailing along on the road.

"You're not wimping out on me, are you?" I used my best weapon.

"Mama's going to kill me." Tara breathed as she hooked her arm through mine. We hurried alongside the weedy ditch full of dusty cigarette packages and beer bottles.

Imo would kill me, too, I thought, but I heard that old devil sitting up on my shoulder, whispering into my ear. "If you don't stop listening to the good-girl side of yourself, Lou, you'll never accomplish anything," he said. "Imo's not your real mother, anyway, and plus, this can't count as a sin if Imo's never said specifically not to come up here. She's even come up here herself to bring food to one of the shut-ins."

The entrance to Dusty Springs looked like a different place that afternoon as we neared it, my heart beating like thunder. We stopped short at the turnoff and Tara withdrew her arm from mine while we stood peering down the road. From where we were, Dusty Springs appeared to be deserted. There were no sounds or movement. Then I noticed a skinny dirt footpath off the road that wound up and to the left and into the common area. I tried not to think of Imo's face as I took a deep breath and crept forward, motioning for Tara to follow me.

She was right on my heels as we stepped up to the back of a dozen dilapidated trailers randomly scattered in knee-length grass and weeds. The closest one was the same sea-foam green as the bathroom tiles at home. An old garden hose snaked up the side of the trailer, hooked into a garden sprinkler setting up on the roof. To keep the place cool, I figured.

Some of the other trailers were suffering just as much, with sheets of clear plastic over the windows and caving stairways. There were wheel-less older model cars with grass growing up through their busted windshields scattered here and there and clotheslines crisscrossing the common area. It certainly was a poor place. There were no flower beds or picnic tables or birdbaths anywhere.

"Should we just walk up, knock on the closest door, show the picture, and ask if they know him?" I whispered to Tara. She shrugged and I stood paralyzed until I smelled some meat frying and slowly, the fear began to lift. The place in front of me shouted possibility. I left Tara standing on a patch of dirt and climbed up the cinder-block steps of the nearest trailer.

"Hello?" I called through a nasty fly-specked screen door that was not quite closed. I thought to myself that whoever lived here must be really trusting to leave their house standing wide open that way. I heard the sounds of a wrestling match coming from a TV inside.

I cupped my hands and leaned in to call "Hello" louder. Finally I resorted to knocking on the wooden frame of the screen door.

"Just a minute, just a minute. What da ya want?" came a gruff older man's voice. He shuffled around the corner, his substantial belly behind a blue dress shirt, spilling over black polyester slacks. I looked hard at his wiry reddish hair, balding on top, with mutton-chop side burns and a couple of chins.

This man looks nothing like me, I reasoned. *Please, God, don't let this be Randy,* I prayed.

With a gleam in his eye, he pushed open the door, looking past me to Tara. "You ladies selling something?"

"Nossir. We're looking for somebody."

"Yeah?"

"Yessir."

"Well, come on in." He stepped aside and held out one arm to welcome us.

"No thank you," I managed, "do you know Randy?"

"Randy who? He in trouble or something?"

"I don't know his last name. He used to live here. Still may. He went with a girl named Vera about sixteen years ago."

"Hmmmm." He leered at us and rubbed his chin, and I felt so stupid standing there. Maybe this *was* him, and he was playing games with us. I searched his face again, and I had a good mind to turn tail and go flying back to Tara's house before I could find out.

"Come on in, ladies," he said, swinging the door open wider, "I don't bite." He chuckled then, looking us up and down hungrily. "Got some fresh white bread and some Spam frying in the skillet. I'll fix us all up a sandwich and then I'll see what I can remember. I been here a good ten years and I may be able to recall better when I've got me some grub in my belly." He patted his stomach.

"You'd better come on, Mary Carol," Tara said in a fake voice, "Daddy's waiting down yonder for us in his patrol car."

I turned to go and saw that she was already back on the footpath, slipping between scraggly pines.

"He obviously didn't know anything about him, Lou," she said as I caught up to her. "I mean, he said he's been there ten years and I bet he knows everybody in those trailers. I bet they *all* know each other like the backs of their hands."

"I'll probably never find my father," I whined. "I know I won't."

"Lou, this is crazy." Tara stopped to pat my back. "Sixteen years is a long time, and you can't expect him to be here after all that long. And you're right, you'll probably never find him."

"But I might," I said. "People find their dads all the time on those TV talk shows."

She hooked her arm through mine. "I sure wouldn't go looking for him, if it was my father who never showed up to claim me," she said. "What if he *is* a scuzzball? Anyway, sometimes ignorance is bliss."

I felt my face redden. "He is not a scuzzball!" I hissed, looking over my shoulder at Buzzard Mountain. I sure wasn't giving up yet.

I decided that what I needed was a little more information, perhaps a last name or another picture. Maybe another peek in Mama Jewell's trunk.

Seven

A Bitter Root

By mid-March the days were warming up some. Early one sunny morning when the girls were off at school and Mama and Little Silas were still sleeping, Imogene packed up their heavy winter clothes and the wool blankets. The things Little Silas had outgrown she put into grocery bags to tote to the Salvation Army.

She folded a navy blue cardigan of Mama's. Mama was definitely getting worse. She was running off a good bit more often, sneaking out to sit in the old pickup truck, or hobbling down along the dirt road toward the bottoms, carrying a long piece of bamboo she called her fishing pole.

One afternoon, when Imo was busy replenishing the mulch on her strawberries, Mama had hopped up out of her lawn chair and walked right by her without notice. It was not until Elmer started carrying on, making a loud racket, that Imo glanced up and ran to turn her around. Another time Mama had managed to climb up into the hayloft at the barn and it took three hours and two firemen to get her down.

These adventures alone would have been enough to tire Imo out, but when you added Jeanette's late hours at the church in Rockmart, and her angry tirades in regard to Mama, and Lou's strange moodiness, what it meant was that Imo's life was tinged with a frantic exhaustion. There never seemed to be enough hours in the day to do it all and she felt like she was doing nothing right. What made it worse was that Imo had always assumed that her sixties would be her golden years—years to garden and read and travel with the Keenagers group at Calvary Baptist, to live life leisurely.

Imogene was well aware how near the edge she lived these days. What she needed was some rock to cling to, a fortress. She fussed at herself when the thought of finding a man flashed across her mind. There were no more Silas Lavenders out there. No more Fenton Mabrys.

But it surely was hard managing all this alone, and every now and again she toyed with the idea of calling one of her girlfriends and just pouring her heart out. Oh, what she would give for a sympathetic ear, someone to help shoulder the burdens of her life! Several times she did go to the phone with the intent to call Martha, but she stopped mid-dial and placed the receiver back on the cradle. Imo had always kept things to herself and carried her own burdens. She liked to think that she was born a private type of person. Also, she knew that Martha had enough to do and listen to as the wife of a preacher. Not everyone, not most people as a matter of fact, kept their burdens to themselves, and many times Martha had let on what a barrage of care and concerns the congregation placed at the feet of a minister's wife.

Still, the most terrible of all Imo's burdens were the memories of her mother's rage and the pain of her stinging words, and somehow, these memories were getting worse with time, instead of fading away.

About the only place Imo could say she was truly happy these days was out in the garden, and it was past ten o'clock that morning before she had the chance to get out there.

Little Silas and Mama were fed and dressed and relatively cheerful by that point. She fastened a wide straw hat onto Mama and settled her in a folding chair in the shadow of a tree not too far from the garden.

"You play right there, sugar," Imo ordered Little Silas, who was pushing a toy dump truck at the edge of the garden. "Stay where Mimoo can see you, and she'll give you some marshmallows when we go back in the house."

Mama fell promptly asleep with her mouth hanging open, and Little Silas made rumbling engine sounds while he pushed his truck. Imo smiled as she paused to ponder what to do first. They'd had a very wet spell, followed by a week that was exceptionally dry, and at the edge of the garden she bent to pick up a cool clod of earth. She was able to easily knock it apart with her thumb. It was, she decided, just the right moisture level for tilling.

Today she would till up the garden and then, if she had time, she would also work in the lime and the compost. Next week should be busy: she planned to harden off her tomato seedlings so they could become accustomed to the outdoors, and then sow her collard and spring onion seeds. Her frost-tender crops—the pole beans, okra, cucumbers, and squash, along with the tomatoes—were still tiny plants in the cold frame, waiting to go into the garden in April when there was absolutely no chance of a late frost.

She entered the shed to grapple with the Troy-Bilt and haul it out to the garden. It was always a big job to till her half acre of a garden (this was down by half an acre since Silas's passing), but she was pleased with the way the machine did the job. She knew how important a well-tilled garden was for a bountiful harvest. The plants were only as good as the foundation that supported their roots.

Thinking about all of this brought Imo's thoughts to Mama. She hadn't ever had the luxury of a rototiller. She'd always worked her garden with a fork, spade, and a shovel. Tilling a garden by hand was backbreaking work. Getting the soil to be loose to a depth of eight inches, and making sure that there were no large clumps of earth, roots, grasses, or weeds took all a body had.

When she was a quarter of the way through tumbling the earth she cut the engine and paused to mop her brow with a hankie. She checked her watch. Eleven o'clock. She glanced at Mama who was still asleep. Little Silas wandered out to see her and she patted his head. "Looks like I may even have time to work the lime in today," she told him, smiling. "May even have enough to get the rows ready for my warm-season vegetables. Now run on along, sweetie, but stay where Imo can see you." He returned happily to his dump truck.

Imo got back to work and just as suddenly, she heard the Troy-Bilt's tine go *thunk* against something. She cut the engine once again and bent to see. A gnarled root as big around as her wrist lay nestled in the dirt. She pushed at it with the toe of her shoe and the thing wouldn't budge. She supposed she'd have to go and fetch the mattock.

She returned to the shed for the mattock and began to chop away at the mean root, grunting with the effort, but to no avail. Dropping the mattock, she bent over to pull at the root with her bare hands, meaning to rip it from the earth.

Imo braced with her feet, drew a deep breath, and tugged with all her might. A pain ripped through her back, forcing her to release the root instantly. She landed on her rump. "Oww!" she hollered. She sat there stunned a moment. She could not get up, she could just barely move.

Now she knew that her back was out. She was in terrible pain as her mind raced over her predicament. What in heaven's name was she going to do? The girls would not be home for four and a half hours, and goodness knew, Mama was not capable of getting Imo up, or getting help either. And Little Silas? There he was scurrying to her side, laughing to see her sitting in the dirt.

"Mi-moo!" he squealed and threw himself onto her thighs.

"Ouch!" she squawked at his impact. She ground her teeth against the pain. Poor me, she thought, I am helpless. She imagined herself sitting there until 3:50 PM, when the school bus rumbled up, of Little Silas's diaper running over, and Mama running off to who knows where. She herself would probably get an awful sunburn.

"Mi-moo boo-boo," Little Silas said, placing a kiss on her nose with a loud *smack*.

She laughed. "Yes, a *big* boo-boo. You're a smart boy," she told him. "You make my boo-boo feel all better. You're a good boy."

Wincing, she lifted him off of her and straightened herself and rolled to her stomach to stretch out against the agonizing pain. She meant to summon up some gumption and slither her way to the house for the phone. She moved one shoulder up to undulate forward and an immobilizing pain ripped through her back. There was no way in this world she could do it. She really was helpless.

At this point of realization, while her face was in the dirt, Elmer appeared. He began to strut in circles around her, blinking and brandishing his beautiful, long train of feathers in a wide fan. He was rattling the train, too, so that hundreds of green and blue iridescent eyes were watching Imo, their jewel colors like a dream.

She sank her cheek down into the garden and closed her eyes. She touched her pulsing back. She wondered how long before Mama took a notion to get up or Little Silas got into mischief. She was afraid. She was mainly afraid for Little Silas. Out here were literally hundreds of perils. Full gas cans, and the old, partially covered well, the Etowah River, the mean bull just over the fence, rusty nails . . . and so many more that just thinking about them sent Imo into a panic.

She should have used her brain and brought the cordless phone out here with them. "Hey!" she said, startled by a sudden idea. "Little Silas!" she thundered, "go get Mi-moo the phone out of the kitchen and she will give you some candy!"

"Candy?" He stopped in his tracks.

"Yes, candy!" she said, nodding and smiling. She tasted dirt.

He clapped his hands as Imo stared past him at the long, winding path to the cinder-block steps of the back porch, and then up those to the door. The back door that was closed tight and liable to stick and need a good strong yank to get open.

The steps would be no problem for him. It was getting to them amid all the temptations of the yard and then getting that pesky door to open.

Little Silas seemed so small, so weak as she looked at him now, compared to not an hour ago when he was a complete handful. She cleared her throat. "Candy for you if you go up the steps and into the kitchen and get the phone and bring it outside to Mi-moo's hand!" she urged, her voice high and silly with desperation.

He looked at her and cocked his head to one side.

"Get the phone." She nodded her head. "Candy! Candy!" she sang out.

Finally he headed toward the smooth footpath worn into the grass. He wound around the camellias, and the scuppernong arbor, and the birdbath.

"Good boy!" she called to his small back. "You're getting closer!" Imogene felt really crazy as she began to holler out "candy, candy, candy!"

When he made it past the pole full of white gourds without distraction Imo's heart lifted up a bit. She glanced at Mama. Her mouth was still open and she was snoring away. Thank heaven for small miracles, she thought, and for the modern miracle of cordless telephones.

She held her breath and returned her gaze to Little Silas. Her body was tense, straining futilely to go running after him as his small boot landed on the bottom step. She made herself grab two fistfuls of dirt and squeeze them hard. This was pure torment. To be so helpless. Completely at God's mercy.

"Candy!" she hollered in desperation as his hand reached for the doorknob. "Candy! Candy!"

He turned, smiled, and waved at her.

Oh goodness, she thought, maybe it's time to hush up. She closed her eyes. *Please Lord,* she prayed, *let him get that door open.*

She let her head fall into the cool dirt again and she felt her own breaths envelop her face. She would be fooling no one now. She was truly at the end of her own devices. This was all so humiliating. No matter what had held her back before, she had to reach out for help now. She panicked. Who should she call? Assuming Little Silas made it back out with the phone, that is. Well, he would just have to, that was all there was to it. She would concentrate on him doing that.

"Get the phone, get the phone," she murmured down into the dirt. She took a deep breath and allowed herself to glance back up toward the door.

He had it open! Hallelujah! Now the problem was that he stay focused on getting the phone and not getting distracted by anything else or, heaven forbid, trying to climb up onto the counter to reach the bag of Mary Janes way up high in the corner cabinet.

Come on, she pleaded silently with the little figure now inside the house. *Get the phone for Mi-moo.*

After an eternity, the door opened again and there he stood, clutching something. A bag of Jet-Puff marshmallows! Imo suppressed the urge to shout "No!" She spread out her fingers in a fan and waved. "Good boy!" she hollered. "Now, go get the phone, too, and bring it to Mi-moo and she will let you eat that whole bag of marshmallows!"

When he turned to go back inside the house, Imo sighed and dropped her forehead on her fist. Things could not get any more desperate.

But they did.

Mama grunted loudly. She began her backward and forward rocking. With another large "hunh!" she managed to propel herself to her feet. She stood there shakily for a moment, turning her head this way and that, mumbling something that Imo couldn't make out. Then she proceeded to amble down the road toward the bottoms.

Imogene felt like an actress in a Laurel and Hardy comedy. Heart pounding, she watched Mama. Now it was all a race against time. She had no idea what Mama would do when she reached the Etowah. Hadn't Mr. Dilly pulled her from the Great Pee Dee River just in the nick of time on many occasions? She couldn't swim. Those two times Imo had stopped her lately, she was still a good bit away from the edge of the water.

"Honestly, officer, I couldn't save her." Imo practiced what she'd say to Sheriff Bentley and then the coroner. "She looks old and decrepit, that's for sure," she would say, "but she can be as nimble and as spry as a teenager when she takes a notion to do something. And when she does, you just can't stop her. Plus, I couldn't get up off the ground to go chase her. My back went out on me. Hasn't done it in forever, but it did it today."

Imo closed her eyes against the sun. There was nothing to do but wait.

"Mi-moo!" Here came Little Silas down the steps. He had the Jet-Puffs, Imo's giant plastic container of Tums, and . . . was it the phone? Yes! He had the phone! Hallelujah!

"You wonderful child," she gushed. She felt like kissing the ground. "Come to Mi-moo!" She chewed her lip as he made his way slowly to her and threw the phone in the dirt at her shoulder. She curled her hand up to get it and a sharp pain shot up her side.

"Oww!" she howled. The phone was sticky and encrusted with dirt. Imo held it a moment to ponder. Here she was. No other way to do it but call someone to come and help. It had to be done.

But who? That was the question. She summoned up all the numbers she knew by heart. She spotted Mama, now a tiny speck on the road, and she toyed with the idea of not calling anyone. Just grabbing ahold of Little Silas's ankle, pulling him down, and pinning him underneath her, with room to breathe, of course. Holding him there, feeding him marshmallows and telling him stories until the girls arrived.

Mama's death, if she drowned, would indeed be natural. But then, how would Imo explain the fact that she held a phone? Maybe it would be justice if Mama did drown. Maybe Imo could bury the phone in the garden and just play dumb when Jeanette looked for it later. Buy another one at the Radio Shack in Cartersville on Saturday.

Imo's hand on the phone shook. But if she did let Mama drown herself, would that solve anything? Make anything better? There'd been enough pain in their relationship already and it had to stop somewhere. Imo forced herself to mash the green button to turn the sticky phone on. She dialed Martha's number.

"Lord have mercy!" Martha hollered out the window of her Dodge, kicking up a cloud of dust as she screeched to a halt right at the garden's edge. She sprinted to Imo's side. "You weren't pulling my leg, were you, hon?" She shook her head wonderingly.

Imo lay very still and allowed only her eyeballs to look up. Her face was covered in dirt and Little Silas was pinned securely beneath her.

"Martha"—Imo was breathless—"please, you've got to run fetch Mama down to the river before you help me." She gave one vigorous nod in the direction of the river. "There's no telling what she's gotten herself into," she said. "Better hurry. She's spryer than you'd think."

"Oh my stars," Martha said, shading her eyes and peering down the dirt road. She looked back and forth between Imo and the road. "Don't you move," she said, then sprinted off toward the Etowah.

After a long while Imo saw their two heads appearing over the dip in the road and she blew out a relieved whoosh of air and released Little Silas. He ran to Martha.

Imo watched Martha bend to pick him up, hug him, and swing him up onto her hip. Then she wrapped her free arm around Mama's shoulders.

Imo sank down into the warm dirt and waited for Martha to get them into the house and situated and come back for her. She had to admit it felt good not to be in charge for a change.

"They're looking at TV together, Imogene," Martha said as she squatted next to Imo and grinned like she was the funniest thing she'd seen all day.

"Thanks, Martha," Imo said, "you're truly an angel."

Martha shrugged off the compliment. "Give me your hand," she ordered. "We're going to get you in the house and into the bed. Call Dr. Perkins. Then we'll get us a washrag and clean you up."

So here Imo was, wincing with indescribable pain, and leaning on Martha as she half carried her around to the front of the house where there was only one tiny step up to manage. What was swirling around in her brain was that the house was in the worst mess ever. The kitchen sink literally overflowing with dishes, dust balls rolling around under everything, smelly heaps of laundry in the den, and rings in the toilet and tub that a gallon of bleach couldn't cut. Got to swallow my pride, she thought, and accept Martha's help.

Imo's bladder pulsed from her morning coffee. "Stop me by the bathroom, dear." She tugged at Martha's arm.

Imo left her dignity at the bathroom door, and holding tightly to Martha's arm, she lowered herself painfully onto the toilet. She felt like Mama must feel—no longer master over her own self, depend-ent on the kindness of another.

Martha helped Imo creep into her bedroom, sat her on the bed while she plumped the pillows, eased off her Keds, and swiveled her around. "Where's the number to Dr. Perkins?" she asked.

"In the drawer yonder."

Martha's voice as she talked to Dr. Perkins was comforting, and soon she was on the phone again, calling the pharmacy to deliver some pain pills.

Sleepily, Imo listened to the bedroom door open and close several times. Conversations rose and fell in the den. This must be heaven, Imo thought, in a half-dream state. Her eyes closed as her head sank deeply into the pillow. The bed felt like a soft cloud to her exhausted body. For that matter, to her exhausted mind and spirit, too. This was worth the back pain any day, to lie here in this blissful state.

Ahhhh, she said, covering her head and feeling her body fall like lead. Her dream smelled warm, and peppery, and tomatoey. Sleepily, Imogene opened one eye.

"Medicine's here." Martha held a tray with a prescription bottle, a hand towel, some iced tea, and a steaming bowl of vegetable soup. In the pocket of Martha's apron, which was actually Imo's, there was a stack pack of saltines. "Doctor says you've got to stay in bed till your back's one hundred percent better, or you'll be sorry. So don't you worry about finishing the garden. The girls are home, having a snack. I made oatmeal cookies. Then we're going to get homework tended to." She set the tray down, placing a crook-necked straw into the glass of iced tea. "Little Silas is busy coloring and your mama's watching her story."

Imogene peered at her. "Pills?" she asked, conscious of a spreading pain.

Martha nodded. She shook out a white tablet and placed it on Imo's tongue. She held the tea glass level with the bed and placed the straw between her lips. "Swallow, dear. Be just a little bit and you won't feel any more pain. Then we'll prop you up and get this soup down you."

"Oh, Martha," Imo said as she swallowed the tablet and tried not to cry. "I don't know what I'd have done if you didn't come when you did. You're an angel. A saint."

"Don't be silly, dear," Martha said. "It's my pleasure. This is what friends are supposed to do."

Martha seemed so vital, so capable a person to handle Imo's tangled-up life. It certainly looked as if she needed no instructions to step right in and manage things to a T. No wonder she was such a good pastor's wife. Imo settled down into her covers again. The pain was lessening.

As Martha scurried around the bedroom, sweeping, gathering piles of dirty laundry, and dusting, Imo lay in bed and slept like a baby. The months of sheer physical and mental exhaustion vanished. Now the frayed corners of her life seemed to be so far away and when she did occasionally surface, she felt a surge of courage.

In the kitchen, late in the afternoon of the second day, Martha started a pot roast and a big boiler full of navy beans. She came into the bedroom to gently shake Imo's shoulder and ask did she have any fatback to season the beans. Then Imo heard her flying around the house entertaining the girls, Little Silas, and Mama.

At seven she breezed into Imo's room with supper and some warm Rice Krispy treats. "I'm going to stay again tonight, dear. May stay tomorrow night, too. And the next one. So, don't you say a word about it. I *want* to."

That's fine and dandy with me, Imo thought, closing her eyes again, savoring the warm nest of covers. I'm absolutely thrilled.

Day after day Martha was there. Often she came in to bring food, administer a pill, and laugh over something Mama said or to report on Little Silas and the girls.

"How are we feeling?" she asked Imo so many times that she lost count.

"Guess I need a little more rest," Imo always replied. "But you really shouldn't mind me. I imagine Lemuel's just falling apart without you at home." Then she rubbed her back and looked as pitiful as she could manage.

"I imagine he is that!" Martha laughed. "It'll just remind the man how much he needs me, now won't it?"

By the fifth day, Imo reckoned that she was as good as new and could get up and at it if she wanted to. But Martha was doing so well—better than she did. One more day couldn't possibly hurt, Imo decided as she rolled over and snuggled down.

Eyes closed, arms and legs akimbo, she sank into another deep sleep. She dreamed and in the dream she was a girl again, with her heart beating so hard she thought it might rip through the skin across her chest. She was crouched behind the linen-press in her room, hiding, while Mama screamed out cuss words and made loud footsteps as she scurried down the hall to hunt for Imo. She came closer and closer.

"Imogene Rose! Come out *now*!" Mama yelled. "*Right* now! You don't come out and I'll do you worse than I'm already planning to."

The door to Imo's bedroom opened and went *bang!* against the wall. Imo held her breath, her heartbeat booming in her ears. She closed her eyes and her nails dug painfully into her palms. It was coming. Mama had the hickory switch with her.

Imo's crime was that she'd left a big hunk of fatback in a pot of beans on the burner too long and turned it black. The beans were blackened, too, but that was not as great a sin. Beans were cheap, but fatback was treasured. It was used over and over again to flavor beans until it was worn out.

"There you are, you little wench!" Mama shrieked when she spotted Imo's stricken face. "You're in for it now, I'll teach you to waste our fatback!"

Pleading silently for mercy, Imo pressed herself against the smooth back of the linen-press, covered her head with her arms, and waited for the blows. The switch whipped through the air, stinging her arms and back. She choked down the tears.

"No, Mama, no!" Imo pleaded. "I'm sorry!"

Martha's gentle hand broke through the dream. She stood at the edge of the bed staring down at Imo. "Imogene, sweetie, you've had a bad dream. I imagine it's all those pills you've been taking." She stroked Imo's arm. "Everything's all right. Don't you worry about a thing."

Imo awoke with hesitancy. She lay on the disheveled bed and sought Martha's face. "Only a dream," she murmured. But the fact of the matter was that it had been a dream based on her real life.

❊   ❊   ❊

During the night, Imo sat up in bed, blinking into the darkness. There was a human shape at the foot of her bed. Was it another dream? She checked the digital clock: 2:04 AM. She decided it was Martha checking on her.

"Martha?" Imo said softly.

"It's me," Loutishie said.

"Hello dear. It's late. What are you doing up?"

"Couldn't sleep." The child stepped closer.

"Well, sit down, sugar foot. You can sit on my bed now, it doesn't hurt me."

Lou sat on the edge of the bed. Imo turned the switch on her bedside lamp. A pool of warm yellow light fell across the bed.

"Got things on your mind?" Imo asked.

"Yessum," Lou said weakly.

"Martha been treating you well?"

"Mmm-hmm. She even helped me study for my algebra test. I got an A."

Imo smiled. "Well, now. Sounds like she does better than me in arithmetic."

"Imo?" Lou was looking down at her knees. "Does anybody ever die of their back going out on them?"

"Goodness me, no," Imo said, chuckling. "Just lands a person flat on their back for a spell." She rubbed Lou's thin shoulder. The child's concern and innocence were touching, and she felt a twinge of guilt over not being there for her over the past days. "You've been giving Martha a hand with Mama for me, haven't you?" she asked.

Lou nodded her head.

"Well, I feel much better now. Like a brand-new person."

"You do?"

"I surely do. I needed this bed rest. Been a godsend. Martha, and you, too, dear, have been my salvation."

"Really?"

"Yes indeed."

"But Martha said she's going home tomorrow . . ."

"Reverend Peddigrew must be missing her after all these days away from him, and I'm all healed up and ready for battle. I'll need your help to catch up on my gardening."

"But what if it happens again?" Lou asked. "If your back goes out again, or if you get sick?" She twisted the spread in her hands.

"Well, we don't have to worry about that. Martha said she'd come right back at the drop of a hat if I needed her. All I've got to do is pick up the phone."

Lou jumped up, walked to the other side of the bed, and slid in next to Imo. "That's real good," she said, grabbing and squeezing Imo's hand. "Cuz Martha sure knows how to settle fights between Mama Jewell and Jeanette."

"Does she now?" Imo asked, and it dawned on her that she hadn't heard any major knock-down, drag-outs since Martha'd been there. "How in tarnation does she do it?"

"Well," Lou said, "first of all, she got that little bitty old black-and-white TV down out of the closet and she put it in there in front of Mama Jewell's La-Z-Boy, and she fastened a wire coat hanger onto it so it'll pick up the stations, and she moved the big color set into the dining room, on top of the sideboard, for Jeanette."

Imo laughed at the thought of Mama chewing Martha out. "Bless poor Martha's heart," she chuckled. "I must've been out cold because I sure didn't hear that fight."

"There was no fight."

"What?!"

"Mama Jewell was totally happy to have the black-and-white set."

"You're kidding me. I tried that myself, and Mama pitched a royal fit about not seeing her stories in color. And then when I gave the old black-and-white TV set to Jeannie, she threatened to throw it into the river. It doesn't pick up her stations."

"Well," Lou said, giggling, "what Martha did is she told Mama Jewell that it was 1952, and they hadn't invented color TV yet."

They lay there, giggling in fits and starts, and Imo marveled at Martha's ingenuity. She looked over at Lou and said reverently, "You know what, sugar foot? That Martha has the very wisdom of Solomon. Yes, indeed. I thought there was no way on earth those two would ever stop fighting and fussing at each other over the TV. I figured it was just one of those things I had to learn to endure."

When Lou was gone, Imo rolled over onto her back. She laced her hands across her stomach and stretched out to think.

Martha sure seemed to think that Imo had it made. She galloped in every so often, all tickled and laughing hilariously at Mama's words and doings like she was just the cutest thing God had ever placed on this earth.

Why, Imo reckoned to an outsider she did have it made! Two sweet girls, Little Silas, and a mother who was a laugh a minute!

Caring for Mama would be exhausting still, surely it would, but wouldn't it be satisfying and just if Imo didn't have to lug around all these awful memories? It was the memories and the ugly feelings they brought that were hurting her. Some part of her wanted to holler out that she was entitled to these feelings, she had earned them. But the truth was, she could not pretend that she was okay with these feelings. She could not hide from her own heart. Her heart gave her no peace on the matter and she tossed fitfully in her bed.

It was close to five when a mild tingle ran up her spine at the sudden realization that the first step toward wholeness was to empty out all the bad memories stored up inside her. Surely there had to be some way she could unload them. They were sucking the joy out of life, and she *wanted* to be free of them so badly, and surely, somehow, with God's help, she could find a way to release these burdens she had clung to for so long.

Now, there had been times during these past days when Imo had almost told everything to Martha, but the right moment never came. "You help me to find the right time, dear Lord," Imo whispered out into the darkness. "You help me find some peace." A wave of hope settled over her as gently as a down comforter as she drifted off to sleep.

Loutishie's Notebook

My next chance to gather more clues on my father came one afternoon when Imo asked me to keep an eye on Mama Jewell while she ran into Cartersville for some milk and diapers. She said she couldn't wait to get out and see the world after being in bed so long.

"Yessum, I'd be happy to," I said, envisioning myself rifling through the trunk for more clues.

Things looked promising as Mama Jewell was asleep in her La-Z-Boy with her mouth hanging open when Imo left. I watched Imo backing out from the shed and walked down the hallway to peer into my bedroom. Little Silas was napping and Jeanette was on the phone.

My heart was lifted high. The perfect chance!

Entering Mama Jewell's room, my conscience was silent. I marched boldly to the foot of the bed and opened the trunk. A musty waft of air coated my face as I stuck my hand in to lift the top layers out. The same postcards, faded corsages, and photographs I'd seen earlier.

It was time to dig deeper.

A bit nervous over having enough time to sift through everything, I hurried past piano recital programs and newspaper clippings of obituaries, until I came up on a clump of photographs I hadn't seen yet. I recognized my mother's face in some school pictures and I saw Mama Jewell and Granddaddy Burton sitting together at a table draped with a white tablecloth and a sheet cake that had a big twenty-five on top. She looked normal. I imagined she was in her forties then. In the black and white of the photo, the skin on her movie star face was perfectly smooth. She wore a dark tailored suit and pearl ear-bobs. She and Granddaddy were smiling as they held hands behind the cake.

Could this really be that same senile old warthog, as Jeanette called her, who sat in the other room with her mouth hanging open and so many wrinkles she looked like an elephant's leg? Jeanette loved to say how we'd all be happier, especially Imo, if Mama Jewell croaked. "She's just a drain on us," Jeanette said, "all she does is eat, sleep, crap, and bitch at everybody."

Though I wouldn't utter the words aloud, I sure enough agreed with Jeanette. And the Bible says as a man thinks in his heart, so is he.

I laid that photo aside and slowed down, searching at my leisure through two more armloads of mementos. There were boring pictures of family reunions and Garden Club Christmas parties and retirement dinners. There were interesting pictures of Imo at various ages, and pictures of my granddaddy Burton standing in his cornfields.

I paused to read poems cut from magazines and inspect the stubs of movie tickets. It was absorbing to get this glimpse into my family's history and I dug deeper and deeper as the minutes passed, lingering at all kinds of interesting things, till all of a sudden I hit pay dirt! There was his face! Tiny, but unmistakably him. Just barely breathing, I pulled the photo closer. It was a full-body shot. He was wearing boots, jeans, and a checked shirt open at the neck. Long sideburns and a mustache, leaning confidently against the side of a blue van with his arms crossed. Behind him was a flat cinder-block building. Peering even closer, holding my breath, I read the sign above the overhead doors of the building. It said Randy's Van Conversions.

I flipped the photo over. *Vera—Here's me at my new shop* was scrawled across the back. My dad was a business owner! I knew he wasn't a scuzzball. Or a jailbird. I saw myself proudly showing this to Tara. Then I saw us tracking him down in no time.

I sat there, holding my future in my hands, imagining me and my father at father-daughter suppers, fishing together, and playing Yahtzee on cold winter evenings. I looked at his face again, and I felt a warmth spreading all the way down to my toes. I closed my eyes to try and picture him, to see what he was doing at that very moment.

All of a sudden I heard the back door slam, and like lightning I sprang to my feet, stuffed the photo into my back pocket, scooped up the pile of stuff on the floor, jammed it back into the trunk, and dropped the lid. I rushed to the kitchen, but it was only Jeanette, chasing after Little Silas. I stopped at the kitchen window to glance out at the shed—no Imo yet. I let go of the big breath I'd been holding and headed to the den.

My heart dropped to my toes when I saw that Mama Jewell's chair was empty!

I did a lightning-quick search of the house, ran outside around the yard, and peeked inside the well-house, the shed, the barn, and the old pickup truck. No luck. I ran back to the house.

"Jeanette!" I hollered, "you seen Mama Jewell?"

"What?" She was standing on the back porch, lighting a cigarette.

"I can't find Mama Jewell anywhere. Guess she's run off again. Help me look for her before Imo gets home, please."

"Ain't my fault she's lost." Jeanette inhaled deeply, then blew a long, white stream of smoke.

"Please, Jeannie," I wailed, "please help me. I've got to find her."

Jeanette let more smoke out in a long, exaggerated sigh. "All right, kiddo," she said, "where in tarnation do you suppose the old warthog got herself off to this time?"

"I dunno. You check the yard and the garden, and up toward the big road," I shouted over my shoulder, "and I'll run down to the bottoms."

"What a pain in the neck," I heard Jeanette muttering as I tore down the steps.

Both peafowl and Bingo were right on my heels as I jogged down the rutted road, searching left and right frantically. She couldn't have gotten too far on her old feeble legs, I told myself, and I kept half expecting that Jeanette would find her somewhere up at the house and ring the bell.

I yelled out "Mama Jewell!" as I went tearing along. The funny thing was, depending on where she was in her memory, she could respond to one of a half dozen names—Mama, Mama Jewell, Jewelldine, Jewelldine Anne, Miss Pridemore, or Baby Girl.

But right now, the problem wasn't figuring out what to call her, it was finding her at all. I didn't want to even think of what Imo would say if she got home and Mama Jewell was still missing, so I concentrated on the hunt while I kept hoping to hear the bell.

I felt my heart beating faster and faster as I neared the Etowah. The late afternoon light made the leaves on the trees along the river look brighter. Breaking through a tangle of weeds and knee-high pines at the bank, I stopped and surveyed the water. It was the same earthen red as the banks that held it in, flowing along peacefully enough.

I held the stitch in my side and sank to my heels a minute. Elmer strutted along the bank, and Bingo's nose nudged my arm. "Well, boys," I said, breathing hard, "I don't see her anywhere here. Let's go search downriver a bit and then I guess we ought to head on back up to the house. I don't see how she could've got this far anyway." I was fairly certain she hadn't made her way through the thicket of brambles along that part of the water's edge, the place where the river was all grown up and wild with underbrush and brambles. But we wandered along, searching and calling. At last I stopped, looking around for Dewy Rose. "Where's your girlfriend at?" I tickled Elmer's feathers playfully. "Come on, I bet we'll find her and Mama Jewell somewhere up at the house together."

I turned to go, casting one final glance downriver, and I thought I saw the gray-white flash of some winged animal. Again, it fluttered and in that instant, I made out a gray head, a blue shirt, and perhaps a fishing pole slicing through the air. I stopped and held my breath for a split second, then I tore down the overgrown path alongside the river, scrambling closer to see. "Shoo, scat!" I yelled at Bingo and Elmer, who were getting underfoot.

A hundred yards downriver, sitting on a broad, flat rock out in the middle of the water, was Mama Jewell. She held a long piece of bamboo between her knees.

"Mama Jewell!" I waved my arms overhead, but she was oblivious. How had she gotten herself out there? I half slid, half leapt down the bank to the water's edge. "Mama Jewell!" I hollered, "look at me!"

She didn't budge. No telling where her mind was. I searched my brain frantically. Probably she was back in her childhood days, judging by the way she was sitting like a grasshopper, with her knees up around her jaw, and her wet skirt bunched at her thighs, rocking her torso forward between her knees to hold the bamboo. What did they call her when she was little?

"Jewelldine!" I tried.

Nothing.

"Jewelldine Anne, you listen to me this instant!"

Nothing.

"Baby girl, sweetheart, this is your mama. Time for supper!" I called in a syrupy voice.

That was all I could think of. But still she sat there.

"I found her, Jeanette!" I screeched, knowing full well she couldn't hear me way up at the house and all the while shucking off my shoes and plunging into the edge of the cold water. *Please stay put, Mama Jewell,* I breathed, and I didn't even feel the sharp stones or branches on the slippery bottom of the Etowah like I usually did. I was like Wonder Woman as I sank to my middle and pushed my hips through the water.

"Annalea," Mama Jewell said in a surprised voice when I reached the rock, pulled myself up, and sat down beside her dripping wet. I'd heard the story of her cousin Annalea dying of lockjaw. Annalea was nine and Mama Jewell was eleven when Annalea stepped on a rusty can out front of an old shanty where she and Mama Jewell were playing dolls, and six days later she was dead.

I said, "Hey. Caught anything?" There was no line, hook, or bait on the bamboo.

"Four big enough to be keepers," she said, "but I'm gonna hafta git us seven. One for everbody at supper."

"Good, good." I nodded my head, trying to think of how I could coax her back across. Thankfully she had chosen a relatively gentle bend in the Etowah, a place not deep; plus, I told myself, she *had* managed to get herself out there. One thing in our favor was that she was almost pure fat, so she could float if she lost her footing, and I could keep a hold of her arms and just guide her back to the bank like a raft.

"Ooo, look at this, Jewelldine," I said, leaning over and swishing my hands vigorously in the water and pretending to scoop up fish. "Here's three more good ones. Let's get them home to Mama to fry."

"Reckon auntie'll fry us up some hush puppies to eat with them, Annalea?" Her old eyes were shining.

"Mmm-hmm." I nodded. "She sure will. And we'll have us some slaw and some taters, too." She seemed satisfied with this and I stood up, grabbed her elbow, and said "Upsy daisy!" She didn't protest as I tugged her to her feet, keeping one arm hooked through hers while I gathered up an imaginary bucket. We shuffled to the edge of the rock and she held on to that piece of bamboo like it was gold.

I hopped into the water while she sat down on the edge of the rock and put only her feet in. Slowly, I eased her all the way in, talking foolishness all the while—about our fish dinner and about Bingo, who was barking wildly on the bank.

"He's hoping we have some leftovers," I said, laughing. It was going fairly well and we were inching along through the water, about a quarter of the way across, and I was praising myself for being so courageous when all of a sudden, a huge surge of water swelled over us like a tidal wave. "Lord God up in Heaven!" I yelled as we tumbled forward. Lucky I was holding on to her so tight.

The dam had opened up! With all my talking, I had not heard the warning siren that the Army Corps of Engineers sounded every time before they released the water. Right then I started thinking it was all over. My life wasn't flashing before my eyes, though. All I was thinking of was how Imo would be disappointed in me, and her sad face at our double funeral.

We got carried downriver fifteen feet or so until I felt a small boulder bump my feet. I managed to lock my legs around it and hang there, swallowing lots of water. I got to thinking that maybe I could get us safely to the bank if I could just keep hanging on to the boulder and to Mama Jewell until the river calmed down enough.

Gulping water, I managed to get Mama Jewell onto her back. Pinecones and sticks battered us, but she wasn't saying a word. Her bamboo pole was long gone. The muscles in my thighs began to burn from clinging to that rock. Then they started shaking. Thankfully, Mama Jewell didn't struggle, she just lay there afloat with wide eyes. "It can't be too much longer," I said, "we can make it."

But in the next second I noticed Elmer heading downriver toward us. He was swirling around and around in a little eddy. "I'll get you, sweetie boy!" I screamed at the back of his neck as he did a 180-degree turn. He was just about within my reach. My feet gripped onto that rock with a new unction as I let go of Mama Jewell with one hand to strain out toward Elmer. But I was still inches away from him, waggling the fingers of my hand so frantically it may as well have been a mile.

In those next two seconds I had to make the toughest decision of my life. It was Mama Jewell or Elmer. I could not continue to hold on to her and reach out that extra bit to get ahold of him. Who to rescue? My mind fired off like popcorn. Elmer! No, Mama Jewell! Elmer?! Mama Jewell?! Thoughts screamed of how Mama Jewell had already lived long and was pretty much gone mentally, her so old and just a drain on everyone anyway. Then thoughts of how Elmer still had a good life ahead of him and how Dewy Rose would be sad and how much I loved him and how I didn't even *like* Mama Jewell. Wouldn't it be doing her and us a favor to let go of her?

But in that final moment, I reckoned that with what I knew about God, I'd see Elmer again. He'd be happy to get up there to heaven and meet Uncle Silas; plus, even though Mama Jewell doesn't know who she is ninety-nine percent of the time, she's still Imo's mother and my grandmother.

Like a dream, I watched Elmer churn upward and then finally underneath the water and out of sight. The river began to calm back down. It always did, but it seemed like an eternity before I could move. When it was smooth, but five feet higher, I did the lifesaver stroke to haul Mama Jewell toward the bank.

When we made it, I struggled to pull her up because when she was wet she weighed a ton. We flopped back onto the slick clay with dirt and leaves stuck all over us. My thighs ached and my arm muscles quivered. I was totally wrung out.

"Annalea," Mama Jewell breathed, turning her face toward mine, "father's gonna be mad at me for getting my new dress wet." She covered her face with her hands and started to bawl.

I turned to her then. I was furious. "You're worried about your *father*?!" I shouted so hard I saw red. "*You* almost drowned, *I* almost drowned, Elmer *did* drown, and you're worried about *your father*?!"

She looked at me then, confused. "But Annalea, he's going to beat me with the strap."

"Yeah, well," I said meanly, "you deserve it."

"You don't care about me." Mama Jewell tucked her chin to her chest and looked at me like I was the meanest thing ever. "You really don't."

I lost it then. "Dern it, woman!" I yelled at her again. "Get into reality!"

She cowered. "Annalea," she said meekly after a moment, "aren't you scared of getting into trouble?"

"You are out of your mind, Mama Jewell!" I screamed. "Look what you've done. You've killed Elmer!"

Startled, she turned her head and looked over at my angry face.

"You don't have a father! He's dead," I shouted into her ear, "and further-more, I am not Annalea! I am not Sheila either! Or Vera!" I picked up my leg and stomped the ground hard. "They are all dead, and so is your husband! And this is the river along the bottomland of your daughter Imogene's house, and I am Loutishie. I am *your* granddaughter! Daughter of your daughter Vera!"

"Yes," she agreed in a strange voice. She raised her arms from the mud and wrapped them around herself.

"You are a very sick person," I growled. "Crazy as you look. You know that, don't you?"

"Yes," she replied. She hugged herself tightly and looked at me with downcast eyes. "You are angry with me, Loutishie, daughter of Vera," she said as she extended her right arm and placed her hand on my forearm.

She's *apologizing*, I realized. This is her way of saying "I'm sorry." A tiny part of my heart went out to her stricken face, to her pathetic body lying there all helpless on the bank.

The soft purple gray of predusk in the woods encircled us as I lay there unable to move, listening to Mama Jewell's sobbing. Something jabbed my calves, and I opened my eyes to see Dewy Rose. She was making such a fuss. "You're looking for Elmer, aren't you, sweetie?" I said, and that's when a flood of hot salty tears began to pour out of my eyes.

Along about then I heard the slap! slap! of Jeanette's shoes as she ran down the trail above us. "Lou? Lou?" she called, and I heard Little Silas echoing her. "Oh my God!" she shouted when she saw us. She set Little Silas down on the rise and dropped to her fanny to slide down the bank. "Are you all right?" She grabbed my shoulders and shook me so hard that my teeth rattled. I could not speak.

"Answer me this instant, Loutishie Lavender!" she yelled into my face. "You all right?"

I managed a nod.

"You get caught in the dam water?"

I nodded again.

Jeanette put her hands on her hips. "Well, that was real stupid, Lou. Now get up and I'll help you haul this old warthog up to the house."

"Elmer's dead," I squeaked out.

"Huh?"

"I couldn't get to him and hang on to Mama Jewell, too."

"He's in the river?"

"Yep." I was shaking.

"You're shittin' me." Jeanette's voice was quiet.

"No," I whispered, "I saw him go right by me while I was hanging on to Mama Jewell and the rock."

"I bet he can swim," Jeanette said. "Ducks swim, and I bet he's downriver just swimmin' up a storm." She patted my head. "Stop crying now, Lou. We'll find him."

"He cannot swim either." I stared out at the woods.

"Good God, Lou. Then why the hell didn't you let her go and grab *him*?" She was shaking her head in wonder.

I didn't know how to put it into words.

It was close to eight when Imo got home that evening. Jeanette told her how I'd rescued Mama Jewell from the river, and Imo dropped her armload of groceries, galloped over with terrified eyes and hugged me to her, and just cried and cried. "You've got a heart of pure gold, Loutishie, dear," she said at last as she pecked my cheek, leaving a whiff of gardenia eau de parfum in the air. She didn't even ask me how come I hadn't been watching Mama Jewell like a hawk.

Imo's words made it easier to bear my own loss, but still, the memory of Elmer swirling out of reach haunted me and I couldn't bear to go near the Etowah for an entire week. But Mama Jewell kept wandering outside, calling for Elmer. It was plain she had no memory of the scene down at the river.

Late one night, several weeks after that terrible day, I was in bed, huddled against the cool wall, memories of Elmer coming so fast and furious that I couldn't sleep. I watched the covers over Jeanette rising and falling in the glow of the night-light next to Little Silas's crib, and I could tell that Jeanette wasn't asleep either.

I sniffled a bit to get her attention.

Jeanette flipped over to look at me. "What's wrong?" she asked.

"Just thinking about Elmer," I said.

"Mama Jewell's a real pain, ain't she?" Jeanette said.

"Yep," I said, feeling a little shiver of pleasure run through me.

Jeanette giggled. "You know what, Lou?" she said. "We ought to tell her that the Baptists are holding poker games on Wednesday nights, and serving liquor drinks. You know how worked up she gets over folks playing bingo. Calling it the devil's game, calling it gambling."

"Ha-ha!" I laughed. Enjoying this thought, I felt my insides unkink a tiny bit.

Jeanette was delighted at my reaction. "It would be great, wouldn't it, Lou?" She slapped the mattress.

Jeanette's idea made me feel giddy. It was the first time in a long time that I felt anywhere near peaceful or happy. It also made me feel close to Jeanette, warm and connected in a way I hadn't been in forever. And I guess she noticed it, too, because after several minutes she crept out of her bed and sat on the foot of mine. She pulled her legs up and rested her chin on her knees. Her eyes were shining.

"I think he's falling for me, Lou," she said dreamily. "Last night he *kissed* me!"

A mixture of horror and excitement tingled through me. It was a sensation I didn't know what to do with. Jeanette was taking me into her confidence and it was really thrilling to hear, and it was also hard to believe that he was the same man who was a minister of God.

"Well?" Jeanette asked, leaning forward and squeezing the covers over my feet. "It's taken him a while, hasn't it? You know, to get the hint." Her voice was high and excited. She laughed. "'Bout had to hog-tie the man. But last night, definitely, *he* made the first move. It was worth the wait, too, Lou. We kissed in the choir robe closet."

I lay there rigid. I heard Little Silas shifting positions in his crib, and an owl hooting far away. I could feel Jeanette's excitement like electricity bouncing off of her. I thought of her and the Reverend Montgomery Pike in the choir robe closet. His dark swoop of hair and those tattoos.

"Hey," Jeanette was wiggling my feet, "don't say anything about it to Mama just yet, hear? She thinks I'm in it for the religion and I don't want to burst her bubble."

"All right," I said as I rolled to my side, contemplating telling Jeanette *my* secret about the trip to Dusty Springs and the photos I had underneath my mattress. But before I worked up the courage to say anything to her, she got an idea.

"Let's give ourselves perms tonight, Lou!" Jeanette pointed toward the closet. "I bought a couple of those Lilt Lotion home perm kits from the Buy-wise!"

It was way past midnight, and though I truly wanted to keep the close feelings going, I had no interest in getting, or assisting with, a perm.

"School tomorrow," I said, sounding like Imo.

"Screw school," Jeanette said, "I'm thinking of dropping out of school."

I pulled myself up to my elbows and looked hard at her. "But you can't,

Jeannie!" I breathed. "You don't have that much more to go. Don't you know Imo like to have *died* when you tried to drop out of school when you got pregnant! Do you know how proud she is that you're sticking it out now? It will kill her if you drop out."

Jeanette just shook her head. "She'll get over it. After all, I'll probably be getting married real soon." She sat there chewing her nails for a few minutes while my mind was racing. "Anyway, Lou," she said quietly, "I've got a D in math and an F in English."

"You can go to summer school and . . ." Before I could finish my sentence, Jeanette was on her feet, walking over to the closet. She tugged the cord to the lightbulb inside the closet and pulled out a brown paper bag. From this she removed two pink boxes that said "Lilt" in swirly black letters.

"Come on, Lou," she said, beckoning for me to join her at the pool of light from the closet.

Stubbornly, I lay on my side. Though I longed to keep her so happy, in the back of my mind I was thinking that if I did let her give me a perm, it would be a silent way of saying I approved of her dropping out of school, and approved of her chasing a reverend, of tricking him by singing in his choir under false pretenses. I mean, here she was, with no thought about anybody but herself. No thought about Imo, or getting a good education.

Well, I had promised Jeanette I wouldn't tell Imo about Montgomery Pike, but I hadn't said a word about not telling Imo about Jeanette planning to drop out of high school.

Eight

❧

Imogene Saw the Light

Imo wished that there were a fitting way she could say thank you to Martha for all she'd done for her while her back was out. Clearly, she was indebted to her friend.

By mid-May, the bliss of what she privately referred to as her "vacation" was fading to a sweet memory. She had returned to the rhythm of caring for Mama and Little Silas, getting by with the cooking and cleaning, and stealing moments to go outside to the garden.

The garden was coming along nicely. Imo had made a habit of carrying the phone along with her since the incident with her back, and when it rang today as she was retying a tomato vine to its stake, somehow she knew it would be bad news.

It was terrible news.

In a soft, solemn voice Maimee Harris informed Imo that Martha was in critical condition after a car wreck.

Four sad days had passed when Imogene pulled into the visitors' lot of Northside Hospital in Atlanta. She dreaded what she might find today. Her stomach knotted as she walked through the sliding glass entrance and the familiar waft of antiseptic surrounded her.

She'd heard the story umpteen times by now, and still each time it sent a chill up her spine. It went like this, though there were no eyewitnesses, and Martha's recollection was patchy: Martha had left home at 8:00 PM last Tuesday, a rainy night, to drive to Shiftlet's for a carton of whole milk and some fudge ripple ice cream, and when she was on her way home, a dog darted out from a thicket of trees just as she was turning onto Harvey Odelle Road, causing her to startle so that she completely missed the turn, careening down a steep embankment where her Dodge rolled over and over until it slammed to a stop against a large boulder.

The paramedics told Lemuel it was a miracle Martha was even alive, and Dr. Chapman offered few words of hope as he spoke gravely to the family in the hallway outside of Martha's room.

Martha was the needy one now. The tables in life had certainly turned. Between Wednesday, when she first heard, and today, Saturday, Imo had spent what seemed a lifetime arranging her responsibilities at home to get here and be with her friend.

It certainly took an act of Congress to juggle schedules and find sitters for Mama and Little Silas while the girls were at school, let alone muster the strength to fight Atlanta traffic and fold laundry at midnight.

Ashamed of such selfish thoughts, she hurried to the elevator. Martha needed Imo more than ever now. She was not getting any better. Though it was hard for Imo to keep the disappointment out of her voice and off her face when she saw Martha hooked up to all those machines, she determined to be extra cheery today. It was her duty to offer comfort and hope.

With a huge smile plastered across her face, Imo pushed open the door and tiptoed into Martha's room. "Hello!" she said brightly when she saw that Martha was awake. "What a lovely day for a drive to see you!"

Martha smiled. She was lying immobile, flat, her gray hair fanned out on the pillow.

"Yessum. Sun just a-shining so pretty," Imo said, "it was a lovely drive." She sat down on the vinyl recliner beside Martha. She glanced around the room. "Lemuel go home?"

"Cafeteria," Martha said.

"Good, good. Went by your place on my way. Got the mail and the papers. Pretty day outside, too," Imo said. "Did I already tell you that? Brought some supper for Lemuel." She patted a brown paper bag at her feet. "Fried chicken breast, pimiento cheese sandwich, potato salad, and some pound cake. With lemon icing on it. Tea in that thermos there."

"Real sweet of you, Imogene."

"Don't you think a thing about it. It's my pleasure. After all you've done for me." Imo patted Martha's wrist. "Yes, such a pretty day," she added.

"Well," Martha said.

Imo could read nothing from Martha's eyes, but her hands were all clenched up on top of the sheet. Did that mean she was in terrible pain?

Tears glazed Imo's eyes, but she willed them not to fall. It would not do to bring anything but a hopeful feel to this room. Imo was proud of herself. Each day so far she'd managed a cheerful monologue. She'd sat right here and talked up a blue streak of anything but Martha's condition. She'd brought only positive news—words from the Garden Club, the county agent's report, the sewing circle from church, and their book club discussion group. This she managed while her thoughts scrambled around disjointed and weary, and above all, scared. Emotionally, Imo was so fragile that once she left Martha's hospital room, the tiniest thing could provoke her to tears.

Now she would give anything to have her life back the way it was just weeks ago. As terrible as it had all seemed then, as hopeless as that situation felt with keeping the peace between Mama and Jeanette and battling the awful memories, it was heaven compared to watching her dearest friend teeter painfully at the edge of life.

She reached for Martha's water cup, held it level with the mattress, and positioned the straw. "Drink up," she told Martha, "you need to keep your fluids going good." Then she purposefully drew a deep, loud lungful of air. "Yessum, it certainly is the prettiest day we've had in quite a while. The daffodils are blooming away and your yard is as pretty as a postcard. Yes it is!" But in the next breath, Imo wondered if it weren't making Martha feel worse to hear about all the good things she was missing. She decided she ought to bring up the one topic that always got a giggle out of Martha.

Mama.

Imo had been busily telling all the crazy stories from home for the past three days; relaying Mama's words and shenanigans while Martha cackled. "The Adventurous Life of Mama Jewell," Martha had named the stories.

"Mama went to pieces last night," Imo said.

"Old lady giving you trouble again, Imogene?" A smile crept across Martha's face.

"Goodness gracious, yes. Came a quick little lightning storm. No rain, but lots of thunder and lightning, and Mama went to pieces. Acted just like a two-year-old."

"Tell me."

"Well, first she practically flew up out of her La-Z-Boy, as spry as you please," Imo said, and she noticed that Martha's hands were unclenching a bit on top of the sheet. "And she crawled underneath the dining table with Bingo. I lifted up the corner of my nice white tablecloth to check on them, and there she was, just a squeezing that poor dog so tight his eyes were bulging! Then, and now this is the kicker, Martha, hon, Mama whispered right into Bingo's ear that she knew he must be as terrified as she was and that she was planning to let him sleep in the bed with her."

Imo laughed. "Poor dog, I don't know what he thought was worse, the thunder or Mama chasing him around the house later that night."

The covers shook as Martha laughed. "She still running off a good bit, too, Imogene?"

"Oh, goodness, yes!" Imo was laughing now. "Found her up in the loft of the hay barn yesterday evening."

This tickled Martha. "The hayloft?"

"Yessum. Sitting right up there. Had on one of Silas's Feed 'n' Seed caps. Singing 'When the Saints Go Marching In' and slurping an Orange Crush."

"You're not serious."

"Serious as I can be. Had her big black handbag up there with her. And a Mason jar full of pickled watermelon and a little can of Vienna sausages and a flyswatter."

She glanced over at Martha to see her eyes still dancing with amusement, a grin from ear to ear and her hands open loosely now.

After a spell Martha closed her eyes and began to snore softly.

Imo sighed. It was a little disconcerting to bear the burden to keep on entertaining and distracting Martha. But what else could she do? She had to do it. She felt the tears welling up again as she set Lemuel's brown bag and the mail on the lamp table, alongside a flower bouquet spilling out of the top of a ceramic goose.

The next day, Sunday, as Imo drove past Calvary on her way to Northside Hospital, she sped up. She willed her eyes to stay on the road in front of her. But out of the corner of her vision she could tell that the parking lot was deserted and that several letters had fallen off of the roadside marquis that Martha was so proud of.

Imo figured the place was falling apart without Martha. And without the Reverend Peddigrew. For he spent every second at the hospital. Sometimes when Imo was there beside Martha she felt like she was intruding. Like she shouldn't be there at such a personal time. She thought of the way the Reverend moved his long-fingered hands along Martha's face.

That was how she felt today as she breezed into Martha's room and leaned over the cool metal rails of her bed. "Howdy, howdy, hon," she said into Martha's face.

The Reverend stood against the far wall. He was tall and gaunt, in a pair of billowing overalls held up by red suspenders. He wore a haggard expression that made him look almost as bad as Martha. Dark bags under his eyes, cheeks sunken, and skin so pasty it was gray. Maybe the doctors ought to check him out, too.

Imo said, "How're you holding up, Lemuel?"

"I'm right tired, Imogene," he said, shaking his head slowly from side to side.

"You need to rest then," Imo said. "I'll be here until nine or so. You go on home and try to get some sleep, you hear?"

"I don't think I can leave her side," he said.

"Look at you, though," she said, "you look awful."

He held up his hand. "I don't care how I look. How I feel either. I can't leave her." He fiddled with one suspender and cleared his throat. "I can't bear to think of her slipping away while I'm not here." His eyes swept over Martha.

Imo watched him curiously. Life's trials were just as hard on a man of God, she thought. For some reason she'd half expected him to laugh in the face of calamity, to rise above earthly pain.

Hollow-eyed, he wrung his hands together. "I can't bear to let her go," he said softly.

"I know, you love her so." Imo fumbled with the words.

"I've *begged* God. Pleaded with Him, 'Take me first,' I asked Him." He raised his face heavenward. Tears dribbled from his eyes.

Imo felt tears in her own eyes.

" . . . can't bear it," the Reverend was saying. "I'm not handling this too well. My life. She is my life, my heart's desire." He swallowed hard. He pounded his fist into his other palm. "You can't possibly know," he said, looking to Imo.

"I do know," she said. "It wasn't three years ago I lost my Silas."

He regarded her a moment. She did not blink. She held her ground.

"You're right," he finally said in a hoarse whisper.

"I know exactly how you're feeling, Lemuel," she said, hugging her arms against the ache inside. "You feel angry. You feel scared. Hopeless. Sometimes you feel like an actor in a play."

He nodded. Shuffled his feet just like a small child.

"You'll get better," Imo said, her voice shaking. "Given time, you'll be stronger. Believe me, you'll be okay when she . . ." She stopped herself just in time. "But she may pull through! We shouldn't talk like this! We have to hold on to our hope, you hear me, Lemuel?"

He nodded again.

Yessum, she thought, *you had to cling to hope. You couldn't just crumple up and give in.* But a wave of despair swept over her, as familiar as her own skin it carried with it a hopelessness borne of exhaustion. For Martha, for Lemuel's sake, she had to cast it off. She must. It would not do for her to crumble, too.

She bustled around the tiny room, tidying the flower arrangements lining the deep windowsill and then fishing Lemuel's supper from the hamper on the floor near her handbag. There was a still-warm pork chop, rice, black-eyed peas, and some candied yams. She unwrapped a corn muffin from a pouch of tinfoil and set the ever-present thermos of sweet tea near his elbow. She'd brought the newspaper, too, and a paperback of crossword puzzles along with a sharp pencil. She fluffed the bed pillow he'd brought from home.

She noted that his overalls were stained all down the front. "You have more clothes you can change into?" she asked him. He shook his head.

"Well, I'll fetch some on my way in tomorrow. Then you can give those to me and I'll wash them and press them and bring them back for you."

He cocked his head. "What?"

"I said I'll get clean clothes for you," she said. "Your razor, too. Your hairbrush, comb, whatever you need."

"You don't need to do that," he said. He slumped into the chair and stared at Martha. "It's good of you to be here with her. That's enough."

"Lemuel, it's nothing. It's the very least I can do. I *want* to be here," she said with a shake of her head. "Eat," she said, "keep your strength up."

The fork trembled in Lemuel's hand. "This is real good of you, Imogene. You don't know how—"

The door opened and a nurse came in. "Time for our bath," she said. The Reverend rose from his chair in an awkward, almost shy manner. Imo could tell how uncomfortable he was.

I should go on home, she thought, *let him deal with this private matter alone.* "I'll see you tomorrow, Lemuel," she said, "and I'll bring you some fresh clothes and things." She left quickly, walking numbly to the parking lot.

She drove back to Euharlee only vaguely conscious of the other cars on the road. Her thoughts were on coping. How could she handle this? Today had been the first time Martha had not woken up to speak to her. And it was excruciating to see the way Lemuel's eyes rarely left Martha, as if he were scared to turn away lest she fly away. Every time Martha moved, or made a noise, Imo saw how stiff he became, how he even seemed to stop breathing. Martha just couldn't die on them.

Imo walked into the house to find Lou sitting at the kitchen table in her nightgown doing her lessons. She looked young and vital there with the light above the table shining on her soft brown hair. She'd been very withdrawn lately. First there was Elmer's death that hit her hard, and now there was Martha's critical condition, which meant Imo had to rely on her so much.

Lou looked up as Imo appeared, holding her pencil in midair. "Hey," she said.

Imo sat down across from her. "Hey to you, sugar foot." She watched the child's face. She could almost see the despair in her eyes, too. "Things go all right while I was gone?"

"Fine." Lou chewed her lip.

"Get enough supper?"

"Yep," answered Lou.

"Mama behave?"

"She did okay. Fussed with Jeanette some."

"That's no surprise." Imo smiled, reached across to pat her arm. "I surely do appreciate you watching Mama so I can go see Martha." She glanced at the book near Lou's elbow. "Doing your arithmetic?"

Lou nodded and looked into Imo's eyes. She could tell from the girl's hesitation that she wanted to say something more. "Well," Imo said, "that's good. Keep up your lessons and make good marks and you'll go far. Soon school will be out for the summer, won't it? And we'll have to have us a graduation party for Jeanette. We can make us a cake with a diploma out of icing on top." She smiled at the thought.

There was a long moment of silence.

"Jeannie hasn't been going to school. She hasn't been in weeks," Lou said in a high, thin voice. "She said she's already flunked math." She watched Imo. "English, too. She flunked English."

Imo's jaw dropped. She felt like she'd just been punched in the gut. She looked over Lou's head, to a skillet hanging on the wall. A reminder that Jeanette couldn't cook worth a flip. No education. No homemaking skills. A sure recipe for a sad life. For herself and that sweet baby. "Jeannie *can't* quit school!" Imo sputtered. "I swannee, Lou, I don't know how she can be so selfish! Who does she think will raise Little Silas if she can't earn a living? Hmm?" She raised her eyebrows as she looked at Lou.

"Beats me," Lou said, shrugging. "I tried to talk her into staying in."

"What did she say?"

"Nothing. You know how stubborn she can be."

"Hmph!" Imo looked at Lou's expectant face. "Don't you worry over it, sugar foot. I'll try and talk some sense into the girl," she promised.

*   *   *

Now a week had passed, and still Imo had not confronted Jeanette. She stood in the garden, refurbishing the mulch around her okra and lima beans, keeping an eye on the low, threatening clouds overhead as she worked.

These days she timed her trips to the garden with Little Silas's naps and Mama's TV shows, and as she left the house, she carefully locked the deadbolts to the front and the back doors. The keys and the phone rattled around in the same pocket as the baby monitor receiver.

In the afternoons, Imo put Lou in charge as she made her daily trek to Northside Hospital. Martha came in and out of consciousness, with no apparent improvement according to Dr. Chapman. Though today was Garden Club day, they'd unanimously agreed to cancel this month's meeting. Anyway, Martha was the president and the program chairman, and what Imo feared, what they all must fear, judging by Florence Byrd's voice over the phone, was that the club would disintegrate without Martha.

A sharp ache filled Imo's chest as she pinched a sucker off a tomato vine. A cold something hit the back of her neck. Was that a raindrop? Were those clouds up there fixing to let go? She raised her face to see, and her cheeks and forehead were pelted with rain. Well, she shouldn't resent the rain—they surely needed it. Euharlee had been dry as a bone for the past month and she had half a mind to stay outside anyway. After all, this was her paradise, her little bit of heaven on earth.

But the rain began to beat down harder, darkening the dirt and making the tomato leaves shimmy, and a bolt of lightning lit up the sky. "Well, well," she said to herself, "reckon I'd better get on back in the house."

Mama was reclined in the La-Z-Boy with her mouth open, her raucous snores filling the den. Imo turned off the TV as she passed by on the way to the bedroom to change out of her damp clothes. She returned to the kitchen and fixed herself a cup of coffee.

Too bad about the rain coming when it did, she mused as she sipped her coffee. Her one little window to get out there in the garden.

Got to make hay while the sun shines, Imogene. She could hear Mama saying this. She squeezed her eyes shut tight and buried her face in her hands to fight against the terrible memory that threatened.

But it was inevitable, and sitting there in the gray kitchen, with her hair still damp, and dirt underneath her fingernails, Imo could feel every nerve in her body standing alert. She was thirteen again, standing on the porch staring through the screen as Mama, furious and rigid, breathed down her neck. In this remembrance, torrents of rain were falling. Lightning flashed, and when it did, a bright picture of the morning's laundry still on the line, hanging in sodden clumps.

"I'm sorry," Imo murmured as her forehead fell against the screen, "so very, very sorry, Mama. Please, forgive me."

Mama's agitation only increased with each plea from Imo's lips. "Such an idiotic thing you did, girl! . . . Left it out there . . . where was your mind? . . . When will you ever learn? . . . You've got to make hay while the sun's shining, Imogene Rose!" she cried. "I just don't know what's going to become of such a stupid girl as you. I'll teach you to forget! Out, out." She shoved Imo outside into the raging storm and locked the door behind her.

Imo stumbled out into the driving rain. She fell to her knees at first, covering her head from fear of the lightning all around her. At last, she got to her feet. Chin quivering, she half ran through sloppy puddles, stumbled over bits of grass, then practically fell forward into the small stone building that was the well-house. Leaning against the cold wall of this sanctuary, she cried bitter tears, her chest heaving.

She stayed until the distance between her and Mama was enough.

From the receiver came Little Silas's cries. Shaken, pulling herself out of memory, Imo rose to get him. She passed by Mama, who was still asleep and still snoring away. Darn her, thought Imo, darn her for making it so hard to love her. To forgive her. To take care of her.

At five, Imo was on the way to Northside Hospital. She was carrying supper to Lemuel—meat loaf, scalloped potatoes, green beans, and rolls. She was also carrying a heart full of her own troubles. She hadn't slept in two nights from worrying over Jeanette, and now she was reeling emotionally from the day's terrible recollection.

You must leave your own troubles at the door of Martha's room, she admonished herself. It wouldn't do for her to bring anything but cheer to the sickbed of her dearest friend.

She knocked softly, opened the door, and swept in with as bright a face as she could muster. She was alarmed to see Reverend Peddigrew sitting there, wringing his hands, with red eyes, a pink nose, and the shadowy stubble of a beard.

"She's not . . ." escaped Imo, as her eyes frantically sought Martha's face. No, she wasn't. A weak smile spread across Martha's lips as her eyeballs cut over to Imo's direction.

"Well, hello there!" Imo exclaimed. "Got ourselves some rain today! Yes, we did. And, oh, it was heaven-sent!"

She could feel Lemuel's eyes on her and she met his gaze. *I'm glad you're here,* it said.

"Why don't you go get a cup of coffee, Lemuel," Imogene said. "We've got some girl-talking to do." She bent toward Martha to tell her about the fertilizer she'd put on her early-flowering bulbs.

"Yessum," she said. "Got that on before the good rain came." She smiled again. This was so difficult.

"You look tired, Imogene," Martha murmured, her brows knit in concern. "I reckon I'm running you ragged with coming to see me every day."

"No!" Imo said, "you're not! It's not you at all!" She held her breath. What could she blame it on? "It's my allergies!" she said, laughing like that was the funniest thing on earth.

"You don't have allergies, Imogene Lavender." Martha's head moved ever so slightly from left to right. Her eyes penetrated Imo's face. "Tell me what it really is. If it's not me, and it's not allergies, what's bothering you, hon?"

Imo's mind churned. She hadn't even begun here, today, to bring cheer, and now her plan was crumbling. She cleared her throat and swallowed, buying time. "Well," she said finally.

"Well what?" Martha said.

Imo drew a deep breath. "Jeanette wants to drop out of school," she blurted with a teary laugh.

There was a brief pause, then Martha sighed. "Oh, Imogene. Why in the world haven't you called Wanda about it? She could straighten the girl out. Wanda dropped out of high school three different times before she went back and got her diploma!"

"You're absolutely right!" Imo exclaimed, her mind racing to thoughts of Wanda, whose high school diploma hung proudly in the Kuntry Kut 'n' Kurl, right above the hair dryer, and beside her beauty college diploma.

"Wanda comes by every morning to see me, Imogene, and I'm going to tell her to have a talk with Jeanette," Martha said. "Always good to have that diploma. Shows you finish what you start." Then Martha really grinned. "Plenty of good reasons to stay in school, Wanda says. She says she decided to dig her heels in and graduate because she realized you can't depend on a man." Martha's chest shook with laughter. "And you know how many men that girl's been through!"

Imo smiled. "Thank you, Martha. I surely do appreciate you doing that for us."

Martha nodded. She didn't look dismayed over Imo's troubles one bit. On the contrary, she was noticeably brighter. "Glad I could help," she said. She lay there quiet, but seemingly happy. "Got any new 'Adventurous Life of Mama Jewell' stories for me?" she asked after a bit.

"No," Imo sighed, "sorry, but I most certainly do not."

"You don't?" Martha looked disappointed. "No more about her running off? No more stories on the great Depression or about the Baptists?"

"No, no." Imo folded her hands in her lap.

"There's something else wrong, isn't there, hon?" Martha said. "I can tell. I can see it in your eyes."

"No," Imo insisted. "I'm just a bit tired is all."

This was not true. For some reason, it was today's recollection of her early life with Mama that had pushed Imo to the breaking point. She was bone weary from shouldering the burdens at home and from fighting the bitter feelings toward Mama.

"You're wore out on account of me," Martha said. "You've been running the wheels off your car and wearing yourself out to tend to me and Lemuel." She stuck her bottom lip out and knit her brow so that she looked sad. "I feel just terrible."

Imo stiffened. "It's not that a bit," she said. Now she was torn.

"Tell Martha," Martha said.

Imo flushed under her scrutiny. "It's Mama," she stammered, squeezing her hands into fists.

"Tell me all about it, dear," Martha said softly.

God, give me strength, Imo prayed as she drew a deep, long breath. "Martha," she began, "life with Mama hasn't always been so hilarious or so entertaining . . . and I've got a confession to make. You've got to believe me when I say I've wanted to pour my heart out to you a jillion times about this. I mean it. I said to myself not long ago, I said, 'Imogene, why can't you tell your dearest friend in all the world about how you're feeling? About your relationship to Mama when you were growing up?' But you've got to understand, Martha, it hurts me to even think them, much less say them aloud. Yes, it physically hurts, and I'd really rather just ignore the past and move on along. But I realize I can't. Since Mama's come to live with us, I can't escape the painful memories and the ugly feelings." Imo shook her head. Her heart was beating like crazy.

Imo placed a hand on Martha's wrist. "I know I should have told you all this before and I hope you're not angry with me. I'm going to tell it all to you now. I really am."

Martha's eyebrows were high and her eyes opened wide. "Okay, tell me, Imogene," she insisted, "you ought to know you can't shock me. I'm a minister's wife, I've heard it all and then some."

Imo began slowly, her fingernails cutting pink moons in her palms. "Growing up, Mama mistreated me. Fussed me out and made me feel worthless more times than I can count. Cussed me. Screamed. Threatened. Hit me with the hickory switch. Locked me out of the house. Over nothing, really, I realize now. Nothing but childish mistakes. She did it out of pure meanness." Imo closed her eyes with a sigh. "Or mental illness, I really don't know which."

Martha opened her mouth. "I'm so sorry, Imogene," she murmured finally, tears pooling in the corners of her eyes. "It really hurts, doesn't it, dear?"

Imo had been staring off into space. "Yes," she said, "it really, really does." Her nose was running into her mouth.

"Get you a tissue on that table over there, hon. Blow your nose," Martha ordered. After a moment, she spoke softly to Imogene's back. "I wish I could erase all those ugly memories for you," she said, "you sit back down and tell me every single thing. Don't leave anything out."

Imo took a deep breath. She would do just that. Every detail she could remember, she would speak aloud here in this tiny hospital room. A part of her sensed that this would be what would lighten her load. Whether it would be by allowing her to release the burden of guilt over hoarding her pain to herself, or by just airing it out in the open, like laundry on the line, she did not know.

She was conscious of nothing else but Martha's intent gaze looking up at her as she let the words tumble out, every last shred of her memories.

"What hurt even worse, Martha," Imo continued, "is that she used to say the ugliest things to me. Like how she wished I wasn't ever born, or that I was a boy. Or that I was stupid and would never amount to anything. I can't forget them and I can't forgive her and it hurts me so bad." Imogene slumped into the recliner beside Martha's head and buried her face in her hands.

There was a long pause. Imo sat there, feeling like she'd just been run over by a long train.

"Do you see why it's hard for me to have her there with me now, Martha?" she asked finally. "Bending over backward the way I have to, to tend to her?"

"Listen, Imogene," Martha said, "I don't mean to sound ugly, but why in heaven's name have you taken her in?" She was genuinely puzzled. "I mean, wasn't she living in one of those old folks' homes?"

"She's got no money left. Nothing." Imo cleared her throat. "Plus, Martha, the Bible says," her voice began to tremble like crazy, "to honor your mother and father." She covered her face with her hands. "I guess I'm just not doing too well with that commandment, now, am I?"

"Wait a minute here now. Just wait a minute," Martha said, "you shouldn't be beating yourself up about that, because you *are* honoring her! You certainly don't *have* to take her in. No one's holding a gun to your head and forcing you to do it."

Imo nodded, though she had no idea what Martha was getting at.

"So, it's your *choice,* hon. Out of the goodness of your heart you're doing this. You're returning good for evil. You're not looking for any thanks. You're the bigger person for treating her so well. In the book of Romans," Martha continued, "it says not to repay evil with evil, not to take revenge. God says 'Vengeance is Mine, I will repay.' He says if your enemy is hungry, feed him. If he's thirsty, give him a drink. It says when you do that, you're heaping coals of fire on his head." Martha nodded. "So, of course you're honoring her, dear! You're overcoming evil with good. I think you're doing a great job!"

"You do?" Imogene said, a bit giddy now.

"Shoot, yes, hon," Martha said.

"I don't *have* to do it," Imo said. Then she was silent a moment as a bit of relief washed through her. She listened to Martha's labored breathing, the click and whir of all the machines hooked up to her. Her mind began to turn again, however, and she realized that her confession was incomplete.

She turned halfway in her seat, her face to the wall. "I have another confession to make, Martha," she began in a repentant tone. "I still feel the meanest things you could imagine toward her. I don't seem to be able to let it all go." She stomped her foot. "And I *hate* feeling this way. I don't want to live like this!"

Martha gazed up at the ceiling. "It's a heavy load to bear, isn't it, Imogene?" she said at last. "A heavy load of bitterness and resentment."

Imo nodded. "I can't turn around but there's another recollection coming at me just like a raging bull, with a big load of ugly, hateful feelings." Imo tightened her grip on the chair's armrests.

Martha's eyebrows knit in deep contemplation. At last she nodded her head happily. She took a moment to gather her thoughts. "Why, I know what you should do, Imogene Lavender. The Good Book says to dwell on the fine, good things. It will help you if you can just train yourself to think about the good things in your mother. When those bad memories come at you, when you're feeling angry and bitter toward her and mad at yourself because of it, drag up some good things about her and just dwell on them." Martha looked very pleased with herself then. She smiled and sighed.

Imo looked at her incredulously.

"Surely there is something good she gave to you, dear," Martha said. "Some wonderful thing about her that she passed on to you."

Imo bit her lip. She searched her brain furiously. "If there is, I cannot think of it!" she exclaimed. "In fact, I am sure of it, there is absolutely nothing good to dwell on in Mama. Nothing she gave me in my raising-up years. All I ever wanted from the time I knew any better was to get away from her and all these memories. To be free! And look, here I am, the one having to take care of her. There is nothing good she ever gave to me!"

Martha smiled. "Don't be so sure about that, dear."

Imo stood and turned to face the window. "You've got to help me, Martha," she said. "I honestly can't think of a single good thing about her."

"Give it time," Martha reassured her, "you will discover it."

As she drove along home that evening, Imo was not exactly sure what had happened. She was still exhausted, yes, but unfathomably lighter, and strangely clean. She was feeling clear of mind like a sharp, cold winter day, and wondering just who had brought cheer to whom back there at Northside Hospital.

Loutishie's Notebook

Dewy Rose won't fly up into the low branches to roost at night anymore. Maybe the memories get to her too bad. Since Elmer drowned she's taken to sleeping in the barn with Bingo. He lies sprawled on his side up on a smelly pallet of old croker sacks, and she is a perfect fit for the space between his paws.

I saw them there this morning before dawn as I made my way down to the bottoms to think. I sat on the banks of the Etowah and watched it flowing along without a care in this world as the sun slowly rose. *The river gives and the river takes away,* I thought, as I stirred a stick in the water's edge.

I had thought my love for Elmer was stronger than the river, but I should have known by then that you can't count on forever for anything. I shouldn't have been the least bit surprised when he went swirling away. Because it was here, along this very stretch of river, that Uncle Silas had told me about his cancer. And thinking of dying, Jeanette had said the previous evening that Martha Peddigrew was going to be death number three. "Martha's fixing to croak," Jeanette said. "I saw them towing her car the day after the wreck and it was flat as a pancake where the driver's seat is."

I didn't doubt Jeanette. Martha was in such terrible shape that Imo went every day to see her. She'd come home saying stuff about how Martha was going to rise up out of that hospital bed and go home, but no one else believed her. I was proud to help Imo out by keeping an eye on Mama Jewell while she went to the hospital, and I had sense enough by then not to let the old woman out of my sight. It was boring, all right, but I kept thinking it might somehow help atone for my sins, which had gotten to be so many by then that I couldn't even keep track of them.

Watching the river glide on by, I knew if Jesus came to blow the trumpet, I would be left sitting right there. Certainly Imo would be gone, and pure Little Silas. They'd be up there in heaven with Uncle Silas and Fenton Mabry and I'd be stuck down here with Jeanette. Fear clutched at my heart.

I considered Mama Jewell. Would she rise up? Mama Jewell's eternal fate was anybody's guess, though she certainly didn't seem to be worried about it. She was seldom worried about anything for long, and she never worried enough to lose a night of sleep over what was going on today or what tomorrow might bring.

To add to my misery, I was worried that Imo was heading down Mama Jewell's path. It sure seemed like she was slipping. "Want me to help you?" I had asked her the previous Saturday. She was standing in the garden, tying up the pole beans.

"No, Loutishie," she said, shaking her head. "You run along and play with Jeanette."

I didn't say a word, but me and Jeanette were way past playing. At the time, I figured she must be going backward, in reverse, like Mama Jewell, and she must have thought me and Jeanette were back to ages six and nine or something.

I looked real hard at her and I noticed her eyes weren't really connecting with the pole beans she held, but it was her undereye bags that really worried me. She had deep, puffy gray pouches, and so I decided she was just wore out from going back and forth to see Martha all the time.

Still, it hurt me that she didn't want me underfoot. I craved to talk to her about finding my father. I wanted to ask her if she knew anything about him. But I couldn't do it because we were in the middle of that same old stick-your-head-in-the-sand game that we always played when unpleasant things came up.

So I held a little pity party for myself. Imo was exhausted, Jeanette kept her mind on beautifying her outsides and chasing Montgomery Pike, and Mama Jewell was as crazy as ever. And that left me with no one in the whole wide world. At school I did see Tara, but since Imo depended on me to watch Mama Jewell each afternoon and on weekends, too, I felt like the loneliest soul on earth. An island unto myself.

What I was pinning my hopes on, still, was finding my father. With my new clue, I would find him, I knew it. And when I did I wouldn't be alone ever again. I dreamed of the two of us together a lot and I didn't allow myself to even think of not finding him. I *had* to find him.

I concentrated on my plan, which consisted of trying to wrangle a time to get myself over to Tara's house and convince her to go back up Buzzard Mountain with me. I figured since I had more information on him, surely someone there would know something. Every morning I thought to myself, maybe today—though I never mentioned this to Imo. I always said "Sure, I'd be happy to" whenever she asked that ever-present question about keeping an eye on Mama Jewell for her while she went to visit Martha.

Day after day went by like this, with me cooped up in the house watching Mama Jewell. I got a terrible case of cabin fever, until finally, one Saturday, I was free. It was late in the day and I stood on the back porch. The sky was low and threatening, but still I didn't want to hang around inside the house for another minute. What I needed was the wind in my hair and the open sky above me.

I slipped out and followed the dirt road down to the bottoms, whistling for Bingo, who did not come. He was deathly afraid of storms, and more than likely huddled up underneath the back porch with Dewy Rose, as close to the door of the house as he could get, hoping Imo would take pity on him and let him inside.

Being alone at this exact moment was not altogether bad. I wanted to use the solitude to think, to plan my strategy for getting back up Buzzard Mountain.

The Etowah looked like frothy chocolate milk, with bubbles here and there at the edge of rocks. I heard a few birds making noise in the woods on the other side as I walked along beside the water, hunting for Indian arrowheads. To the east the sky was almost pitch black, but looking over my shoulder to the west, there were only long streaks of wispy gray clouds.

By and by, I chose a spot to sit down and stare at the water. I thought of the most comforting things I could. I pictured me and Tara walking boldly back up Buzzard Mountain, meeting my father and us laughing as he carried us in his customized van into Cartersville to the Shoney's to meet her dad. We ate strawberry pie. Tara wished her dad could be as handsome and fun as mine.

I'm not sure how long I was there, it must've been close to an hour, but I hardly noticed when the clouds let go of the rain. Under my canopy of leaves, I sat happily dreaming of my future. I wanted nothing more than to feel myself in my father's strong, secure arms. I wrapped my arms around my knees.

The storm arrived in full force, with jagged flashes of lightning and thunder that shook the ground underneath me. Finally, it was enough to send even me back up to the house.

As soon as I pushed open the door I knew something was different. I paused in front of Mama Jewell's empty La-Z-Boy. The den was gray and still, the loud silence too strange. I glanced out the window and saw the Impala underneath the shed.

They're all outside, I told myself, as a tremendous boom of thunder shook the house. It also cleared my head of that crazy idea. I walked into each of the bedrooms, flipping on every light and lamp as I went.

No one.

There was not another living soul in the house. Naturally, I figured Imo had left a note for me, so I walked into the dusky blueness of the kitchen. No note. I checked the answering machine. Nothing there either.

Finally I walked out to the well-house, the potato house, and the barn. I opened up the driver's door of the Impala just to be sure they weren't sitting inside for some reason.

No need to panic, I tried to convince myself. Surely there was some logical explanation. I walked back to the house where Bingo joined me hesitantly from his dry spot underneath the porch. I slapped my thigh and Dewy Rose emerged as well. I let them come into the kitchen with me. We made our way into the den and turned the TV on pretty loud until another huge blast of thunder shook the pictures on the wall. I unplugged the TV and sat there on the rug with Bingo and Dewy Rose.

Into the silence came these questions: Where in the world would all four of them go together on a late Saturday afternoon without the car? Mama Jewell sure couldn't walk too far, and Jeanette wouldn't leave the house without her pocketbook, bulging with cigarettes, a mirror, a makeup pouch, her round brush, and a tiny bottle of Aqua Net. It was hanging on one poster of her bed. And Imo wouldn't leave me like this without a note.

I felt the hairs on the back of my neck stand on end.

Bingo and Dewy Rose lay down together on the rug, and I decided to call over to Tara's. I dialed the number and in my mind I could see the pink poodle-shaped phone in her room ringing amid her collection of plastic quarter horses. Thirty-nine rings and no one picked up. I stood there waiting for something to happen. Outside it had gotten as dark as midnight with the rain coming down in sheets and a tiny new moon. I could feel the current of electricity raising hairs all over my body. Bingo came to me, stiff and alert. In response to sirens far out on Paris Road, his throat quivered. "Arrooo," he howled seriously.

In my fuzzy brain, I connected the sirens with car wrecks, and the car wrecks with those scary bumper stickers about the Rapture; the ones that say Warning: In Case of Rapture, This Car Will Be Unmanned. I pictured the roads in and around Euharlee with cars crunched bumper to bumper, some off on the shoulders, upside down, tires still spinning.

A sudden and utter helplessness washed over me. It was definitely the

Rapture! The time was at hand and I had been left behind! I dropped to my knees in a panic, thrust my damp hair out of my face, and extended my arms heavenward. I began to beg for mercy and grace and pardon. "Please, Most Gracious Heavenly Father," I pleaded, my words tumbling out crazily, "please take me up, too! I'm sorry for all my sins. I repent! Please! My heart is sorrowful! I know I am a sinner, and I don't deserve Your mercy, but please, Lord, you've got to forgive me and let me rise up through the clouds with the saints! Please, Lord!" Bingo cocked his head to regard me curiously as I fell prostrate on the floor.

"Please, please, pretty please," I moaned finally into the rug, having nothing else left to say. Bingo crept over to me and began to lick my face. Deep in my brain, I knew that I'd been left behind rightly. My heavenly account was so far in the red, there was no way I could have heard that trumpet blowing. I had sure enough blown it.

At that point I went into the kitchen and lay down on the dingy linoleum. I just wondered how in the world Jeanette had made it. Then I decided that she'd probably got salvation sometime recently, at one of her choir rehearsals. I hadn't really talked to her for weeks. Hadn't she gone to one of Reverend Pike's special Wednesday night services last week? Perhaps she'd gotten her slate clean then and it had been easy enough to keep it that way for just a few days. That girl had squeaked by! She'd grabbed onto the Reverend Pike's coattails and gone sliding through those pearly gates in the nick of time.

That didn't seem fair. Babies had it easy, too. Their capacity to sin was so small or not even there. And really old people could repent of all their sins, and then keep their slates clean easily enough. They'd had their fun, gotten it out of their systems, and righteousness could come easily. But for people in my age bracket—the young, unmarried, able-bodied, and hormone-driven— the odds of being ready for the Rapture were low.

I sat at the kitchen table, still in shock, and I wondered if God realized how unfair His system was. Look at me, I said to myself, I am beyond salvation, so I may as well go on and go all the way now.

I strode over in an angry huff and reached above the Frigidaire into a dark corner of the cabinet for the dusty bottle of rum Imo used each Christmas to make rum balls. Unscrewing the cap, I sniffed it. It was so strong it made my eyes water, but I held my nose and forced myself to swallow a good bit of the nasty stuff. I leaned against the counter and waited for the worldly pleasures Reverend Peddigrew talked about to begin.

I was beginning to feel fuzzy-headed and kind of giggly as I walked to the bedroom and got down Jeanette's carton of Marlboros. I carried them into the kitchen. It took me a while to get one lit up and take a puff on it, and when I did, I almost choked to death. It sure looked easy when Jeanette did it.

I opened the Frigidaire and drank the last Pepsi while I thought about things. It was all Mama Jewell's fault that my heavenly account was in such bad shape. If she hadn't come to live with us, then Imo wouldn't have gotten wore out and Jeanette wouldn't be fighting with Mama Jewell all the time and making Imo so upset, and I wouldn't have had those evil, impure thoughts about wanting Mama Jewell to die. I would have been content enough with my life and I wouldn't be having to search for my father, which is what caused me to lie and steal. I shook my head. If if if.

Well, I shrugged, slumping down and not feeling too bad at all by then, I would just have to face the music and live in this big house by myself. That got me to thinking about who else was going to be left down here. Definitely Tara. Her mom, too. That woman was the definition of gossip.

But it was sure hard to imagine the world's population without any babies or small kids and not too many old folks. Imo told me once that she reckoned just about all the politicians would still be here after the Rapture. She also mentioned a few folks at Calvary Baptist she thought would stay around. All the movie stars would still be here, too. As far as students and teachers at Euharlee High went, it was hard to say, but Tara and I could talk about everyone that was gone.

To get some peace of mind, I focused on the bits and pieces I remembered from Reverend Peddigrew's sermon, where he talked about what happened to people left behind. A person still had a chance to make it into heaven if they missed the first boat, but I thought I remembered him saying it was going to be hard. Back then I was just so sure I was going to make it on the first boat that I paid little attention to that part of his sermons.

It hurt me no end when I realized that I could have been talking to God and Uncle Silas at that moment if I'd only kept my feet on the straight and narrow path. I could have asked God what they were planning to do with all the animals. I walked through the house then, filled with an endless stream of regrets for my sneaky ways. Bingo kept up his howling with another slew of sirens, so I fed him a pack of ground beef Imo was saving for tomorrow night's hamburgers. I certainly couldn't eat all that by myself and it would hush him up.

When the rain began to ease, I picked up the phone to try Tara again. Dead. I decided to walk to Tara's. It would be hard to walk the five miles past all those wrecked cars and bawling folks, but I would have to get out there and connect with what was left of the human race at some point.

"Come on, boy," I said to Bingo, heaving myself up and trying to will some life into my flesh. I felt like a boneless chicken in the vitality department.

I went slowly at first, with Bingo miserably slinking along beside me. I thought about heaven and this picture formed in my brain of Imo, Mama Jewell, Jeanette, and Little Silas running into Uncle Silas up there. He asked them, "Where's my Loutishie?" and then, crazy, like a delayed reaction, tears started streaming out of my eyes.

About that same time the rain started up again but I hardly noticed it as I trudged along like a zombie in *The Twilight Zone* reruns. I kept biting my lower lip to make sure that this was really happening.

Bingo and I were halfway to the Dairy Queen when I realized how dizzy I was. I thought it must be on account of being hungry, but still, I didn't even want to think about eating. "C'mon, let's run, boy!" I hollered to Bingo, and broke into a wobbly trot to get the journey over with. I really needed to see Tara's face.

There was a stitch in my side by the time I spied the DQ sign over the treetops, and then, around the bend in the road, came the blue lights of the sheriff's patrol car. Here was Euharlee's ambassador to reassure the unsaved fragments of society left out in the rural areas! For a moment I was ready to wave him on by and holler that I already knew all about what had happened. But then I decided that a ride to Tara's would be nice.

"Hey, little lady." Sheriff Bentley pulled over and slid his window down.

"Hi," I said, wondering if he could smell the rum on my breath.

"Where you headed to, Lou?"

"Friend's house," I said.

He took a deep breath. I could tell he was fixing to tell me something serious. I shivered in my soggy clothes.

"Get in a minute," he said gently.

I knew it! I told Bingo to sit and I climbed in as the windshield wipers slapped at the rain. The sheriff adjusted his gun holder and cleared his throat. "There's been a little trouble," he said in the saddest voice.

I said, "I know. I know." I held up my hands, palms toward him.

He got quiet.

"Yep," I said. "No need to tell me. I know all about it."

"But your aunt told me you didn't have no way of knowing. Said they was in such a state that when the ambulance got there she plum forgot to ring the bell."

I had trouble computing all his crazy words. "Huh?"

"Yessum," he said. "She tried to call you from the hospital, but your phone line was out. The little fellow, Silas, I believe she called him, broke his foot. He was jumping off the back of the couch. Thought he'd broke his whole leg . . ." He was nodding and looking down at his lap.

I couldn't think of one thing to say. It was not the Rapture! I sat there shaking my head until Sheriff Bentley said, "I imagine we ought to get you on back home, little lady." He whistled for Bingo and opened the back door of the patrol car for him to jump in. I sure had a hard time getting to sleep that night. I couldn't stop turning the day over and over in my mind. Naturally, I felt a great sense of relief, and slowly I began to relax, stretching out flat in bed. I couldn't help thinking how jumpy and uptight I'd been over the whole incident and my cheeks flushed warm from embarrassment. Oh well, no one but Bingo and Dewy Rose knew about my stupid goof.

I decided then and there to ease up on myself. I determined to stop dwelling on the Lord coming back every second. I would stop fretting over the next life and have some fun living this one.

So I was going to loosen up some, but not totally. I still had a healthy respect for God's all-seeing eye and I reckoned that the day's events had been His wake-up call—telling me that I'd better straighten up and fly right. What I needed to do was come clean with Imo.

I was going to confess my lying, and my stealing, and my trip up to Buzzard Mountain to hunt my father, and also my plans to go back again.

Nine

The Promise

*I*mogene pulled two yellow crookneck squash from their vines. Still warm from the sun, she cradled one in each palm. Out of the corner of her eye she spied some cucumbers ready for picking.

The fruits of her labor were here! The garden was burgeoning with colors and shapes. Each summer she was as excited as a child at Christmas when it was time to pick the first of the season's produce. Sometimes she felt like the first person ever to harvest something to eat from a tiny seed she'd started. And yet it was all so familiar she could not explain it. Something she'd always known, something she wore like a second skin, or did unthinkingly, like breathing. She drew in a deep breath of warm marigolds and crushed tomato leaves, the smell of summer itself. A smell that sent her to a good place. It was especially good today as she contemplated making her daily trek to Northside Hospital.

She looked over at Mama now, asleep in a lawn chair near the edge of the sweet corn. A straw hat sat askew on her head and her mouth hung open stupidly in sleep. Her handbag sat on her lap, the sun glinting blue off its shiny black-patent side.

The burden that Imo had carried all those years was definitely lighter. Yes, Martha, the Lord bless her soul, had been right about one thing. Imo certainly didn't *have* to take care of Mama like she was. This was a pure gift Imo was giving, her choice to take care of someone who'd hurt her so deeply.

There was a tremendous sense of freedom and power inside of her whenever Imo let this knowledge soak in, when she realized that no one was holding a gun to her head, forcing her to take care of Mama. She took another deep breath. She was stronger now, though the healing was not complete because she was still searching for that fine, good thing in Mama to dwell on.

If Mama stayed asleep a while longer, and the baby monitor in her pocket stayed quiet, Imo would work on the mulch and also get her sweet potatoes planted. But even if Little Silas did wake up, the cast on his leg made him much easier to keep an eye on. The thought of unfettered time in the garden filled Imo with joy. She needed this to get herself pulled together before she went to see Martha.

Imo felt a pang for Martha. She ran her fingers along the tendril of a gourd vine, thinking *It will happen soon. It's been six weeks now and Martha is no better. She will certainly leave this world behind.*

Truly Martha was weaker. There were many visits where she did not speak. Yesterday, the light in her eyes was much dimmer. She was growing faint in the fight to keep herself alive and this was all scary to Imo. So unfathomable that Martha might leave.

Don't think about that, Imo. Think of the sturdy tomato vines, and the stalks of sweet corn shooting up a foot every day, and think of the beautiful okra blooms. Think of slicing open a Crimson Sweet watermelon on the picnic table over yonder. Think of carving a pumpkin for Little Silas in October. His sweet, dimpled cheeks . . .

But Imo could not shake an image of Martha's face from her last visit. In a way, Martha seemed to be almost relieved. Though physically much worse, she was somewhere above her circumstances; almost lightweight, floating, and so peaceful, as if she knew something no one else did. Imo felt her heart stop as she recalled how Martha went in and out of reality at times. One minute she was totally connecting with the world around her, engaging Lemuel and Imo in conversation, and the next going off somewhere else entirely. Unreachable.

Imo wondered where Martha went at those moments. She didn't think it was anywhere terrible, though, judging from the smile on her pale lips. Imo always sat numbly during these times. Breathing and just being. Pretending things were ordinary.

"It's time!" Mama bellowed, interrupting Imo's thoughts. Mama slapped the arm of her lawn chair, her head erect and her eyes like bullets. "It's time for my stories!"

Imo shook her head to clear it. She looked from Mama to the garden and back, and a hint of irritation rippled through her. *You could tell her off, Imo, then ignore her. Leave her be and just plant your sweet potatoes the way you want to. Because, like Martha said, you certainly don't have to pander to her now. She doesn't deserve to have you be this good to her.*

Imo grabbed the hoe from the wheelbarrow. She struck at the dirt hard. *Whack! Whack!* She went on making holes for the sweet potatoes. But after a minute of digging, she stole another look at Mama. She was sitting there expectantly, with that purse perched right up on her knees.

"Alrighty, Mama," Imo sighed, laying the hoe back down in the wheelbarrow, "let's get you on inside."

At four o'clock, Imogene backed the Impala out of the shed. She patted a sack of cucumbers on the seat beside her.

The day was sunny, with a sky as blue and clear as you could ask for. She could almost drive to Northside Hospital blindfolded by now and she barely noticed the traffic.

Frantically she was trying to think up pleasant chitchat to offer once she was there. Her hope that Martha would arise from her bed seemed pathetic now. Imo could put on a smile and act like things were wonderful, but inside she was crumbling.

The elevator stopped on Martha's floor. Imo clenched her teeth together and made her way down the hallway past the nurses' desk, where the women sitting there felt like family.

"Hello, Miz Lavender," one of them said, "so nice to see you." Was there something solemn and disturbing in her voice today, Imo wondered? Something different and cautious? Like she knew something Imo did not? Maybe a bit, well, sad?

Imo slowed down some, feeling uneasy as she put her knuckles against the door and knocked softly.

"Come in," Lemuel said.

Imo walked into a somber room. Lemuel looked worse than ever. Bent over, and defeated, he raised his whiskery head off a pillow in the recliner next to Martha. The flower bouquets were all drooping. A morgue of Styrofoam cups lay on the floor at his feet.

And Martha! She was asleep, but visibly smaller, shrunken almost. Her eyelids were a crepey gray and tissue thin.

Saddened by despair, Imo placed the sack of cucumbers on the floor. "How is she today?" she asked.

"No better," Lemuel said flat out, with no expression.

"First ones of the season." She patted the cucumbers, and he looked up at her.

"Thank you, Imogene," he said, then returned his gaze to his knees.

"Brought you some supper. Roast beef, potatoes, and carrots. A tat of corn bread, too."

He nodded his head ever so slightly in acknowledgment.

Imo's eyes moved to a hospital tray of lunch. Salisbury steak white with cold grease, and congealed lima beans. "You haven't eaten a thing today, have you, Lemuel?"

His head shook a tiny bit.

"But you *need* to eat!" she exclaimed. "Martha's going to have to get on to you!"

He shuffled his feet a bit and hunched forward even more when she scolded him. Imo noticed his shoulder blades protruding underneath the cotton back of his shirt and realized how rail thin he'd gotten.

Imo wagged her finger and spoke more sternly. "Eat!" she said, unloading the roast beef and the corn bread, arranging them on a Chinette plate. She brought out the potatoes and the carrots and sprinkled them with salt. Next she poured a glass of tea from the thermos and cut his meat into bites. She placed all of this on a tray with a napkin and a fork and set it atop his knees.

He looked up meekly. His face was drained. He peered into Imo's eyes and whispered, "Dr. Chapman says it's just a matter of time now."

Though Imo had known this instinctively, she felt like someone had punched her in the gut. She pounded her fist on her knee. "No!" she cried, spitting the word out. This couldn't be true! He was just befuddled from exhaustion and hunger. The same thing happened to her when she was weak physically. "No! No!" she said, pushing against his shins with her fists.

Somehow she had to get out of there. Stupidly she stood up, patting the front of her blouse. "I forgot to bring your dessert," she said to Lemuel. "Pecan pie. I'll just run home right now to fetch it." She bent to pick up her purse, feeling strangely detached, and turned so furiously with it that it slapped against a bouquet of mums on the windowsill, turning them over. A trickle of water made its way to the edge of the sill and drip, dripped.

"Don't go," Lemuel uttered, pathetically reaching an arm toward her as she stood with her hand on the doorknob. His eyes were so desperate, they fastened on her face and she felt them like the heat from a fire.

Something clutched in Imo's throat. It hurt her to speak. "All right," she managed to say, "I won't leave you." She returned to his side and reached for his hand.

He squeezed her fingers, his eyes fastened on Martha's face. "Could be any moment now."

Imo bit her lip hard. She had to talk with Martha. She felt her heart aching with a sense of urgency, of needing to speak with Martha at least one more time before she left. "Martha!" she pleaded, willing her to connect. She leaned closer, praying she'd come to.

Suddenly Martha's eyes fluttered open and sought Imo's. "Hello, hon," she murmured. Her cheeks were a feverish pink. "Glad you're here."

"Yes," Imo said, relieved, "me, too."

"You're a true friend. Lemuel tells me about every morsel you've been bringing to him," Martha said. "How your cooking's near about as good as mine is!" She tried to laugh at her own joke, but winced instead.

Martha's sudden chattiness worried Imo. "You don't have to talk, Martha," she cautioned, patting her shoulder. "You rest and I'll do the talking." Gentle things, she thought to herself. I'll say gentle things that won't make her laugh and hurt.

"But Imogene, there's something I need to ask you—"

"Hush now. Anyway, Martha, I've got the best news to tell you. Yes indeed." Imo sighed. She smiled at the memory of Wanda and Jeanette. She leaned over to tell it in an excited voice. "Wanda came out to the house Saturday. To wash and set Mama's hair, as usual, and she got through and she came on in the kitchen, where I was cooking up a mess of butter beans for supper. And so Jeanette came in, too. She always likes to visit with Wanda, you know. She sat down at the table and next thing I know, I'm putting a dollop of bacon fat into my butter beans and I overhear Wanda telling Jeanette that with her flair for doing hair and makeup and fingernails, that if she'd go on and go to summer school and finish up and get her high school diploma, that she'd pay her way to beauty college and make her a business partner at the Kuntry Kut 'n' Kurl. Course, I was acting like I wasn't listening. If Jeanette knew I was behind it, she'd pitch a fit. So I played dumb. Acted like I didn't hear a thing. I hummed. I rustled through the cabinets. Didn't even turn around. But I was just standing there smiling, stirring my pot of beans. Pretty soon I heard Jeanette and she said a cuss word. But not in a bad way. It meant she was excited. She says those words sometimes when she can't quite believe something. And she got all happy, jumping up and down and saying it was her destiny. Said she was going to get her diploma, and that nothing could stand in her way now. I was so tickled, Martha, I about burned up my butter beans. Plum forgot to turn them down to a simmer once they were boiling."

Martha started to laugh, but she winced again. Lemuel's fork stopped in midair.

"Don't you laugh!" Imo exclaimed quickly. "I shouldn't have told you I burned them. Jeanette will get her diploma now. She will have a future and that means Little Silas will have a future." Imogene gave one swift nod.

Martha stared up at her. "Now, Imogene, there's something I really need to—"

"Uh, uh, uh," Imo said, and wagged a finger at Martha. "You just leave the visiting to me."

"Please," Martha pleaded, "let me."

Imo could see the urgency in Martha's eyes. "Only if it's not funny," Imo replied.

"Oh, it's not funny." Martha's brow knit up.

There was a long pause, then Martha tried to mouth something to Imo. Her eyebrows scooted way up with the effort.

"Come on and let it out," Imo encouraged her. "Let it come on out." She laced her fingers, cocked her head to one side, and smiled thoughtfully.

Still, no more words came from Martha.

Imo looked hard at her. Definitely there was something Martha felt she needed to say, but at the same time was hesitant about. It was unthinkable for straightforward, heart-on-her-sleeve Martha to be tongue-tied. Imo decided that she was just choked up. Probably she was going to thank Imogene for feeding Lemuel, and visiting her daily. That was absurd, it was the least a person could do for their dearest friend.

"So!" Imo said cheerfully, "got my sweet potatoes planted. Surely did. Started to this morning, but Mama had to get back inside to her stories and Little Silas woke up when we went in, and I had to wait a little spell and put them in just before I headed to see you." Out of the corner of her eye, she saw Lemuel fork up a bite of meat.

Martha's brows shot way up high again. "Get close," she whispered so faintly Imo wondered if she'd really heard her.

She leaned in and moved her ear just inches from Martha's mouth.

"Send Lemuel out," Martha whispered, again so indistinct Imo could hardly hear her.

Imo was puzzled. This was certainly odd. Why in heaven's name did she want Lemuel to leave? And just when he was eating! She pulled away and looked hard at Martha. Searched her face for some kind of dementia, but all she saw were clear, pleading, dark brown eyes.

"Would you fetch me some coffee please, Lemuel?" Imogene turned to him.

He nodded, set the tray on the floor, unfolded himself from the chair, and moved silently out.

Imogene laced her fingers together in her lap, leaned forward, and smiled. "He's gone, dear. Now what did you want to say to me?" She held her breath and waited.

"He's helpless without a woman, Imogene," Martha said. "When God said it was not good for man to be alone, He meant it."

"Well," Imo said, startled by this comment and stalling for time, too. What was she supposed to say back to that? What comfort could she possibly offer to someone who was acknowledging her own impending death? "Um . . ." she said, "um . . . don't you worry about Lemuel. All us Garden Club girls are taking good care of him." That sounded so feeble! "You know we will keep looking in on him. We'll set up a continuing rotating schedule of meals, and do his laundry, too, when you're . . . ." Imo couldn't bring herself to say the word *gone,* so she put on a big smile and thought frantically of how to change the subject. "Speaking of Garden Club, Myrtice called me yesterday," she said, "wanted to know what I was fixing for the bake sale. I told her I'd do my red velvet cake and some pecan tassies, too. Those seem to sell fairly well, if I remember correctly."

"I'm going soon, Imogene. I need to get things in order." Martha's voice had a warning note in it.

"But you can't go, Martha. I—"

"Imogene!" Martha fixed her with a look. "What a selfish thing to say! I happen to know that the alternative is wonderful," she said sternly. "The best is yet to be. I know that now."

Martha seemed happy with what lay beyond. Ready, almost, to cross on over to Glory. Almost, but there was this thing she had to say first. Would she get it said? Imo could not fathom what it might be. "Lemuel will be back in a minute," she said, burning with curiosity.

"Lemuel," Martha murmured, with her eyes closed. "Lemuel James Peddigrew. Man of my heart."

This alarmed Imo. Why was she talking this way?

"A man who'll be alone," Martha said, "not good for him to be alone." She raised her chin, fixed her eyes on Imo's.

"Not good," Imo repeated. What was she supposed to say?

"I have to ask you something, Imo, dear."

"Okay. Ask then."

"Would you do something for me if I asked you to?"

"I'd do anything for you, Martha. You know that."

"Anything?"

"Anything."

"I want you to marry him."

Imo stared at all the tubes running from Martha's body. At the wafer-thin pillow behind her hair. At Martha's earlobes, covered in fine white downy hairs. Was this a dream? She blinked, she pressed a fingernail into her palm. It hurt. She must not be dreaming. Obviously, she had to be thinking to determine that she was not dreaming.

"Imogene?" she heard Martha's voice calling to her from a far-away place.

She squirmed in her chair. She closed her eyes.

"Oh my lands!" Martha whispered after several minutes had passed, "I've sent you into a spell. Oh my, oh my." She began to cry.

This brought Imo back to her senses. "I'm sorry, Martha," she said, "you just surprised me so." Her brain was in a tizzy, with a million different thoughts and memories—pictures of years past, specifically one from back when Silas was alive and the four of them rode up into the mountains to look at leaves one autumn, and how wonderful it had been, and now look! What was this crazy notion?! Why, she could not marry Lemuel!

She blinked against that thought. She swallowed hard.

"Well?" Martha whispered, eyeballs rolling up and beyond Imo to the door to make sure Lemuel was still gone.

Could she say "yes" to give Martha peace enough to go? Then get herself out of it? No, that would be lying. There was God to answer to, too. Surely there was a way out of this one. She could just offer to cook and clean and do for him. Like a wife but not a wife. She'd scrub that parsonage to a fair-thee-well. Organize his appointments. Do his laundry. Darn his socks. Cut his toenails, even. She smiled. "Now, Martha," she said happily, "I'll tend to everything. Don't you worry. We don't need to be married for me to take care of him. He won't lack for a thing!"

"But I *want* you to marry him, Imo." Martha laughed a loud guffaw. This time she didn't wince. "But, of course, I plan to ask him, too. I just thought I'd ask you first."

"I cannot imagine that he would say yes to such a thing." There, she'd gotten out of that one.

"But if he *does* say yes, you will?"

"Surely." Imo smiled. She could not even picture such a preposterous scene as Lemuel proposing to her.

"And one more thing, dear," Martha said, "before I go."

"Don't talk like that!"

"Sorry, then, Imogene. One more thing."

"Yes?" Imo's heart was thudding in her ears.

"Will you take over as president of the Garden Club? I have a feeling the group will just drift apart if someone doesn't take charge."

After the first question, this one was a breeze to answer. "Yes!" Imo practically shouted at Martha's startled face.

Martha's chin quivered a bit. "Thank you, dear." She sighed.

"Well, you're just as welcome as you can be."

There was a silence in the next few moments before Martha began a long, labored monologue about Lemuel's likes and dislikes. She described his morning back rub and how he liked his blanket layered on the bed in winter, with the wool blanket between the quilt and the cotton throw. She also told Imo where to find the canvas tote bag that held all of the Garden Club things.

The door opened and Lemuel placed a tepid cup of coffee into Imo's hand, then dropped small packages of nondairy creamer and sugar on the table at her elbow.

"Thank you," Imo said.

He nodded and sank back down into the chair at the window.

Imo pretended to sip the coffee. Martha was dozing peacefully now, the sheet across her chest rising and falling.

Imo stole a glance at Lemuel. He *was* a sweet and thoughtful man. Passable in the looks department. A fine, upstanding pillar of the community. She searched her heart a minute and she guessed she loved him in the sense of a dear friend, rather like a brother. But could she go through with such a thing as marrying him if it came to it? She could not even wrap her brain around the idea. It was unfathomable. *Surely he won't agree to marry me,* she thought as they sat there in silence. She didn't know what to do or say at the moment. Should she get up and excuse herself and head on home? Maybe. Or should she just stay right here until Martha crossed over? No, she couldn't, because then her friend wouldn't have the private chance to talk to Lemuel, who would surely say no, and then Imo would feel beholden to her promise and have to marry him. It was late, anyway, be dark before long, and her girls needed her. Mama needed her. And Little Silas did, too.

Wonder if Martha'll go before I can get back to see her tomorrow, she thought, hugging herself and feeling goose bumps rise on her arms and the back of her neck.

"'Preciate you coming," Lemuel said in a low voice, "for bringing the supper, too."

Was that her signal to go? She turned to him and met his eyes uneasily. He regarded her with an otherworldly smile. She watched him arise and walk toward her, and there was nothing to do but say good-bye and give him the chair at Martha's bedside. She couldn't say a thing, however. Couldn't utter the word *good-bye.* She gathered her handbag, bent to kiss Martha's cheek and stroke her hand, and walked out.

On automatic, she floated to the parking lot, drove to the highway, and headed toward Euharlee. Cars whizzing by her, the lighted signs of fast-food restaurants and gas stations dotting the night, the houses with cars parked on their driveways—all of these made Imo feel that she wasn't a part of what was real. She pulled underneath the shed at home and cut off the engine. Closing her eyes, she took a deep breath. If only it were not the real world! If only there was not this terrible feeling of a world without Martha.

She answered the door early the next morning with a knowing inside and her hand pressed against her heart.

Lemuel stood on the front porch.

"Come in," Imo said, noting the dark hollows underneath his eyes and the way he twisted his hands together awkwardly. "I'll make us coffee."

He shook his head. "I can't stay," he said in a hoarse whisper.

"She's gone?" Imo asked.

He nodded, eyes on the ground.

Imo let her body collapse against the door frame. She shook her head slowly. "I'm so sorry, Lemuel," she said after a spell.

He went on standing there, not meeting her eyes.

"You were good to come and tell me." She took a step over the threshold to enfold him in a clumsy embrace.

When he'd gone, she walked to the edge of the porch, leaned against the rail, and stared numbly into the gray haze of dawn. It was still and quiet out. She turned and sat on the porch swing. After a while she rose and returned to the kitchen, walking more quietly than usual. She saw Martha's face in her mind's eye, small and distant like a snapshot.

It was almost impossible to compute that Martha was no longer alive.

This fact would, Imo supposed, soak in over time. When the days passed with no exchange between them. The only thing Imo could do right now was just to keep putting one foot in front of the other.

Seven days passed, along with Martha's funeral, and still her death seemed unreal to Imo. Early one morning as Imo was watering her tomatoes, she remembered the memorial garden at the covered bridge in downtown Euharlee. Martha had been the instigator as well as the sustainer of the camellias and gardenias and impatiens they'd planted there in honor of Garden Club members who'd passed away, and it had been Martha who faithfully arranged for rotating members of the Garden Club to prune, feed, weed, water, and mulch the pretty area. As dry as it had gotten, Imo was sure it was severely wilted, if not dried up altogether.

"Myrtice?" Imo was breathless as she held the phone. "Hi, dear. How are you? Listen, I just realized that we need to tend to the memorial garden down at the bridge." She paused. "Also, I guess it's time to add Martha's name."

"Why, you're absolutely right!" Myrtice said. "It plum slipped my mind without dear Martha around. How is Lemuel making out?"

"Bless his bones, he's terrible," Imo said reverently. "Looks like he's lost fifty pounds, if that's even possible. I can hardly get a word out of him." This was true. Imo had been trying to determine if indeed Martha had asked him the million-dollar question, and, if so, what fate held in store for her. But there seemed to be no way to broach the subject with him. She was just as glad, however, preferring blissful ignorance for the time being.

"Well, you can count me in for the memorial garden. If there's any way we could pay tribute to dear Martha, this is it. I'll call Viola and Glennis. Maimee, too. When do you want to do it?"

"Oh," said Imo, "how about this evening? Seven? I'll call the Trophy Shop in Rome and get them to do a little brass plate with Martha's name inscribed on it. I can pick it up this afternoon."

"Suits me, dear. Let me get off and call the girls then."

Imo hung up. Thoughts of the Garden Club tending the memorial garden without Martha seemed like it might be a way for her to finally accept that Martha was really gone and that life would move on without her. Though Imo knew this was a necessary thing, and though she loved spending time with the Garden Club girls, her trip into Rome for the nameplate was tinged with a palpable sadness, and her eyes stung as she fetched the hose, the clippers, and her gardening gloves from the shed.

At five she rang the bell to call everyone for an early supper. After a quick meal of vegetable soup and corn bread, she asked Lou to keep an eye on Mama for the evening, washed up the supper dishes quickly, rinsed out an empty gallon milk jug and filled it with sweet tea, and grabbed the transistor radio she and Silas used to carry fishing with them. "Bye now," she called as the screen door slammed shut behind her.

She was the first to arrive and she climbed out of the car and stood gazing at the sight of the ragged, neglected flower garden. It had indeed become a wilting tangle of dusty plants grown up in weeds, sprawling haphazardly at one end of the bridge.

She made her way first to the teak bench with the brass name-plates of former members fastened along the backrest. She patted the smooth, cool rectangle in her pocket bearing Martha's name. The bench was practically engulfed by johnson grass. "Oh, this will not do," she murmured to herself as she bent forward to yank some of the clinging strands away from its legs. "This will not do at all."

"I see London, I see France!" a voice from behind Imo teased. She straightened up quickly to tug her dress down and turned to see Glennis.

"Oh, hi, hon," Imo said, "glad you could make it."

"Well, I am, too, to tell you the truth." Glennis cackled and slapped her thigh. "Let me tell you, though, Imogene, I like to never got out the house. Swinson Caudelle came by with something for me to notarize for the Rotary Club and I did it and then he got to talking a mile a minute about some pork barbecue supper they're doing and never took the hint that I had to go. I'd say, 'Well, I've got to be getting along now,' and ease on over toward the door, with my handbag slung across my arm, jangling my keys, you know, and he'd keep right on going about vinegar- versus ketchup-based barbecue sauce. Finally I just opened up the door, marched down the steps out to my car, and he was *still* at it. I cranked the thing, backed up, put it in forward, did put the window down, however, so I could still hear him, I sure didn't want to be ugly about it, and he followed me clear past the mailbox, just carrying on. Finally, I had to holler at him to please lock the door handle to the house when he took a notion to leave."

"Gracious me." Imo smiled at the thought of Swinson running down Glennis's driveway and talking to her exhaust fumes.

Glennis surveyed the memorial garden with her hands on her hips. "There's lots to do out here, isn't there?" she asked.

"Lands, yes," Imo said. "It's a mess. I knew it would be after all this time. But yonder comes Maimee and Viola to help."

Glennis slipped into her gardening gloves. "Many hands make light work!" she said. "But isn't it hot as fire this evening? I heard it hit ninety-eight on the bank's thermometer."

"Sure enough?" Imo said. "Seemed like it was ninety-eight in the shade to me. I brought us a jug of tea."

"Hi ladies," Maimee said, jogging up with her eyes narrowed on the garden. "I say we pick up all this unsightly litter first off." She kicked at a faded Dairy Queen cup in disgust.

"That's fine by me," Imo said. "Let's go on and get started. Myrtice should be here before too long. She said she was coming." She tugged her gloves on and stood for a moment, feeling the late sun on her shoulders. It struck her as odd that there was no one else about. Downtown almost felt like a ghost town. There was no hum of lawnmowers or distant tractors, no pedestrians strolling along, no one fishing in the creek. Perhaps everyone was inside, eating supper, or getting a tub-bath to clear away the day's sweat before tomorrow's Fourth of July celebration.

Glennis noticed this, too. "Hey, girls," she exclaimed, "it's like we're having our own private garden party out here! Why don't you put us on some music, Imogene?"

Imo twiddled the dial on the radio until she came to some soothing instrumental music.

"We'll fall asleep to that," Glennis said. "Find something lively."

Imo tuned in to a station out of Rome playing oldies.

"Shake it up, baby, twist and shout . . ." came John Lennon's voice.

Viola began to shimmy a bit. "Haven't done this in ages!" she said, laughing.

"Least you can still do it," Glennis said. "I've gotten stiff as a board."

"Oh, you could do it if you tried, hon," Maimee urged. "Come on!"

Glennis rotated her shoulders to the right and her hips to the left. She winced. "Ow! You try it, Imo."

"Oh, I don't know," Imo said, "I've never been much of a dancer."

"Come on, hon." Viola grabbed Imo's wrists and twisted her a bit. "Let it all hang out. Ain't nobody watching us."

Imo found herself moved by the beat of the music, and she jittered and twisted a bit here and there right where she stood. It felt good to dance. Amazingly good.

"Woo-hoo!" Myrtice called, jogging up to join them. "I didn't know we were having a *party* out here. You're looking sharp, Imogene, with all that twisting."

"Sorry, I got carried away," Imo said. She stopped moving. "We're here to work. Plus we've got serious things on our minds."

"Don't apologize." Maimee put her hand on Imo's shoulder. "I think Martha would *want* us to enjoy ourselves," she said. "She wouldn't want us out here moping around like a bunch of old sad sacks while we tended to the memorial garden. Might kill the plants."

There was a thoughtful pause.

"Maimee's right," said Viola. "We should celebrate our memories of Martha tonight!"

"Well," said Imo, looking furtively at Glennis and Myrtice.

"I think it's a fine idea," Glennis said. "What better way to celebrate her than doing what we all love best? Hmm?"

Myrtice nodded. "She's right."

"Well, crank up that music then!" said Maimee.

"Yes," said Imo, "of course." But still she was a tad hesitant as she turned the volume dial louder. The Everly Brothers were singing . . . "All I have to do is dree-ee-ee-eam . . ."

"Yes," said Maimee, "that's a nice tune to work to." She moved around the area plucking up cigarette butts and gum wrappers in time to the beat.

"Do y'all remember the time Martha got that natural pest-control expert to come talk to the club?" said Myrtice, yanking up a tall pink stalk of poke sallet. "Man that told us to put out saucers of beer to drown slugs?" She guffawed.

"Well, it worked," Viola said. "You can't deny that. Fred wasn't too happy about me using his beer like that, but it did the job sure enough. Also, that same feller said to plant scented geraniums to attract ladybugs to gobble up aphids. Said they'd eat their weight in the things every day. That worked, too! Martha sure did plan us some great meetings."

"Oh, yes," said Imo. "Speaking of pest control, I was thinking the other day about that time Martha was having trouble with folks stealing her watermelons."

"I remember that!" said Viola, smiling. "She was so mad. She'd waited all summer for her patch to get ripe and every time she turned around, somebody had stolen one."

"She finally saw some of those Llewellyn boys sneaking off with one," Imo added, "and what she did was, she carried a can of Crisco outside and she greased up every last one of the rest of her watermelons."

"That Martha," Glennis said softly. "She was one in a million. There'll never be another like her."

There was a long pause. Imo drew a deep breath. It felt very natural to talk about Martha. Yes, this had been a good idea tonight. She hadn't realized how much she needed to talk about Martha. "Hey, girls," she said after a bit, "was it three or four Julys ago that Martha had us marching in the Fourth of July parade?"

"Believe it was three," Maimee said. "I remember that all fifteen of us made it. Hot as the blazes that day!"

"Sure enough," Viola said. "Seemed like we walked a hundred miles."

"Wasn't but three quarters of a mile." Glennis laughed. "We wore gloves and carried hoes and spades and watering cans and the like. What was it Martha had on that sign she carried? Something about keeping America green?"

"It said 'Red, White, Blue, and Green. Keep America growing!'" Imo said. This memory settled over her gently as she dug up a patch of dandelions.

"I'll say one thing," Viola told the group after a spell, "those folks who planned the parade that year must've been city slickers."

"What makes you say that, dear?" asked Myrtice.

"Well, it was tough enough dragging ourselves through all that heat, carrying our gardening tools," Viola said, "but having to side-step all that horse manure just beat all I ever saw!"

"We did have a time of it," said Myrtice. "I remember now. But the folks I felt the sorriest for were all those little majorettes, twirling and dancing right ahead of us. Imagine putting horseback riders at the beginning of a parade!"

Everyone laughed, working happily.

After a bit Imo made her way to the broad stepping-stones leading up to the bench. It was a relief to kneel and pluck out the weeds that had infiltrated the lovely creeping jenny nestled between the stones. She heard the distant chirping of birds—*happyo! happyo! happyo!*—in the trees across Euharlee Creek. The day's warmth radiated up from the ground and bathed her face as she ran her hands across the plants, her fingers feeling the satisfaction of their work.

"Looks like the impatiens are doing right good," Maimee remarked, standing with her hands on her hips.

"Yes, dear, but everyone knows impatiens *thrive* on neglect," Viola said.

Imogene sat back on her heels to admire the smattering of snow-white impatiens encircling the bench. Such sweet little blooms, she noted, so cheerful and steady and dependable. All they needed was a bit of weeding and a nice soaking and they would be as good as new. However, she was almost afraid to turn her head and look closely at the camellias.

Martha had chosen to plant a *Camellia japonica* variety called Aunt Jetty, as it was sun tolerant. In their prime, the gorgeous double-flowered blooms were a hearty blood-red, speckled with white. She'd planted five of these nestled together on the right side of the bench. They were indeed dropping their leaves and shedding many withered buds.

"They do look bad," Myrtice said, "but would you just look at the *gardenias*!" She threw up her hands in a gesture of dismay. All heads turned to the other side of the bench where five Cape Jasmine gardenias appeared to be dying. Their once shiny, dark green foliage was yellow and scattered blossoms lay shrunken and brown like dirty tissues on the ground beside piles of withered leaves.

"Well, looks like we've got our work cut out for us, girls," Glennis said. "It's a shame if those gardenias are dead."

"They're not gone yet," Imo reassured her. "It *looks* bad, yes, but really all it'll take is some tender care, and I'm just about done tidying up the creeping jenny here."

There was something very invigorating about the prospect of reviving the memorial garden and Imo felt pleased in a funny sort of way that it was as far gone as it was. She was almost giddy with the purpose and anticipation of it all.

An ever so slight breeze had begun to sweeten the air and the sky stretched above them clear as it could be. Euharlee Creek flowed smoothly beneath the covered bridge and Elvis was singing "Love Me Tender." Five straw hats were bobbing to the beat as the girls animatedly examined the plants. Imo paused to pluck a sturdy little impatiens and tuck it into her buttonhole.

They decided to tackle the camellias first. Maimee took over as boss and began to direct the pruning. First they removed the leggy branches on the outside, then thinned out the weaker branches on the interior of the plants, finally trimming the bushes off to a height of twelve inches from the ground. When they were finished, a knee-high pile of clippings lay in a heap and there were five well-formed camellias.

"Now this is satisfying!" Glennis stood back to admire their work. "We water them real good, and put down some mulch, and they'll be back to their former beauty in no time at all."

Imo passed the jug of tea around. When it got to Myrtice, she paused to blot the sweat from her upper lip before she drank. "Did y'all hear about Carletta Hughes?" she whispered.

"Uh-uh." Viola shook her head and leaned in closer. "Tell us."

"She's left Billy."

There was a collective indrawn breath. Carletta Hughes worked as clerk at the courthouse and her husband, Billy, was the bailiff there.

"Just up and ran off on him. Took the dog, her grandmother's sil-ver pitcher, and the TV—"

"Not their new big-screen TV!" cried Maimee, eyeing Myrtice incredulously.

"Mmm-hmm, surely did. Took right off with it. But directly she phoned Billy from this little hotel down in South Georgia, The Pink Flamingo, I believe it was called. Told him that it was either her or C.J."

"Who's C.J.?" Imo asked, clutching clippers close to her bosom.

"C.J. is the woman on that *Baywatch* TV show. Played by Pamela Sue Anderson."

"Well," Glennis said brightly, "least it isn't a real person."

"Why, she *is* real to him," said Myrtice. "Carletta said to Annie Mae that Billy keeps a big poster of her up in their bedroom!"

"Poor Carletta," said Viola, "reckon she's just jealous on account of being so stout? Because I'm as sure as the day is long that Pamela Sue Anderson won't have nothing to do with Billy Hughes."

"I don't know," Myrtice said solemnly. "I've a good mind to give that boy a talking to. I taught him Sunday school in the fifth grade and maybe he'll still listen to me. He couldn't have a finer woman than Carletta."

"Don't go getting yourself in the middle of things," said Glennis. "I bet it'll all work itself out in time."

There was a pause. Maimee closed her eyes and Imo shook her head gravely.

"Well," Imo announced brightly after a bit, "time to tackle the gardenias." She led the girls into the midst of them. "There's one a piece, just like the camellias," she said, eyeing the shrubs. "First let's clip out all the dead stuff, water and feed them real good, and then I've got some peanut hulls and rotted oak leaves in my trunk for us to mulch with. Need to put down some mulch under those camellias, too." She dabbed at her sweaty forehead.

It was cooler standing among the six-foot-tall gardenias, and Imo drank in a fusion made from the rich odor of the creek bank and the almost-sickening-sweet perfume of the flowers.

"Smells like my great-aunt Bebe's toilet water in here," laughed Viola, twiddling one of the pure-white double blossoms between her fingers.

"Smells like a French whorehouse to me," Maimee said.

"How would *you* know?" teased Myrtice as she clipped away a dead branch.

By eight-thirty it was almost a pleasant temperature to be outside toiling so hard. Myrtice, Imo, Maimee, Glennis, and Viola had achieved a satisfying rhythm as they worked, chatting about flowers, birds, children, and grandchildren.

"I feel like we've wrought a miracle here," said Maimee as they were putting the mulch down underneath neatly trimmed gardenias. "I think Sheriff Bentley ought to give us an award for downtown beautification."

"Sure enough," said Viola, and they all stood for a long while, swilling tea from the gallon jug, admiring the garden by moonlight, and listening to Elvis sing "Blue Suede Shoes."

Imo turned the radio off when the song was finished. "Girls"—
she spoke in a hushed tone—"it's time to put Martha's nameplate on
the bench." Solemnly she walked to the Impala for the drill and a
screwdriver, and when she returned everyone was already gathered
in a semicircle around the teak bench.

"I'm thinking we ought to put her right here," Imo said, pointing to
the center of the backrest, between LaTrelle Oglesbee and Nanette
Finch. "Is that agreeable?"

Glennis smiled. "I think that's fitting."

Everyone nodded.

"Let's all bow our heads in silent prayer for a moment," Imo
admonished. She closed her eyes and sent up a word of thanksgiving
for the beautiful gift of Martha Peddigrew, and when she raised her
head she saw everyone else smiling through tears just like she was.
"Alrighty," she announced brightly, "I will commence to drilling."

She ran her fingers over the letters on the small rectangle of
brass as she positioned it to mark where the holes should go. There
were two short shrill bursts from the drill and Imo slid the plate in
place. "Who will do the honors?" she asked, offering her palm with
two tiny screws.

Maimee reached out for them and fastened the plate onto the
bench ceremonially. "Well," she said when she'd finished, "let's all
raise our right hands, as representatives of the Euharlee Garden
Club, and vow that we'll all stay together and keep our club strong!"

"Amen to that," said Myrtice. "I think Imogene should lead it."

Touched, Imo raised her voice and led them in a brief oath of
allegiance. "I'll call the others tomorrow and let them in on everything," she said as she gathered her things to go.

Early the next morning Imo went outside to the garden. The sun
was shining but it was still fairly cool. There were tomatoes and butter beans and cucumbers and green peppers and sweet corn that
needed picking. She also wanted to pinch some suckers from the

tomato vines and soak the garden really well. The prospect of all this filled her with happiness.

She made her way to the shed for her gloves and the wheelbarrow. Inside the shed it was dim and Imo stood for a moment letting her eyes adjust. She breathed in the dusty, sharp smell of the things lining some metal shelves along the back wall. There were cans of gasoline, gear oil, thirty-weight motor oil, bags of 10-10-10 fertilizer, lime, and insecticides. This fusion was as familiar to her as her own face, and it was pleasing in the way that odors can remind a person of happy times. Imo paused to rearrange some items on the shelves, straightening and refastening the various containers. As she righted a fallen bag of Sevin dust on the bottom shelf, her gaze fell upon a tiny black metal watering can that was wedged between the wall and the shelf.

In automatic, Imo's hand reached out to retrieve the can, but just as quickly she drew in a sharp breath and snatched her hand back to herself, holding it against her chest. The watering can was part of a set of junior-size gardening tools her mother had given her for her seventh birthday. There had also been a small hoe, a spade, a trowel, and a pitchfork.

She felt a memory begin to swim into her consciousness. First there was that tightening of the skin that announced déjà vu, and then her heart began to race. *Fight it, Imogene,* she admonished herself, *you were feeling so much better today, after that nice experience at the memorial garden yesterday evening. Don't let another bad memory get you down.*

Imo tensed herself. She traced the letters *G-A-S-O-L-I-N-E* on a red can at eye level. She shook her head. To no avail. This memory was wound up in her being with threads as strong as steel and it came on as surely as the dawn arrived each morning. There was nothing to do but get through it.

All at once she saw herself as a small girl crouched in the garden as she set in a tiny tomato seedling. A warm finger of morning sun stroked Imo's back and Mama's hand was on her wrist, guiding her while she patted the dirt around the plant. "You did a lovely job, Imogene Rose," Mama said, "you're a natural. Born with a green thumb, I reckon." These beautiful sounds of praise spilled from Mama's lips, and then, with a gentle voice she offered instruction to Imogene. "Mind you water that next hole there real good, sweetheart, before you set the seedling in, and then we'll come along and give them another good drink after we get them all settled in. I am so proud of you."

Imo remembered the warmth of Mama's skin, her smile, and the peaceful, relaxed curve of her body as she knelt in the garden beside her. The memory of all the gardens of her childhood came flooding in. She saw the years roll back and the new tiny set of tools lined up along the edge of the garden.

Imo felt her body relax. She smiled. Mama had an infectious joy when it came to growing things. Imo recalled her happy, sparkling eyes whenever they were out in the garden and the way she drew in deep lungfuls of peaty air and sighed. Those early days of spring each year were Mama's favorite times. Something about the garden brought out only the best, the pure and the good, in Mama. It was in those moments in the garden that the wild beast in Imo's mother was tamed. There were no enraged eyes or seething words. Moments of pure joy and sanctuary were theirs together beneath God's blue sky.

Imogene paused to ponder these forgotten memories of her childhood. They were, she decided, her legacy. A pure gift Mama had passed down to her! Mama had nurtured in Imo's tiny being a love of gardening, of working the earth. A love that remained to this day and was often Imo's deliverance.

Imo let herself bask in this memory for a long time; barely breathing, standing in the dim shed, and gazing at the tiny watering can. "Hey Martha," she said at last, "you were absolutely right, you know. I never should have doubted you. I found that fine, good thing about Mama that I need to dwell on."

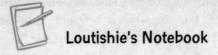

Loutishie's Notebook

Not too long after Martha's funeral, I decided it was time to come clean with Imo. It was a steamy Saturday morning in late July, and I figured I'd hunt her down, wherever she was, and do it before I changed my mind.

Imo still seemed distracted in a peculiar sort of way and she'd been more absentminded than usual, walking around with her head up in the clouds, saying things to herself like, "Well now, who'd have thought it? I never dreamed he would say that." I had no idea what she was mumbling about. I figured it was just her grief talking.

In the den was the sound of *The Price Is Right* and I could smell nail polish hovering like a cloud. I stuck my head around the door frame. Jeanette lay with her hands and feet stretched out like she'd been electrocuted, bits of cotton balls between her toes. "Hey Jeanette," I said.

"Hey." Jeanette's voice rose over some audience member really whooping it up as they hopped onstage to Bob Barker. I saw Mama Jewell asleep in her La-Z-Boy and Little Silas on the floor with a plastic laundry basket full of toys.

"C'mere Lou," Jeanette said, "I've got the perfect color for you." She crooked one hot pink fingernail to beckon me over. On a TV tray next to her head was a stack of beauty magazines and an array of nail polishes.

I stared at Bob Barker offering showcase number one to a fat woman dressed like a bumblebee. "No thanks," I said.

"Just your toenails, then," Jeanette said.

I knew she was offering a chance for us to bond. Another try from her to include me in her world. But this was my perfect chance to talk to Imo in private.

"Nah," I said, "can't right now. Maybe later. Where's Imo at?"

"Out in that dern old garden again," Jeanette said.

"Great!" I said over my shoulder, sprinting barefoot down the back porch steps to the garden. I ran past the squash and pepper rows and Imo's compost heap, stopping to squiggle my toes in the silky dirt at the edge of where Imo was picking tomatoes.

She jumped and spun around. "Loutishie!" she breathed. "You snuck up on me!" Then she smiled. "Mama still out?"

"Yep," I said, "asleep in her chair."

"Well, I'm glad. I've got so much to do out here, you know."

I nodded. "I can help you."

"Good, good. I need to finish harvesting the ripe tomatoes and cucumbers. Need to water a bit, too."

I could feel her happiness out there and I knew that this was the right place and time for my confession. Still, I decided that I would have to ease into it.

"Tomatoes are sure looking good," I said, knowing her soft spot.

"Yes'm," she said. "It's a huge crop this year. Enough to eat bountifully on, some to give away, and plenty to put by." She eyed the vines. "May end up canning several dozen quarts of tomatoes this summer."

"Quarts of 'Maters, you meant to say," I said, watching her face. "'Maters!" I said again. I knew the story she loved to tell by heart. It was Imo's memory of some old country boy insisting to her and Uncle Silas that tomatoes were called 'maters. It would put her in a good frame of mind.

She laughed and the lines around her mouth smoothed out some. "Mm-hmm," she said, "sure enough. 'Maters they are." Skillfully, she retied a tomato vine that was laden with fruit to its stake. She turned and patted my shoulder. "You're a big help around here, Lou. Thank you for all your help with Mama. You allowed me to be with Martha so much at the end."

"You don't have to say that," I said.

"Why," she said, "I surely do. Not many teenage girls I know of would have given up their evenings and weekends the way you have. You can't possibly understand what a help you've been to me." She placed a gloved hand on each of my shoulders.

"I've got something I need to tell you," I said quickly, wanting to get it in during our warm, fuzzy moment. I took her silence as a sign to go ahead. "I have sinned against you and God," I began.

Now I had her attention. Her eyes were on me, steady and forgiving, as I spilled everything from stealing the photos out of Mama Jewell's trunk to knocking on a door at the Dusty Springs Trailer Park. I ended with a grave "I'm sorry. I've lied some, too. Please forgive me. But I needed—I still need—to find my father."

She swallowed hard, stroked my cheek, and I knew from the soft look in her eyes that she forgave me, and at that moment I felt whistlely clean inside, the way your mouth does when you suck on a strong peppermint. Mentally I saw my heavenly chalkboard being wiped spotless by a gigantic eraser.

For a while neither of us said a word. Just stood there in the warm garden.

"Now, Lou," she said finally, cocking her head toward her right shoulder a bit and wrinkling up her forehead, "you know that your mother was . . . a young girl when she met your father." I could tell she had a hard time saying that last word.

I nodded and smiled that I understood this.

"We all do crazy things when we're young, Lou, and sister fell hard for a wild young boy. Believe he'd been in and out of reform school. Don't remember much about what she said about his home life, except that he lived with a grandmother and they were right poor. The world can be a hard place on some folks, you need to realize. It's been close to sixteen years . . ."

"I know," I said, "of course I know that."

"Well," she said hurriedly, "what I'm trying to say is that sometimes people get their hopes up about something, dear, and it doesn't work out the way they imagine it will."

I pictured the photo of my dad, a young, smiling man leaning against a van. A *customized* van from his very own van shop. "He's got his own business," I said. "He's cute, too."

Imo dropped her hands from my shoulders. "I just don't want you hurt, Lou." She paused. "You've put a lot of thought into this, haven't you? I reckon I could make a few phone calls."

It was as easy as that. Imo turned quickly and moved to the next tomato vine.

I grabbed a pail from the wheelbarrow, went over to the snap beans to pick and to think. I didn't want to get hurt either, and I sure didn't want Imo hurt any more than she was, but I refused to consider the fact that he might not be all that I desired in a dad.

The next morning, barely dawn, rubbing the sleep from my eyes, I crept into the kitchen for some juice. Imo was sitting at the table in the kitchen drinking her coffee. No one else was out of bed yet and the house was mighty quiet.

"Morning Loutishie," she said softly.

"Morning." I looked over at her. Underneath the bright light fixture and with her hair flat from sleeping, she looked very old.

"Like to take a drive with me this afternoon?"

"A drive?"

She nodded. "I made a few phone calls."

This took me completely by surprise. "You did?" I asked incredulously. "That was quick."

"Yessum. So, want to take that ride with me?" She patted my wrist.

"Of course!" I said. "When?"

"Well, let me get dressed, get Mama up and dressed and fed, too, because I reckon she'll have to ride with us. Be close to eleven, I imagine, Lou, by the time I tend to everything. I'll ring the bell for you."

"Where's he live at? Dusty Springs?"

"No," Imo whispered over her coffee cup as she leaned in close to me, "he lives in the Campo's Mill Community."

"Great," I said, though I knew nothing about this Campo's Mill place. But if my father was there, it had to be wonderful. Surely it was nicer than Dusty Springs.

"Just don't get your hopes all up, Lou," Imo warned as I skipped off down the hall to get dressed.

"Okay," I called back, lifting my chin. But it was too late. My hopes were way up high. I dressed quickly, galloped outside, and whistled for Bingo. He wasn't too long coming and as I bent down to hug him, Dewy Rose meandered up, stretching a leg here and there. "Y'all want to take a walk with me this morning?" I asked, breathing in their familiar smells.

"Guess what? I'm going to see my father in a little bit," I said as I skipped along down toward the bottoms, my heart feeling lighter than the cool morning air. The sun was just over the tops of the trees as I plopped down onto my behind to watch the light glinting on the surface of the Etowah. I rubbed Bingo's ribs and watched Dewy Rose hunting for bugs.

This day had been a long time coming, and now, after all my impatience and anticipation, it was finally here!

When the sound of the bell drifted down to the bottoms, I fell all over myself getting back up to the house. Imo had the car idling when I got there and Mama Jewell sat in the backseat, her chin poking out like she was in a fighting mood and her big black shiny purse on her lap.

I fished a comb out of Imo's purse and fixed my hair as we passed the Dairy Queen, then spit on a napkin to freshen my face. It didn't take us half an hour to get to Campo's Mill. There was no sign, but Imo said she knew it was the right place as she turned off the main road. We cruised along a narrow gravel road, slowing down at the first of a dozen tar-paper houses. They were long and narrow, like trailers, only they sat up on cinder blocks and the front door was on the short end. Dirt yards with a sprinkling of dandelions and trash ran between them and the road.

"Well, here we are, Lou," Imo said.

I know I looked disappointed to Imo, sitting there eyeing those dilapidated shacks with my mouth hanging open.

"Lots of the folks that live here are old, Lou, too old to get out and tend to things." She patted my shoulder.

But my father wasn't old, I reasoned. He couldn't be over forty. I told myself that he was the manager, the able-bodied caretaker of the Campo's Mill Community.

"Alrighty!" Imo said with a false cheerfulness I could hear, "we're looking for number one-eighty!" She crept along the shoulder of the road, searching each mailbox.

Mama Jewell craned her old neck like a turtle's to peer out the window. Suddenly she perked up. "Why, this here's the mill!" she exclaimed. "Freda

Jane Johnson's daddy works at the mill! He's a weaver *and* a loom-fixer."
She was beaming. "Let's go see them! Pay them a social call!"

"Mama," Imo said gently, "Campo's Mill is no longer in operation. Closed
down years and years ago."

"Why it is, too! How you think there's going to be food on Freda Jane's
table if her daddy doesn't have work?!" Mama Jewell looked alarmed. Then
she reached into her handbag and pulled out a jar of chow-chow. "Here's for
Miz Johnson." She patted it proudly. "Be a real nice hostess gift. Got me a
blue ribbon with this, you know, Sheila." She turned to look at me.

I nodded as Imo came to a stop at a leaning mailbox. "Can you make out
that number there, Lou?" she asked. "Is it one-eighty?"

"Yep," I said, in a kind of daze, "one-eighty." I looked hard at the tiny
house not fifty feet away from us, my heart beating in my ears so loud I was
sure Mama Jewell and Imo could hear it. I put my hand on the door handle
but did not open it.

"Let's go, sugar foot." Imo gave me a swift glance.

"We're *all* going?" I said.

"Of course. You don't think I'd let you go up there by yourself, do you?"
Imo said, swinging her door open and stepping out to open the back door.
"And I can't leave Mama out here. She'd swelter in this heat."

Mama Jewell climbed spryly out with her jar of chow-chow held aloft.
"This surely doesn't *look* like Freda Jane's house," she said, narrowing her
eyes. "Looks like somebody's fallen on hard times."

"Come along, Mama," Imo said.

I slunk out and walked along behind them up to the house, glancing
around the yard. There was a rusty old dishwasher lying on its side, and a
row of white tires sunk halfway in the dirt and the rotting bench off a picnic
table covered in green moss. A dirty white Trans Am with a pair of red fuzzy
dice hanging from the rearview mirror sat right up next to the house.

We paused at the bottom of the steps.

"Mama and I will stay down here, Lou," Imo said.

"Okay," I said, "fine." Strangely reluctant now that I was there, I stood on
the balls of my toes, fingering the photographs in my pocket.

"Go on, Lou," Imo urged.

I climbed the steps, stood at the screen door, and gazed in. The floor was littered with clothes and trash. If Imo hadn't been standing down there waiting, if she hadn't been so sure of where he lived, I would've turned tail and run. "Okay, here goes," I whispered under my breath, knocking timidly.

Two things happened then, and I was so unprepared for either one of them that I almost forgot being scared. From somewhere inside came a growl—a throaty warning, followed by a sharp, deep bark and the feel of something, a presence, crouched and ready. It was a *huge* dog, I could tell that much. Probably the kind that could rip right through the mesh of the screen. I held my breath, paralyzed.

Next came a voice I knew so well rising over the fierce growling. "Freda Jane?" Mama Jewell sprinted up beside me. "Call off your dog, Freda Jane," she called through the screen. "I've come to pay you a social visit!" She reached for the handle of the screen door and she swung it right open.

The dog, its teeth bared and looking like a wolf with wild eyes, sprang at Mama Jewell. But she barely noticed the taut streamlined missile of that dog coming at her. She didn't flinch, she just stepped right into the house as she brought her arm with the purse in it way behind her like a batter fixing to swing, then flung it forward with sheer power, smacking the stunned animal upside his head hard. He let out a high-pitched whine and slunk away, cowering behind a couch with white stuffing oozing out.

Mama Jewell shook her purse strap to her forearm. She stood with her hands on her hips, looking around. "Freda Jane's gotten slovenly," she said.

"Mama?!" Imo came bustling up behind us and past me, right on into the house beside Mama Jewell. "You come on out of here, Mama," she hissed, "this is not Freda Jane's house!"

Mama Jewell wrenched her arm away from Imo's grip. "Well, I reckon it is, too. Freda Jane!" she shouted at the top of her lungs. "Oh, Freda Jane! We're out here standing in your parlor!"

Then came a man's voice out of the gray hallway. "Rex?" he said. "What the hell's going on out here, boy?" A figure lumbered into the room. I strained to see him. He reminded me of a wrestler with his massive hulk of a body, his long, stringy brown hair, and an even longer beard with a scraggly mustache. He wore a stained T-shirt and faded, torn blue jeans stretched over massive thighs. He was barefoot.

I tried to see the person past all that hair and the sleep-swollen face. I felt a sudden shiver as I recognized the eyes from the photographs. My eyes.

He stopped and stood there a second, looking at all three of us, and he blinked. "Who the hell are you?" he snarled, rubbing sleep out of his eyes.

"Hello," Imo said, putting on her social voice. She cleared her throat. "I am so sorry we barged in on you like this. My mother thought it was the home of a childhood friend." Mama Jewell was looking around crazily, the jar of chow-chow hanging like a jewel from her hand.

"Where's Freda Jane!?" Mama Jewell moved up close to the big man.

He shook his head. "Huh?"

"I *said,* where's Freda Jane?!" she thundered. "You deaf? I aim to pay a social call on her." Mama Jewell was bouncing around like a flustered hen, her little stick legs shaking.

"Ain't no Freda Jane here," he said.

"Well, pray tell what you have done with her then. I've a good mind to call the law on you," Mama Jewell threatened.

"Shoo." He waved his hand like she was a fly. "Get on out of here, all of you."

"I won't do it," she said, planting her support shoes firmly onto the dingy linoleum.

I was numb as I watched him reach out to grasp both her shoulders with his massive hands. He began walking her toward the door. "Go on, now. Git." He waved his hands.

"Randy," Imo said.

He stopped dead in his tracks. He looked hard at Imo and nodded ever so slightly, a look of surprised recognition coming onto his face.

"Imogene Lavender"—Imo touched her chest—"the former Imogene Wiggins. Vera Wiggins's sister." Imo put a hand on Mama Jewell's back. "This is Jewelldine Wiggins, Vera's mother, and this"—Imo motioned backward at me—"is your daughter, Loutishie."

Numbly, I stepped forward into that crazy room rank with dog and cigarettes. "Hello," I said as I met his bloodshot eyes. He studied me hard, scowling and rubbing his chin. There was no warm sense of connection between us, no overpowering sense of family; he didn't melt and enfold me in his arms. I wasn't sure I wanted him to anyway.

First he laughed a bit nervously, then he shrugged and ran one hand through his beard. "Vera," he pondered slowly. "Man, that seems like another life. I seem to recollect hearing that the girl had done died," he said finally.

"She passed on giving birth to *your* daughter," Imo spat as she put her hands on her hips.

Something in her stance, a mother-bear fierceness along with her flashing eyes, made me feel protective of her. "Come on, Imo," I said. "Let's go. He doesn't want me." I wanted to add *And I don't want him either,* but I constrained myself. "He's not my father," I said. "I'm sure of it."

I thought we were all done there, and moving out the door, back to the sanctuary of the Impala, when something clicked inside of Mama Jewell and she became as stiff as a two by four.

It was the calm before a storm.

"So *you're* the piece of white trash," she said through clenched teeth, "what knocked up my Vera!"

His mouth opened in surprise as she flew at him, slapping the side of his head with her shiny black purse. "You sorry, good-for-nothing, low-down piece of white trash!" she screeched. The chow-chow clattered to the ground, shattering open and looking like vomit at his feet.

"Shit, man!" he cried, stepping away and covering his face. "That hurt. This old broad's crazy!"

"Imo," I pleaded, cringing at the thought of what he might do. I knew he could easily snap all three of us in two if he took a notion. I backed out onto the tiny stoop. "Come on," I called. "Let's go."

Imo stood there with her mouth open, watching Mama Jewell.

"White trash," Mama Jewell hissed, still not ready to quit. She backed up, dropping her purse and punching the air like a boxer, headed for him again. This time she battered his chest with her fists.

He started to laughing then, as if it were the funniest thing he'd ever seen, all the time shaking his head. "You wanna fight, do you?" He balled up his fists and held them in the air, playfully bouncing on the balls of his feet in a boxer's pose. I could see panic rising in Imo's face as she raced forward.

"Let's go, Mama," she said as she pulled Mama Jewell's arm. "It's time to leave."

"No!" Mama Jewell yanked away from Imo. "I need to kill him, Imogene. The Bible says an eye for an eye!"

"It also says that vengeance belongs to the Lord!" Imo said gently. "Leave it to the Lord."

"The Lord smite him then!" Mama Jewell roared. "Now, Lord! Do it now!" She thrust her hands up to heaven and closed her eyes. "Avenge Vera's untimely death, Lord!" she shouted.

I watched Imo tugging at Mama Jewell's elbow, and I saw Mama Jewell twirl herself away from Imo toward the center of the room. It was unreal. My father stood there with his mouth open, his face frozen in disbelief. Mama Jewell bopped him again, this time with her purse.

That seemed to satisfy Mama Jewell, and Imo was finally able to convince her to go. By the time they turned toward the door I was already moving so fast down the steps and across the yard that everything was only a blur. That sun felt so wonderful on the top of my head and the stifling interior of the Impala was like heaven.

All three of us were silent as we pulled away from the curb; however, I did cast one backward glance over my shoulder. The man was standing on his doorstep, dumbfounded. After a good while, Imo reached over and squeezed my arm and left her hand there. "Lou, dear," she said softly, "-everything's going to be okay. Talk to me about how you're feeling."

I shook my head. I focused on the dashboard, blanking out my mind. I didn't really know how I was feeling yet. I knew I would have to acknowledge that hollow spot in the pit of my stomach sooner or later, and the pang of sadness grabbing at my heart, but at that moment all I wanted was to pretend that the scene behind me had never happened.

∘   ∘   ∘

Early that evening I made my way out to the barn to find Bingo and Dewy Rose. When I got to the well-house and peeked in, there was enough light to make out Bingo sprawled on his side and Dewy Rose cozy between his paws. The sound of my feet startled them awake and they both eyed me groggily.

Feathers were everywhere. Dewy Rose was molting, just like peafowl are supposed to do after mating season. Bingo stretched his front legs, eased up slowly on them, and began stretching. There were feathers stuck all over his nose and paws. "You're turning into a peacock, boy," I teased him. "How about you two birds come down to the river with me?"

As we made our way slowly along, the sky was darkening, the sun sinking behind the tops of the trees. We sat on the bank of the Etowah, listening to whippoorwills and owls calling across the water. I watched Dewy Rose wind herself around Bingo's legs and look adoringly at him. I wondered if it ever dawned on her that she was a different creature than he was. Maybe ignorance *was* bliss in some cases. Clearly some things were better left unexamined.

I told myself that I was going to pretend that yesterday had never happened, that this life here and now was all I'd ever known or would know. I reached into my pocket and tugged up the two photographs of him, and, without glancing at them a last time, tore them to shreds and flung them into the water.

I was walking back to the house when I saw Imo out in the garden picking the sweet corn. She stopped when she saw me. She cleared her throat. "Sugar foot," she said, "come here." She removed her gloves and tossed them onto the wheelbarrow and reared back to look hard at me. "Looks like it's time for us to have a little heart-to-heart talk."

Stunned, I blinked at her. A heart-to-heart talk? That was a rarity around our house.

"About parents, and about lots of other things, too," she said, placing her hands on my shoulders and steering me over to the glider, where we sat down.

As she began to talk I fastened my eyes on Mama Jewell, who was asleep in a lawn chair near the garden's edge.

"We don't get to choose who our parents are, Lou," Imo said. "Mama was not the best of mothers to me, not by a long shot. There was a time I couldn't even bear to recall my childhood, much less speak to her." She put her arm around my shoulders. "It hurt me, Lou. Really, really hurt."

I swallowed hard. I patted Imo's hand. "I always figured something was wrong between you two," I said.

She nodded her head and squeezed me. "But it's okay now. I've moved on. Made my peace with Mama and with my own self. I'm stronger now, even."

I told Imo I was sorry. "That must've been awful," I said, "you didn't deserve it."

"Well," she said, "I just shared that to let you know you aren't the only one to feel let down in the parents department. What I'm trying to say is I don't want you to let a root of bitterness take hold inside of you in regard to your biological father. You had a daddy, Lou. Your uncle Silas adored you. No one else on earth could have loved you any more than he did."

"I know that," I said, and feeling like I was about to start bawling, I stood up quickly.

"One more thing I need to say," Imo warned, "and you really need to be sitting down for this one. Please, dear."

I sat.

"I'm going to marry the Reverend Lemuel Peddigrew come December," she said very matter-of-factly. "It's what Martha wanted," she added when she saw my face.

The weeks flew by, and there we were, with a packed house at Calvary once again. Montgomery Pike was the officiating minister, and boy was Jeanette all tarted up and excited. She wore a skintight, pink, crushed-velvet dress, three-inch heels, and tiny silver bracelets up and down both arms. I felt sad for her on account of the fact that she had confided to me earlier in the month that Reverend Pike told her that though he had deep feelings for her, he was a man of God and needed to keep his faith in mind with respect to their new relationship. He said for her not to come early to Praise Squad rehearsals or stay late, either one, that they couldn't be alone together like that where he would be tempted.

Reverend Pike was up there on the steps facing Imo and the Reverend Peddigrew, reading some vows to each of them so that they could repeat them to one another. They exchanged rings and then he turned them around to face the congregation.

"Family and friends," he said, "I'd like to introduce to you the Reverend and Mrs. Lemuel Peddigrew." There was an appreciative murmur among the congregation, and he acknowledged this with a smile and a nod. Then, somehow, he managed to work an altar call in.

"People," he began as he slung his blue-black forelock of hair and let his eyes comb the sanctuary, "these two before me are not only joined in holy matrimony, they are joined in the *faith.* Two believers, evenly yoked, to walk hand in hand down the road of life. Two. Two to divide the load of one another's sorrows and two to double their joys."

He paused here a moment for drama, and it seemed to me that his eyes sought out Jeanette's. "Perhaps there are some of you sitting here today who would like to join ranks and walk with the believers," he said. "If that is the case, I invite you to come now, and lay your life down at the Master's feet. Today you can receive His forgiveness and you will have eternal life." He swept his hand out toward the altar rail and stepped forward to wait.

At that Jeanette stood, her rapt face tilted up to the Reverend Pike's. She plunked Little Silas right into a surprised Mama Jewell's lap. "'Scuse me, 'scuse me, 'scuse me," she said, teetering on her heels as she slipped along the pew and out into the center aisle. Jeanette made a beeline for the altar rail, where she knelt down and bowed her head. "Amen to Jesus!" she cried, throwing up her arms full of tinkling silver bracelets.

Reverend Pike dropped down to his knees beside her and placed his palm on top of her head. He murmured some words to her as she nodded her head. Finally he stood, turned, and said, "I'd like to introduce to you my newest sister in the faith," and Jeanette turned to face us amid several faint "amens" from the congregation.

We moved into the fellowship hall for a reception, where a long table was laden with punch, cheese straws, sausage balls, and a tall white cake. Imo wore a peach-colored skirt with a matching blouse, a purple-flower corsage, and a serene smile. Graciously she spoke to each person, clasping a long line of well-wishing hands.

Jeanette sat on a folding chair off to one corner, subdued. After a bit, I saw her lean forward, twist her hair around her fingers, and mutter to herself in low tones—her thinking pose. I had a pretty good idea what she was thinking about, and I was not surprised to glimpse determination in her eyes as everyone spilled out into the cold parking lot to see Imo and the Reverend Peddigrew off.

"All the single females come right over here," trilled Miss Lillian Tatum, who was an unclaimed blessing in her fifties. A handful of us flocked to the bottom of the church steps. Imo appeared in the doorway of the fellowship hall, wearing her nice London Fog raincoat for traveling. She held her bouquet of white roses out like an offering.

I stood with hands folded, listening as Miss Tatum instructed Imo to turn her back to us and fling the bouquet over her shoulder. All at once I watched that bouquet come sailing through the air, down the steps, while Jeanette managed to elbow both Evelyn Culpepper and Sally Ward *hard,* and also to simultaneously knock Miss Tatum down onto her rump, as she performed the single most amazing leap I have ever seen to catch that bouquet. She held it up then, waving it around proudly as she sought the Reverend Montgomery Pike. I saw her catch his eye and I saw him blush.

She was still clutching her prize tightly while the rest of us threw rice at the back of Reverend Peddigrew's truck as he and Imo left for two nights up in the Great Smoky Mountains.

After the honeymoon, Reverend Peddigrew packed up his things at the parsonage and moved out to the farm with us. But even more earth shattering than that change was the news that the Reverend Montgomery Pike had decided he missed his alone time with Jeanette so much that he wanted to make it all official by marrying her! Two reverends in the family, now that was something.

Come January Imo spread manure over the garden and the Reverend Peddigrew happily plowed it under for her. But that April, when it was time to sow the seeds and transplant the seedlings, he shrugged and raised both his hands in a futile gesture. "Never been able to grow a thing," he said. "All I've ever done my whole life is kill plants. Born with a black thumb, I reckon."

I watched Imo's face as this registered. She was carrying a tray of tomato seedlings from the cold-frame to the edge of the garden. "Okay then, dear," she said calmly. "Lou and I can be the gardeners. But you can be a big help by keeping an eye on Mama for us when we're out in the garden." She caught my eye and gave me a secret wink.

As we finished setting out the seedlings, dusk was falling, and streaks of a brilliant gold-and-crimson sunset stretched above the horizon. Imo surveyed the garden and drew in a huge breath. She released it with a satisfied sigh and turned to me with a beautiful smile. "Lou," she said, "it's going to be a wonderful spring."

"You think?" I said, eyeing her a bit incredulously.

"I surely do. Mama really seems to like Lemuel. She listens to him like he's God. Plus, we've got Jeanette's wedding to the Reverend Pike to plan, not to mention her starting at beauty college next fall."

I nodded as I crouched down to lean back on my heels and take a deep breath. I knew then that Jeanette had found her way and that Imo was at peace and that we were mending as a family. The air at twilight was soft and healing. The garden, still fledgling at that early date, held the promise of a harvest to come, and I felt myself filling up with hope for what lay ahead.

Ten

At the Close of Day

*I*n May the days were warmer and longer, the seedlings in the garden had turned into sturdy plants and the grass was growing rampantly. All sorts of flowers were bursting into bloom, so that it seemed to Imo that the entire earth was burgeoning. She was able to get out in the yard and work in the garden to her heart's content, as Lemuel was always more than willing to keep an eye on Mama.

These days when Imo saw Mama, it was only as a pathetic old woman; frail, at the mercy of others, and tortured by a sadness no one had diagnosed. Imo's epiphany in regard to Mama allowed her a great measure of peace in her thoughts, and this made all the difference. She smiled often and sometimes she even laughed aloud at Mama's antics. This meant that the entire household was happier. She felt much stronger, with the pain and rage her servants, getting better with each passing day.

Lemuel, however, was only just now gradually working his way back up to being a full-time preacher and tender of his flock. Martha had been gone for a good ten months at this point, and Imo and Lemuel had been joined together in holy matrimony since December. However, in Imo's opinion, their union was not so much a marriage as it was an extremely close friendship. They'd not been intimate yet, had not even seen each other undressed for that matter. Though Imo was constantly aware of the possibility of physical interaction, such as when their feet bumped underneath the covers at night, or as they sat on the couch together to watch the evening news, Lemuel seemed to view their relationship as satisfactory the way it was. He meant, she supposed, to keep some sort of distance between them until his heart was fully strong enough. She planned to give him all the time he needed.

Imo stood at the sink musing on all this as she washed up the breakfast dishes. Lemuel had coaxed himself into heading to Calvary for the early part of the morning. The girls were gone, too, along with Little Silas, and the house was quiet except for the sounds of Mama's TV show trickling into the kitchen. When she'd cleaned the last fork and hung up her apron, Imo paused to consider what she would do with her morning.

She glanced at her watch, grabbed her straw hat from the back porch, and stepped out into the backyard. It was a glorious day, full of birdsongs and cool breezes. Bingo appeared at her heels and followed her out to the garden, where she stopped and patted his head. "Not much that needs doing out here today, is there, Bingo?" she said. The hard work of tilling and sowing and planting was behind them, and besides keeping it watered and plucking a random weed now and then, there wouldn't be much to do for several more weeks yet. "How 'bout we go around front and see about the daylilies, boy," she offered.

The daylilies had been right on the verge of bursting into full bloom for several days now and Imo was waiting expectantly for the extravagant emergence of yellow and orange that would cover the bank along the front of the farmhouse. No matter how many times she'd seen them, when the daylilies came forth in all their glory, it never failed to take her breath away. Imo and Bingo strolled along past the glider and the birdbath and the oak leaf hydrangeas blooming all along the side of the house, and they rounded the corner so that the front yard was in full view.

Imo stopped short. She gave a high-pitched squeal of glee that sounded like it could have come from Little Silas. Breathlessly she bent to hug a startled Bingo. "Would you just look at that!" she gushed into his ear. "It's never been prettier!" After a moment she stood up and shook her head in a wondering sort of way as she jogged to the edge of the daylilies. She reached out to stroke a velvety petal, marveling at the intricate interior of the flower. "Isn't this the most gorgeous sight in the world, boy?" she turned to say to Bingo, but he'd sprinted off to rustle a squirrel up under the acuba bushes.

After a minute or so, it seemed oddly flat, sad even, to be admiring all this beauty alone. Something began to tug at the hem of her consciousness. Telling her that there was someone who'd appreciate this sight just as much as she did.

Imo bent to snap the sturdy stem of a daylily and twirled the flower between her thumb and forefinger, hardly believing that she was actually thinking what she was. Then, shaking her head that a moment like this would ever come, she ran in a reckless, headlong way back into the house to show it to Mama.

"You're not going to believe this, Mama!" she sang out breathlessly, laughing, as she bounded through the front door bearing the daylily. Rounding the corner into the den, she held it out in front of herself as an offering.

She noted that Mama's eyes were closed. It was odd for Mama to be sleeping so early in the day, particularly in front of her favorite story, which was blaring loudly from the TV. Imo mashed the button to turn it off. "Please wake up and look at this, Mama!" she said, shaking the old woman's shoulder.

All at once the silence seemed unusually deep. Imo dropped to the floor at the side of the La-Z-Boy. "You sleeping, Mama?" she whispered. She shook Mama gently, but her eyes remained closed. Imo picked up Mama's wrist from the armrest and the remote fell with a thud to the floor. Her arm was far too heavy, an inanimate object.

Oh, great God in heaven, Imo thought, *Mama's dead.* She studied Mama's face. Her expression was peaceful, a slight smile at her lips.

The silence that followed was so deep that Imo felt suspended in time. She rose after a spell and with trembling hands she laid the daylily across Mama's chest.

It was a balmy afternoon with a cloudless sky as everyone piled into the Impala for Mama's funeral service. The Reverend drove and Imo sat in the middle of the front seat next to him. She was subdued, wrapped in a jet-black church dress, with a white mum fastened at her shoulder. Jeanette and Little Silas and Loutishie rode in the back, strangely quiet as well.

There were only a handful of people there to mourn Mama Jewell's passing—several Garden Club ladies, a tiny clump of people from Calvary, and Mr. Dilly from the Carolina Arms. The Reverend climbed the steps to the pulpit somberly and rested his Bible on the lectern.

"It was not too long ago," he began, "that I was on the other side of a funeral. *I* was the one who needed comfort. I didn't really know how to reach out and ask for comfort, as I was always the one giving the comfort up till then. But my dear friend, Imogene, helped lift my spirits up from the abyss of hopelessness. And she's still lifting them. And now we are gathered here to say good-bye to her mother, Jewelldine Pridemore Wiggins, and it is my turn to comfort *her* heart.

"Imogene's mother lives on in the gifts she bestowed upon her daughter. Oh, not in silver or gold, for Jewelldine Wiggins married for love, and could not offer much materially to her daughter. But my wife has let me know, on several occasions, that her mother bequeathed unto her a love of the earth. Fashioned in her a delight in growing things, and this legacy, if you will, is a part of Jewelldine that will live on and on."

Imo began to nod. She reached over to one side and squeezed Lou's hand and then to the other to squeeze Jeanette's. Jeanette laid her head on Imo's shoulder. Her lashes were spiked with tears. "Who'd a thought it?" Jeanette whispered through her sniffles, "I'm really going to miss the old warthog."

Imo wasn't sure how to feel about Mama's passing quite yet. She was torn. The house seemed strangely empty and quiet without Mama and her antics, but Imo figured that now her feeble old mind was released from its prison, and that she herself could finally rest.

Still, she had to admit that it worried her quite a bit that the tears weren't flowing from her eyes.

One Saturday in June, after the supper dishes were washed, dried, and put away, Imo hung up her apron and made her way out the back door. She went down the steps, past the islands of showy watermelon-colored azaleas and the buttery jonquils along the footpath to the garden, where she stood at the edge of the tomatoes.

In the twilight of evening, the lemony scent of warm tomato leaves enveloped her as she reached out to touch the hard, smooth skin of one green orb hanging from a vine. "It won't be long now till they're ripe, Mama," she said softly.

And she cried then. She cried for those things that bound her to Mama, those things that had separated her from Mama, and those hard things she had learned in her life that had made her stronger.

Imo cried for her mama and the tears darkened the dirt at the edge of the garden. It was then that a warmth filled her. As gentle as the evening sun, it wrapped itself around her and blanketed her with peace.

A RECIPE FOR
'Mater Biscuits

Of all the southern staples, buttermilk biscuits and home-grown 'maters top the list. Put them together and what have you got? A melt-in-your-mouth union of tender, flaky pastry and the juicy zing of summer.

> 2 cups sifted all-purpose flour
> ½ teaspoon salt
> 1 teaspoon sugar
> ½ teaspoon baking soda
> 3 teaspoons double-acting baking powder
> ¼ cup lard *or* 6 tablespoons butter
> ¾ cup buttermilk
> 2 large homegrown 'maters, thickly sliced (see NOTE)

Preheat oven to 425 degrees. Sift together all dry ingredients in a mixing bowl. Cut in shortening until mixture resembles coarse corn-meal (you can use a pastry cutter or two knives). With a light hand, stir in buttermilk until the dough follows a fork around. Turn the dough out onto a floured board, knead gently, and pat to a ¼-inch thickness. Cut with a biscuit cutter (I use an upside-down floured drinking glass of 3-inch diameter), place on an ungreased baking sheet, and bake 10 to 14 minutes, till brown. When biscuits have cooled to the touch, slice 'em open and stuff 'em with a thick, juicy slice of homegrown 'mater.

A NOTE on the superiority of homegrown 'maters: *Nothing* can compare to the flavor of a sun-kissed homegrown tomato—spicy, sweet, and juicy. So grow your own if you possibly can, and if not, stop by one of those roadside produce stands. Store-bought tomatoes are bred to stand up to rough picking and shipping techniques, then harvested while they are still green and ripened with a dose of ethylene gas—that's why they don't taste like anything.

Acknowledgments

I would like to say "thanks" to the following, whose support and encouragement have been priceless to me. First, I am indebted to the superb and untiring team at Simon & Schuster's Touchstone/Fireside division, especially Amanda Patten, whose shrewd eye worked literal miracles page by page. As with most everything else in my life, I had to rely on help from a warm circle of family, some of whom honestly deserve a paycheck for all their practical help, and all of whom are a joy to me every day. A humongous thanks goes to my better half, Tom, for absolutely *everything*; and I must also single out my memaw, Nancy Nell Ellenberg Lowrey, and my granny, Geneva Grizzell Lewis, for loving to garden, and for being different in every conceivable way from Mama Jewell, who I created for this story. A special thanks goes out to Augusta Trobaugh, a generous soul, and a sister both in writing and the faith, for her encouragement and delightful lunches at the Golden Dragon. Finally, I give my endless thanks to God, who, by His grace, sustains me day by day.

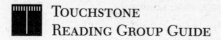
'Mater Biscuit

1. The narrator of 'Mater Biscuit tends to focus on what Imo sees happening around her, and what she's feeling. Some sections, though, come from "Loutishie's Notebook." What does this diary add to the book? How well does Loutishie understand what's going on in Imo's household? Sometimes the narrator describes events from Imo's perspective, and then Loutishie describes the same event in her notebook. How does Loutishie experience events differently than Imo does?

2. In chapter 4, Martha helps Imo realize that "she was sandwiched in the middle of two very demanding generations." Imo thinks of herself as the filling in a 'mater biscuit. "Every day she fell further and further behind in her own life; she had less and less time for the filling." How is this realization significant for Imo? Does she successfully reconcile her duty to her mother and her younger charges with her need to spend some time on herself?

3. Soon after Imo brings her mother to live with her, she tries to speak with two ministers about the burden she has taken on and the hard time she has honoring her mother. Reverend Lemuel Peddigrew isn't able to help her find peace of mind, and Reverend Montgomery Pike isn't any more successful. Compare these two conversations with Imo's conversation with her friend

Martha in chapter 8. What is it about this conversation that makes it so much more healing for Imo?

4. Why do you think it took so long for Imo to tell Martha how much her relationship with her mother troubled her? Why did she choose to confide in the Reverends but not in her friend? Even after the Reverends aren't able to help her, she doesn't share her troubles with her friend. "But it surely was hard managing all this alone and every now and again, she toyed with the idea of calling one of her girlfriends and just pouring her heart out." But Imo doesn't reach out. "She liked to think that she was a born private type of person." What does Imo deny herself when she prevents herself from talking to her friends?

5. Even Imo's good friend Martha asks Imo why she took Mama Jewell to live with her in spite of their disturbing history. Caring for Mama Jewell, with her fitful memory, would be difficult for Imo even if she had untempered love for her mother. Why does Imo bring her mother home? How does her faith play into this decision? Does Imo feel she lives up to the challenges she sets for herself?

6. How do the other characters, especially Lou and Martha, see Imo? How do they help carry some of her burdens? After Imo injures her back, Martha comes to stay with her, take care of her, and help keep her household running. Imo is afraid that Martha won't respect her after seeing her piles of laundry and dirty dishes. Why do you think Imo is so afraid that Martha will judge her? How does Martha help Imo to see herself in a more positive light?

7. Shortly after Imo recovers from her injury, she asks Lou to mind Mama Jewell while she runs some errands. Lou doesn't see Mama Jewell sneak out to the river. When she finds her, they both get

caught in the dam water. Lou hangs on to Mama Jewell even though this means she is powerless to save Elmer as he floats by her. Why does she work so hard to save Mama Jewell when she "didn't even *like* Mama Jewell"? How does Lou's faith or her sense of duty help her make this decision? Why doesn't Jeanette understand the choice she made?

8. How would you describe Loutishie, and how does her relationship with Jeanette reveal her character? Lou puts an awful lot of pressure on herself to behave well, and her sneaky prying into her grandma's trunk weighs heavily on her conscience. The night little Silas breaks his foot and Lou's family takes him to the hospital without telling her, Lou thinks they've all been swept up in the Rapture without her. What does she learn about herself that night? What does Lou do differently after that, and how do her relationships with Imo and Jeanette change?

9. Loutishie is secretly looking for her father at the same time that Imo is busy coming to terms with Mama Jewell and her childhood. When Lou finally meets her dad, she recognizes her resemblance to him but says, "He's not my father . . . I'm sure of it." Why does she say this? How do Imo's troubles with her mother help her to talk to Lou about her disappointment?

10. Why does Martha ask Imo to marry her husband, Lemuel, after her death? What does Martha hope for Lemuel to gain by marrying Imo? Is she worried about Lemuel's ability to take care of himself? Imo thinks, "Surely she could just offer to cook and clean and do for him. Like a wife, but not a wife." Is that what Martha is asking for? Later, after Imo and Lemuel marry, Imo thinks their "union was not so much a marriage as it was an extremely close friendship." Do you think this was what Martha had in mind?

11. Shortly after Martha's death, Imo asks the Garden Club to come out and tend the Memorial Garden and install a plaque with Martha's name on it. This is their way of honoring Martha. Still, the plaque isn't the only way they memorialize their friend. How else do they remember her, and how does their informal memorial also help them to heal?

12. The last memory of her mother that Imo shares is one in which the two of them plant seeds in the garden together. This is the memory, the one fine thing that helps Imo make peace with Mama Jewell. Gardening is a solace for Imo many times during *Mater Biscuit*. What is it about gardening that helps Imo find peace?

LOOK FOR **JULIE CANNON'S**
FIRST HOMEGROWN NOVEL

TRUELOVE
& HOMEGROWN TOMATOES

"Hilarious, poignant . . . I look forward to the next installment of Imo's search for love."
—Ann B. Ross, author of Miss Julia Throws a Wedding

a novel by Julie Cannon

Join the Euharlee Garden Club to stay up-to-date with the lives of Imo, Jeanette, and Lou. Members will receive the *Hot Off the Vine* **newsletter** filled with homegrown news from Euharlee, a complimentary seed packet, and a membership card! Sign up by sending your name and address to **hotoffthevine@simonandschuster.com.**

0-7432-4588-1 • $13.00

TOUCHSTONE
A Division of Simon & Schuster
A VIACOM COMPANY